G

*Peabody Public Library*
*Columbia City, IN*

FICTION M STAND
Standiford, Le
Presidential De
/ Les Standiford.
1st ed.

JUL 1 6 '98

DISCARD

# presidential
# deal

ALSO BY LES STANDIFORD

*Deal on Ice*
*Deal to Die For*
*Raw Deal*
*Done Deal*
*Spill*

# presidential deal

## deal

A Novel

*Peabody Public Library*
*Columbia City, IN*

# Les Standiford

HarperCollins*Publishers*

Though I love South Florida and the surrounding waters just as they really and truly are, this is a work of the imagination, and I have taken certain liberties with the land- and seascapes. May they please the innocent and the guilty alike.

PRESIDENTIAL DEAL. Copyright © 1998 by Les Standiford. All rights reserved. Printed in the United States of America. No part of this book may be used or reproduced in any manner whatsoever without written permission except in the case of brief quotations embodied in critical articles and reviews. For information address HarperCollins Publishers, Inc., 10 East 53rd Street, New York, NY 10022.

HarperCollins books may be purchased for educational, business, or sales promotional use. For information please write: Special Markets Department, HarperCollins Publishers, Inc., 10 East 53rd Street, New York, NY 10022.

FIRST EDITION

*Designed by Elina D. Nudelman*

Library of Congress Cataloging-in-Publication Data

Standiford, Les
    Presidential Deal : a novel / Les Standiford — 1st ed.
      p.   cm.
    ISBN 0-06-018655-0
    PS3569.T331528P74  1998
    813'.54—dc21                              97-31642

98 99 00 01 02 ❖/RRD 10 9 8 7 6 5 4 3 2 1

*This book is dedicated to Brian Standiford . . .*
*and to his parents, Craig and Bethann, heroes all.*

All our lives we fought against exalting the individual, against the elevation of the single person, and long ago we were over and done with the business of a hero, and here it comes up again: the glorification of one personality. This is not good at all. I am just like everybody else.

*—Vladimir Ilych Lenin*


No pain, no palm; no thorns, no throne; no gall, no glory; no cross, no crown.

*—William Penn*

# Acknowledgments

Deal and I would like to extend a special thanks to those who have helped: to Kimberly who kept me going; to Bill Beesting, Rhoda Kurzweil, and James W. Hall, my trusty readers; to Captain Robin Smith, for his advice on nautical matters; to Lieutenant Tony Rodriguez and Assistant Chief Ray Martinez, Miami P.D., for their input on police procedure; and finally, to those former members of the intelligence community who must remain anonymous—your input was invaluable.

# Prologue

**Near Coconut Grove, Florida**

Late May, on toward evening of the perfect boater's day. In the distance, hovering over the Biminis, a towering bank of cumulus reflecting the last pink glow of the sun. Stretched out just ahead, the waters of Biscayne Bay. Going steely now. Soon to be indigo, along with the night.

*Now or never,* Deal thought. It was why they'd come out here, after all. Stop stalling.

He nodded to himself, reached for the controls, shoved forward, opened up the twin diesels on the *Miss Miami Priss.* He was wondering if he'd finally gotten things right, if the big engines were going to finally fire in synch, thrust him forward over the swells like something shot out of a sling. Just as likely, though, the balky SOBs would erupt in a thundering explosion that would put an end to all the agony. That's what he was thinking when he saw what was on the surface of the water up ahead.

At first he thought it might be a cluster of lobster buoys, broken loose from their traps in Biscayne Bay, drifted out toward the Gulf Stream, but that wasn't right. Too many of them for that, the color, the shape, the movement all wrong.

Some kind of floating debris tossed from a cruise liner headed for the islands, that's what crossed his mind next. There were ship's captains who liked to save a few bucks that way—why have your garbage hauled by surly Teamsters in the Port of Miami when you could just chug out past the limit, dump it in the unprotesting sea?

But it wasn't that kind of debris, either. He was close enough to see that now. And was cursing the fact that for once in his life, his mechanical abilities had held.

The engines had kicked in just the way he'd dreamed. He'd felt the pop at the back of his neck, the kind a schoolboy yearns for when he sees a powerful car. *Miss Miami* was a forty-five-foot Bayliner with a flying bridge and a patched-up hull. She was a charter fishing craft well past her prime, the kind of boat you see in a backwater marina in the wrong part of the Keys—you might drive by and notice her and think to yourself, *She must have been something once.*

Her glory days were long gone. There were a million younger, faster,

1

*Peabody Public Library*
*Columbia City, IN*

better-designed boats out there now. But *Miss Miami* had belonged to his father and she was his now—another albatross he should have had the good sense to stay away from, but it was all he had left of his old man, really—and he'd poured everything there was to pour into her, and she had responded. Here she was now, just trying to please, show him she had a few moves left after all. An over-the-hill fishing boat hurtling over the waves like she was trying to get up on plane.

"What the hell is that?" Vernon Driscoll cried in his ear. Driscoll, in keeping with his bulk and his methodical ex-cop's nature, was not an excitable man. But he had just come up from the galley, a couple of Red Stripe beers in one of his big hands, had not been ready for this.

Deal didn't have time to answer. He shoved the throttles forward, threw himself against the wheel. The *Miss Miami* banked hard, riding up high against the waves, pushing out towering sheets of spray ahead of their starboard side.

Driscoll lost his footing and careened across the cockpit. The beers flew from his hand, one sailing over the rail, the other exploding like a grenade against the windscreen.

Deal sensed the stinging of glass shards at his cheek, saw from the corner of his eye Driscoll slam head-first into the console, felt the thud as the big man went down. Deal wanted to go for him, but he couldn't. He was holding desperately to the wheel, praying to God they wouldn't flip, praying to God they'd miss those people out there. All those people, bobbing in the waves just ahead.

**Nineteen of them** altogether. Nineteen women and children from Cuba and he'd nearly driven his boat through them as if they were a school of sea cows spread out to die.

He pulled the last woman over the transom, screaming back at her in his fractured Spanish, "Yes, yes, *tenemos su niña*, we have your baby."

She heard him, but he couldn't tell from her expression if she believed him. Still, she allowed herself to be dragged into the boat.

Once he had her aboard, Deal sagged back against the rail, gasping from exertion, staring at the ragtag cargo before him. All of the women wore orange life jackets, most of them so old they tied rather than snapped together. A few of the children had jackets, but most were too small. They'd had to cling to their mothers as they bobbed in the sea. They were still clinging, screaming, crying. The *Miss Miami Priss* had become a little corner of Hell.

Driscoll was still propped in the corner of the cockpit where Deal had dragged him, beginning to stir now. His eyes flickered open, blearily surveyed the scene around him, closed again.

"You want to change the channel?" Driscoll called, his hand lifting to the makeshift bandage tied about his head.

Deal nodded. He'd love to change the channel, find the one where two guys finish their cruise on the bay without incident, put in at Matheson Hammock Park, eat yellowtail snapper and drink island beer at the Red Fish Grill. But that channel seemed to be on the blink.

He'd used his T-shirt to wrap the gash on Driscoll's forehead, had cinched it tight, but the fabric was already soaked through with blood. Plenty of stitches to come, he thought. Probably a concussion, too.

*No time for lollygagging, Deal.* He pushed himself up, heading for the wheel.

One woman who had no child clinging to her was fighting at the far rail of the boat, screaming, while two of her companions struggled to hold her.

"For God's sake," Driscoll said. He was struggling up now, his movements awkward and drunken, though the beers he'd been carrying when he'd come up on deck would have been their first.

"Yeah," Deal answered, making his way toward the scene. The woman wanted to dive back into the water, he didn't have to know Spanish to understand that much. Nor to understand why.

He and Driscoll staggered through the bodies sprawled on the deck to the opposite rail, helped the two friends pull the distraught woman back.

"Is her son," one of the woman cried to him in broken English. "Her son."

Deal stared out over the empty water. "Where?"

The woman stared back at him, her face a mask of despair. "*En la agua,*" she said helplessly, waving her hand over the sea.

Driscoll was still out of it. "What happened? How'd they get out here, anyway?"

Deal shook his head, scrambled up onto the flying bridge, turned a quick circle to scan the water. The light was going fast now. No ships in sight, though maybe something out there, a smudge on the eastern horizon.

Then, closer to the *Miss Miami,* he saw it, a dim shadow, just below the surface. Maybe a bread bag slithering in the current. Maybe a chunk of cloth. Maybe the backside of a T-shirt, ballooned up with air.

He kicked off his deck shoes and dove.

He came up to get his bearings, found Driscoll at the bridge now, pointing, shouting, "Twenty feet. That way."

Deal turned, began to stroke the water wildly.

He was still trying to force himself to calm—no good comes out of panic—when his hand came down with a smack on the boy's back. He stopped, steadied himself, treading water, got the boy turned over, his puffy face under the crook of his chin, out of the water.

He glanced up to find Driscoll at the wheel of the *Miss Miami*, the blood-soaked shirt making him look like some kind of latter-day pirate. He eased the *Miss Miami* toward them and Deal saw the gunwale of the boat sidle up, saw all the grasping hands descend. The boy was lifted up, the inert form dragged over the rail, and then Deal had Driscoll's meaty hand in his and followed.

The boy was sprawled inert on the deck, his burr-cut head lolled to the side, the mother, a thin woman with a ribboned scar down one cheek, screaming, trying to claw her way toward him. "Hold her back," Deal commanded the women closest to her. No one had to translate.

He bent over the boy, checked his air passage, thrust his hand beneath his neck. He bent, pressed his lips to the boy's cold and clammy flesh, began mouth-to-mouth.

"They didn't wreck," Driscoll was calling down as Deal gave his breath to the boy. "I thought maybe their boat sunk. It wasn't that at all. Some sonofabitch put them off in the water."

Deal left off his breathing, rose to push down on the boy's chest. He watched water erupt from the boy's lungs, glanced briefly up at Driscoll.

"Contract smugglers," Driscoll said, nodding at the woman who'd been speaking halting English earlier. "The bastards saw a boat, thought it was the INS, they were going to get busted. They threw one life raft in the water, forced the rest of them off at gunpoint."

"Where's the raft?"

Driscoll barked something like a laugh, then winced, his hand going back to his head. He reached out, steadied himself against the rail. "It lasted about two minutes before it came apart."

Deal was back at work on the boy now. A familiar story, he thought. But he'd heard worse. Contract smugglers who promised passage from Cuba, from Haiti—pick any agonized nation—the bastards collected their fees, carried their passengers out to sea, then simply shot them. Land of the brave, home of the free. Streets paved with gold. Dear Lord.

Wailing above him, wailing within. He pressed his lips to the lips of the boy and gave it all he could.

**News item:** *The Miami Herald*, Friday, May 28:

## Contractor Pulls Twenty from Sea

John Deal has contributed more than his share in a career dedicated to the restoration of Dade County's architectural treasures, but nothing compares to what he managed Thursday. Deal, son of legendary Miami builder Barton Deal, was out for a test run off Soldier Key late yesterday, on a boat that had belonged to his late father, when he came upon a group of Cuban refugees, women and children tossed overboard in the aftermath of an apparent contract smuggling operation gone sour.

Deal, 38, and his companion, former Metro Dade detective Vernon Driscoll, 51, were on their way into port at about 7:00 P.M., aboard the *Miss Miami Priss,* an aging forty-five-foot Bayliner Deal had been restoring, when they spotted the group floating in the water about six miles off the coast. . . .

". . . I just did what anyone else would do," Deal said as he left Coast Guard headquarters in Coconut Grove, where the refugees were delivered. "Vernon Driscoll is just as responsible as I am for saving these people."

Deal is the owner of DealCo Construction, a firm that helped to sculpt the Miami skyline in its heyday. DealCo was the principal contractor for the Dorado Beach Hotel and several other luxury hotels constructed on Miami Beach in the 1950s. In the 1970s and early 1980s, Barton Deal and several associates spearheaded the development of the Brickell Banking Center, as well as downtown's First Federal Tower, still the tallest building in South Florida. Stung by a building glut and an economic downturn, the firm went into receivership in 1989, and Barton Deal committed suicide soon after.

The younger Deal fought to rebuild his father's firm from the ashes, however. Following the devastation wrought by Hurricane Andrew in 1992, he turned the company's efforts toward the rebuilding of several of the area's architectural landmarks, including the Denby estate in South Dade and the former Vanderbilt family compound in Coconut Grove, LaGloria, now occupied by computer tycoon Terrence

Terrell. "It was either that or build strip malls the rest of my life," Deal said. "I didn't have to think too long about it."

As to what took him out on the water late yesterday: "The *Miss Miami* is about the only thing my father had left when he died. It had been sitting down at Monty Trainor's marina for years, just rotting away. He loved the boat, and I finally decided it was time to put the old girl back in service. She's been a money pit, but I'd have to say it was worth every penny I put in her now. I think my old man would agree."

# Part 1: Primaries

## Washington, D.C., June 6

"I'm thinking this was not such a good idea." It was the man in the plaid Bermuda shorts and purple Georgetown University sweatshirt speaking.

He wasn't looking at Salazar, who sat in stylish linens on the marble bench beside him. He had his gaze fixed instead upon the enormous, brightly lit visage of Abraham Lincoln that loomed in its niche nearby.

It was a balmy night, not quite ten, the early summer heat dissipated into invitation, even promise, the stars glittering overhead. Tourists still lolled about the Mall. Knots of schoolchildren roamed here and there, shepherded by their chaperones, chattering, shrieking, clambering up and down the ghostly steps of the monument.

"And why is that?" Salazar responded, his voice mild.

He turned, saw that Salazar was watching on a willowy girl in a plaid uniform jumper and knee-high socks standing several yards away. The girl, tall, serene, her features about to transform themselves from childish beauty into loveliness, had drifted apart from her group, an especially rowdy bunch, to stare up at the statue of Lincoln, intent.

"No one who works in this town ever goes sightseeing," he said.

"Yes," Salazar said, his eyes still on the girl. "And that is why no one you know will see you here."

The girl turned. Sixteen, possibly seventeen, going on ageless. She couldn't have heard, but it seemed as if she had. Her glance flickered over him, held for a moment on Salazar. He had learned long ago that his was a face that did not attract the attention of women. He did all right at close quarters, but someone with Salazar's dark allure, well . . .

There was some shift of expression there, a narrowing of the girl's eyes, maybe . . . then she turned away, moving back toward her group with a toss of her long hair.

*She knows what this man is,* he found himself thinking. *And still she would have him.*

"I have presented you with the solution to all your problems," Salazar said. His eyes followed the knot of schoolchildren as they drifted away into the darkness. Finally he turned. "And now it is time for you to accept my proposal."

He shook his head. He'd known it was coming. He cursed himself for even agreeing to meet Salazar this night. But there had been times when

9

he'd needed Salazar, hadn't there? He owed him the courtesy of a face-to-face, at least.

He drew a breath, met Salazar's gaze. "I've thought about it, but we'll take our chances by ourselves," he said.

"And you will lose the election."

"You seem awfully certain."

"I've read the same reports that you have, my friend. Malcolm Jesse is *your* analyst, not Senator Hollingsworth's, is it not so?"

He stared back, poker-faced. Malcolm Jesse had produced three sets of data: one for official release, with projections on the race so sunny he doubted even the dullest readers of the daily newspapers believed them; the second was a slightly less rosy set designed for unofficial "leakage" and intended to offset skepticism concerning the official report. The third set of figures told the truth, so far as Malcolm Jesse and his statistical gnomes could determine it. How Salazar had gained access to those carefully guarded figures, he had no idea.

"I have lived long because I make it my business to know such things," Salazar said.

He turned away, trying to hide his discomfort. What the hell was it? He'd been at the right hand of the President for nearly four years, had traveled the halls of power another dozen before that. He'd bluffed foreign leaders, sold transparent lies to U.S. congressmen. But Angel Salazar, provocateur, mercenary, lifelong opportunist, could look inside his head and read the thoughts as clearly as if in screaming neon: *Find a way to take Florida or we're dead!*

"President Sheldon cannot go hat in hand to Jorge Vas," he said flatly. "The man makes the NRA look like a pack of flaming liberals." Vas was the leader of the Cuban émigré community in the United States. His authority was unquestioned, as were his politics. And if Malcolm Jesse's third set of figures was to be believed, Vas held the key votes; he alone had the power to deliver the state of Florida, and the election, into Frank Sheldon's hands.

"If we proceed as I say, your president will not have to go hat in hand," Salazar said. "We will stage our little incident, laying the blame at the feet of the international cabal of communism, and your president will issue a stinging rebuke of these actions, and Jorge Vas will have appropriate reason to lend his support as a result. It is perfect public theater and everyone can save the precious face."

He heard the bitterness in Salazar's intentional twisting of the phrase. There was a child's shriek from somewhere in the darkness, an answering burst of laughter. He conjured up the face of the young girl whom he had watched, teetering on the cusp: on one side all the ideals chiseled in marble, on the other the truth of Salazar's leer.

"What's in it for you, Salazar?" he asked.

Salazar raised his shoulders in the slightest of shrugs. "There is some expense involved, of course," he said, pausing thoughtfully. "Let us say five million dollars."

He stared. "You're crazy."

Salazar shrugged again. "One million now. The rest after the election." He smiled. "Politics aside, I'd prefer the continuity. It's always difficult, breaking in a new administration."

He stifled the urge to laugh. "Just call up the Treasury, have them cut a check, is that it?"

Salazar's smile never left him. "You have a war chest, my friend. This is war."

He stood, fed up. Most of his adult life had been spent cutting deals, proclaiming an interest in spreading democracy, then sitting down with men like Salazar to do the opposite, all in the name of necessity. Two steps forward, one step back, that's how the process was justified, but it more often seemed like one step forward, two steps back. Now Salazar wanted five million dollars to stage a "controlled" riot in Miami—like saying he wanted to pull the trigger on the A-bomb but cut off the reaction before the mushroom cloud appeared, wasn't it?—so that these dances of deception could continue indefinitely.

"You've wasted my evening," he said. "Even if it worked . . . "

"It *will* work," Salazar cut in.

"Forget it." He turned abruptly, jostling a tourist who'd been backing toward them, camera pointed at the monument and his beaming, snowy-haired wife.

"Excuse me," he muttered at the man, moving away across the Mall. He heard more shrieks from the darkness, no answering laughter this time. There was a distant wail of a siren, but it seemed to be receding, not approaching.

He had taken half a dozen steps, no more, when he felt Salazar's hand grip his arm. Thumb by his elbow, fingers in the soft flesh beneath his biceps. He started to turn, to order the man away, when he felt the incredible pain. Though he willed himself to keep going, he felt his breath constrict, his legs go leaden. If Salazar had not been holding him tightly, he would have pitched face-first against the pavement.

He saw a park policeman up ahead, the officer hurrying off toward the darkness and those unending shrieks. *Call out for help,* he thought, *put an end to this insanity once and for all.*

"You *will* help me," Salazar repeated, his voice rasping, the man's breath hot at his cheek. "We have too much history, my friend. And the world will learn everything, every last detail, every little secret, every agreement, every favor I have arranged at your behest. You, your president and his precious liberal's façade, there is too much at risk here, do you understand me?"

He felt the pressure loosen at his arm then, and the pain disappeared, as if by magic. He could breathe again, and he stumbled forward, feeling his feet regain their rhythm. He felt a renewed burst of outrage, and though the park policeman had vanished into the darkness, this was something he could take care of on his own. He was an important man in this town, for God's sake, even if he was, at this moment, wearing some idiot's disguise of floppy shorts and purple sweatshirt, and he would not be treated this way by a subhuman creature who had been well paid for a few necessary favors. He would never agree to his plans in a million years.

He drew a breath and turned, ready to set Salazar straight once and for all. There was Lincoln gazing down from his perch, sirens and shrieks behind him, flashbulbs and nervous glances into the darkness . . .

He met Salazar's eyes. "Goddammit," he said, his chest heaving. He paused, drew another breath, felt the weariness rising like a tide until it seemed he would choke on it.

"A controlled disturbance, you said. Break a couple of windows, fire a few shots in the air. That's all . . ." He heard the words coming from his mouth as if from a stranger's.

Salazar in turn was nodding, his smile playing about the corners of his mouth. "Do not concern yourself with details," he said soothingly. "I am very good at what I do."

He stared back, feeling exhausted, as if he'd just stumbled to the end of some marathon run. His head was leaden, and throbbing . . . and he was nodding in response, a motion almost casual, seeming quite apart from will.

What awful cries from the darkness now.

## News item: *Washington Times*

### Heroes' Ceremony Moves to Miami
#### Washington, June 24 (UPI)—

The White House announced today that the National Medal of Valor ceremonies, a Rose Garden staple since the awards were conceived in 1963, would be held this year in

Miami, Florida, during a campaign stopover by President Frank Sheldon. Earlier this week, Miami had been added to the list of cities the President would visit during his "Town Meeting" tour. Recipients of the so-called Local Hero awards are individuals nominated by various governmental and civic agencies around the country in recognition of "acts of valor and courage on behalf of others well beyond the norm." It is a designation often referred to as the civilian equivalent of the military's Medal of Honor.

"This is a further reflection of the President's commitment to carrying government to the people, beyond the Beltway," advisor John Groshner said during the weekly press briefing. "And Miami is the perfect site for this year's Medal of Valor program. The city and its people have a long history of quiet heroism, having provided safe haven for untold thousands fleeing dictatorships and political oppression in Latin America for the entire last half of this century."

Response was immediate from the camp of Senator Charles Hollingsworth, the President's opponent in the forthcoming election. "It's nothing more than an attempt to add luster to a failed campaign strategy," a Hollingsworth aide said. "The President's slipping so badly in the polls that he'd promise to move the White House itself if he thought it would get him the votes he needs."

Two A.M., a hot June night, humidity pumping in off an Atlantic easterly, so much moisture in the air, you ought to be half fish just to be able to walk around, or so Ray Brisa was thinking. Maybe he was half fish himself, maybe his lungs had these pink feathery fringes growing already, maybe one day he'd wake up and find himself with a pair of gills sprouted from the coppery skin just behind his ears. Fish-man, they could call him. Or Gil. Or 'Cuda.

*Cuda* had the right ring to it. Bad-ass fish, more teeth than you could count, stick your hand in Ray Brisa's water, see how much comes out. He smiled at the thought of it, at the way his mind worked, surprise a minute, million minutes in a day.

He heard the sound of an engine, then glanced down the deserted street toward Biscayne Boulevard, the direction from which Zito and Luis would naturally come. He'd been waiting for an hour and a half, breathing in all the seawater air that was turning his skin to scales, keeping an eye on the building, making sure that when and if the other two showed up, they'd be alone, though there wasn't too much to worry about, the neighborhood that surrounded the area of warehouses and shops where he waited being so bad that even the lowlifes hung out someplace else.

Ray wasn't personally concerned. He knew no one from this or any other neighborhood was about to mess with him. No one ever messed with him, no one in his right mind, anyway. Not that he was so big, not that he worked on looking so bad, it had just always been that way, from the time he was four years old, it was as if the other kids could feel something pulsing out of his brain, some signal on the street-kid wavelength that said, "Leave *this* twisted mother alone."

Ray couldn't remember actually doing much to create this apprehension beyond the fact of always coming out on top of the usual street-corner scraps, though he could date his understanding of just how feared he had become back to the time six other kids jumped him and held him down and one kid on top of him with a baseball bat aimed at his head—Ray saw the look in the kid's eye and knew the kid wanted to kill him out of pure fear, like "Wipe this sonofabitch out before we *all* die"—but then, wouldn't you know it, a police cruiser happened around the corner and Ray got to live after all, the kid with the bat moved away with his family a week or so after.

14

Ray leaned back against the wall of the building, found the edge of a brick he could use to dig into the muscles of his back, work out some kink that had arisen there. A hell of a thing to remember, wasn't it, you're maybe eight or nine years old and realize another person wants to kill you for reasons you don't even know?

Meantime, still no Zito, no Luis. He checked his watch. He should have gone along with them, and would have, except that he never liked to take a chance on being surprised, never again. There could be somebody with a bat come up on you when you least expected it, that was Ray Brisa's philosophy, one of the many hard lessons of his youth.

Nothing he'd worked consciously on, of course. It was just the way his mind worked. Like the one law of physics Ray remembered from his desultory years of high school, a cartoon movie with some Donald Duck character demonstrating, pound one end of a teeter-totter with a big hammer, the other end fires your ass into outer space—for every action, there is an equal and opposite reaction, so if you've got trouble in mind, stay far the fuck away from Ray Brisa.

End of story, he nodded, for Zito and Luis were pulling up to the curb in a shiny new Suburban now, both of them grinning, jerking around in their seats to the beat of whatever song they had tuned to the max on the sound system of the vehicle they'd stolen. Big Zito behind the wheel, his pupils shrunk to the size of pencil points, whatever he was taking, Ray was surprised he could even see. Probably he couldn't. It was Luis looking around for where Ray might be, half-assed kind of looking, of course. Ray shook his head, stepping out of the shadows toward them. If he was a barracuda, any kind of fish, then these two had to be sea worms.

He hit the hood of the Suburban with the flat of his palm and the two inside jumped. "Whoa, man," Luis said as the passenger window glided down. "Scare the shit out of me."

"Then there'd be nothing left," Ray said. "Turn that radio off."

Luis obeyed.

"There a hitch on this thing?" Ray asked.

"You said get a truck with a hitch, that's what we got," Luis said. "There was a big-ass boat behind it, too. Zito wanted to take it along, drop it somewhere we could come back to, but I told him we didn't have time."

Zito gave Luis a look. "Was Luis wanted the boat," he said.

"Fuck you," Luis said.

"Shut up," Ray said. "Both of you."

There was silence.

Ray listened to the purr of the big V-8 beneath the hood of the Suburban, calming down, readying himself, arranging every atom for the task at hand. Not even sea worms, he thought. What was it that fish ate? Plankton, wasn't it? Then that's what Zito and Luis were, plankton with arms and legs and faces.

"Everything else in back?" he said, glancing toward the rear of the Suburban.

"Sure, everything's in back," Luis said.

Ray didn't like the tone of Luis's voice, but he put the thought out of his mind. They had less than an hour to get where they were going. "Then take it up over the curb, Zito," he said. "What are you waiting for?"

Pinholes for pupils or not, Zito could drive. He had the big Suburban in reverse and over the high curb in seconds, stopping just short of the heavy iron gates protecting the store's entrance. By the time Ray got to the back of the vehicle, the rear window had already slid down. He glanced up the deserted street once again, then dropped the tailgate.

He reached in, pulled out the six-foot length of anchor chain they'd adapted for their uses, handed one hooked end to Luis, who wrapped it around the door grating. At the same time, Ray bent to loop the other hook around the Suburban's heavy-duty hitch. He gave Zito the high sign and the Suburban lunged forward, jouncing down over the curb. There was an awful screech of metal on metal, the sound of a thousand metal comb fingers across glass, and then the heavy steel doors burst out of their concrete casing and crashed to the sidewalk.

Ray heard an alarm bell clanging as the clatter died away, but he doubted the sound could carry to anyone who gave a shit. For that matter, he was fairly certain the place had a direct-wire alarm as well, but that didn't concern him, either. Inside was what he needed. Short of nuclear response, nothing was going to keep him from it now.

Before the concrete dust had drifted from the ragged opening where the doors had once been, the three of them were inside, Luis wielding the twelve-pound sledge on the display cases they'd scouted earlier in the day, Ray and Zito right after him, lugging the heavy pry bars they'd need for the steel-barred racks. Emergency lights atop the alarms had popped on, illuminating the place in a garish, otherworldly fashion. Mostly they made it that much easier to work.

There was the sound of shattering glass, of shrieking, splintering wood. Zito out with one canvas sack of goods to toss in the back of the Suburban, Luis close on his heels, Ray already busy with the bar of the second rack.

By the time Ray had finally popped the retaining bolt free, the other two were back to help him load, everything going about as well as he could hope. He motioned Luis out the door and led Zito toward the prize of the night, an antitank rocket launcher that the owner had mounted on a pedestal like some god of gun shops. It wasn't on the order list, but what the hell, if the people they were working for tonight didn't want it, *someone* would pay good money for it.

The stand had been bolted to the pedestal, but it hardly mattered. Four blows with the twelve-pound sledge, the thing was free and slung across big Zito's shoulders, Ray fast on his heels, dragging the heavy box of shells through the debris.

Zito dumped the launcher into the back of the Suburban, then turned to help Ray heave the wooden box in after. Luis was behind the wheel now, moving them away from the curb before Ray and Zito had slammed their doors. They were at the end of the block in seconds, two more quick turns onto Biscayne, half a mile to the entrance ramp of I-95, and joined with the light but never-ending Miami traffic, like the Chinese that could line up and march forever into the ocean, Ray thought, checking his watch again, total elapsed time, from gates on the sidewalk to rolling down the highway, less than five minutes. Assuming the shop had been wired, assuming best-case response, the cops wouldn't be arriving on the scene for another minute or so.

*Five minutes' work, twenty-five thousand dollars,* Ray thought. He settled back in the plush leather seat, allowed himself a smile. "You know where you're going, Luis?" he asked.

"Man," Luis said in his whiny voice, "why you keep asking shit like that?"

"Just the way my mind works," Ray said evenly. "The way it does."

**They'd scheduled** the drop for a warehouse district near Tamiami Airport, a noncommercial field far to the south and west of the city. Ray favored it as a place to do business, partly because it offered his customers a ready way to move or store whatever goods he was delivering, partly because he knew a dozen ways in and out of the canal- and lake-encircled place, and partly because it was remote and otherworldly, to his city-bred tastes, anyway.

He could pick out a spot, give someone a route in, he'd take another, and know of three or four more out, in case of emergency. He'd get there early, post Zito and Luis in places where they could do some good should anything go wrong, then kill time all alone, out there on the edge of civilization, in the middle of tall pines and sawgrass a couple of miles from where the Everglades began for real, just chill out, watch the clouds scud by the moon, by the time whoever it was showed up, they'd find Ray Brisa all alone in the middle of nowhere, composed, in control, ready to do any kind of business at hand.

Like right now, for instance. Ray lounging with his back against the warm grillwork of the Suburban, arms folded across his chest, watching some kind of owl whisk across the night sky like a big bat, light on a tree branch twenty yards away, take up his own post. Ray couldn't see the creature's eyes, of course, but he could feel them. The owl staring right down at him when it was supposed to be hunting the rats that favored the area. Ray cocked his head, staring back at the blunt-shouldered silhouette, and swore he saw the owl copy his motion. There was a soft coughing sound from somewhere, and Ray glanced off in the direction where Luis was supposed to be. He listened intently for a moment, but there was nothing else. When he turned back, the owl was gone.

He heard the distant sound of an engine then, the sound rising and falling as the driver made his way through the twists and turns of the route that Ray had provided. It was another full minute at least before he saw headlights, saw the late-model sedan, an off-white top-end Chevy with smoked glass—except for the windows, the kind of car a cop with some suck might ride.

The front doors opened then and two short guys got out on either side of the car, careful to keep what they could of steel and glass in front of them. After a moment, the guy who'd been driving turned and said something into the back. A rear door opened then and a taller guy in dark jeans and a turtleneck got out. The tall guy looked around, smiled, held his hands out from his body as if to show the owls and the looming trees that there was nothing to be afraid of.

A couple more moments of silence, the guy reached into the car, came out with a briefcase, put it on top of the Chevy, opened it up. He turned back, making a slow semicircle before all the nothingness in front of him: a warren of U-Store-It warehouses connected by a maze of alleyways. He held the briefcase by the lid with one hand, shone a light down on the contents with the other.

Ray could see the guy's face in the reflection. Handsome guy himself, shiny scar up the side of his neck just like Ray had been told. Fine. Right guy, right time, the money looked right. All that remained was to live through the rest.

Ray stepped out then, and one of the guys at the front of the Chevy whirled around, just about shit himself. The guy dropped onto a knee behind the hood of the Chevy, pistol out, all kinds of excited Spanish coming out of his mouth, most of it having to do with the fact that there was a cop coming out of the darkness toward them.

"Shut up," the tall guy said, and Ray felt an instant identification. The gunman's excited rattle stopped.

Ray came straight ahead, ignoring the two thugs, both of whom had drawn down on him now, edging in a jerky, sole-grinding way a safe distance alongside him, pistols raised in two-handed stances. Sawed-off, banty-rooster versions of something they'd seen on American TV, was what Ray thought.

Ray stopped a couple of paces from the boss, jerked his head at the two thugs. "They still watching *Scarface* down where you come from?"

The tall man glanced at the gunmen, turned back to Ray. "Policemen make them nervous," he said.

Ray nodded, took off the uniform cap, unpinned the badge, tossed it in the cap, handed both items to the tall man. He gave the two thugs a significant look, then moved his hands to his gun belt, undid the clasps, handed that to the tall man as well. The tall man checked the mobile phone resting in its pocket, beeped it on and off. He popped the holster strap, inspected the weapon, replaced it, tossed everything in the back of the Chevy.

He turned, regarded Ray's crisp uniform shirt, the dark brown slacks, the permanently shining black brogans that Ray was wearing.

"You have brought everything, then?"

Ray reached into his pocket, ignoring the pistol that one of the thugs brought to within an inch of his cheek. He withdrew something that resembled a small TV controller, pushed a series of buttons on the keypad. One of the warehouse doors behind him began to grind upward.

After a moment, he pressed another button and the doors came to a halt. There was just enough room to see the antitank gun set up on its tripod, the wooden box of shells nearby.

The tall man sent his flashlight beam traveling over the weapon. "Interesting," he said. "The rest of the items are inside there?"

Ray pushed another button, and the door began to grind back down. "You wish," he said, giving the guy a smile of his own.

"What happens is, you give me the money, I give you the keypad. I drive out of here, and in about a minute or so, I call you on that phone I just gave you, tell you a code. You punch it in, then another one of these doors is going to open up." He swept his arm toward the darkness behind them. "Then you walk in and get your badges, your uniforms, your sidearms." He broke off, nodded in the direction of the door that had closed itself.

"You too can be Miami cops," he said. "You want the tank gun, it's another ten thousand."

"And I am supposed to trust that you will do as you say," the tall man said. "Just give you the money, let you drive away?"

Ray shrugged. "You don't know me, I don't know you, but I know the people who put you in touch. First thing, these people explained to you something like it was going to work, so this is no surprise. Second thing, I live here. I have to keep on doing business with these people. You think I'm going to screw with that for your little bit of money?"

The tall man considered it. He had another look at the uniform Ray was wearing, glanced at the stuff in the back seat of the Chevy. Finally, he nodded. He turned to the other two, made a gesture. They stepped back, stowing their weapons. The tall man took the briefcase from the top of the Chevy, handed it to Ray, who found it satisfyingly heavy. He riffled a couple of the packets at random. Twenties, through and through. He closed the case, tossed the keypad to the tall man who caught it against his chest.

"How about the tank gun?" Ray asked.

The tall man opened his palms at his sides. "It does not fit into our plans," he said.

Ray pursed his lips. "I'd make new plans if it was me."

"Thank you for the offer," the tall man said.

"Sure," Ray said. Too bad, but he would have no trouble finding a buyer. He was already edging away, moving backward, his eyes locked on the tall man. Nothing was going to happen, he thought, that didn't begin with some word, some gesture from the *jefe*. That was the rule with sea worms. And as for the tall man, he didn't seem dumb enough to try anything at this point, but, take all the precautions you want, you still had to keep your guard up.

"Just hang tight," Ray said. "A minute or so." And then he was gone.

**Down the tight passage** between two of the mini-warehouses, over one chin-high fence, another passage so tight he had to move sideways, a quick right down an alleyway, then a left and over a block wall, he was moving as fast as one of the rats that loved the place, faster even, and he imagined the owl up there in one of the tall pines, watching him go, guy looking something like a cop with a briefcase banging his leg, one more quick turn and there was the big Suburban right where he'd left it, Ray jumping inside, screwdriver for a starter good as if he'd had a key, one straight run between the offices of an air-conditioning repair service and an appliance warehouse, big bilingual banner draped across the front, "EXPORTAMOS—WE EXPORT."

"Me too," Ray called out, the pedal of the big truck on the floor. He wondered briefly what a bunch of Salvadoran drug scammers intended to do with the stuff he'd delivered, but it wasn't a major hold on his attention. It'd be some serious deal, of course, involving much more than what he'd take home from his night's work, but the risk was so much greater. You might make a half-dozen drug scores just fine, but sooner or later your action would attract someone else's action, and that wasn't where Ray Brisa wanted to be. He'd found his niche.

In a city like Miami, being a thief was like taking up the civil service work of crime. Everybody expected to be stolen from, even the cops. Long as you didn't actually hurt anybody while you were at it, they kept their attention directed at the murderers, and the serial grandmother rapists, and the drug runners who were into serious weight. There just wasn't time for anything else.

Ray congratulated himself once again on this wisdom: Maybe he was not yet old enough to vote, nor to legally purchase a drink in the state of Florida, but at age twenty he had acquired a status and a security within it that would elude most of his peers all their lives. He swung the Suburban into a hard left turn, down a lane that would have seemed more like a walkway to anyone else.

It *was* a walkway, in fact, but Ray knew exactly how wide it was, and where it led, pity anyone using it to actually walk to work at this hour of the morning, though. He hit the berm of an elevated drain, and the right fender of the Suburban veered a few inches off course. The collision took a twenty-foot gouge out of the plaster wall on one side, and his correction was a bit too strong, sending the other fender into a slightly shorter furrow down the side of the building on the left.

He noticed the rich trail of sparks he left in his rearview mirror, but that wasn't what he was looking for. Important thing, there were no headlights in his wake.

He nodded and turned back to his driving. A yellow barrier pole had been planted at the mouth of the far end of the passage. He must have been doing forty by the time the Suburban hit it, flattening it as if it were a wooden stake.

He was behind the south end of the warehouse complex now, barreling across a vacant parking lot and fishtailing up onto a grassy dike-top road that paralleled a broad canal. A hundred feet ahead was the gate to a bridge that only the water management people used, which he had jimmied earlier. On the other side of the canal was a similar gate that opened onto a lane that led into the streets of a development, and from there one-point-two miles to the entrance ramp of the Florida Turnpike.

He swung through the open gate, the Suburban's tires roaring on the wooden bridge planks. At the top of the bridge's incline, he hit the brakes, and the Suburban slid to a halt. Something rolled in the rear compartment, thudding into his seatback. Loose equipment, he thought, or maybe the briefcase, but then he remembered he'd tossed that into the seat on his right.

He'd secure whatever it was in a moment, for he had two more pressing items to attend to. First, make the call he'd promised; and then he'd give Luis and Zito exactly thirty more seconds to show up here at their planned rendezvous. After that, the plankton would be on their own.

He dialed in the number of the phone he'd left with the tall man, heard the connection make after the first ring.

"I am here," the voice came.

Ray was scanning the open space between the warehouse complex and the canal, checking for signs of Zito and Luis.

"You're going to be sorry, you didn't take the tank gun," Ray said.

"You have some numbers for me," the voice said.

Ray knew the guy was over there in the middle of the warehouses, a mile or more from where he sat, but it sounded like he was right in the seat beside him. The cellular phones he was accustomed to stealing were often noisy, always cutting out in the middle of conversations, okay for free, but why did the people who paid for the things put up with such quality? he'd often wondered. This new digital technology seemed a major improvement, though. He would try to steal only those from now on.

"You see a couple of my people over there?" Ray said. "Big guy and a little guy?"

"I would like those numbers, my friend."

"Yeah," Ray said. "Sure." Not that he cared a great deal what happened to the sea worms, but he was curious now. "Punch six, six, six," he spoke into the phone.

"Clever," said the tall man.

"The way my mind works," Ray said. He imagined he could hear the wheels of the warehouse door grinding upward. He was also thinking he'd have to give up on Zito and Luis, let them make their own way home.

"You see your door?" he said into the phone.

"Yes," the tall man said. "It would seem as though it is working."

"Then *hasta la vista*," Ray said into the phone.

"*Hasta*," was the tall man's reply.

Ray cut the cell phone connection then. He took a last glance in the direction Zito and Luis might have come, then shrugged. He patted his briefcase, dropped the Suburban into gear, was about to ease on down the other side of the bridge when he remembered the thing sliding around loose in the back of the truck.

He flipped on the dome light, turned, stopped cold. The carpet in the rear compartment was glistening wet with something that looked like oil. He reached out his hand tentatively, felt it warm and sticky, knew what it was before he brought his fingers back into the light.

He wiped his hand quickly against the uniform shirt, raised himself so that he could see into the crevice between the front buckets and the platform. If he hadn't been ready for it, the sight would have knocked him backward.

Skinny Luis down there, staring sightlessly back up at him, an impossibly big smile on his mouth. Impossible because it was his throat, in fact, laid open from ear to ear, or so it seemed to Ray, who was already pushing himself away, little sounds of fear popping involuntarily out of his gut like bubbles of awful gas.

He twisted back into his seat, his hands clamped on the wheel, gasping for breath. *Control, Ray, control.* Sure, it was a shock, seeing Luis like that, enough to scare anyone. But he was far away from the guys who'd done it. Just hit the gas, he told himself, zip right on through suburbia, those guys could never find him. *You're cool, Ray, you're just fine . . .*

. . . and then his eyes fell on the briefcase.

He could visualize the stacks and stacks of twenties inside, feel the satisfying heft of the thing . . .

. . . and suddenly he was clawing for the door handle at his side, jerking it so hard he snapped the pot-metal lever—cheap stuff they used despite the fact that these days a glorified van cost $40,000—because he'd somehow leaned on the automatic door lock button and had to hammer every goddamned thing on the armrest that looked like a control until he finally heard the little pneumatic *thunk* as the lock disengaged and he had the handle by its little nubbin, didn't matter that he sliced his finger open doing it, he would have used his tongue on the ragged metal if he had to.

He jumped down from the cab, took one step, then two . . .

. . . and then the blast came and the door he'd tried to hurl shut came right back after him, slamming into him like the business end of a bus, taking him out over the canal, weightless as an astronaut . . .

. . . only it wasn't an astronaut, it was Ray Brisa, thinking *fucking brief-case, fucking money*, hurtling through a soundless black sky like heading to another dimension, and then, finally, the wall of fire caught up and took everything.

# Part 2: Campaign Trail

# 3

". . . I'll have to admit, it wasn't what I had in mind, Frank." She had her gaze set out the window of the airy hotel penthouse. Blue skies, even bluer sea, a scattering of sailboats, toy-sized at this distance, free and glistening in the tropical sun. That's where she wanted to be. Who wouldn't?

"Why don't you call me Mr. President," he said, giving her his trademark grin. "It might remind you why you volunteered."

His idea of a joke. She turned to watch him as he stepped into his trousers. Sure enough, one leg at a time, just like anyone else. Maybe she ought to bring in the photographers, let them snap away at Frank in his flopping boxers. It was the sort of thing that had once aided the presidency, wasn't it: LBJ showing his scar, Gerald Ford clonging his bald head on an airplane wing?

"But you're going to miss it. It's right up your alley," she said. "Cops, soldiers, derring-do." She noted that he sucked in his breath before he snapped the waist button of his slacks. A damned shame. You could be chief executive and your waistline still be beyond your control. Not that she had any room to talk, of course. She'd paid twelve hundred dollars for the suit she was wearing, and if the wall of mirrors behind her husband was to be trusted, about a thousand dollars' worth of the fabric was stretched over her behind.

Frank disappeared into the bathroom, pulling his shirt on, and she turned, trying another angle, trying to convince herself it was just the way the light struck the fabric. There was a knock at the bedroom door and she glanced at her watch. One of the aides, she thought, hurrying them along. "They're baying at the door, Frank . . ." she began, and then the door flew open.

"I don't give a damn what Malcolm Jesse says," the first man through the door was saying. It was Larry Chappelear, who'd been with Frank from the beginning, the man who'd helped transform him from a professor of political science into a state representative, a governor, and ultimately a president. They'd all been classmates at Mizzou together, once upon a time.

The normally placid Chappelear was red-faced now, nearly shouting at John Groshner, Frank's special advisor, who was coming through the doors on Larry's heels. While Larry had been with them since forever, Groshner had come aboard in Washington last year to help lay the groundwork for this campaign. Larry was down-home, even rough about the edges, and, while forthright, a strategist who preferred to play behind the scenes. Groshner was Ivy League through and through, stern but brilliant, a Beltway insider who loved the spotlight. Frank didn't care for Groshner's style, either, but she knew he trusted the man's brutal instincts, counted on him for the ruthless take on things, something Frank worried that Missouri politics had not prepared him for sufficiently, even to this day.

"Getting in bed with these people is like taking a hum job from a rattlesnake . . ." Larry was saying to Groshner. He broke off when he noticed Linda staring at him.

"Sorry," he said, glancing about the room. "Where is he?"

"In the bathroom, Larry. Do you mind . . . ?"

Chappelear didn't hesitate. He was through the open door before she could get another word of protest out.

"You can't do this, Frank," he was saying.

"I can't take a leak?" she heard Frank call back.

"Forget Florida . . ." Chappelear continued.

Groshner hesitated, gave Linda a look that was supposed to be apologetic, then barged into the bathroom after Chappelear. "He can't forget Florida. Not if he wants to be president . . . "

"He *is* the president," Chappelear called out. "How do you think he got there?"

"Stop it!" Linda heard Frank cry over the sound of the toilet flushing. "Both of you!"

She saw Groshner backing out of the bathroom, followed by Larry, both of them being driven along by Frank, who was zipping himself up. He glanced at Linda, shaking his head. "You believe this?"

She shrugged. She'd come to believe just about anything over the past four years. She was just happy she'd had her clothes on.

"It's a mistake, Frank. You can set a major precedent here—" Chappelear began again.

"And become the first president to shoot himself dead in front of the American public." Groshner broke in.

Frank closed his eyes, held up his hands for quiet. "The matter's been decided." he said.

"But, Frank . . . "

Frank opened his eyes, shaking his head, holding a finger to his lips. "I said 'decided,' Larry. Now both of you, get out of here and let me finish getting dressed."

Groshner flashed a smile of triumph, but Frank didn't acknowledge it. He clapped Chappelear on the shoulder, met his hangdog look. "We'll make this work, Larry."

Chappelear started to say something else, but saw the set of Frank's chin. He nodded quietly then, and went out the door after Groshner.

Frank went to the door, examined the knob. He turned back to Linda. "No lock," he said. "Amazing."

"It wouldn't matter," she said. "Groshner could ooze in through the cracks." She knew how Larry Chappelear felt, after all. He'd spent a dozen years at Frank's side, helping him hone policies that were both humane *and* workable. Larry, who'd written his dissertation on Latin American politics, had won the admiration of commentators and politicians on both sides of the floor for his work to extricate the country from entanglements with the sleazier of those regimes, to embark upon more enlightened policies in the region. Now, here he was, faced with the prospect of seeing all his work obviated by Groshner, pragmatist extraordinaire.

"That's not fair, Linda. John's got a point of view, but . . . "

"He's an android," she said. "They don't think, they're programmed."

"Are you going to grind me about this meeting, too?" he asked. His voice had risen a notch. He looked at her as if he might suddenly be wondering where to place her: for him or against him. This could be his last battle, except for maybe where to build the library to house his presidential papers, she understood that much. But she also worried that the point of waging the war in the first place had been lost a long time ago.

She shook her head. "You need to do what you think is best," she said. She managed a wan smile. "I'll do my part. Just tell me where to go, who I'm supposed to do it to."

He gave her a look meant to convey gratitude, though perhaps it was just relief. "It's the same goddamned drill, Linda," he said. "Pretend it's the Daughters of the American Teapot Association or the Homeless People of the Mississippi Delta, something you're interested in."

She knew he was trying to joke, but it still came off as a dig. "Maybe you can do it that way," she said. "I can't."

He rolled his eyes, struggling with a cuff link. Twenty-two years in political life, he still couldn't get a cuff link in place. She stepped forward, took hold of his sleeve, guided the nub through the tiny embroidered holes.

A set of cuff links she'd bought him once, she realized as she smoothed the fabric of his shirt. Tiny fishing flies under amber-cast domes. For an instant, she saw him as he had been in his twenties, when they were both graduate students, she on a Fulbright to Oxford, he come over for a summer exchange program at Cambridge. They'd tramped Wordsworth country together, picnics, fly-fishing, lovemaking in fields of daisies. Yes, her heart *had* leapt up.

She took his other sleeve, held her hand out for the other cuff link, took care of that one as well.

He nodded his thanks, she gave him a smile. They could be out there on that glistening bay, she thought. He casting, she reading a book. Sure. It could happen. In about four and a half years, in fact. Four years sooner, if the election were to be lost. A distinct possibility, if Malcolm Jesse, the gloomier of their in-house pollsters, were to be believed. That was what Larry and Groshner were really wrangling about: those distressing figures and what might be done about them.

"Linda," her husband said, in his famous aggrieved but patient tone. "When Groshner talked me into doing this thing in Miami, I didn't think there was a chance in hell of making any inroads with the Cubans. But if they want to talk, then I'd be a damned fool not to talk."

Until yesterday, there'd been no prospect of inroads, no meetings with exile leaders, nothing but the standard photo opportunities and the Medal of Valor ceremony, a pleasant enough event, but politically insignificant: there was a fundraiser attached, and there would be several hundred party faithful in attendance, but for Frank it would be like preaching to the choir. He'd been morose, worried that the whole trip had been wasted: why hadn't they stayed in the Midwest, worked harder on Ohio . . .

. . . and then Groshner had come in with the news: Jorge Alejandro Vas, archconservative leader of the Cuban exile community and longtime pretender to the presidency of a liberated Cuba, had agreed to meet with Frank after all. Vas was the man who could deliver Florida. That was the thinking, at least. To meet with Vas meant that Frank would need a replacement for the Medal ceremonies, though, and that's where Linda had come in.

"I'm happy to stand in," she said, though she knew her tone didn't exactly support the statement. "But I'd still like to know what John told Mr. Vas in order to arrange this meeting."

"What does it matter? The point is, I have the opportunity to try to talk some sense into the man." He gave her the sincere look that all the reporters loved. But they didn't live with the man. When he used it on her, it meant he was being less than forthcoming.

"Tell me the truth, Frank. What do you have to give up?"

He was checking his cuff links again. "That's not the way I do things, Linda. You know me better than that."

"You're going to undo all of Larry Chappelear's work just to get this man's blessing?" She was well aware that Chappelear had been campaigning from the moment they'd arrived in Washington to soften the U.S. stance toward Cuba, to open meaningful negotiations there. There'd been more talk recently, vague references to the "new strategy" down there, and she knew something was in the works, though she hadn't asked Frank and he hadn't volunteered any information. That was just fine with her; her interest in the intricacies of Latin American political affairs rated right up there with flower arranging. But in this case, she sensed her husband being whipsawed. And *that* was something she took an interest in.

He glanced up at her. "I'm not going to undo a thing. I'm going to point out to Mr. Vas that he's got a hell of a lot more to gain by allying himself with the inevitable process of rational policy-making than by getting in bed with an opportunist like Charles Hollingsworth."

"Good luck," she said. "From what I've heard, I don't think Vas understands the word 'rational.'"

Frank rolled his eyes at her, but he didn't respond. Partly because he wasn't interested in having this fight, partly because deep down he shared her feelings about the far right.

Still, he was going into a meeting where he would have to make nice with an ultraconservative power broker who would not merit five minutes of their time in any other context. Thank God it was Frank, she thought. Thank God it was he who had to cover and compromise and concede every day of his life. She knew what was required but had never become comfortable with it. Oh, at first, perhaps. When it was still local politics, nothing that mattered outside Missouri, and nothing much in Missouri that everyone didn't feel basically the same about, or so it seemed in relation to the way things were in Washington.

Nearly four years in Washington later, she'd finally come to understand the true meaning of politics. Now all she could think about was getting out, and Frank just as desperately wanted four more. Not that any man wouldn't, not that she had ever expected otherwise. She could understand that, but at what price to *her* soul, that was the question she'd been wrestling with, though she understood how presumptuous it would seem to share such a thought with anyone.

*Get a grip,* she told herself. *You are the wife of the president of the*

*United States. Get a grip. You do not have feelings of doubt, insecurity, hesitation, depression, or yearning for a life other than the one you have. Give anyone the idea that any such thoughts have so much as passed through your mind and . . . well . . . look at the field day the media had had with Fergie, Diana, Pat Nixon, with Hillary, for God's sake . . .* she realized that she had drifted off, that Frank had taken the opportunity to move away from the subject of Vas and what Groshner had or hadn't intimated.

". . . think you're going to enjoy this, Linda," Frank was saying, shrugging into his suit coat. "All these people are heroes. They get their pictures in *Parade* magazine, they inspire others, they stand for all the worthy values."

"They're probably all huge," she said. "I'll have to stand on a box to get the things over their necks."

"There's a lady cop from Oakland," he said. "Second-generation Vietnamese-American. She pulled ten people out of a hotel fire. I'll bet she's not an inch over five feet, probably goes about a hundred pounds."

She nodded. "I never said it wasn't a worthy occasion, Frank."

"There are all kinds of people," he said. "One guy's from Miami, some kind of contractor who saved all those Cuban folks out in the Gulf Stream."

She nodded vaguely. Lady cops, heroic building contractors, local SWAT team members. Not that she didn't appreciate their good works, not that she was unaware that they were capable of greater acts of courage than she would ever be capable of . . . it was just that behind every Herculean deed was a story of human tragedy, and even if it was, in these cases, tragedy aborted or averted, she was not entirely consoled. For every good work, for every heroic act, how many tragedies had gone forward unimpeded, how much cruelty had been gleefully and freely expended, how many evil intentions had been carried out undeterred?

Loony to see things this way, she could not argue with that, and she had never been one to see her glass as half empty. But perhaps that was the toll the office had taken upon her, even her slight part in it. She'd heard others talk about it, how many fine men had come to Washington, full of the best of intentions, only to find that the immense Leviathan that was the entrenched bureaucracy had been steaming along for years, its course unaffected by any single captain's will—and it would continue to be that way long after she and Frank were gone.

One could garner personal power, one could reward friends, one could make a show of doing things differently, but the days when one man could change the world were gone forever. Even JFK had been forced into alliances he'd personally abhorred, had he not? She glanced at her husband and shook her head.

"What's that about?" he said. He was checking the knot of his tie now, staring back at her through the mirror.

"Nothing," she said, forcing a smile. "You look handsome." And it was true. He was still handsome. If anything, age had only dignified his features, which, when he was young, had been almost too perfect. A touch of gray at the temples, squint lines at his eyes, a weathered look on his burnished skin. The Marlboro Man in city dress, refined, at ease.

"You want me to talk to John? He could handle the ceremony. It wouldn't have the same flair, of course."

He'd probably do it, she thought. And yet there was something withheld in the offer, something left unsaid. As if she could calculate what it might cost or, to put the best possible light on things, what it could add to have her there, draping the heroes with their medals, how many more photos would be lifted off the wires with her doing the honors—laurels from the First Lady—than if gruff John Groshner were there. And then it crossed her mind that the entire business was a setup, that her husband, this consummate politician, might have calculated that she would outshine even his star in that particular context . . .

. . . but that was being too cynical, even for Frank, who, after all, was hell-bent to capture the state of Florida and its twenty-five electoral votes from Jorge Alejandro Vas. That was where his thoughts were focused, not on some photo opportunity.

"Go," she said wearily. "Go talk some sense into Jorge Vas. I'll handle the heroes." She smiled to show she understood.

He smiled in return, and she thought she saw a moment's flash of that boy she'd met in England so many years ago. He'd been fly-casting, showing off for her, stepped off backward into a deep pool and filled his chest waders, she'd had to dive into the fast-flowing stream to get him untangled before the current swept him away . . .

. . . had dragged him—a president-to-be who couldn't swim—gasping and choking to the bank, where he finally caught his breath and grinned up sheepishly at her. *He's something special,* she'd thought back then, *and yet he needs me too.* A long time since she'd thought of that moment, thought of saving him . . .

Then, just as quickly, the flash was gone, and he had bent to brush her cheek with his lips and she caught a hint of his cologne. "You'll knock 'em dead," he told her, and then he was out the door.

33

*Peabody Public Library*
*Columbia City, IN*

"You look pretty spiffy," Vernon Driscoll said. The ex-cop leaned in the doorway of John Deal's bedroom, working a toothpick in the corner of his mouth. He wasn't looking at Deal, though. His eyes were on the television atop Deal's dresser, where a weatherman was tracing the development of yet another tropical storm, a sizable whorl of red and green weather bands advancing toward the Caribbean.

"Thanks," Deal said. He didn't feel spiffy, not at all, and the prospect of another storm system grinding their way didn't do much for his mood. He checked his reflection in the mirrored sliding door of his closet: the one decent suit he owned, a dark wool pinstripe he hadn't worn in a couple of years, pinching him now at the waist and shoulders, a white button-down shirt that seemed to have shrunk one size at the neck. When DealCo had been a major player among South Florida builders, when his old man had still been around, he'd spent plenty of time in suits.

But that had been a decade or more ago. Before his old man had sent the firm into ruin, then painted the walls of his bedroom with the insides of his head. Now Deal spent most of his days moving from job to job, keeping his crews moving, a hammer in his own hand as often as not. You couldn't really swing a hammer while you were wearing a tight suit.

"Too bad they switched this heroes shindig to Miami, though," Driscoll said. "You're going to get pretty hot in that outfit."

"At least it's not raining," Deal said.

"Give it a couple of days," Driscoll said, pointing at the television.

Deal nodded glumly, though it really didn't matter about the heat or the prospect of another storm. When he'd received the call about the award, he understood that the ceremony would be held in Washington, D.C. He'd spent a week working out a plan with Janice, his estranged wife, had intended to pick up his daughter, Isabel, in St. Pete, take her along, make a sightseeing trip out of it. Nearly seven now, she was old enough to appreciate such things. But a few days ago, there'd been another call from the White House and Deal had gotten it straight: The President was coming to Miami, the presentations would be made there. No sightseeing trip after all. And no visit from Isabel, either, at least not right now.

"You promised her a trip to Washington, Deal. And now you're canceling," that's how Janice had put it. "You just don't do that to a child her age."

Making it his fault, somehow, piling on the guilt. The upshot was, Janice was using her vacation from the gallery in Naples where she worked to take Isabel to Orlando and its associated fantasy worlds for the week; Deal could have his visit with his daughter another time. It was illogical, and maddening, but in Deal's mind pushing Janice would have been like squeezing a fine teacup, one of those with all the spidery fracture lines just beneath the glaze. His wife, so lovely on the surface, so fragile underneath.

But she'd been doing better, they'd been making progress, edging back toward one another. He was determined not to do anything that might blast that possibility apart.

"You gotta admit," Driscoll said, breaking into his thoughts, "Miami's the perfect place to pass out the awards. Number one in tourist murders, hurricanes, money-laundering, it only stands to reason we ought to attract more heroes than anyplace else. You know, like a lot of bears just naturally migrate to those spillways where the codfish try to swim upstream?"

"That's salmon, Driscoll."

"Them too," Driscoll said. "You follow my reasoning."

Deal simply nodded. Getting into the fine points of an argument with Driscoll would be like inviting legal discourse from Yogi Berra. Better to let the matter stand, let cod displace the salmon in the waters of the Pacific Northwest.

He turned back to the mirror, gave his sleeves a tug, as if that might stretch the fabric out a size or two. There were a couple of sport coats in the closet that he would have greatly preferred, but he thought the suit was the appropriate thing, under the circumstances. He glanced at Driscoll, who was wearing a version of his retirement uniform: cutoffs, rubber flip-flops from Kmart, a black Pig Bowl sweatshirt with the sleeves cut out, a snarling, slobbering boar's head stenciled across the chest.

"You ought to be part of this, you know," Deal said. He'd said as much to the White House aide when she'd called, as he had to every reporter whom he'd talked to following the incident, but it was a waste of effort. From day one, Driscoll, in his typical fashion, had shunned the limelight, refusing to take any shred of credit for their adventure on the bay.

"I was just along for the ride, buddy-boy, that's all."

"Bullshit. What about that last kid we pulled up?"

Driscoll shrugged. "You did all the heavy lifting while I was having me a siesta." He touched the scar on his forehead. The stitches were gone, but the hair they'd had to shave where the gash had run up his scalp was still thin. "I might have bled to death if it wasn't for you."

"I doubt it," Deal said. "You're too ugly to die."

"I appreciate it," Driscoll said, cocking his finger at Deal. "And I owe you."

"You owe me nothing," Deal said. Stacked up against all the things Driscoll had done for him and his family, Deal thought his payback seemed minuscule.

Driscoll shook his head. "You ought to take a minute, consider what you did, my friend. There's twenty people out there chasing the American dream this very day because of you."

Deal glanced at him. "The whole thing was a stroke of luck for everybody. And I'd have never saved that kid without your help."

"Sure you would've," Driscoll said. "Just accept it. You're a hero. The President's gonna shake your hand."

Deal bit his lip in frustration. About as easy to argue with Driscoll as it was with Janice. *Maybe* he could have brought the kid back to the *Miss Miami* in time, then brought everyone in safely, but he sure as hell wouldn't have wanted to try. Even with Driscoll's help, he'd been as exhausted that night as he'd ever been, mentally as well as physically.

The fact that those women and children had been cast into the water like so much excess baggage had weighed upon him more than anything. He'd helped save that group, sure, but nothing had changed the conditions that led to them being out there in the first place.

"How many boats in the Gulf Stream right now, full of people trying to make it to Florida, Vernon?"

Driscoll shrugged. "Probably a couple as we speak. What's your point?"

"Who's going to save the next bunch when their boat swamps or some scumbag tosses them over the side?"

Driscoll stared at him. "Hell, I dunno. But that doesn't take away from what you did."

"The real hero," Deal said, "would be the one who could change why those people are climbing into the boats in the first place."

"That's probably why the Prez is coming down," Driscoll said. "He's going to hang that medal around your neck, then make a big announcement, normalize relations with Cuba . . . "

"When pigs fly," Deal said. In Miami, even the mention of such a notion could get you shot.

"Naw, I got it all figured out. He's going to buy out Fidel, send him to a

Swiss chalet somewhere, appoint Jorge Vas the new president. Vas'll get the casinos going again, all the boats'll be heading the other way, steaming into Havana harbor."

It was Deal's turn to stare. Jorge Vas was the ultraconservative leader of the Cuban exile community. Detractors claimed he dreamed of returning to his homeland as the new Batista. "That's your solution, is it?"

"It's about as likely as anything else on the board," Driscoll said, then gave Deal a more serious look. "We got a time-honored tradition of mucking around in other countries' business, especially south of the border. I don't see it changing anytime soon."

Deal gave him a glum look. Cuba. Haiti. El Salvador. Nicaragua. Panama. Colombia. Peru. Mexico. An unbroken roll call of disasters for U.S. foreign policy. Maybe Driscoll was right. Forget the big picture. Be happy he'd saved those poor people. Take his medal. Smile for the cameras. Go back and build good houses. Maybe one of the kids he'd hauled out of the water would live in one someday.

He forced himself from his thoughts, gave Driscoll a grudging nod. "You could at least come along for the ride," he said.

Driscoll shook his head. "Not my kind of deal, pards, you'll forgive the expression. But you give the Prez a kiss for me, okay?"

Deal regarded him for a minute. "I think that's the French president," he said finally, "where you get a kiss." He was trying to twist his neck free, find some room inside the noose of his tie. Dark blue silk, a knot that felt the size of a fist, about a thousand tiny Snoopy images knitted in the fabric. He wasn't sure the tie was dressy enough, but it was the only one he had that matched. Besides, Isabel had given it to him last Father's Day. It was going to have to do.

Maybe there'd be a picture in the Orlando papers, he thought. Maybe she'd see he'd worn the tie. That would be something, at least.

"Don't worry about how you look," Driscoll said. "I saw the roster. Most of the people going to that ceremony are either cops or some kind of military. Next to them, you're gonna come off like the Duke of Earl."

"I can expect a lot of 'PIG AND PROUD OF IT' T-shirts, is that what you're telling me?"

"Nothing that dressy," Driscoll said. "Fact of the matter, I knew a detective from Fort Lauderdale won one of these things a few years back. He stumbled onto that heist out at Gulfstream, took out three guys by himself, talked the fourth guy into surrendering his hostages."

Deal nodded. It was a vague memory, something from another era of Miami history, when crime had been a grander, somehow classier endeavor. Now most of the criminal minds around seemed to be focused on blowing away 7-Eleven clerks or assaulting grandmothers. He'd taken a crew to lunch the other day, they'd come back to a job site at the far south end of Old Cutler Road to find their power cords stolen.

Fifty bucks of worn and patched cord to replace, but he'd lost the labor of six men for two hours while someone drove all the way to Shell Lumber (Deal refused to trade with the ubiquitous chain supply stores), then he'd had to send two concrete trucks back to the plant because the footing forms hadn't gotten done, and finally he'd had to scratch the rest of the day altogether when a thunderstorm, typical for an early summer afternoon, came crashing in just as they were ready to go to work again.

"Jiggs McCullom was this cop's name," Driscoll was saying. "He used to wear a sport coat looked like a blanket he took off one of the nags at the track. Only coat I ever saw him in. No question that's what he wore to pick up his medal. If he even bothered to go, that is. I guarantee you one thing, if the ponies were running, the Prez had at least one no-show that day. The whole thing was sheer accident to begin with—Jiggs had one shining moment as an officer of the law, and he hit the quinella with it."

"Maybe *I* should stay home," Deal said.

Driscoll snorted. "Don't give me that. You're dying to go. I would be, too. I'm just jealous, that's all."

"Why'd you nominate me, then?"

Driscoll glanced at him. "Nominate you for what? The Prez has people that read the papers, the newsmagazines, watch Ted Koppelman."

"Ted Koppel," Deal corrected.

"So he had his name changed." Driscoll shrugged.

It was true, Deal thought, there had been plenty of public fuss over their adventure, but the aide from the White House who'd called to inform him of his selection had made it clear: civilian nominees were put forward officially by mayoral or gubernatorial offices from around the country, and Deal's name had come from the mayor at the behest of the chief of police. No question in Deal's mind where the process had begun. Driscoll might have left the department, but his influence lingered on.

"Thanks anyway," Deal said.

Driscoll reached out to clap him on the shoulder. "I'm proud of you, pards. You go on down to the Hyatt, rub shoulders with the Prez, mention D & D Security in your acceptance speech. We'll have a drink when you get home."

D & D Security, Deal thought. The result of an impulsive gesture that would have been more typical of his old man. Deal had fronted Driscoll a thousand dollars for office rent and supplies, that had made him a partner in the security business. Driscoll had come home with the cards, calling Deal his silent partner. "Besides," he'd said, "D & D makes it sound more like a *company*."

Deal gave Driscoll a look. "They're handing out thirty-five of these medals," he said. "I don't think there are going to be any acceptance speeches."

Driscoll offered another of his patented shrugs. "Take some cards, then. Slip one to the Prez while he's giving you a kiss. All the stuff people try to dig up on him, he ought to have his own counterintelligence consultants."

"He has a couple already," Deal said. "They're called the FBI, the CIA."

"I'm talking about people that can get in there, do him some real good," Driscoll said, unfazed.

Deal rolled his eyes, took the card that Driscoll extended toward him. "I'll be sure and pass it along."

"You're a national hero," Driscoll said. "He'll listen to you."

"Give it up, Driscoll."

"There's money to be made in private security. You want to spend the rest of your life driving nails, building strip malls?"

"I can think of worse ways to make a living, Vernon."

Driscoll feigned exasperation as Deal tucked the card away, then checked his watch. Less than an hour before his scheduled arrival, no more time for banter.

Besides, Driscoll understood how Deal felt about his work, perhaps even envied him. He understood what he could get his hands on, was less certain about things he couldn't, that was the simple truth. He knew wood and concrete, how they could be shaped, what could come from the application of his efforts with saw, hammer, and chisel. He was no artist, but he considered himself a fair artisan. He could measure the worth of a day by what stood where nothing had a few hours before. He took great satisfaction in restoring an older home another builder might dismiss as a "tear-down," took pride in seeing places he'd put up weather hurricanes, and a corresponding sadness when neighboring structures toppled for the lack of simple craftsmanship or worse, because someone, builder or owner, had wanted to save a few hundred dollars.

Sometimes, he thought, he must have been the only kid who'd ever truly paid attention to the story of the three little pigs, and sometimes he worried that his care and his attention to detail had spilled over into so much of his life that it made him seem stodgy, if not downright pig-headed, but there'd been some pretty fearsome wolves coming after him and his family the past half-dozen years or so, hadn't there, and not one had been able to blow his house down yet. He gave himself a little inward nod of self-congratulation that might have actually held, but for the sudden troubling thought that intruded: Hadn't a couple of the little piggies who used to live with him moved out?

The question was enough to shake him from his reverie. *Think too much, you could always find a way toward trouble, Deal.* Time to get in motion. He punched the power button on the television, passed out the doorway of his bedroom, moved down the hall and into the kitchen, where Driscoll was rummaging in the refrigerator for a beer.

"Make yourself at home," he called toward Driscoll's formidable backside, checking his watch once more: plenty of time, no more than twenty minutes, this time of day, from the fourplex, on the edge of Little Havana, to the Hyatt in the middle of downtown.

Driscoll came up out of the refrigerator's maw with a Red Stripe in his hand, saluted him with it. "Not bad," he said to Deal. "I been buying Old Milwaukee recently," he added.

"You've always bought Old Milwaukee," Deal said.

"Yeah, but it used to be because it was cheap. Now, since I read that *Consumer's Digest* report that says it's number one, I realize it's because I got good taste."

Deal regarded him for a minute: the sweatshirt, baggy plaid Bermudas, the foam oozing from the already-popped Red Stripe. Two hundred and forty pounds on a maybe six-foot frame. Taste?

Deal considered two or three responses, but then he looked into Driscoll's guileless, I'll-step-in-the-way-of-a-truck-for-you gaze. Finally, he shook his head. "I'm out of here, Vernon. I'll give the President your best."

"Do that," Driscoll said. "And don't forget to explain what we can do for him, either."

"I've got the cards," Deal said, heading toward the curb, his neck chafing anew in the heat.

"I'll be right here, manning the phones," Driscoll said.

"Who told you to bring a unit back here?" the man in the suit was saying.

Salazar towered over the man, who had to look up into the sun to find his features. The sun was so bright that the eyes of the man in the suit had begun to water even though he was wearing dark glasses.

Salazar thought he looked convincing, even natural, in the uniform of the American police, though he no longer favored uniforms. The pin on his breast pocket was stamped with the name "ESCOBEDO, D." He had no idea what the "D" had stood for when Escobedo was still among the living, but he knew what it stood for now. He also knew that the man speaking to him came from somewhere in the northerly regions of the United States and that he was not used to the heat or the humidity or the punishing angle of the subtropical summer sun.

The two of them were standing by a service dock at the rear of the great hotel. There was a City of Miami cruiser not far away, where Salazar had parked it so as to block the narrow service path, and a bank of garbage Dumpsters off to the side, where a slope fell away in a tangle of unidentifiable tropical foliage toward the broad and listless estuary known as the Miami River. The sun had turned the Dumpsters into cauldrons, reeking with castoff shellfish and the remains of carved red meats and whatever else had not made its way into the stomachs of the pampered guests up above.

"Humping-A," the man in the suit said as he took off his dark glasses and wiped his brow with a handkerchief. "I'll be glad to get back to Washington."

Salazar knew that the man's remark was not directed at him. The man was disgusted with his superiors, with the need to be in this place at such a time of year, with an assignment that required him to be standing outside less than a dozen feet from a veritable shipload of rotting garbage, giving orders to a simple-minded local officer of the law who likely did not speak English and who would never know the pleasures of a good steak dinner in an air-conditioned restaurant in Georgetown where the ferns hung in well-tended clumps and the women had fair skin and were willing to look a man squarely in the eye when they were interested.

As the man wiped the back of his neck with his handkerchief, Salazar noted the thin curl of wire that led up out of the man's ear to loop and dive down again under the collar of his jacket. When the man put his handkerchief away and turned to continue his questioning, Salazar held up his palm and spoke in a quiet but concerned tone of voice.

"You are with the detail of the President?"

The man stopped what he was about to say and gave Salazar a closer look.

"Of course I am. What . . . ?"

"I think it is something you should see," Salazar said, cutting the man off once again. He turned and moved quickly toward the rear of the cruiser, motioning for the man to follow.

Salazar inserted a key into the trunk of the cruiser and unsnapped the lock. He glanced back at the man in the suit and indicated that he should look at whatever was inside.

"What the hell . . ." the man in the suit said when he caught sight of the officer who lay staring up out of the trunk into the brilliant sky without so much as a blink or a waver.

The man in the suit sent his hand under his coat. Possibly he had been reaching for his phone, intending to call in news of this startling development. Or it could have been that the situation had unfolded itself before him in an instant and he was actually reaching for his sidearm. Wherever it had been traveling, his hand stopped suddenly, at the very instant that he sounded a sharp intake of breath. The knife so slender, so sharp, it would take a moment for the pain to register. But the pain would come, bright and sharp and awful, and the man might even have lived long enough to cry out, except that Salazar's free hand now clamped his mouth shut, and the last thing he could have seen was a red film bathing the palm-lined world as he tumbled, and the lid of the trunk coming down like night.

"Base to Steam Cleaner, Base to Steam Cleaner. Everything okay back there?"

A single touch to turn it on, and after that the device operated on simple voice activation, the better to keep one's hands free in case of emergencies, Salazar noted, fitting the earpiece more snugly into place.

Salazar gave the appropriate response in rapid but carefully accented English. He had once been trained, after all, by that very agency. There was a pause, and Salazar wondered for a moment if perhaps something had gone wrong.

"Check that, Steam Cleaner," the voice answered then, and then skipped off to monitor the next agent.

Salazar turned to face the opposite bank of the turgid river, making the prearranged gesture. It was a distance of a hundred yards or more, but still he heard the sound of the boat's engines firing, saw the craft swing away from its docking place. Two more police cruisers had swung into position at the head of the narrow lane that led down from a side street to the secluded loading dock. One of the officers who stepped from the cruisers gave a wave to Salazar, who returned it easily.

Salazar checked his watch. Out in front of the grand hotel, where the crowds had gathered to both cheer and decry the arrival of the American president, another group would be moving into place, its work yet to come. He nodded, wiping the slender shaft of his weapon carefully on the handkerchief he had availed himself of. He tossed the soiled handkerchief into the mouth of one of the Dumpsters and walked through the fetid air toward the ramp of the loading dock.

"Would you please come with me, sir?"

Deal stared back at the man who had spoken to him. Guy with a strange-looking ID badge clipped to his suit. He was in his early thirties, wore his hair carefully trimmed, regimental tie, white shirt, dark wool suit not unlike Deal's own, if a notch lighter in weight and stretched a bit more across the shoulders and chest. Deal suspected he hadn't built his pecs by swinging a hammer or carrying hod, though. He also suspected the question wasn't really a question.

"Sure," Deal said. He checked his watch, then followed the guy across the gleaming marbled lobby of the hotel.

The guy seemed like a jerk, but Deal was happy to be inside in the cool air-conditioning after the frantic twenty-minute hike he'd made from the Metrorail parking lot. The Metrorail lot was as close as he'd been able to get to the Hyatt, a hotel that had been built by DealCo, in fact, but that had been twenty years ago, back when his old man had been running the company show, riding high, and headed for an equally long fall.

Deal had tried to explain why he was headed to the hotel to a traffic cop, leaving out the part that he'd helped to build it, but the cop had stared back as if he were crazy, had given Deal a choice, move the Hog or submit to arrest, though not exactly in those terms. Deal supposed it hadn't been unreasonable, some guy wearing a wool suit out in the Miami summer, driving what had once been a Cadillac sedan now sawed and chopped and converted into some kind of pickup truck from a loony-bin dream, stops in the middle of the street and says he's a hero, take me to your president. Sure, Deal thought. He was lucky the cop hadn't just drawn down and fired on the spot.

The security type, meantime, had stopped, was holding a finger up to indicate Deal should stop, too. His other hand had slipped inside his coat. They were in a quiet little room off the side of the lobby now, the carpet heavy, the furniture gilt-trimmed and massive, the drapes long and thick, enough velvet there to be used in most of the movie theaters of his youth. It was the sort of place that made you sleepy just being in it. If the guy had his hand on a gun, Deal thought, he could fire with impunity, the sound wouldn't travel a foot.

"I have someone named Deal here," the security type was saying, apparently to himself. His eyes flicked up at Deal. *"John* Deal?"

Deal nodded, noting the wire coming out of the guy's ear. They waited for a moment, staring at each other, though the security man's gaze seemed to focus somewhere else.

"Is this going to take a long time?" Deal asked.

The guy looked at him, but didn't say anything.

"I'm part of the program," Deal said. "The Medal of Valor program."

The guy nodded, ran his eyes over him, then glanced away.

"Uh-huh," the guy said finally. "Right." His eyes seemed to refocus, as if he'd snapped out of standby mode.

The guy had his hand under his coat again, came out with some kind of security wand. He used it to scan Deal from head to toe, pausing twice: once for Deal to fish out his keys, a second time to examine his Swiss Army knife.

"Picture ID, Mr. Deal?"

Deal reached into his hip pocket for his wallet, noticing how the guy watched his every movement now. "Sorry I forgot the letter," he said.

The guy nodded slightly, the sort of acknowledgment you give an alien who's about to assume his true, frightful form.

"I read about a guy swallowed a pound of plastique, ground his fillings together, the sparks set him off like a rocket," Deal said as he watched a local television crew bustle past. "Took out an entire dental group."

The security guy looked him over. "I could make another call, you know."

"I didn't ask to come here," Deal said. A couple more exchanges, he figured, any chance of making it to the ballroom would be gone. He envisioned the headlines: "LOCAL HERO GOES BERSERK, ASSAULTS PRESIDENTIAL SECURITY DETAIL—AWARD RECALLED." His mind wandered on, pictured Isabel reading the story, asking her mother to explain "berserk."

Deal had seen the look in the man's eyes. For a moment, he felt the absurdity of the situation. It was true, the implication in the eyes of the security guy. Deal had no business here, mingling with cops who put their lives on the line every day, mothers who had chased gang-bangers and drug runners from their embattled neighborhoods.

All this was Driscoll's fault. Deal could have been with his daughter in Orlando, going hand-to-hand with some ride operator at Disney World instead of this.

"Picture ID," the guy repeated. It wasn't a request this time.

Deal withdrew his wallet, flipped it open to display his license. The guy took the wallet, studied the license as if there were some code in there to be broken. After what seemed like a long time, he glanced up at Deal, his expression doubtful.

"This expired three months ago," the guy said.

Deal nodded. They'd offered to send a car for him. Why hadn't he accepted? "Is it important?" he said. He checked his watch again.

"Just hold on." The guy turned away, saying something into his invisible mike. There was a rumbling noise from out in the lobby, a couple of workers pushing a dolly full of banquet chairs, and the security man opened a door to an interior office. When Deal started after him, the security man held up his hand to indicate he should stay where he was. He waved the wallet at Deal as if to say he just might return, then closed the door, still talking into his invisible mike.

There was a terrific crash in the lobby outside, and Deal turned to see that the chairs had toppled off the dolly onto the marble. The two workers were shouting at one another in Spanish and a manager was converging rapidly on the scene. Deal glanced at the doorway where the security man had disappeared with his wallet. No sign of him.

"Mr. Deal?"

Deal turned back toward the lobby. The man he'd taken for a hotel manager was hurrying toward him, maneuvering around the toppled chairs and the gesticulating workmen without so much as a glance.

"We'd nearly given up on you." He was florid-faced, silver-haired, his hand extended, an impressive bank of teeth on display.

"Monroe Fielding, Special Assistant to the President," the man said. He reached out, clipped one of the security badges on Deal's suit coat. He took Deal's arm. "We'd better hurry along."

Deal hung back. "My wallet's in there." He pointed at the door to the inner office.

"Excuse me?"

"One of your security men took my ID."

Fielding rolled his eyes. He hurried over to the door, tried it, found it locked. He banged on it with his hand, but there was no response.

"Anyone in there?" Fielding called, but no one answered. Fielding checked his watch, then glanced at Deal. For a moment Deal wondered if Fielding believed him. What if Fielding demanded ID?

"I assure you we'll have your wallet returned, Mr. Deal," Fielding said, smoothing his hair into place. It was impressive hair, Deal thought. The kind someone like Fielding would want to keep smooth. "Let's get you up with the others, then I'll take care of it."

Deal glanced at the silent doorway. Along with the expired license, he had maybe fifty dollars in the wallet, a wad of receipts and notes, Driscoll's business card. Maybe they'd lose the wallet, he could say he'd been carrying a fortune.

"What say we go on upstairs, Mr. Deal?"

Deal turned to him. *What say?* Deal thought. *What say?*

"Sure," he told Fielding finally, and followed the man away.

"There'll be local photographers—maybe something extra because we've got that Miami person in the mix—and the usual contingent from the national press and newsmagazines, as well as someone from the White House staff, of course, but it's the guy from *Parade* we have to spend some serious time with."

It was Leslie Blanding, one of the aides who'd stuck from the days in Missouri, who was briefing Linda as the Secret Service team led them down a hallway to the room they'd be using before the ceremony began.

"Frank didn't mention anything about a special shoot," she said. But Leslie seemed not to hear. Linda sighed. She was still holding out hope of a few minutes in the sun before the day was out. Wasn't that what Florida was about, after all?

She hadn't been in the state since she'd come to Fort Lauderdale with some girls from her sorority her sophomore year, but the minute she'd stepped out of *Air Force One* into the warm bath of air, the memories had been sneaking back with surprising clarity, maybe because it was the last time she could remember being so foolish.

Like any other winter-frozen coed who wanted to get the most out of five days in the sun, she hadn't even unpacked before she had hit the beach with the others, blanket spread, lathering herself with a mixture of baby oil and iodine, drinking beer until she was woozy and burned to a crisp. The following morning, a maid at the motel where they'd crammed six to a room had walked in to find her alone in bed, wracked with chills and frozen with fiery pain. The maid took one look at her skin and disappeared, to call for help, Linda had supposed.

A few minutes later, the maid had reappeared, carrying what looked like a dusty spear tip in her hand. It had turned out to be a leaf she'd sliced from something called an aloe plant in the motel's courtyard. She'd split the inch-thick leaf open to expose a gelatinous inner material so vividly green it looked radioactive. The maid reassured Linda that the Seminole tribe—of which she was a member—had been using the plant for centuries. She scooped some of the green stuff into her palm and began to spread it gently across Linda's shoulders. The effect was instantaneous. Linda felt as if she had been dipped into a tub of cooling liquid anesthesia. In less than an hour the chills were gone and she was able to sit up straight again, the pain a whisper of what it been. She had tried to give the maid money, but the woman refused and Linda had settled for buying the woman a huge basket of fruit and leaving it in the room upon their departure, along with a card of thanks. Lucy, her name, the desk clerk had told Linda. Sure, you get sick, Lucy'll have something for you to try.

So odd, she thought as Leslie Blanding ushered her inside the waiting room. One trip, so long ago, and such details still vivid. She'd spent the rest of the week in the shade of a clutch of coconut palms at the edge of the beach, her pink and peeling nose in a series of books, while her sorority sisters cooked themselves bronze and flirted with a group of lazy-eyed college boys from South Carolina who spoke in melodious drawls of such mysteries as barrier islands and beach music.

It had been as if she were an invalid parked in a deck chair on a cruise ship while exotic scents and tropical scenery glided past. She could still feel the giddiness born of the palpitating heat, the tang of cocoa butter everywhere, the faint grittiness of sand that clung to her skin no matter how many cool showers she took, the soft *crash-crash* of the coconut fronds above her head, and the easy smiles of the boys from coastal Carolina who danced in the sand, some slow jitterbug step they called the "Shag" that seemed to lend itself to almost any song.

Truly odd, Linda thought, walking to the window of the waiting room to stare out over the hotel's marina at the calm waters of the bay. Something about that visit she'd never really gotten over. Some vision of paradise born of a sheltered Missouri girl's postadolescent experience, and though nearly a quarter-century had passed, and she had traveled the world, and taken degrees, and practiced law and married a man who had turned her from a career-driven attorney into the First Lady, she still indulged that improbable, exotic vision of a life under the cocoa-buttered palms.

She turned to Leslie Blanding, who was standing nearby, studying her notepad. "Did you ever come here, Leslie, back in college, I mean?"

Leslie gave her a curious glance. "To Miami?"

"Well, you know, Fort Lauderdale, spring break, *Where the Boys Are*, all that."

Leslie smiled, shook her head. "I was a California girl, remember. We always had the beach."

"Right," Linda said. "I'd forgotten." Blonde, slender, self-assured, untroubled Leslie. She looked like she'd grown up in a place everyone else had pined for. No pent-up longing for a life in some far-flung paradise for her, Linda thought. No yearning to escape small-town life and small-town thinking. None of the Midwestern baggage of self-doubt, the Gatsby-like compulsion to prove yourself on the bigger stage. What must that be like, she wondered? No Calvinistic baggage of guilt, no innate tendencies toward self-denial. Leslie Blanding had probably had one of those mothers who took their daughters in for birth control pills as casually as Linda had been fitted for braces.

She laughed then, chiding herself for her silliness. Good grief. Projecting all this on poor, sweet Leslie, who worked like a Turk and by all accounts idolized her and her husband, who never failed to mention how fortunate she felt to have such a job as this, attending to a million and one trivial details of protocol and public relations most hours of her waking life.

"Something wrong, Mrs. Sheldon?" Leslie was staring at her uncertainly.

Linda gave her a smile she hoped was reassuring. "Just thinking about the last time I was here," she said.

"I don't remember that," said Leslie. She was clearly puzzled now, obviously trying to reference some forgotten affair of state.

"I was just a girl," Linda said, and waved her hand in dismissal. "Now let's see that speech that Frank was supposed to read. I'm sure there's plenty of testosterone we'll have to boil out before *I* can read it."

Leslie Blanding smiled then, and Linda thought she caught a glimpse of something cross the face of the Secret Service man who stood at attention just inside the door to their room, though whether it was amusement, amazement, or disapproval, she couldn't tell, and it really didn't matter. She had come to be who she was, and she was comfortable with that, she thought as she took the sheaf of papers from Leslie. Anyone who wasn't, they would just have to vote for another First Lady, now wouldn't they?

"This is really some *do*, isn't it?" The voice rose over the din of conversation that filled the room.

Deal shielded his face from the lights of a television crew panning the hospitality suite and turned to the person who had spoken to him, an ebony-skinned man in his late twenties wearing a cream-colored sport coat, dark brown slacks, checked shirt, knit tie. Despite what Driscoll had said, the guy looked like he'd stepped off the pages of *GQ*.

"It's something, all right," Deal allowed, watching as a pair of security men hustled the camera crew toward the doors. He was still wondering about his wallet. He supposed it was safe in the hands of a Secret Service agent, but still he felt a little undressed without it.

The two of them were standing by a table laden with finger foods and iced-down soft drinks at the back of the crowded staging suite where Fielding had delivered him. It was the rest of the heroes milling about the room, Deal assumed, though he hadn't stopped to check any name tags.

Four burly guys in short haircuts and the kind of clothing Driscoll had described stood at the other end of the table, devouring tiny sandwiches by the handful and cracking jokes in rapid-fire accents that bespoke the outer boroughs of New York. They were the most obvious cops in the room, though Deal was sure there were others, even the two long-haired, emaciated types in a far corner who were either heroic hippies or narcs who had brought down untold weight.

For the most part, however, the group resembled an Amway dealers convention or some kind of casting call for a latter-day Norman Rockwell crowd scene: There seemed to be a fair complement of housewives, slightly paunchy middle-aged males, a goodly representation of blacks, several Hispanics, a couple of Asians. Also the hippies, the cops, a couple of younger men in Western-cut jackets talking together near the doors. There was one dark-haired woman wearing a black form-fitting cocktail dress standing alone near the center of the room who seemed uncharacteristically striking. Maybe she'd wandered into the wrong party, Deal thought.

"Myself, I think she humped a bad guy to death," the black man at his side said.

Deal turned, feeling his face redden. "I was that obvious, huh?"

The black guy shrugged. "Everybody else been staring at her, why wouldn't you?"

Deal laughed, and the black guy held out his hand. "Roland Wells," he said. "What did you do to deserve this?"

"I've been asking myself that very question," Deal said, shaking hands. "My name's John Deal."

There was a pause and then the black guy snapped his fingers, pointing at Deal's chest. "I remember. You're the guy that pulled all those folks out of the ocean."

Deal nodded, the feeling of discomfort welling up inside him once again. "It wasn't like I went out hunting for them," he said.

Wells gave him a look. "I know what you mean, all this fuss," he said, glancing about them. "Same way with me. I was driving home from work one day—I live just outside Columbus, that's the Ohio one—I see a cop pulling a guy over up ahead, I don't think much about it." Wells took a sip of his Diet Coke, let his eyes travel to the knockout in the form-fitting dress.

"By the time I pass by, the cop's just getting out of the cruiser walking up on this trashed-out RX-7 when all of a sudden the guy floors it and takes off."

Wells stopped himself, turned back to Deal. "But you didn't ask to hear this, now did you?"

"I'm interested," Deal said. Something about Wells's unassuming manner had engaged him. "What did you do when the guy took off?"

Wells raised his brows. "Nothing, at first. I mean, who the hell wants to get involved? Like I said, I was just on my way home." Deal nodded, and Wells seemed to make some decision. He closed his eyes momentarily—it might have seemed just a blink in any other context—then took a breath, let it out in a sigh.

"What happened was I glanced down—I'm driving my van, see, I install tile for a living, got my own little shop—and I realize the guy's right beside me, trying to crowd in off the shoulder, and about the time I realize what's really happening, the guy points a gun at me, like get your black ass out of the way."

"You didn't get out of his way," Deal offered.

Wells shrugged. "I sure as hell intended to, but I was in a solid line of traffic and I guess I wasn't fast enough. The next thing I know the guy's shooting, the glass is blowing out of my windows, I'm under the dash, one hand on the wheel and crossing myself with the other." He gave Deal a brief smile as he continued. "*Then* I feel something slam into the side of the van, I realize—insult to injury—the guy's trying to run me off the road."

Wells stared at Deal as if he'd understand the outrage of it all, and Deal thought maybe he did understand. "Just what had this person done, anyway?"

"I'm getting to that," Wells said. "Meantime, all I know is he's an asshole trying to kill me and I just got the van out of the body shop that week, five hundred bucks for a big ding my wife put in there pulling out of a parking space. I mean, I know it's not rational, but I am pissed. When the shooting stops, I come up out of my seat and I don't even bother to see if the guy's still got his gun out, I just pull hard right on the wheel of the van and smack back into him and all of a sudden, there we are, like a couple of billy goats butting head to head, going about sixty miles an hour by this time, chewing a big cloud of dust right down the shoulder of the road."

Deal was hooked by now, was reliving flashes of a not-so-dissimilar encounter of his own, on his way to work one sunny Florida morning, when a cretin in a car he'd unwittingly cut off in traffic had pulled a gun and nearly killed him.

"What was happening with the rest of the traffic?" he asked Wells.

Wells's face broke into a grin. "Oh, man, they were flying every which place, just trying to get out the way."

Deal felt himself identifying more and more with Wells, this fellow hardhead who was just driving along, minding his own business, when trouble came calling. It reassured him in a way. If he and Wells had found themselves at such a gathering, then surely others in the room had ended up here under similar circumstances. Maybe there should be a special category of the awards, he was thinking; call it "Accidental Heroes." Maybe he'd feel like less of an impostor, being here.

"We might have gone on like that until the guy reloaded or we ran out of gas, one," Wells was saying. "But then I saw we were coming up to this underpass for I-70."

Wells paused, his expression sobering. "I'll never know if the guy saw it coming, 'cause I know I caught sight of it just in time to hang a big-time left." Wells shrugged. "My van clipped the support pillar on the rear end, but the asshole took it head-on. His car just blew up, man, burned to a cinder."

Wells gave Deal a look. "He'd have been dead already, of course. I hope he was. Even with what he'd done, I'd hate to think about somebody burning to death like that, even him." There was something almost pleading in his tone, something that made Deal nod in agreement.

"You were going to tell me what the guy had done," he reminded Wells gently.

"Yeah." Wells sighed. "Turned out he'd robbed some pissant little bank out in Grove City, marched three tellers and the woman manager into the vault and shot 'em in the back of the head."

Wells shook his head. "One of them lived, but she's in a wheelchair, can't even say hi to her kids. The guy got six thousand dollars. It burnt up in the crash."

He was staring at Deal hollow-eyed now. "Thing I can't figure out," Wells said, "what the hell have we come to, anyway? I mean, the guy had the money, wasn't a soul going to contest him for it. He didn't even have to shoot those women in the first place."

Deal shook his head. "I don't know," he said. "It's not the same world I grew up in. I know it must sound dumb, like it's something my old man probably said in his time, too, but . . ." He trailed off, feeling helpless before Wells's answerless question.

"I don't have the first regret about doing what I did," Wells said. "I just don't feel like any hero, you know what I'm talking about?"

"I know," Deal said. "I know."

Wells managed a smile. He raised his hand in a fist, sent it forward in a slow tomahawking motion, tapped Deal lightly on the chest. "Didn't mean to go on like that," he said.

"It's all right," Deal said. "I'm glad you told me."

"I'm gonna get me another Coke," Wells said. He gave Deal a glance. "Probably be busting a kidney before this thing's over. You want something?" He pointed to the nearby table.

"You find a Red Stripe in there, you can bring me one," Deal said.

"That's a beer, right?"

"The best," Deal said.

Wells laughed. "Yeah? Well, then, I'll bring us both one," he said, and moved away toward the table.

Deal watched him go, thinking that his expectations for this event had already been exceeded. *Just goes to show you,* he thought. *You can't get too cranky, can't turn yourself into a recluse. You just never know where or when you might meet a kindred spirit, somebody who just might have the same, nearly inexpressible feelings you carry around day in and day out.* He turned to toss his own soda can into a trash receptacle, wondering if Wells were married, if he had trouble at home as well . . . when he heard a woman's voice at his shoulder.

"Mr. Deal?"

He turned to find the dark-haired woman in the cocktail dress standing before him.

"I'm Valerie Meyers," she said, eyeing him carefully. "*Are* you John Deal? The pictures they sent out in the packets weren't very good, you know."

Deal caught the subtle scent of some perfume that even he knew had to be expensive, some mixture of exotic flowers that grew only in France and Nepal and then got ground up into a powder along with hundred-dollar bills. Her skin was pale and flawless, her hair even darker up this close. He had to will his gaze away from the plane of her chest. *Act like a human being,* he told himself, *show her there are men of higher purpose in the world.* He ignored the donkey's bray that sprang up from somewhere to accompany these thoughts.

"I'm John Deal," he managed. *Now there's a suave rejoinder, Deal.* What on earth *had* she done to find her way into this company? Why hadn't he bothered to read the packet of material the organizers had sent along?

She reached into a small bag, withdrew a business card. "I'm with Far Horizons, in Los Angeles," she said, holding out the card to him. He took it speechlessly, turned the card over a couple of times in his fingers.

"We make films, feature films," she continued. "I've been wanting to talk to you."

Deal felt himself shaking his head dumbly. "You're a movie producer?"

She smiled in response. "I work with Carson Parks."

Deal shook his head again.

"He made *The Last Brotherhood, Three Friends, Shiver Rules.*"

When Deal didn't respond, she paused to give him a closer look. "Is there something wrong?"

"A producer," Deal said. He was feeling a bit giddy all of a sudden. He turned to the buffet table, but Wells was nowhere in sight. "Sonofabitch."

"Excuse me?" she said. She was still wearing her Isis-like smile, but now he saw some shadow behind this appearance, something he might never have spotted from across the room. Dark red lipstick, flipped-under hairstyle something like the pageboys from his distant past; he realized she reminded him of the gangster's moll John Travolta danced with in that movie about good-hearted killers. A guy could spend the rest of his life trying, Deal thought, no thing he could do which would ever get a rise out of this woman.

"Nothing," Deal said. "There was a guy here wanted to meet you, that's all."

"Well," she said. "Carson and I have been talking. He's very interested in your story . . . "

"You came all the way to Miami to talk to me?" Deal asked. He felt an odd jangling somewhere behind his eyes, synapses firing at cross-purposes, messages derailing, little sizzles where they plowed into slumbering gray matter.

She glanced about the room, her smile widening a fraction. "There were a couple of people Carson and I discussed, actually, but you're very high on our list. We think there's a property here, a potential . . . "

"As in make a movie out of what happened with me out testing my boat?" Deal heard his voice rising. He tried to imagine it: himself a dashing hunk behind the wheel, the young boy he'd given mouth-to-mouth transformed to some babe in a see-through sarong.

"As in get to know you, Mr. Deal," Valerie Meyers said easily. "Talk. See if there might be something to explore . . . "

Explore exactly *what*, Deal thought. He'd stumbled into all this to begin with, and the people he'd pulled into his boat were in that water because they'd risked everything for a decent life. He and Valerie and Carson were going to sit down and talk about how that might make them all rich?

Deal felt his throat go tight with anger, felt his hands begin to tremble. Serious mental weather, look out, storm about to come ashore . . . and then, just as quickly, everything kicked over into calm. That old standby, psychic circuit overload, he thought, the weird safety mechanism that had rescued him more than once from going absolutely haywire.

"Gee, I wish I'd known," Deal heard himself saying. He was surprised at how calm his voice sounded. He shook his head in a way that was meant to seem rueful. Maybe this was the tack that the wolf had taken just before he gobbled up Grandma.

Valerie Meyers shook her head. "What do you mean?"

"I already signed," Deal said. He was careful to keep his expression glum. "With Robert De Niro, a guy from his company, I mean. Like a binder or something?" He glanced at her as if for help.

"An option?"

Deal copied Roland Wells's gesture, made a pistol of his fist. "That's it. An option."

She gave him a careful glance, but Deal kept himself fixed on rueful. Part of him wanted to tell Valerie Meyers to take a flying leap at the moon, another part yearned to dump the half-melted bowl of ice over her lovely head, but he focused on rueful and restrained and prayed that if she did nothing more than pass on his absolutely fanciful information to her boss, he would have achieved a greater effect.

He took her hand, which was firm but delicately boned, and replaced the card she had given him in her palm. "I appreciate the thought, though," he said. "Maybe some of the other folks haven't been taken. There's a lot of heroes here." He swept his arm about the room good-naturedly.

"Maybe you should keep the card," she said. "In case things don't work out . . ."

"Everything's just the way I want it," Deal said. His expression felt as bland as wheat. He grinned happily, hoping that wasn't laying it on too much.

"Well," she said. "Good luck."

"Oh, I've had plenty already," Deal said. She smiled back, a bit uncertainly, he thought, and then she was moving across the room away from him, her hips winking in that black dress in a way that made him just the tiniest bit sorry he hadn't heard her out.

"Did I see what I thought I saw?"

It was Roland Wells approaching, Diet Coke in one hand, can of ginger ale in the other. "Always happens to me," Wells said. "Every time I go to the bathroom, I miss a good part." He handed Deal the ginger ale. "You were talking to her? She came over here and talked? And you let her get away?"

Deal thought about it for a moment. He fixed Wells with a forlorn expression. "She's a man," he said. Wells stared back at him, then craned his neck for a better look across the room.

"No way," he said. "No way."

Deal gave the shrug he'd picked up from too many years around Vernon Driscoll, the gesture that was meant to lend credence to almost anything. Wells might even have bought it, but Deal would never know. For in the next moment, Monroe Fielding was back in the room to tell them it was time.

"Do you enjoy a good cigar, Mr. President?" It was Jorge Vas, reaching into his suit coat to withdraw a dark leather case.

He and Frank Sheldon sat alone at a table in a pleasantly appointed atrium where they'd retired after lunch—as alone as it was possible to be with the President in a public setting, that is. Secret Service agents were arrayed at the doors and along the hallways beyond; more agents—as well as Vas's own security detail—in the main dining room; and a cadre of city and state police along with other Secret Service men outside the Little Havana restaurant Vas had insisted upon. There were probably agents hidden under the phony boulders and amongst the ferns and rocks of the grotto-like atrium, but Sheldon wasn't going to bother looking for them.

Going to Vas on such short notice had required considerable logistical effort, but Sheldon was willing to concede where trivialities were concerned. Besides, he'd enjoyed the food, which was a welcome change from the usual rubber-chicken banquet offerings and health-conscious fare Linda was always pressing on him: a thin-cut palomillo steak pan-fried in a garlicky butter and smothered in chopped onions, black beans and rice, fried plantains, even a Hatuey beer, which Vas took pains to point out had once been brewed in Cuba but now was a product of the Bacardi U.S. operations. They'd had a delicate flan and a robust espresso in the atrium, and now there was also the possibility of a cigar? He tried to imagine Linda's reaction—a steady diet like this, he wouldn't have to concern himself with the actions of some lunatic, he'd be assassinated via lunch.

"I'm going to guess that's *not* from Cuba," Sheldon said, pointing at the fat unwrapped Churchill that Vas held up for inspection.

Vas glanced past the cigar, grunted something like a laugh. "El Credito," he said. "The tobacco is Honduran, grown from Cuban seed. And it is fashioned by Cubans, though in a shop only a few hundred yards from where we sit. A fascinating place. Perhaps you would like to see it?"

"I wish I had the time," Sheldon said.

Vas nodded his understanding and extended the case. Sheldon hesitated, then took one of the cigars. There was a waterfall burbling somewhere. It sounded like distant rain.

"It takes a person a year to learn how to roll a cigar like that," Vas said.

"And most of a lifetime to learn how to do it well." He replaced the case, raised the unlit cigar to savor its aroma.

"These, for instance, are made for me by an old woman named Perla Valdez." Vas reached into his pocket, found a cutter that operated like a miniature guillotine, used it to snip the end of the cigar neatly away.

"Her husband worked in a cigar factory in Havana," Vas continued. "When he persisted in passing along news accounts smuggled back from Miami for the factory's *lector* to read, Castro had her husband's thumbs cut off." Vas produced a wooden match, flicked it into life with his thumbnail. He paused to stoke the big cigar into life, then held out a match to Sheldon.

"It's a terrible story," Sheldon said, shaking his head at the offer of the match.

"Such stories fuel our passion," Vas said. "There are many of them."

"And I appreciate your feelings."

Vas waved the remark away. "Enjoy the cigar at your leisure. If you are pleased, let me know. Perla Valdez would be honored to fashion *los puros* for her *presidente*."

"That's very kind of you . . . and Ms. Valdez."

Vas nodded. "And it is kind of you to agree to this meeting on such short notice."

Sheldon nodded dutifully. "It's *my* opportunity," he said. "I want you to know I think we can work together in the next administration. I'm convinced that between the two of us, we can fashion some solutions to some longstanding problems where it comes to Cuba."

Vas nodded thoughtfully. "I would like to think so myself, Mr. President . . . "

"Well, then—" Sheldon began, leaning forward across the table, his cigar raised for emphasis.

". . . but it is impossible."

Sheldon stopped short, staring at Vas. "Impossible?" The sound of the waterfall seemed to have increased into a torrent.

Vas puffed on his cigar, stared at Sheldon through the cloud of smoke that billowed between them. "I have heard distressing rumors," Vas said after a moment.

"That's usually just what they are, rumors," Sheldon countered.

Vas shrugged. "Reports that an agreement has been reached for the opening of diplomatic relations between this country and the present government of Cuba."

Sheldon stared back levelly. "People have talked about that for a long time."

"Indeed they have," said Vas. "But there has never before been a president who would lend credence to such a notion."

"I can assure you that no one in this administration . . . "

Vas waved his free hand back and forth. "It is not necessary for you to issue a denial, Mr. President. I simply want to explain to you why it is impossible for me—for any Cuban—to support your candidacy."

"Hear me out," Sheldon protested.

"I've seen with my own eyes," Vas said. "Documents which make clear your intentions."

"I don't know what you've been looking at . . ." Sheldon began.

"You intend to make a deal with the devil," Vas said, his voice quiet but firm.

Sheldon stared at the man, momentarily at a loss. It was true, certain preliminary documents had been prepared, but they were a long way from anything formal, and nothing his advisors would let out. The best-case scenario suggested announcement of trade agreements with the Cubans a year or so after the elections, and he and Chappelear had agreed they would keep their cards close. Vas had to be bluffing.

"I can assure you that no policy changes with the Cuban government would be entertained without consulting with you first," Sheldon said. "Anything you may have heard is pure speculation."

Vas waved his hand. "You would like to win a second term, and you would like to leave behind a legacy," Vas said. "I understand all that. As I understand that it would be suicidal for you to announce your intentions before the election. But I can promise you that this legacy will not be built upon the backs of the Cubans who want their country returned to them."

"You misunderstand my intentions," Sheldon said.

"Then prove me wrong," Vas said.

"And what would that take?"

Vas waved his hand again. "Certain assurances." He reached into his pocket, withdrew a folded sheet. He spread it flat and laid it on the table before Sheldon, tacking a corner with his finger. Sheldon understood that the document was not being passed along.

Sheldon scanned the short list, then stared at Vas. How many of his predecessors had seen this document, or a version of it? How many had had this conversation, or one similar to it? And where had it gotten them?

What Vas would require of him would tie his hands, undo all of

Chappelear's work, just like Linda had said. And even if he were to concede, how could he be certain Vas could deliver what he claimed he could? John Groshner was convinced Vas held the keys to the kingdom, but Sheldon wasn't so sure. In any case, make a half-dozen deals like this, what would winning accomplish? He took a deep breath, spoke firmly over the sound of water tumbling over artificial rocks.

"The world has moved on, Mr. Vas. I'm sure you realize that in your heart of hearts. I'm going to win this election, but I was hoping you'd agree to work with me. I'm sure we can find a way to represent your interests and the interests of the people who depend on you for guidance."

Vas nodded, and a thin smile crossed his lips as he folded up the document and replaced it in his pocket. "It was a pleasant lunch, Mr. President. I am sorry we do not see eye to eye. Perhaps you will come again when you have more time to spend with us."

Sheldon stood. The phony waterfall seemed to be crashing louder now. He extended his hand. "Please consider what I've said."

Vas rose to take his hand and nodded, but if there was any hint of acknowledgment in the gesture, Frank Sheldon missed it altogether.

"We are ready."

Salazar's voice was flat, unaccented, emotion-less, and though it came through a portable phone, and the incoming signals might have been detected by any number of scanning devices, sophisticated and unsophisticated alike, they would have been manifested to any other listener on earth—computer hacker, spy, pervert, all the same—as a mad scramble of indecipherable static. Access to such technology was just one of the privileges of power, one more reminder of the need and the duty to maintain the public trust.

"Then proceed," he responded. "Just as you were instructed."

"You are certain?" Salazar's voice came again.

He thought briefly of what was about to happen. "A disturbance," he said. "A managed disturbance."

"Precisely," Salazar replied.

"Nothing serious, but the point will be made."

"Absolute discreditation," Salazar intoned, reciting now. "Public the-ater. An event that will demonstrate just how volatile the communist forces truly are, how politically unstable. At the very moment that the chief executive of the United States agrees merely to meet with the leader of the Free Cuba movement, see what these men, blinded by their pas-sions, will do . . . "

"That's enough," he said, realizing that Salazar was feeding his own rhetoric back to him now.

"Do not worry," Salazar said, his voice reassuring now. "One day you will write of all this, of how simply the world was changed, once and for all."

He felt a momentary breathlessness and then, on its heels, that instant of clarity when madness and logic join and metamorphose into something greater, beyond the sum of the parts. Once past that moment, he was calm and certain and unassailable, he always would be.

"Then do it," he ordered. And switched off the phone.

**11** Vernon Driscoll was at the kitchen window of the apartment he rented from Deal, a pair of binoculars raised to his eyes, muttering softly to himself in the moments before the bulletin came over the television. "Come on, you bastard," he was saying. "Uncle Vern's got a surprise for you, baby."

He edged the focus down with one finger, brought the intruder into sharper focus. This one had come over the back fence just where he'd expected, a place where a thick spray of Florida holly from the untamed yard next door hung over into Deal's property. It shielded that part of the yard from the street, providing the perfect cover to enter and exit without being seen, and after the last time, Driscoll had found smudge marks and scratchings at the top of the stockade fencing there.

He'd thought about driving a few punji stakes into the ground just beneath that spot, but after a bit, he'd set that idea aside. What if Isabel were to come visiting, after all? Or what if it slipped his mind he'd even done it, he found himself out there helping Deal with the grass trimming, all of a sudden he discovers he's impaled himself?

No, he'd done the right thing. Always better to prevent the crime from happening in the first place. He nodded, though he glanced down at the rifle on the counter nearby and thought that if all else failed, he wouldn't hesitate to use it.

He turned back to the binoculars, discovered he'd lost his mark. He dropped the binoculars again, scanned the backyard quickly, caught a flash of movement behind one of the oak trees there. He raised the glasses again and nodded in satisfaction. "Uh-huh," he said. "Up to your old tricks, but it's not going to work this time."

He caught another flicker of movement then, and suddenly the sonofabitch was visible in full profile, swinging around the oak, ready to make his move. After that, things happened quickly.

The squirrel that he'd been watching had climbed at least six feet up by now. It dipped into a four-legged crouch, bringing itself chest to trunk against the tree, as if it were doing some kind of vertical push-up, then sprang away backward into space. It had to be a good ten feet from the trunk of the oak to the place where the bird feeder hung down, Driscoll thought, but the creature soared across the space easily, as if it had little furry wings. It hit the side of the Plexiglas feeder, slid down, and, even though the whole apparatus was swinging wildly by this time, caught the feeding ledge neatly in its claws.

"Little prick," Driscoll muttered. He'd seen the whole process once before, just after he had hung the feeder from a cord he'd strung from his second-floor balcony railing all the way across to the utility pole at the corner of the property, all that so there'd be no convenient tree limb for the thing to shinny out on. He'd been sure he'd foiled the squirrel that time, but the fact that he'd had to move the feeder half a dozen times prior should have been a tip-off.

By now, of course, it had become a matter of professional pride. How could he bill himself as a security consultant if he couldn't keep a goddamned squirrel from ripping off a five-pound supply of birdseed moments after he'd replenished it, and never mind if nobody knew about the problem but himself and the other tenants of the fourplex, currently Deal and his erstwhile housekeeper, Mrs. Suarez.

Of course, Deal, who made no end of fun at his expense in the matter, could always make some crack in front of the wrong person, and Mrs. Suarez was a gossip of the first order. She could start the Cuban tom-toms beating down here in Little Havana, inside of twenty-four hours word would have spread to Hialeah, where Driscoll had his most lucrative account with the string of Zaragosa Drive-ins. Hector Zaragosa might still be telling everybody about how his new security man had nailed the *pendejo chingado* who'd been robbing his stores by dragging him bodily through the drive-up window, shotgun and all, where he'd proceeded to beat the living rice and beans out of him in full view of the staff and front-area patrons, but Zaragosa was in fact the only account Driscoll had, and he didn't need to be taking any chances. Lose the job and he could find himself puttering around some valet parking lot in a golf cart with the rest of the broken-down rent-a-cops. No thanks. No thank you very much.

Meantime, the squirrel—who was so sleek and fleshy that Driscoll had no doubt it was the same one who'd been deviling him since the day he'd brought home the bird feeder, a present for Deal's young daughter actually, and wasn't that a sad state of affairs, her and her mother gone away instead of being here a part of things—this rat with a furry tail had steadied itself on the feeding ledge of the feeder, which had stopped its wild rocking and settled into a rhythmic sway in the breeze coming in off the bay. The thing took a last look around, probably to be sure there was no fat ex-cop in bermudas and flip-flops creeping up on him with a machete or a flame-thrower, then bent to the business at hand, which meant scooping every last kernel out onto the ground in about fifteen seconds so that it could hop down and pick out the big black sunflower seeds that it favored.

Only this time, something was different. The squirrel made its usual pawing movements at the trough, then stopped, glancing about the yard again.

"Hah!" Driscoll barked, a smile coming over his face.

The squirrel began pawing again, but again no seeds flew. "Hah-hah-hah!" Driscoll's bark had turned to near-maniacal laughter.

Thirty-nine ninety-five, it had cost him, down the street at Ace Hardware, or Ferreteria, as it was known in this neighborhood. A bird feeder that looked just like every other bird feeder in the world except this one had a spring-loaded feeding ledge fitted below the trough. The last time Driscoll had gone in for another fifty-pound sack of birdseed, the clerk had taken him aside and explained to him—primarily in sign language, since Driscoll's store of Spanish was limited to *cerveza*, which meant beer, and *una otra*, which was a vaguely redundant way of asking for more—that the delicate mechanism of this new feeder would support the weight of a bird (they had hollow bones, Driscoll had learned, since discovering this new and wholly unexpected passion, a sure sign of aging and the onset of Alzheimer's, he was certain), but not the comparatively Jupiter-like mass of a squirrel. Let some creature of bulk climb—or leap—upon the ledge, and it would sink down an inch or so, bringing along a clear Plexiglas cover to slam on top of the birdseed trough itself.

Driscoll particularly liked the notion of the Plexiglas, that the squirrel would be able to *see* the birdseed it couldn't get, claw as he might, maybe even suffer a nervous breakdown as a result, and even though this smacked of sadism, he thought it was a pretty mild case, given the fact that he'd spent twenty-five years as a cop and, for instance, wasn't sure that capital punishment helped a goddamned thing.

Which was why he would never have used the air rifle he'd unearthed from the trunk that held a bunch of his boyhood items he'd brought down from Lakeland a couple of weeks ago. Just a couple of weeks now since his father had finally passed away in the nursing home and the attorney had called to tell him the house would go on the market at long last.

Driscoll shook his head. Ninety-five years of age, the old man made him promise not to sell the house even though he'd been in the home a dozen years, he was going to get better and move back home any day, if not this week, then the next, boy. That's what he'd told the nurse who found him rolled out of his bed and onto the floor, in fact: "Tell Vernon I'm going home;" couple of minutes later he'd died.

Driscoll found that his view through the binoculars had blurred for some reason, though he could tell that the squirrel was in the midst of an absolute shit fit now, clawing and scratching, and the bird feeder dancing on its line like something alive. He put down the binoculars and blinked himself back into focus and unscrewed the cap end of the BB gun and tilted the barrel forward into the sink so that the shot could roll out and down the drain. Too late he realized he'd used the wrong side of the sink, but he supposed a disposal could probably eat up a little bit of copper shot in time.

He recapped the empty rifle and set it aside, then picked up the old bird feeder that he'd unhooked an hour before, and tucked it under his arm, and picked up the new sack of feed. The screen door slammed behind him on his way out to the yard, and he noted that the sound sent the squirrel diving to the ground. The creature was across the band of intervening St. Augustine grass, up and over the fence—exact same place it'd come in, Driscoll noticed—in moments.

Driscoll walked to the spot where the feeder hung, worked the hook off the chain, then out of the eyelet on its phony shingled top. He bent down, set the new feeder aside, rehooked the old one, stood and clipped it back on the chain. He scooped seed out of the bag until the old feeder was full again, then picked up the seed sack and his thirty-nine ninety-five squirrel-proof miracle and walked back to the house.

He thought he could hear the scratching of tiny claws on the fence top behind him, but he was okay with that. Little bastard can fly, then a person just ought to let him, Driscoll thought.

He went back to the kitchen then and glanced at his television and, frozen, took a second look, remembering what real problems were made of.

**12**

"... now give you our First Lady, Ms. Linda Barnes Sheldon."

It was Monroe Fielding at the podium, finishing his enthusiastic introduction. The band just below the risers where Deal and the others were seated burst into a reprise of "Gonna Fly Now," and the sound would have been loud enough without the amplification that sent it roaring out of massive speakers hanging behind the makeshift stage.

Deal turned one ear from the speakers, tried holding a finger to the other, but it didn't do much good. Both were still ringing from the opening processional that had had them all marching down the central aisle of the ballroom in the eye of several spotlights while the music blared and the crowd, which must have numbered five hundred or more, roared and applauded as if they were a bunch of pro footballers returning with the Super Bowl trophy.

Onstage now, he leaned close to Roland Wells, where Deal had planted himself despite the organizer's attempt to keep the group lined up in alphabetical order, tried to make himself heard above the music. "The President *and* the First Lady?" he said.

Wells shook his head. "Nobody told you?"

"Told me what?" Deal said.

"Fielding made an announcement in the waiting room, before you showed up, I guess. President was called away. The First Lady's a stand-in."

The music died away at "stand-in" and Wells's phrase sounded loud enough to carry to the first rows of the audience. A couple of shushing noises came from in front of them, and Deal straightened back in his seat. Maybe it was just as well Isabel hadn't come. Though he was just as willing to accept his accolades from the President's wife, he wasn't sure what kind of weight first ladies carried with the second-grade crowd.

There was no such question in the ballroom, however. Outspoken Linda Sheldon might have cut a controversial figure in the press, but here she was among friends. Her ascent to the podium was buoyed by the stroboscopic effect of hundreds of cameras flashing and a wave of thunderous applause. Even as the applause began to fade, there came whistles and shouts of approval, and a burst of laughter when someone in a foghorn voice called out, "You the wo-*man*."

A regular political rally, Deal thought, not a bad showing for a liberal president in a town that had come to be dominated by political thinkers who found Genghis Khan a bit too far to the left. While he'd been offered a half-dozen tickets for his own use, Deal had heard that most of the invitees to the ceremony were party regulars who were expected to cough up a thousand dollars for the privilege of seeing him and the others decorated.

The stuff of an election year, he mused. And if not for that fact, the President would never have come to Miami, and Deal and the others would be in the Rose Garden, sweltering in the summer heat of Washington, and his daughter would have been there . . . and if and if and if, he thought. If the dog hadn't stopped to take a leak, he would have caught the rabbit, too, that's what his old man would have said.

Deal glanced out at the audience, wondering briefly if Valerie Meyers were out there somewhere, going down her checklist of heroes to turn into movie-of-the-week subjects. And it also occurred to him, with a curious pang, that were his old man still alive, he'd certainly be out there with a score of fellow movers and shakers and their wives, holding court in the hotel he'd built himself and toasting his heroic son.

Deal, who expected a fair amount of the blah-blah-blah associated with any speech to be delivered at a quasi-political event, had drifted into a state of moderate awareness, a part of him wondering why he'd ever come here, another part noting that the First Lady was not only taller but also considerably more attractive than she seemed on her television appearances. Her brownish hair, lit here and there with highlights of blonde, was cut at shoulder length and fell naturally away from a face that seemed less broad and more intelligent in this light. And while her eyes were keen, he could see that the smile she'd given the heckler in the audience was nothing manufactured, but danced steadily at her lips as if she were actually at home doing this dance.

Maybe it was because he was always seeing her in the midst of being grilled about something or another on the television news, he thought— her call for increased spending for the aged, for revamping the workings of the United Nations, for a toughened congressional code of ethics—but here she seemed far more at ease, almost unguarded. He shifted slightly in his seat and satisfied himself even further: the First Lady also had a nice pair of legs.

"She's already spoke for," Roland Wells's whisper sounded at his ear.

Deal turned, shaking his head at Wells.

"She *is*," Wells whispered more insistently. "I know the guy, too."

Deal would have laughed but for the circumstances. One of the borough cops had turned to fix a hard stare on them, and Deal nudged Wells, who widened his eyes and made his gun-shooting gesture at the cop.

Deal turned back to the First Lady, who, he realized, was not going to indulge her audience with the usual opening banalities.

"Something has gone terribly wrong with our world," she announced, her chin coming up to underscore her statement. "I don't like to say it, and you don't like hearing it, but if you're anything like me, it's something you've probably said yourself, or at least thought about, every time you pick up the paper or turn on the news and hear about another act of terrorism, another heinous crime, another senseless act of violence." There was a murmur in the audience and Deal thought that even his fellow guests of honor had shaken off a bit of their finger-food- and soft-drink-induced torpor, were suddenly leaning a degree or two further forward.

"Even if you have never been a victim, and there are fewer and fewer among us who can say that these days," she continued, "these events cause so many of us to feel unjustly threatened, defenseless, even helpless. It is understandable to be diverted by those who propose quick fixes: more prisons and longer prison terms, widespread use of the death penalty, monumental increases in our spending on intelligence gathering and antiterrorist measures."

She paused to brush back her hair and glance about the crowded room. Rapt faces, Deal thought. Also, a uniformed officer with automatic weapon in shoulder sling at every doorway, a score of Secret Service men scattered about.

"More moderate voices call for attention to the social conditions and the inequities that foster criminal behavior." She hesitated once again, seemed to make a decision. "I could take this opportunity to address my husband's array of solutions, but I will not." She turned to regard the group seated on the stage behind her, and Deal felt the force of her gaze momentarily. Not a woman content to go to tea parties, he thought. No wonder the establishment press was always sniping at her. He'd cast a write-in vote for Harry Truman, last presidential election. Maybe this time, he'd give it to Linda Sheldon.

"Instead, I want to speak to you today about something even more important," she said, "something more essential than a political platform, no matter how worthy I believe it to be." Deal noted that Monroe Fielding, who'd taken a seat just behind the podium, leaned to whisper something to John Groshner, the dour special advisor to the President who'd opened the ceremony with a brusque explanation of the President's absence. Groshner stepped unobtrusively down from the stage, bringing a cell phone to his ear. Deal could imagine the message being relayed: *SOS to the President—there she goes again!*

"I think that all of us, no matter how we feel, no matter what remedies we might propose . . . "

She gripped the podium tightly now, leaning forward to drive her words out into the audience. "Irrespective of our politics, every one of us is familiar with that ground-zero response to bombings and sabotage and senseless murder, the shudder in our emotional underpinnings which is an assault upon a sane and rational existence itself."

Deal stole a glance at Roland Wells, who seemed as absorbed in her words as he was. The audience too seemed caught up, though he wasn't certain whether it was involvement or outright stupefaction. He couldn't imagine that this was the speech any American president would have intended to make before a group of backslappers.

"When I was growing up," she said, "we were aware of such a lurking presence of doom. The Bomb, we called it, and we spoke of how man had created the possibility to annihilate the world. When the Cold War ended, it seemed that this shadow had vanished, and that we had embarked upon a new course—that we could bend our efforts toward the making of a better world."

She paused, and when she began again, her voice was quiet. "Now this. A wave of crime, violence, terrorism on our doorstep, so much of it as to have been inconceivable only a few short years ago. So much of it, in fact, that the very concept of the value of human life erodes before our eyes, the very concept that makes democracy possible vanishes, the very concept that undergirds the notion of civilization itself threatens to disappear into some awful void."

The murmur had grown in the audience and she raised her voice again in response.

"And that, ladies and gentlemen, is what makes this ceremony today so very important. For we have gathered to celebrate a group of fellow citizens, of everyday people like you and me, whose actions remind us not only of the sanctity of human life, but show us—compel us to realize, in fact—that we can combat these forces which assail us, that there is hope, that each of us can have a profound influence on the workings of the our world."

Applause broke out in the audience then, a smattering at first, then growing to a solid roar punctuated by shouts. She waited, then turned to indicate their group with a gesture.

"Despite what a listing of their feats might suggest, not a soul up on this stage is wearing a cape, not a one of them is able to leap tall buildings in a single bound . . . "—she paused before concluding with a sweep of her arm—"but every one of these individuals is as powerful in deed and in spirit as any superhero ever was. And I am as proud to be in their presence as you are!"

At this the audience rose and roared its approval. The band had struck up again, and he turned to Roland Wells with a questioning look—forget being heard over this clamor—wondering if it was appropriate for *them* to applaud as well.

Wells was wearing the grin Deal had first seen in the waiting room, the slightly bemused expression that said that even though they hadn't asked for any of this, they might as well enjoy it . . .

. . . when something suddenly changed. Wells jerked backward abruptly, as though some huge hand had reached from the curtains behind him to grasp him by the collar and yank. As Deal watched, Wells flew forward again, his eyes gone glassy and sightless. A dark round dot had appeared high on his cheek.

Deal flung up his arms to catch him as Wells pitched into his lap. He stared down, uncomprehending, at the unrecognizable mass of tissue that had been the back of Wells's head.

"Roland?" he said dumbly, though the crowd was still roaring, and the sound would never be heard.

Deal raised his hand and stared at the sticky redness that covered it. He felt the warmth of Roland Wells's blood bathing his lap, soaking through the wool fabric of his suit, beginning already to trickle down his legs.

"Roland!" Deal repeated, still stunned. Finally he turned, crying out for help.

The borough cop also seemed to realize something was wrong. He was standing, half turned toward Deal, when an invisible force slapped the side of his face and a spray of red wetness enveloped everything. In the next instant, the big cop toppled backward, taking Deal over as he went.

Deal's grip on Roland loosened as he fell. The big cop's shoulder crunched into him, driving his breath away as they struck the floor of the stage, where he lay gasping under the cop's inert bulk.

The band had stopped playing and the applause and shouts of the crowd had turned to screams, curses, a steady roar that Deal realized was the sound of automatic gunfire. Chairs crashed about him as the others who'd been seated onstage dove for cover. A shoe clipped his forehead, another foot trampled his leg.

Deal struggled out from under the cop, pulled himself to one elbow, stared in disbelief at the scene before him. *Impossible*, his brain insisted. *Absolutely impossible.* And yet it was happening.

The uniformed officers who'd been manning the doors had unslung their weapons and were methodically spraying fire as they advanced toward the front of the room. Audience members ran in blind panic, some toward the stage, only to fall before the withering fire. A woman in a white gown turned as if to protest to the advancing police and the back of her dress blew away in a scatter of cloth and blood.

What in God's name were they doing? Deal wondered. Advancing like some kamikaze unit on whoever had started this . . . how could you possibly justify . . .

His thoughts careened in another direction then as he saw one of the Secret Service men lying prone in the firing position near the toppled podium at the front of the stage, his weapon jolting repeatedly as he fired at the approaching cops.

*It was the cops,* Deal realized then, and now it suddenly was beyond nightmare. *It was the goddamned cops.*

There was an explosion of splinters at the front of the stage and an awful clatter as slugs tore through the metal struts of the risers underneath. The Secret Service man who'd been firing at the advancing cops was flung backward, his body jerking as he rolled over the surface of the stage. But it was the other invitees assembled onstage who seemed to be the focus of the attack. They were cut down in waves as they ran and dove from the stage for cover.

One of the thin, long-haired men whom Deal had marked as an undercover narcotics officer had taken cover behind a clump of potted palms at one corner of the stage. He was bent into a crouch, looking ready to jump down to the auditorium floor, when the clay pots exploded as if they'd been mined. The man disappeared in a froth of black earth, palm fronds, and gore.

Deal heard a scream a few feet in front of him. A slender Asian woman whom he'd seen earlier, passing what looked like family photographs around the waiting room, stood abruptly, a folding chair upraised for a weapon. She began a rush toward the assassins, and Deal ducked as the firing swung toward her. He heard the wet, thudding sounds above the roar of the weapons and her groaning inrush of breath, and he caught a glimpse of the shredded chair she'd been holding as the force of the slugs flung it past him like something caught in the gust of a hurricane.

More slugs ripped into the curtains behind him, more slammed into the bulk of the cop who had fallen on top of him, and in the mad whirl that his mind had become—thank God for Isabel in Orlando with her mother, thank God for that, at least—Deal knew that it would only be seconds now before these attackers, these impostor cops, were on the stage to find and finish him.

He felt too numb for fear. He was operating on some less human level, seeing and hearing everything in hyper-awareness, but unable, for the moment at least, to feel anything. He was bathed in a warm stickiness that he knew was blood. The floor of the stage about him was covered in it, the curtains draped behind him dripping with it. But though he'd felt the jolting blows of bullets, the impact had come to him through the flesh of those who had fallen around him. *Soon enough, though, Deal. Soon enough.*

Yes, Deal, some voice called. You must close your eyes now. Lie quietly. Sleep until this awful dream is done and you'll awake and joke with Vernon Driscoll . . .

. . . and then he heard a burst of gunfire coming from a different place and in a different rhythm, and flung his head up in time to see one of the phony cops mounting the steps leading to the stage. The man hesitated, giving a backward glance, then flew forward up the stairs, though his feet had nothing to do with the movements. It was the fire that had caught him from behind that was propelling him now, a jig that ended in a face-down sprawl a few feet from where Deal lay.

Through the thick haze that filled the room now, Deal saw that at least three of the Secret Service detail had commandeered a spot in the corner of the ballroom where a service bar had been set up. The agents had taken cover there and were trying to mount a counteroffensive against the attackers.

Deal saw another pair of the bogus cops go down, but then the others swung their weapons toward the agents and began a barrage that sounded like an automatic cannon on a gunship. A bank of glassware stacked head-high in plastic racks disappeared into shimmering vapor and an agent flew backward in a broken dive. The linens of an overturned table were transformed instantly into tattered sails, chunks of vinyl padding from the bar flew up like pudding, but still there were answering pops of fire from the pistols of the agents.

*Where are the reinforcements?* Deal thought as he stared out at the assault. *Where is the fucking cavalry?*

Deal saw one of the bogus cops lean away from a tangle of fallen chairs he was using for cover, then make a gesture toward the stage. Two more of the killers broke away from the group and began a crablike run toward the platform. *For what conceivable reason?* Deal thought. *What was so damned important up here on this stage. . .*

. . . and then he saw movement behind the fallen podium—a glimpse of beige fabric, a hand raised and then dropped again—and he remembered Linda Sheldon.

He glanced again at the two cops—they had very nearly reached the steps of the stage by now—then pushed himself up from the stage, lunging for the automatic that the dead killer before him had dropped. Deal caught the weapon as he rolled, felt the heat of its still-hot stubby barrel on his palm. He came up on his knees, found the trigger guard by feel, prayed there was nothing complicated in its workings. Driscoll had taken him to the target range once, let him fire an Uzi, a Mac-10, an automatic pistol they'd taken from an Arab counterfeiter that didn't even have a name. It wasn't necessary to aim such weapons, Driscoll had assured him. All that was necessary was the ability to point, and the will to pull the trigger.

Deal had plenty of will. The first killer was coming up onto the stage when he squeezed off his first burst. He'd aimed a bit low, and most of the slugs traced a line half a dozen feet along the floorboards before he could correct. When he raised the barrel, the man screamed, flying backward off the stage, clutching his shattered leg.

The second man turned back toward the Secret Service agents when he heard the fire. He didn't realize his mistake until his companion tumbled past him. He turned, trying to swing his weapon toward Deal.

Deal had not bothered to lift his finger from the trigger. He simply swung the barrel of the automatic in what he hoped was the right direction. His first shots struck the gunman's weapon, sending up a shower of sparks, flinging it off somewhere. The rest carved a path along the man's upraised arm, his throat, his lower jaw. He went over as though he'd been kicked, and only then did Deal stop firing.

He glanced at the weapon in his hand, as if it were a separate part of himself that had acted. Two men, he thought. He'd snatched up that weapon and managed to make it fire, and now two men lay dead. He might have expected the backlash of fear, or even some grim John Wayne–style satisfaction. But all he felt, in fact, was the curious detachment: *Look what you've gone and done, Deal—now get on with it.*

Shouting in what sounded like Spanish came from the spot where the main assault group was stationed, and Deal saw a man gesturing frantically his way. There was a burst of fire, and bullets chewed along the stage surface, spraying him with fragments of wood. Deal flopped down, rolling automatically toward the podium. As he scrambled behind it, more shouted commands came and the firing ceased.

He felt movement at his side and glanced over. She might have lost the bearing she'd possessed a few moments ago, but there was no mistaking who it was. Her knees were tucked up, and she'd pulled herself tightly into a ball, and her chin was trembling now, but her eyes were clear, her lips drawn in a steady line.

"You're one of the heroes," she said quietly, staring back at Deal.

Sure, he thought. Reluctant but present. He'd pooh-poohed the honor, protested his worthiness, joked with Roland Wells. Maybe he should go through it all again for the benefit of Linda Sheldon, maybe she'd get a big laugh out of his Jimmy Stewart routine. Tell her how it wasn't really him with the gun, it was just a mechanical weapon held by an unbidden arm.

"I hope to God you're right," is what he told her. Then rose up to fire again.

Driscoll had the phone tucked under his chin, was dancing on one foot, trying to get his pants pulled up, when he saw the first live video from the scene. It was an aerial shot of Miami International Airport: Don Shula Expressway and a couple of small lakes in the foreground, an undifferentiated sprawl of industry and warehouses in the distance, the grid of runways and hangars in between.

A dark plume of smoke rose from a corner of the airport property and the camera jiggled as the focus tightened down. Flames boiled from the shattered fuselage of a jumbo jet and a nearby hangar and several outlying buildings. Even the tarmac itself seemed to be ablaze. Firefighting units had circled the area and were pumping water onto the flames. There looked to be a sea of Metro green and white cruisers and unmarked units lining the perimeter roads.

". . . as we told you moments ago, reports are that all this began with an explosion inside a Globestar Airlines 747," the announcer's voice intoned over the clatter of helicopter blades. "The plane was said to be out of service, undergoing routine maintenance work, and no one was aboard when the blast took place. We have reports that at least five maintenance workers and a member of airport security have been seriously injured and have been rushed to Jackson Memorial Hospital, and of course we'll follow up on that for you."

If the act itself weren't troubling enough, Driscoll felt a reasonable certainty he knew the plane in question. He'd seen it the day before while he was on break from a stakeout at Zaragosa unit #12, which sat on the south side of 36th Street, tucked into a little slice of private property abutting the maintenance yards of MIA. He'd been sitting at one of the picnic tables set up in the shade of some tall Australian pines in the back, wearing one of the red and white paper hats that all the other burger flippers wore, finishing a large order of fries, watching the planes take off and land in the distance and thinking that he had never heard of Globestar Airlines, which he had decided was either some cargo carrier or a cover for the CIA. And unless he was mistaken, the shady spot where he'd been sitting was now engulfed by a burning lake of aviation fuel, and nearby Zaragosa #12 was in the process of burning to the ground.

Driscoll got his belt buckled, pulled the phone from his ear, and banged it against his palm a couple of times. Twenty rings at least, a direct line into the office of Dedric Bailey at Special Investigations, and nobody was picking up? What the hell was going on? He'd already tried dialing Hector Zaragosa at his office, but that line was tied up, as it was during the most normal of circumstances, Hector and his minions on the phone steadily, checking the register totals at twenty different restaurants, ordering ground meat and onions by the carload, jabbering endlessly with in-laws.

Aurelio Pincay, ubiquitous news anchor for Channel 7, was back onscreen now, working hard to project the authority that Driscoll thought had always eluded the man. "We want to repeat that this is not a crash, that the plane was undergoing maintenance work in a part of the airport far removed from landings and takeoffs. And to remind you, *Air Force One* is not, I repeat, not at Miami International. The President arrived yesterday at the former Homestead Air Force Base in South Dade, where increased security measures . . . "

Pincay broke off then, apparently distracted by something he was hearing in his earpiece. He glanced up at the camera apologetically while his co-anchor, a slender blonde woman whose name Driscoll could never remember, stared on as though waiting to be invited to the party. Apparently there was only one earpiece available on the Channel 7 set, or perhaps Pincay had determined he'd be the only one to pass along the breaking news.

"We're just getting reports in of a disturbance outside the Hyatt Hotel in downtown Miami, where First Lady Linda Sheldon was to present the National Medals of Valor to recipients in a ceremony moved to Miami this year," Pincay said, holding up a hand as if to forestall questions from his listening audience. "We're going to switch you live to Gina Lozano, who's outside the Hyatt in Victory Plaza . . . "

Pincay disappeared then, and after a few moments of snow and static, the image of a young, smartly dressed Latin woman came up. She was standing near a fountain in the bayside plaza just across the street from the hotel, a troubled expression on her face as pandemonium erupted behind her: clouds of what looked like tear gas, a mounted policeman trying to rein in his rearing horse, glimpses of shrieking crowds in a formless stampede trying to escape the gas that billowed about erratically in the swirling breeze.

"We're really at a loss as to what happened here, Aurelio. There were a few demonstrators gathered, some shouting as the First Lady arrived, but things calmed down, the crowd orderly for the most part, and we're not sure what prompted police to turn the gas loose . . . "

She broke off then as a gust brought the gas drifting over the fountain. There was a muffled shout of warning, perhaps her cameraman, and she turned just as the cloud engulfed her. Driscoll heard her coughing, saw her go down on one knee, heard a thud that must have been her microphone falling to the ground. There was muffled cursing and the video image began to wobble, then flipped over altogether. Driscoll saw a careening shot of the skyscraping Hyatt's tower, saw a drifting thunderhead up above, caught a glimpse of a riderless, galloping horse, and then there was only a static-laced blur.

In a moment, Aurelio Pincay was back, his jaw slack as he stared at an off-screen monitor that must have been displaying the same images. Driscoll heard murmuring on the set, saw the hand of the slender co-anchor reach into the frame to prod Pincay, who turned to the camera with the look of a man who'd been caught out sleepwalking. His mouth opened, but no sound came out. Something behind the camera caught his eye and Pincay finally nodded. "Right," he said. "We're going to go to a break now, folks, and when we come back we're going to . . . uh . . . be right back . . . "

By this time Driscoll had stamped his feet into his shoes and was running out the kitchen door, the tails of his unbuttoned shirt fluttering behind him. No wonder Dedric Bailey wasn't answering his phone, he was thinking as he pounded his way across the lawn toward his car. Bombing at the airport, riot at the First Lady's party, President out on the town with Jorge Alejandro Vas. What next? Famine? Plague? Boils?

Driscoll was into the Ford now, which started, as was its wont, on the first try. He gunned the big engine, spun the Ford in as tight a circle as its wallowing suspension would allow, was approaching Southwest 8th Street in moments. Make a left on 8th, he thought, he'd be on his way west, catch Milam Dairy Road, and on to the airport in fifteen minutes, if he was lucky. Or make a right, he could be downtown in just about ten.

Not really a choice, he thought as he hit the broad boulevard in a screeching power slide, just ahead of a line of approaching traffic. He punched the Ford's accelerator, burned through a yellow that was climbing toward red. Hector Zaragosa had twenty restaurants, after all, half a dozen more on the drawing board. Last time he'd checked there was only one John Deal.

*Frigging medals,* Driscoll thought, fighting a waggle in the wheel as the Ford climbed past eighty. *Get you in trouble every frigging time.*

When Deal came up from cover for the second time, he saw that a couple of the phony cops had split off from the main group and were scurrying behind tumbled tables and chairs in a cautious flanking movement toward the stage. Another half-dozen maintained their barrage upon the position the Secret Service agents had taken. He wasn't hearing any returning pistol fire now. Maybe the agents were simply pinned down. Or out of ammunition. Or dead, and in moments the entire group of killers would turn their attention to mopping up this last business onstage, give the contractor with the gun the award of his life.

One of the men advancing toward the stage fired a short burst in his direction, and Deal ducked as the shots flew high, cutting through a banner that had been draped behind the stage: "NATIONAL MEDAL OF" dropped in one huge chunk, along with a section of the heavy curtain. "VALOR" hung on, dangling by a single hook. Deal lay on his back staring stupidly at the swaying sign, at the slash of ruined plaster the gunfire had torn. He felt Linda Sheldon's nails dig into his flesh as she clutched his arm.

Half a dozen men with automatic weapons out there who wanted to kill him, Deal was thinking. He had one weapon, and no extra clip. He wasn't a betting man, but his father had been, and Deal knew what the call would have been. He closed his eyes momentarily, uttered a silent prayer. *Give my daughter a decent, happy life,* he willed. *Dear Isabel.*

He was ready then. Rise up, one last blast, take one of the bastards out, at least? Or wait for them to reach the stage, maybe take them both before their friends joined the rush?

. . . and then he noticed the electrical panel. Had been staring at it all along, in fact, ever since the big section of curtain had fallen. Huge, dull-gray master electrical panel—Square D brand, it looked like—set into the portion of the wall that had been bared when the curtain fell in tatters, the sort of electrical panel you'd need to control the lights in a room like this. It took him half a second to change his plan.

He brought his weapon up, squeezed the trigger, saw the pattern of fire rip into the facing of the service door just to the right of the electrical panel, then a correction, still holding the trigger down, bringing the fire up a bit, to the left . . . and there was a sudden explosion, a fountain of sparking and a quick bloom of flame that leapt out of the electrical panel, extinguishing itself as quickly as it came, and, finally, everything was darkness.

In the momentary silence that followed, Deal heard a strange whirring, clicking noise, and realized he was still holding the trigger down on an empty clip. He tossed the weapon aside and turned to Linda Sheldon.

"Are you all right?" he asked, trying to hold his voice to a whisper.

It took her a moment to respond. "All right?" she echoed. "I'll never be all right." Deal thought she sounded more angry than frightened. A good sign.

Excited shouts in Spanish rose from out in the darkened auditorium, a curse as someone stumbled over fallen chairs. A pistol shot sounded, a puny sound given what had come before, but to Deal, it meant that at least one of the agents was still alive. There was an answering roar of automatic fire, and he knew that the killers would hold their positions for a few more moments, at least.

"We've got to move," he told Linda Sheldon.

"Move? Move where?"

"There's a door at the back of the stage," he told her. "Just behind the curtains . . ." There was more gunfire, and Deal heard a cry from a distant corner of the room.

He didn't want to add anything more, that the door he'd seen might lead into a service closet, that it might be locked, that they might never get far enough to find out.

"Just get on your feet," he said. "Try to keep your head low. Hold on to me."

He felt her scrambling to her feet, felt her hand on his shoulder. He took her hand, guided it to the small of his back, tucked her fingers under his belt.

"Just keep your head low and hang on," he told her.

"I'll hang on," she said, her voice grim.

He heard the sound of footsteps, someone coming carefully up the steps of the stage. Deal paused. He bent down, found the heavy automatic he'd dropped.

"Let go," he whispered. "Just for a second."

"I don't want to," she whispered back.

"Now," he hissed. He felt her fingers slip away from his belt. He edged them carefully away from the fallen podium, then stopped.

He understood now, knew that there would be no random firing in the dark, and that gave the two of them a certain advantage. He turned, reached into his pocket, found his car keys. He hesitated, then tossed them in the direction of the podium. There was a clatter, and then a beam of light flicked on for a fraction of a second, someone aiming a tiny hand-held light in the direction of the sound.

Deal stepped forward, holding the heavy automatic at port arms, the still-hot barrel in his right hand, the metal tubing that was its stock in his left. He drove the butt down sharply, felt a satisfying crunch as metal met bone. He hit the man again as he went down, then turned, caught Linda Sheldon, and pulled her after him.

"Stay with me," he told her. "Whatever happens, don't let go."

"You don't have to worry," she said, her hand clamped again on his belt.

He led her toward what he hoped was the back of the stage, shuffling and stumbling through the debris, stepping over fallen bodies until he felt the folds of the heavy curtain in his hands. He sidestepped along until he found the bare section of wall where the curtain had sheared away, passed the smoldering, stinking ruins of the electrical panel, felt the cool metal door beneath his fingertips.

He found the metal knob, hesitated briefly—*if it's a closet, we're history; if it's locked, same thing*—felt the knob give as he turned, felt a surge of relief as a gust of air surged over them, a breeze full of mustiness and pent-up grease and God knows what, and it didn't matter, because that draft meant it *was* a service passageway, and he yanked Linda Sheldon through the doorway, and closed it as quietly as he could after them.

"Where are we?" she said. "I can't see anything."

"That makes two of us," Deal said. He ran his hands over the inside of the door quickly, searching for a locking mechanism, but found nothing.

He turned, caught her by the shoulders again, spoke quietly but forcefully. "It's a service passage," he told her. "One way will lead to a systems control area, and that's a dead end. The other way'll take us out."

"How do you know all this?" she said.

"My old man built the place," he said. "We built a bunch of hotels. They all have pretty much the same features."

There was a pause, and the sounds of more gunfire echoing on the other side of the door. "So which way do we go?"

"That I'm not sure of," he told her.

"It might have been better if you hadn't told me that," she said.

"We could split up," Deal said. "You go one way, I'll take the other."

There was a pause as she considered it. "I don't think so," she said finally.

A blast of fire struck the wall then, sending plaster fragments and dust raining down upon them.

"So, cross your fingers," Deal said. He took her hand, and they began to run.

*Or hobble, was a more accurate description,* he thought. The passage-way was narrow, its ceiling not quite high enough to stand fully upright. Piping, electrical conduit, and junction boxes jutted out here and there, gouging him painfully every time he tried to pick up the pace. With the door closed behind them, the draft he'd noted at first was gone, but the smells of cooking had intensified. With luck, he was thinking, they were headed toward the kitchen and the central service station. Another fifty feet? A hundred, maybe? How big was a hotel, anyway? It seemed they'd already scooched themselves through a city block's worth of darkness.

"Maybe they'll think we're hiding out there in the ballroom," Linda said. She sounded as if she was gasping for breath, and Deal allowed them a brief pause.

"Maybe," he said. He leaned back against the wall, feeling cobwebs brush at the back of his neck. It seemed twenty degrees hotter in the airless passage. "Maybe they gave up. Maybe some help finally showed up . . . "

He broke off as he felt the draft on his face once again.

"What is it?" she said. Her hand tightened at his belt.

"Somebody just opened the door back there," he said.

"Are you sure?" she said.

When he didn't answer, she added, "Maybe it's help."

Deal thought he could hear the sounds of footsteps now. "You want to wait here and see?"

"No," she said quickly, and urged him forward.

He turned, clipping his forehead on something sharp that protruded from the low ceiling. "Duck," he whispered as he pulled her forward, try-ing to ignore the pain, the blood that was spilling into his eyes now.

He was dizzy suddenly, and the darkness didn't help, but the last thing he was going to do was fall. He lay his shoulder against the side of the passage and leaned forward, propelling himself along, and gradually the vertigo began to lessen. A few more strides and he was feeling like he might be able to stand on his own then, and was actually trying to do that very thing when his shoulder and head slammed into something solid, stunning him again, stopping him cold.

She piled right behind him and he heard her sharp intake of breath as his elbow dug sharply into her ribs. Still, she didn't cry out.

"What now?" she whispered, her mouth at his ear. He could feel the sharp, hot panting of her breath on his cheek. "Why are you stopping?" The sound of hurrying footsteps behind them was unmistakable now.

"Wall," he said, bright lights still pinging behind his eyes. He took her free hand and patted the surface he'd collided with to underscore the point.

"A wall? You built a *wall* here?" Her tone was accusing, even in the stage whispers they'd been using.

"That's what contractors do," he said.

"Goddammit," she said. "Just goddammit."

"Yeah," he said. "I know the feeling."

"What are we going to do now?" He could hear the hysteria building in her voice, as if it weren't fair to get this far only to be stymied, stumbled into a dead end like lab rats too dumb to see what was coming, as if it would have been better to die out there in the ballroom with the rest of the heroes . . .

He had his eyes open now and his thoughts trailed off. Goodbye, sayonara, good night, Mrs. Calabash, his old man had loved that show. Why *had* they built a wall here, anyway? Maybe he'd find his old man in the netherworld, they could have a chat about it . . .

And then he stopped, realizing what he was seeing. He straightened, blinking to be sure it wasn't a mistake, some illusion called up out of desperation and too many blows on the head. But even when he'd rubbed away the sweat and the blood and the plaster dust, it was still there, and he wanted to laugh at his foolishness.

A turn, that's all it was. The passageway made a sharp turn and he'd tried to keep going straight. He knew because he could see it now, an unmistakable glow of light leaking into the passage from some source not twenty feet away.

"Look," he told her, taking her by the arm. "There's our way out."

"Dear God," she said, almost sobbing, and began to run.

He pushed himself upright and hurried after her, his head still reeling from the blow he'd taken. There was still the small matter of the men in the passage behind them, he thought. But once they got outside, they'd have a chance. Maybe a lock on that door . . .

. . . and it *was* a door, he saw as she reached it and pushed it aside and her heels disappeared out into the light. By the time he followed her through, he had formed a plan: he'd send her on for help, he'd stay behind, find something to barricade this opening, trap their pursuers . . .

. . . and then he stopped, the sight before him too surprising, too stunning. A storage room, piled high with boxes and crates. A mop hanging from a hook on one wall, a pair of rubber boots and a bucket just beneath. A man in a suit was seated in a broken office chair that tilted crazily with his weight. His arms dangled at his side and his head was thrown back, his expression fixed in permanent wonder. Another man, also wearing a dark suit, stood with his back to Deal, his arms flung over a pile of flour bags that reached almost shoulder high. There was a dark stain spreading out on the topmost bag where the man's face was pressed.

Linda Sheldon lay crumpled on the floor, one arm upflung, the other at her side. There was a third man in the room, and he was bent over her, his hand at her throat, as if to take a pulse.

This man was wearing a policeman's uniform and Deal tried to tell himself that that was a good sign, though another part of his brain was sending out panic signals in any number of forms and languages. Yes, yes, yes, he thought, he *should* have known better, even before the man stood and raised the pistol that he was holding so that it pointed squarely into Deal's face.

"You *are* a loyal one," the tall man said, almost a smile, a touch of grudging admiration there, and Deal wondered what he might be talking about.

He heard sounds at the mouth of the passageway behind him then, and turned to see, clutching some hope that maybe it was help after all, and before he could resolve to be more cautious the next time he fled from some stifling cave and out into the light, before he could think of anything else at all, the lights went out again.

# Part 3: Damage Control

# Message received at Langley HQ, NSA, 3:14 P.M., July 21:

<u>Encryption Level, Top Sergeant</u>
ACTION ADVISORY

To: Good Pastor
From: Little Lamb
Subject: Assumed terrorist incursion, Ram Man Miami
(This confirms voice communication, 1457 hours)

CONFIRMING RAM MAN STATUS: safe. Repeat, Ram Man safe and
   secured.
Ms. Peep, unauthorized absence. Repeat, Ms. Peep absent without
   leave.

DETAIL MEMBER STATUS: Peep detail, eleven down. Repeat, eleven
   Peep detail down.

CIVILIAN STATUS: One-forty to one-fifty down. Repeat, total one-
   forty to one-fifty down, gunfire and presumed toxic airborne
   vector, source and type unconfirmed a/t/t.

PERIMETER ACTION: Full alert.
INCURSION AGENT: Unconfirmed a/t/t.
INCURSION SOURCE: Unconfirmed a/t/t.
INCURSION PROFILE: Unconfirmed a/t/t.

     SUMMARY ENDS///SUMMARY ENDS///SUMMARY ENDS

**15**

"One lucky boy, you are."

"That's the way you figure it, Doc? That the way the Huns think?" Ray Brisa glanced up, but Jameroski was slipping in and out of focus. The bandages on his face limited his range of vision, made everything fuzzy around the edges, but this was something different going on, something to do with drugs.

"Not so bad on your face," Jameroski said. "This here is bad."

Ray turned his chin on the table top, looked away at the cracks on the scuzzy green wall. "Thanks for the good news."

"*Is* good news," Jameroski insisted. He sprayed something that felt cool on Ray's burning shoulder.

Ray nodded. He wasn't anxious to follow this line of discussion. He'd caught hold of the spin of the drugs now. He wanted to dig in his spurs, ride with them, a big wowser ride. "What'd you give me, Doc? Tell me, so I can score a lot of it when I'm better."

"Yah, yah, I know you like," Jameroski said. "Careful now, is going to hurt."

And Jameroski was right, what he was doing to Ray's back and shoulder did hurt. Hurt like a sonofabitch in that part of him that felt pain. The other part shrugged off the discomfort. That part of Ray Brisa was drifting around some cloudlike landscape like a dark-skinned angel, plunking strings on his little harp and staring down at the poor bastard who couldn't tell where his shirt ended and his charred flesh began.

"Better you go to hospital," Jameroski muttered.

*Fifty years in the United States, he ought to learn the language,* that's what Ray was thinking.

"I already was there, Doc," he said. "I didn't like the way those people looked at me."

"You were in hospital? Sure. When, huh? Who said: 'You! Go now.' Nobody. Shut up. Lean back now. Let me think."

If there were enough brain cells left to do the job, Ray thought. Junked-out Doc Hammer, physician to the underworld stars. You didn't bring your Blue Cross card when you went to see Doc Hammer. He didn't ask you for your insurance number, you didn't ask him for no license.

And the fact was Ray *had* been in a hospital. Some homeowner had dragged him up the bank of the canal where he'd drifted after the explosion, called the paramedics, they'd delivered Ray Brisa to Jackson

Memorial on a gurney just ahead of the cops. Ray waited till the emergency wagon was on its way to scrape up the next victim of the Miami morning, somehow managed to get down from the gurney, made his way outside, hailed one of the cabs idling under the canopy of the emergency entrance.

"Stink up my car, man," that's what the cabbie had told him, they hadn't driven half a block. Sure. Canal muck, blood, fried flesh, it ought to stink. Fifty wet, stinking bucks later, everything was cool, the cabbie helping him through the door of Doc Hammer's clinic, otherwise known as the service entrance to Gould's Pharmacy, a place the old man kept out on the Beach.

"You got great hands, Doc. Anybody ever tell you that?" That was the angel speaking now.

"Shut up," Jameroski said. "Hold tight."

Ray saw the doctor snatch something off his shoulder—what was left of his skin was how it felt—heard a wet slap as something hit a waste can. The angel was strumming his harp furiously, but Ray couldn't hear the music for the sound of the flames snapping on his back.

"Can't put you to sleep," Jameroski said by way of apology. "In hospital, sure. But not here."

Ray Brisa managed a nod. Tears were leaking out his clenched eyelids. He had his hands locked together beneath the table top the doc used for an operating table. Only lucky thing he could think of, there wasn't a brisk trade in gurney rentals. They'd be doing all this on the filthy floor beneath him. Or, maybe, if the pharmacy had already opened for business, the doc would have him lying out there on the counter, passing prescriptions for Dilaudid and Percodans to his distinguished clientele with one hand, flaying him alive with the other.

Who among the doc's customers would care? *You gone kill the bitch, Doc? All right. Hand me my pills first, okay?*

**Ray blinked,** refocused, realized he must have gone out. He was on a cot now in a little storeroom. The doc was sitting on a big cardboard box filled, evidently, with something called DEPENDS.

*Depends on what?* Ray wondered. The pain had gone off somewhere. The angel was back on his cloud, doing some dreamy nod.

The doc was watching a little black-and-white television he'd set up on some steel shelving. Focus on the picture swam in and out. It took Ray a moment to realize it wasn't the drugs, though. The doc jiggled one of the rabbit ears atop the set, and the picture steadied.

"Get the frigging cable, why don't you?" Ray said. His throat felt dry and tight, like he hadn't talked for a long time.

"Shut up," Jameroski said, his eyes fixed on the tube.

Maybe that was it, Ray thought. Bedside manner deficiency. Doc Hammer'd started off losing a patient here and there because of it, he'd gone on drugs to compensate. His whole life went into the shitter because he didn't know how to relate to the feelings of others.

"Ooo, Doctor," Ray said. "I like these drugs you do."

"*Listen*," Jameroski said, making a slashing motion with his hand. "I put you out in street!"

No doubt about it, Ray thought. Serious bedside deficiency. But he kept his mouth shut this time.

". . . these unprecedented acts of terrorism," someone was saying, a voice Ray Brisa thought he knew. "And we will not rest until those responsible are apprehended and brought to account, that much I can promise."

Ray let his head loll to the right angle, stared up at the wavering black-and-white image, caught sight of President Sheldon there on the screen. Palm trees in the background, a skyline that looked familiar. *Pissed off,* Ray thought. *This is a man way pissed off.*

". . . not allow my personal feelings to intrude in this matter," the President was saying. "There have been many victims here today, and we recognize that fact. My heart goes out to the families of the fallen. We will do everything within our power to see that justice is done."

The President turned away from the cameras then, ignoring a clamor of shouted questions and thrust microphones. A cluster of Secret Service agents stepped between him and the pursuing reporters and the scene shifted back to one of the sets of the evening network, where an anchorman in an expensive hairpiece promised Ray and the doctor that he would return in a moment.

"Whoosh," Jameroski said, leaning back, shaking his head.

"How long I been out of it?" Ray Brisa said. His head felt full of cotton.

Jameroski turned to regard him. "Your entire life, I think is safe to say."

Brisa wanted to laugh, but it turned into a wracking cough, which in turn jiggled the flesh of his shoulder into flame. It all finished in tears and Ray gasping for breath on the cot. It had taken him by surprise, that's all, Jameroski with a good line, like a guy with Alzheimer's sometimes gets.

"What's so great on the television, Doc?" he managed, finally.

Jameroski shook his big grizzled head. "Unbelievable, you know? Like nothing I ever saw."

"It looked like Miami to me," Ray Brisa said.

Jameroski glared at him. "You stupid! Of course is Miami. You don't know? Got damn President is here. You don't know?" Jameroski's voice had risen dangerously, Ray thought. "President of United States!"

"I just forgot, okay? What happened?"

The news anchor was back then and the doctor pointed grimly at the set.

". . . where, if you have just joined us, a tragedy of monumental proportions has taken place," the newsman said, his face ashen. "Unconfirmed reports are that a dozen Secret Service agents and as many as forty civilians, including a number of the nation's most heroic individuals, were killed in the gun battle inside the hotel, while more than two hundred onlookers gathered outside the hotel were felled by a cloud of toxic gas loosed by persons unknown. Officials have not yet confirmed this fact, but sources tell us that the First Lady, Linda Sheldon, is missing. I repeat, the First Lady of the United States is missing and may have been kidnapped by terrorists." The announcer paused, as if uttering the words had drained him of something vital.

He sat staring blankly for a moment and then something seemed to jar him from his trance. He pressed his hand to his ear as if listening to some unseen speaker. "We're going to take you live now to Javier Sotolongo, who is standing by with word on that explosion and fire at the airport . . ." he began, and then Jameroski's hand reached out to turn off the sound.

The doctor turned to stare at Brisa with an expression that was less angry than thoughtful. It was a look that made Brisa uncomfortable.

"Maybe *you* do something," the doctor said.

"Do something *what*?" Ray was feeling a little nervous. Jameroski had worked on him half a dozen times: gunshot wounds, stabbings, concussion, a hundred stitches on his knee where he'd run though a plate-glass window just ahead of an angry homeowner who'd been sleeping late instead of going to work like he was supposed to. All those instances, nothing had fazed Jameroski. Did his work, took his money, *hasta la vista.*

"You hear," Jameroski said, waving at the TV. "Somebody kidnap the First Lady. First blow up one airplane, drop nerve gas at downtown."

Ray glanced at the screen, saw what looked like a helicopter shot: office buildings surrounding a park, about a million emergency vehicles clustered down below.

"Wait a minute," Ray said. It was beginning to sink in now. "All this happened in *Miami*? Like when?"

"Today," Jameroski said.

"No shit," Ray Brisa said. He glanced back at the TV, trying to ignore the growing dread inside him. "Somebody did all that?" He noticed Jameroski was still eyeing him suspiciously. Ray started to lift up off the cot, realized heavy straps were holding him down.

"Hey, man, what is this shit?"

Jameroski studied him. "Didn't want you to roll off, hurting yourself while I do the working on you."

"Well, that's over with. Un-fucking-tie me, all right?"

Jameroski made no move.

Brisa tried to shift about inside the straps. "Do the math, doc," Ray Brisa said. "I been with *you* all day. I didn't have anything to do with that shit on the television."

Jameroski didn't seem convinced. "Lot of things to be doing. Have to be a lot of people helping."

Brisa stared at him, not believing it. "Well, *I* didn't," he said. "I'm no terrorist."

"You are talking while you sleep, you know?"

That look again. Brisa felt a panic rising.

"Talking? About what?"

Jameroski raised his shaggy brows noncommittally. "Costing you one hell of a lot, this time," he said.

That's all the old fart cared about, Ray thought. The more serious the crime, the heavier the dime. Always somebody around to grind your ass, no matter what side they were on.

"Somebody tried to kill *me*, okay? Look at my sorry ass." Ray Brisa was thinking about the tall man who'd handed him the briefcase, how he'd wanted to dismiss him as just another South American drug scammer. He was thinking about Luis and his ghastly smile. He was thinking about Jorge. God knows what had happened to Jorge. Guys drive a boat up his ass, maybe.

Jameroski was looking at Ray Brisa all right, but nothing in his aspect had changed.

Ray Brisa found himself squirming under the old man's gaze. Junkie doctor giving him shit, he thought. How about that? Just because Ray Brisa was sick. He hadn't messed around with any crazy shit like Hammer was talking. He hadn't.

He was still trying to convince himself it was true even after the doctor had stood up and walked out. Even after the door had locked shut behind him. Even after the pain had rushed back to claim him and the angel was strumming its ass off again. The way his mind worked, Ray Brisa thought. The way his mind worked.

"Who the hell *are* these people?" The President glanced up from the document Chappelear had handed him. Chappelear was doing his best to exude calm, despite the events of the day.

"No one's heard of them," Chappelear said. He heard the helplessness in his own voice. "These cells splinter, they reform, it's as fluid as the Middle East down there. Maybe more so."

He raised his hands away from his body in a gesture of futility. The communiqué had come off a fax machine in the hotel an hour earlier. Identical copies had rolled off machines in the Homestead offices of the United Farm Workers of America, the Haiti-America Foundation in Northeast Miami, and, for some bizarre reason, the Department of Modern Dance at Florida International University:

"LET THE EVENTS OF THIS DAY MAKE CLEAR THE RESOLVE OF THE FREE PEOPLES OF CENTRAL AND SOUTH AMERICA AND THE CARIBBEAN TO RESIST THE FORCES OF IMPERIALISM AND THE INSIDIOUS SPREAD OF TOTALITARIANISM."

It had been signed *Los Pueblos de Libertad y Justicia*, a group without a history, without a face. A cell within a cell within a cell, for all anyone knew. No demands, no instructions, no mention of the First Lady.

An immediate full-barreled response had solved only one mystery surrounding the communiqué so far: the fax number now belonging to the university's Department of Modern Dance had once been assigned to the Institute for Cuban Policy.

"They're leftist, that much seems certain," Chappelear said. "Maybe an offshoot of Shining Path. Maybe some reorganized Salvadoran insurgents, or one of the Panamanian groups. We just don't know at this point."

The President crumpled the document in his fist, made as if to hammer his fist against the desk before him, but seemed to lose heart midway through the gesture. He turned away from Chappelear, wadded the paper up, tossed it onto the floor. An aide hurried over to pick up the ball of paper before it had stopped rolling.

Frank Sheldon was pale, his features slack, all his fabled, robust bonhomie vanished. This was not a president any longer, Chappelear was thinking. This was a man whose world had disintegrated in the space of an afternoon, a husband who had lost his wife to forces unknowable and unfathomable.

Earlier in the day, the view out these windows had suggested power and privilege and possibility. Now the weather had turned dark, and the bay was a gray slate dotted with whitecaps, the welter of pleasure boats long gone.

"Quantico's got a team of profilers working, Mr. President." It was John Groshner, who'd entered the room on the heels of the aide. "They're saying that the fact we haven't heard anything about the First Lady isn't necessarily bad news. . . ."

"Isn't necessarily bad news?" The President swiveled upon him angrily. "What the hell kind of talk is that?"

Groshner put up his hands helplessly. "They're psychologists, Mr. President. They're working with what they have, which isn't much, admittedly . . ." He trailed off before the President's withering look.

The President waved dismissively, then sat staring down at his desk for a moment. Chappelear thought he could trace the waves of pain moving through him. After a moment, the President glanced up.

"This is your bailiwick, Larry, " he said, an implied question in his tone. "Here we were, ready to open negotiations with Cuba, what everybody down there's been begging for for thirty years"—he broke off angrily, waving his hand at the aide—"and we get this tide of fascism bullshit! What could have prompted it? What's the matter with these people?"

Chappelear noted the use of the past tense. *So much for a legacy of change in Latin politics,* he thought.

"Logic doesn't necessarily enter into it, Mr. President," Groshner ventured. "You met with Vas, that could have been enough to set them off."

"That's just political courtesy . . . "

"In some quarters, maybe."

The President sighed, fell back in his chair.

"Or you could figure it another way," Groshner continued. "Maybe someone hears you're ready to open a dialogue with Castro, that just might mean he's sold out his own principles, their communist butts are finished at last."

The President looked at him in disbelief. "That's lunacy."

Groshner shrugged. "That's how screwed up politics is among the left down there. Vas understands it. That's why he's got so much clout. He maintains one simple policy for the communists. Invite them to the bargaining table . . . then shoot them between the eyes." Groshner leaned forward in his chair. "One thing I can tell you, Charles Hollingsworth is going to be all over the evening news, reminding the country how dangerous it is to consort with the left wing."

The President looked ready to explode. "That's ridiculous!"

Groshner shrugged. "He wants to win an election, sir."

The President sagged back in his chair, covering his face with his palms. "Jesus God," he muttered.

Chappelear sighed, exasperated with Groshner, his simplistic assessments, his obdurate pragmatic focus on the elections in the midst of what had happened. Well, Frank had wanted to hire a bulldog, and a bulldog was what they had.

Chappelear turned to the President, who was still massaging his face with his hands. "We're not even certain this group really exists, Mr. President. Or if they had anything to do with what happened."

The President turned to Chappelear. "We don't know very goddamned much, do we, Larry?"

There was a pause while Chappelear searched his mind for something even remotely comforting.

"I spoke with Jorge Vas a few minutes ago," Groshner said. "He's got a fairly extensive network of informants in Central and South America, probably at least as reliable as ours. He assures us every one of his people has an ear to the ground."

Chappelear eyed Groshner. "As long as we maintain trade restrictions with Cuba, hold the line on those sugar subsidies," Chappelear heard himself saying. Groshner bristled, about to retort.

Sheldon's head snapped about. "I don't want to hear any more of that, Larry," he said. "Am I making myself clear?"

Chappelear realized he was exhausted himself, was letting his emotions get their way. Hardly the way to get through a crisis. "Sorry, Mr. President," he muttered.

"That goes for both of you," Sheldon added.

The President turned a dark glance on the two of them, then softened momentarily. He sighed, raised his hands in a gesture of frustration. "The truth is, if the devil himself were to appear in this room, deliver information we could use to find Linda, I'd treat him like a brother."

He was about to turn away from them when he stopped, fixing his gaze on Chappelear. "That said, let me ask you something, Larry."

"Sir?"

The President's face had taken on an even more sallow tone. "Just speculating for a moment."

"Of course," Chappelear nodded.

"What about Vas? Could he pull something like this, some bullshit stunt to discredit Castro?"

Chappelear looked at Groshner, who stared back as if to say, "Here's your chance."

Chappelear returned his gaze to the President. "It's something we're looking into, sir. We wouldn't discount any possibility at this point."

The President nodded, then turned away gloomily.

"We're going to hear something soon enough," Groshner said. Chappelear didn't think he said it very convincingly, though he understood why Groshner would give it a try.

Chappelear wanted to do his part. He raised a sheaf of the papers that the aide had brought in along with the copy of the communiqué. "We've got promises of cooperation from every friendly government. Quantico's got five hundred special agents on the way down from all over the country . . ."

Sheldon waved his hand to stop him, wandered off to the windows at the far end of the room. He stood there, gazing out at the gloomy sea, his hands clasped behind his back.

"Maybe you shouldn't be standing right there, sir . . ." Chappelear began.

"It's security glass," Groshner said. "Blanked out."

Chappelear turned, about to retort.

Sheldon ignored them both. "It should have been me," he said, still staring out. Streaks of rain silvered the glass now. A gull rose up suddenly, a few feet away, was just as quickly whisked away by a gust of wind.

He turned back to them. "That's what we have to figure, isn't it? All those good people lost because the perpetrators were coming after me."

"Well, sir, we can't be certain of anything just yet . . ." Groshner said.

"I wouldn't blame myself, Mr. President," Chappelear said.

Sheldon stared at the two of them, hands still behind him, chewing on his lower lip. If he had been ready to respond to either remark, he apparently changed his mind. He took a deep breath, glanced down at his shoes.

"I'm assuming that we're maintaining the highest levels of surveillance?"

"Everything's locked down tight, all public transportation, the marinas, the commercial airfields," Groshner said. "We've got checkpoints on the turnpike, the interstates, the major highways. You couldn't move the Invisible Man out of here."

Sheldon gave him another weary wave. "How about satellite imagery? Can that help us at all?"

"They're assembling the readouts right now," Groshner said. "So far as pinpointing anything very specific in the midst of a built-up area such as this, we'll have to be extremely lucky. We may be able to use it to get a pretty good look at boat traffic, but it's a busy place and the imagery's still being evaluated." He gave Sheldon a hapless look. "Half the damn city's out on the water at any given time, it seems. "

"That's where we should have been," Sheldon said quietly. "Out there trying to catch a fish or something."

He stared out at the water for a moment, then turned back to them. "Is it possible she's still somewhere close by?"

"Anything's possible, Mr. President," Chappelear said. "We're going to hope that whoever's responsible didn't go very far. We're going to hope that we get some clearer statement—"

"We're going to hope that she's still alive," Sheldon interrupted, his voice almost a whisper, his face ashen. "If they wanted me, and got Linda instead, then what if . . ." He broke off, leaving his deepest fear unstated.

Chappelear fell silent. Even Groshner looked stricken, he noticed.

Sheldon covered his face with his palms again, massaging the flesh as if he were trying to rouse himself from a terrible dream. Finally he dropped his hands and squared his shoulders. "Whoever the hell it was wanted me," he said. "But they didn't get me, did they?"

Groshner shook his head as if he'd read a script that prompted the gesture. The man exuded all the sincerity of a personal injury attorney, Chappelear thought. He stared back at Sheldon, waiting for whatever was coming next.

"I'll tell you one thing. We are going to move heaven and earth to get my wife back. And I intend to make these people goddamned sorry for what they've done. Are you with me on that?"

"Absolutely, sir," Groshner said.

"Without question," said Chappelear. He wanted to clap Sheldon on the back, lead a cheer, tell him it was the only way to respond, that Frank Sheldon could be counted on no matter how dark the day . . . but he held his tongue.

"Good," Sheldon said. He gave them a grim look in turn, then turned to look out the windows again.

"I still have to be the President," he said after a moment. His voice was forlorn, barely above a whisper.

"The country needs you, sir," Chappelear said gently. "The people need a leader as badly as they ever have."

Sheldon nodded after a moment. "I suppose they do," he said with a sigh.

He turned and took the sheaf of papers from Chappelear's hand, flipped through them until he found something he was looking for. He glanced up.

"Tell Ms. Walters I'll see her in ten minutes," he said to Chappelear. Still exhausted, the lines of worry still etched at his eyes and mouth, but a glimmer of the old Frank Sheldon there, cranking himself up, ready to throw himself back in the fight.

"That's a delayed feed," Groshner protested. "You've got Brokaw waiting to go live."

"We'll get around to Brokaw," Sheldon said. He glanced at his watch, than at Groshner.

"Barbara Walters was the first one of these people ever to take us seriously," he said. "She came down to Jeff City, she and Linda hit it off like sisters. They stayed up half the night talking, and never a peep of any silly gossip ever hit the air."

He turned to Chappelear, trying to muster his energy.

"So go tell her we're going to do these interviews ladies first," he said. "Just as soon as I wash my face."

Chappelear nodded and started for the door.

"One other thing, Larry."

Chappelear turned. "Yes, sir?"

"I'm making you the point man on this investigation."

"But the Service . . ." Groshner cut in.

"I'm not going to have any goddamned quarrels about who's in charge," the President snapped. "Every agency's going to do its part, and Lawrence Chappelear is going to coordinate. I've already sent the order down. Am I making myself clear?"

Groshner dropped his gaze. "Yes, sir."

"I appreciate your confidence, Mr. President. Are you sure . . . ?"

The President reached out to take his shoulders. "Just make sure the job gets done, Larry. I'm counting on you."

Chappelear stood erect, trying to rise above the swell of despair that threatened to engulf them all. "I'll do everything I can, sir."

The President nodded then, and disappeared into the bathroom.

Chappelear turned, glanced at Groshner, who was fighting to keep the anger out of his expression. He wanted to say something to the man, but despaired of coming up with any comment that wouldn't sound like a playground taunt.

Never mind, he thought. There were far more important matters to attend to just now. But God willing, all of this would pass. He would come to terms with John Groshner on another day.

When Deal awoke, his head was slapping something hard, a regular, unfamiliar rhythm that sent a white jag of pain with its every beat. Everything was still dark, and he worried—*blindness, blindness*—until he felt the tight band of cloth wrapped around his head, and realized he'd been blindfolded.

He rolled his eyes upward, straining, could make out nothing. Then down. Little crescents of light there. Vague light. Nothing else.

He smelled gasoline, saltwater, realized the roaring in his head was coming from somewhere else. Engines. Big ones. Chevy blocks, most likely, and he could guess where he was.

Donzi, he thought. Or Cigarette. High on plane, the rhythm that of the hull slamming the waves every fifty feet or so. The kind of boat that did exactly one thing well: go fast at sea. And all the things that went with that, he thought. Even the man who had invented the things had been killed, shotgunned by mobsters outside his own fast boat factory.

Deal struggled to raise his cheek off the rough decking of the hold, felt a pain that turned his stomach over. He eased his head back down, aware now of the rope that circled his throat, that ran down the line of his spine to his knotted hands, then on to bind up his feet, his heels pressed deep in the flesh of his ass. *Trussed like a pig for slaughter,* he thought. And wondered why it hadn't happened already.

He ran his tongue over his dry lips. They hadn't gagged him. Whoever'd tied him knew that much, knew he might drown in his own vomit.

"Are you there?" he tried. He kept his voice low, which was absurd. He could shout at the top of his lungs, no one on deck could ever hear him. You could be standing up top, right beside whoever was at the wheel, you'd have to shout into his ear in order to be heard.

He tried shifting his legs cautiously, an inch at a time. The rope dug into his throat, but he could still breathe. He figured he'd moved himself about a foot along the thudding, vibrating floor when he felt something brush his hands.

He worked his numb wrists carefully inside the ropes, waited for sensation to return, found a lock of hair pressed between one thumb and forefinger. He held tight and leaned away. The cry that came bathed him in relief. *She's alive,* he thought. And then he could see his old man nodding. *Of course you're happy. Misery loves company. Everybody knows that.*

It took him at least twenty minutes to twist himself around without choking himself to death, get his head arranged by hers, swipe the side of his face about the decking until he managed to get a corner of the blindfold lifted enough to see. Her beige suit was a ruin of blood, bilgewater, soot. Her hair was a tangle, her face puffy beneath the tightly drawn band of her blindfold.

"Can you hear me?" he said, speaking more normally now, his lips a foot from her ear.

He repeated the question more forcefully, finally saw her chin bob down a fraction.

"I'm going to try to get your blindfold loose," he said. "Bear with me, my hands are tied."

There was no response, but he assumed she had heard.

He levered himself closer, was judging the angle to use, when the boat hit a heavy swell and flung him down. He heard her groan with his weight, and tried to ease himself onto an elbow, but he was awkward with his hands tied and only ended up falling on her again.

"I'm sorry," he said.

"I think I'm going to be sick," she said. Her cheeks were pale, and slick with sweat.

"Go ahead," he said, "you'll feel better." He tried not to internalize how she must feel: the stifling air, the smells, the constant pounding. Add to that the disorientation of being blindfolded. He'd never been prone to seasickness himself, but if it was ever going to happen, then this might be the time.

She lay quietly for a few moments, the color gradually returning to her cheeks. "It's okay," she said at last. "I'm feeling better. You said you could do something about this blindfold."

"I'm going to try," he said. "Lie still now."

He lowered his head then, until his chin was on her cheek.

"What are you doing?" she said. He felt her start to squirm away, felt the workings of her jaw against his cheek.

"Try not to move," he said.

He felt her sigh, then used his lips to locate the blindfold, took its edge by his teeth.

He clamped down and jerked upward. The cloth began to slide, and he rolled back until he'd pulled the blindfold clear altogether.

She blinked, glanced vacantly around the dim recess of the hold.

"You want to try the same thing on me?" he asked, staring at her one-eyed. "I got it started, but I think I rubbed most of my cheek off on the deck boards."

She stared at him, her expression turning quickly to concern.

"Come on," he said, and bent close to her again.

He felt her bend tentatively toward him, felt her breath on his forehead. "I'm not sure I can do this," she said. "You're bleeding. What if I pull your hair . . . "

"Honest to God, Mrs. Sheldon, I don't care if you pull my hair." *Keep everything calm,* he told himself. *Just pretend it's a game. Couple more minutes, the Secret Service agents will open the hold, tell them it's all been a drill. Sure.*

He could still feel her breathing inches from his cheek.

"My name is Linda," she said finally. "I think you could call me that."

"Linda," he repeated. "I'm John Deal."

"Pleased to meet you, John." She took a deep breath. "I'm going to do this now."

He felt her lips brush his cheek, felt her teeth graze his skin, a moment's pinching pain as she clamped down on the blindfold. "Just hold it in your teeth and roll away," he told her.

He felt her move, felt the cloth sliding away. A monumental achievement, he was thinking. Maybe this was how he'd feel if he'd lost the use of his limbs. Blow into a straw, make your computer type your name. He figured it was a roughly equivalent task they'd accomplished. He tried not to think of the million problems that remained. Go at it that way, you'd flatten yourself.

"Thanks," he said. They were staring at each other now, nearly nose to nose.

"I'm feeling a little sick again," she said.

"Just let me know," he said. "I'll try and get out of the way."

It brought a kind of grateful smile, which she held for a moment. Then she closed her eyes tightly, and he saw the tears begin to squeeze out.

"It's awful," she said. "I'm trying not to think about what's happening, but I'm so frightened . . . "

He drew a breath. "I'm scared too. But if they wanted to hurt us, I think they'd have done it already."

Her eyes were open again, the tears flowing freely now. "I couldn't believe what I was seeing," she said. "I hate guns, I hate violence. I don't even like football. Frank wanted to invite the Super Bowl team to the White House once, and I told him he'd have to do it without me . . . "

She trailed off, starting to shake her head until the rope dug into her throat and she began a strangling cough. After a moment, she glanced back at him, her eyes still teary. "Isn't that a crock? The Super Bowl? The goddamned Super Bowl . . . "

She'd begun to bang the side of her head against the hull flooring, maybe not hard enough to do physical damage, but that wasn't what concerned him.

He could picture it in his mind: the numbness inside her beginning to wear off, whatever wall she'd erected between her feelings and the things they'd already experienced beginning to crumble, first one mental brick popping loose, then another, and another . . . a few more seconds and she'd be buried under that wall.

"Stop it," he said, his voice almost a shout above the roaring engines. "Now!"

Surprisingly enough, she pulled her head up steady, something like uncertainty on her haggard features. Maybe the First Lady didn't get yelled at a whole lot.

"That's just what they want," he said more evenly. "Whoever they are. They want us turned to jelly. That's what they expect."

She stared back at him. "I *am* jelly," she said defiantly. "That's exactly what I feel like."

He shook his head steadily. "I'm sorry," he said. "But you're not. Not even close."

The boat launched itself airborne for what seemed an extraordinarily long time then. When it came down, the impact nearly jolted his breath from him. He saw her lift off the flooring momentarily, her eyes widening. When she came back down, she was biting her lip, fighting to keep herself under control. That tough lady at the podium, he thought, it hadn't been all show.

"We're out in the Gulf Stream now," he told her. "Or else the weather's turning."

She closed her eyes momentarily, but when she opened them again, the determined expression was back. "You're the contractor from Miami, right?"

He nodded. "Born there, lived there all my life."

"I didn't have time to read much about . . . everyone," she said. She bit her lip, then forced herself to keep talking. "It all developed at the last minute, me standing in for Frank . . . it happens all the time."

"If you say so," Deal said.

She stared at him for a moment while the boat continued its steady pounding. *Thud, thud, skee. Thud, thud, skee.* Maybe it was fun up there with your face in the spray, he thought.

"That's part of the job, things come up."

Deal could only nod.

"Are you married?" she asked after a moment.

The question startled him until he realized why she'd asked. "Who's going to be worrying about *you*?" she might have said. And what the hell, he'd pull out family pictures if that's what would keep her calm . . . if he had them, if his hands were untied.

"We're separated," he said. "She's living in St. Pete."

"You have children?" she asked.

"One," he said. Mental picture of a curly-haired little girl who didn't know what meanness was. What would happen when she learned where her father was?

Correction, he thought: When she learned that no one knew where her father was. How would Janice handle this one? he thought. Concern number one billion and one.

"She's seven. Her name's Isabel."

"She's with her mom?"

He nodded again. "In Disney World right about now, I'd guess. She was going to come with me to Washington, see her daddy get his medal . . . "

She watched him carefully as he trailed off. Probably wondering if his own wall was beginning to crumble, he thought.

"We never had children," she said, as if she were simply filling the silence, as if it were something he wouldn't know, as if the tabloid press hadn't had a field day speculating on the reasons why there were none, what the effect of it might have been on domestic policies, on foreign policy, on funding of the space program and the phases of the moon, how it might explain the uncharacteristic and apparently frightening political involvement of the "Barrenness," as one of the more mean-spirited writers had dubbed her.

"I never thought I'd say this, but I think I'm glad about that now," she said. She turned away from him. "I don't mean to be unkind," she added after a moment.

"I'm just glad she wasn't there," Deal said.

She nodded, and there was silence. After a moment, she turned back. "How could this happen, that's what I've been asking myself. How could they pull it off?"

Deal shook his head. "You know a lot more about the security detail than I do," he said.

"Not a lot," she said. "We're drilled on this and that and Frank tells me some things, but I don't get caught up in the details." She looked away for a moment, then came back to him. "I always felt that if you got too wound up in what might happen that you'd go strange, go paranoid, become a different person, you know? The day Frank announced, I told myself, I'll do this because we're probably not going to win and even if we do, I'm not going to let it change me . . ." She drifted off again.

"Still, I never thought anything like *this* could happen," she said after a moment. Then she laughed bitterly. "As soon as I get home, we're hiring a new security service."

Deal wanted to laugh himself. The opening of Vernon Driscoll's dreams. *For God's sake, man, give her one of our cards.*

"You saw the cops," he said finally. "The guys who were supposed to be cops?"

She nodded, her face still averted. "I saw. I thought they were firing at someone else at first and I couldn't believe they'd be so careless and then I realized . . ." She closed her eyes, reliving whatever ghastly moments, he thought.

"I thought the same thing," he said.

She shook her head sadly. "So many innocent people . . ." she said, and he saw the tears coming again, wanted to lose a few himself, though he would stop at that—just wanting to weep, he thought, that was enough, wasn't it?

After a moment she turned back to him. "What in God's name is happening?" she asked him. "What could these people be thinking? What do they want? They must have been after Frank, and then when I showed up for the ceremony . . ."

Deal shook his head. All those questions and more. He'd been running some of the possible answers through his mind, of course, but it was all wild speculation.

Some group of crazies, he wanted to say, thought doesn't enter into it. But that was wrong, that was only his anger working, clouding things. Maybe these people didn't think the same way he or Linda Sheldon did, but they had some logical purpose for what they were doing, from their own standpoint anyway.

They'd taken the wife of the President of the United States hostage for some reason. Which led to the next matter. There was going to be some kind of exchange proposed, obviously. For what, however, he had no idea. And whether it would actually take place and where he might figure in the bargain, well, he had no idea about that either.

*Peabody Public Library*
*Columbia City, IN*

A sudden flood of light washed over him then, and he was blinking, his eyes burning like some cave fish who'd found himself dumped out in the sun. A hatch cover had flipped open, and salt spray showered him as the boat cleaved another giant wave. The draft of fresh air that came with it felt like the breath of heaven. It might have seemed like a miracle, except for the shadowy form that he saw looming there.

Linda too was gazing up at the shadowy figure, and he could see the realization already forming on her face. Whatever order she had recognized in the universe before, whatever logic, whatever reason, it was about to disappear for good.

"Yo, Dedric!" Driscoll called.

Dedric Bailey, chief of the city's Special Investigative Section, glanced up from his desk, the phone tucked under his ear, saw who it was. "Yes," he said into the phone. "Of course. Every single man. Around the clock. Absolutely. Count on it." He hung up the phone, watched Driscoll approach.

"You want your job back?" Bailey asked. Bailey, a black man, was in his early fifties. Normally he looked ten years younger. Today, it was the other way around.

"No thanks," Driscoll said. "It'd screw up my pension." Actually, Driscoll had spent most of his time in Homicide. Aside from the occasional special assignment, he had never worked directly for Bailey, who commanded the more specialized units: Intelligence, Narcotics, the Bomb and Counterterrorism squads. Still, they'd maintained a friendship over the years: Driscoll had always admired Bailey's unruffled approach, just as Bailey seemed to appreciate Driscoll's own steadiness.

Driscoll glanced around the room. Pretty much as he remembered: same battered furniture, same pale green walls, a shade paler with age, same framed commendations that marked the passage of years. There was a picture of Bailey and his wife and son on a shelf behind the desk, picture taken on a college campus somewhere, or so it seemed. Three happy people in a part of the world where logic held sway.

The very notion made Driscoll think of Deal. He tried to tell himself his friend had walked away from all the chaos at the Hyatt, like that Bridges character in the movie about the plane crash. Sure. Deal was sitting in a bar having a couple of drinks. He'd turn up. All this worry for nothing. This nosing around the department, this grave he'd already climbed out of once. Go home, Driscoll. Find Deal loopy drunk on the steps. On the other hand, keep looking for bad news like he was, he was sure to find it.

"We could use you," Bailey was saying. He sighed, leaned back in his swivel chair, rubbed his face with his hands.

"You look like shit," Driscoll said.

"Thanks," Bailey said. "Sit down. I've got about ten seconds."

Driscoll took a seat in a battered gray side chair with stuffing poking out of the armrest. He gestured at the phone Bailey had been using when he'd walked in. "You mustering the Antiterrorist Unit for the feds?"

Bailey scoffed. "Yeah, I got 'em out there directing traffic."

"Come on."

"You know how the Feds are. They know everything, we don't know shit. Give 'em a couple a days to decide which agency is going to be in charge, they'll come ask us if any of us nappy-headed boys know anything. Only by then, anything we have will be stone cold, right?"

Driscoll nodded.

"You remember the Echeverria case, the guy who'd been at the Bay of Pigs, him and his wife got machine-gunned in front of their house down in Kendall?"

"I'm not sure."

"He'd been sending balloons over Cuba, dropping these leaflets, 'Kill Castro,' and all that."

It was gradually sinking in with Driscoll. "So what's the point?"

"Point is, that's the last major case I worked with the Feds. We're stymied on the thing, we discover the guy's got a safe in his house, we get the paperwork done, go out there to open it, see if there's anything inside that might help. I find a couple of suits from Langley waiting there. They tell me, we're going to look at everything comes out of that safe first. We'll decide what's related to your case and pass it along. What's sensitive to our interests, we'll maintain control of. They took a couple of cartons away, they gave me a notepad and a couple of bank statements. Couple of weeks later, they turned over some things might have helped, but whoever did it was long gone. We never did solve the case."

Bailey shook his head, seeming to drift off down the long line of the memory he'd unearthed.

"So you got no word on the First Lady?" Driscoll asked, bringing him back.

"Nada," Bailey said, glancing up at him. "Gone without a trace. Nobody knows if by land or by sea. The only thing they're fairly sure about is nobody noticed any helicopters or airplanes take off from the roof of the Hyatt."

"No one's taken responsibility?"

Bailey shook his head. "There was some bullshit communiqué, signed by an unknown group."

"You have any ideas?"

Bailey gave him a mirthless laugh. "Somebody who's well versed, that's all I know."

"What's the Counterterrorism Unit say? That's still Martinez's bailiwick, isn't it?"

Bailey nodded. "There's half a dozen groups operating out of South

America who have the capability. But there's no skinny on the street."

"Maybe they came from another part of the world," Driscoll said. "Middle East? Europe?"

"Maybe," Bailey said. "Maybe it was aliens." He shrugged wearily. "Unless somebody comes forward, we could be in for the long haul. You know how it goes. Footwork city."

Driscoll nodded. "I was down at the hotel. I saw as much as the *federales* would let me."

"Glad you went?" Bailey asked him. He'd rocked forward in his chair again. His eyes were bloodshot, his normally gleaming skin a sallow shade, Driscoll thought. Or maybe it was just the light. He'd forgotten how shitty the light was in the offices. You didn't have eye problems when you came in, you sure as hell would after twenty-five years.

"I wouldn't've believed it," Driscoll said. "Not if you called and told me about it yourself, Dedric." Bad as a plane crash. Worse, in some ways, knowing there wasn't anything accidental about it.

"We got fifty-nine dead, another two hundred in the hospital, and nobody knows what that shit they turned loose does to you. Maybe the ones that went down with the gas are gonna wake up, maybe not, maybe they're gonna grow feathers if they do." Bailey turned away, his face bitter.

"I wish to Christ I'd retired when you did, Vernon. We could be out in a boat somewhere in the Everglades, grabbing snapper, we'd never even know this happened."

"Right, Dedric. See where *I* am?"

Bailey turned back, gave Driscoll a snort that was supposed to be a laugh. "Why *are* you here, Vernon? Retired but you can't stay away from the big ones? That's head-case city, my man."

Driscoll opened his hands, the mini-version of his shrug. *Tell the man, Vernon. If he's got the news you're after, all this can end.*

He looked at Bailey. "Same people do the plane, you figure?"

"Makes sense," Bailey said, shrugging. "We hear 'bomb explosion at the airport,' what do you think's gonna happen? Half our guys, more actually, go right out of downtown for the airport. Same thing with the Feds. Bunch of them out to MIA, another bunch down to Homestead where *Air Force One* is standing by, another bunch gotta zoom up to Turnberry where the President's giving Vas a hand job."

"Then they turn the gas loose out in front, that distracts the rest," Driscoll said.

Bailey nodded. "You know they chained the auditorium doors shut?"

Driscoll shook his head. "I hadn't heard about that," he said.

Bailey stared hard at him and Driscoll noticed that his eyes were glassy, the rims an even deeper red than he'd thought. Exhaustion? Anger? Anguish?

"What really aches my ass, Vernon, is the thought of these assholes being in uniform, you know? Imagine you're sitting there in some auditorium feeling good about life and the world and even law and order and suddenly here come a bunch of miserable sonsofbitches who look like cops, opening up on you. How would you feel about that?"

Driscoll tried to imagine it, but he knew he couldn't feel it the way Bailey meant. Deal had, though. That much he knew. He found himself thinking of Janice and Isabel. Even if he could find them, what was he going to say when he called? *Say, Janice, we got good news and bad news . . .*

"All those decent people," Bailey said. "It was nothing but a god-damned slaughter. They wanted to take the woman, why didn't they just take her? Why'd they have to do this?"

Driscoll looked back at Bailey. They'd worked Homicide together maybe fifteen years, he'd never seen the guy as much as wince. Lot of people, Driscoll's ex-wife among them, claimed police work made you hard, cut off your access to your more tender sensibilities. Maybe he ought to bring Marie down to headquarters, let her take a look at Dedric Bailey, about to come to pieces, scatter all over his desk.

"Why do they blow up airplanes?" Driscoll said. "Why do they kill babies, grandmothers, pregnant women? Day I figure it out, Dedric, I am going to get myself a talk show and become rich."

Bailey nodded, staring at Driscoll as if he were actually considering his wisdom, but Driscoll knew better. The man was already sidetracked, enough bullshit with a former booze hound and ex-member of the team, time now to go back to the present, stop whining, go to work, try to accomplish something, chip away at the vague helplessness that gnawed at anybody with a brain in law enforcement, no matter how gung ho you might be, like running toward a fire carrying a bucket of water with a hole in it—you knew the basic absurdity of the situation, but how could you not keep running?

"Yeah, well . . ." Bailey had his hands on his desk now, ready to heave himself up, go find somebody to chew on. "My ass is in a major sling here, Vernon. Something specific bring you by?"

Driscoll nodded. No time left. No more dodging the issue. He took a breath that sounded like a sigh. "It's a little crazy at the hospitals, you know. There was a friend of mine in the room, at least I'm pretty sure he was. I thought maybe you'd have a better list . . . "

He trailed off. Why couldn't he just come right out and tell Bailey what he was afraid of? He'd been a Homicide detective for almost twenty years. How many dead people had he seen?

"What I got is a list of the deceased, Vernon. Minus the names of the Feds, of course. They're not giving that to me or anybody else."

Driscoll nodded. "I know what you have."

Bailey stared at him a minute, finally understood. He took a breath, rummaged around the papers on his desk. "What's this person's name?" he asked. He didn't look up, Driscoll noticed.

"Deal," Driscoll said. His voice sounded hollow in his ears. "John Deal."

Bailey looked up this time. "That's the local guy who was getting a medal, right?"

Driscoll nodded.

Bailey paused. "Weren't you on that boat with him? How come you didn't get a medal?"

"It's a long story, Dedric," Driscoll said, absently fingering the scar on his forehead. "Under the circumstances, I'm not unhappy about it."

Dedric nodded. "So this Deal was a friend of yours?"

"I worked the Thornton Penfield case way back when, Deal was the first guy we went after."

Bailey nodded, but it was clear his mind had drifted elsewhere once again. "I knew his old man," Driscoll said. "I rent an apartment from Deal now. We drink some beer."

Bailey bent back to his list, his jaw set firmly now. *We drink some beer*, Driscoll thought. Like code talk between old drunks. If it was a woman they'd been discussing, it would have been as if Driscoll had told Bailey: "We're in love."

Bailey flipped his list over, then back again. He glanced up at Driscoll, a glimmer of hope in his eyes. "Name's not here, Driscoll. You sure he's not in the hospital somewhere?"

Driscoll shrugged. "Maybe. It's pretty crazy at the hospitals, like I said."

"Maybe he just walked away after it was over," Bailey said.

Driscoll gave him a stare of his own. "Were they just letting people stroll away from the scene?"

Bailey seemed annoyed now, all his compassion used up, his patience going with it. "It was pretty crazy there, Vernon, that much I can tell you. I'll get something coherent from the hospitals pretty soon. I'll check that over, give you a call if you like."

"Sure, Dedric. You got a lot to do, though,"

"I said I'd call you, Vernon. He'll turn up."

"I appreciate it," Driscoll said. He was nodding agreement with Bailey, both of them up and walking toward the door now, Driscoll trying to ignore the troubling thought that had occurred to him.

"They took the First Lady," he said, stopping Bailey at the door. "What if they took John Deal, too?"

Bailey stared at him. "He's just a citizen. Why the hell would they do that, Driscoll?"

"I don't know," Driscoll said. "But it could've happened."

"So what?" Bailey said. His mind was clearly elsewhere now, Driscoll thought. Couldn't blame him for that.

"So what if they did?" Bailey repeated.

Driscoll stared back at him as if the answer were obvious. "Then I'd have to find him, that's all."

# 19

"Shall I apologize for the accommodations?" the tall man said. He had swung easily down through the hatch to stand atop them. Though his face was still shadowed, Deal could see that he was Latin, with fine features and a fair complexion.

The man didn't seem concerned that they'd worked their blindfolds off, or that neither of them responded to his statement. He dropped into a crouch, his face a couple of feet from Deal's. The boat's speed had dropped off, and the roar of the engines had abated.

They were off plane now, and Deal felt the wallow of the hull in the water just beneath him. Heading in, he thought, whoever was at the wheel lining up a path toward channel markers, or, more likely, getting ready to pick a passage over shallows or through a reef. These boats, for all their size and speed, didn't draw much water. He didn't suppose there were many islands, even the least among the thousands dotting the waters of the Caribbean, that they couldn't approach. He tried to calculate just how far they might have traveled, but without knowing how long he'd been unconscious, it was a hopeless task. It was only fifty miles to Bimini, little more than an hour's run in a Cigarette. Another half-hour and the possibilities for landfall grew exponentially, became virtually limitless.

He'd like to think there was some chance they'd been tracked, that even now a great flotilla of rescue ships and planes was being assembled somewhere, but the logical side of him discounted that hope. The truth was that the Coast Guard had an impossible task stopping suspicious craft *entering* U.S. waters, where anything resembling a harbor was well charted. With all the pleasure craft and commercial traffic plying these waters, the notion of tracking a boat going in the other direction was ludicrous: it would be like asking the Metro Police to find an unidentified car with something hidden in its trunk during rush hour.

"We will be putting in now," the tall man told them, watching Deal as if he understood what he might be thinking. "I think you will be more comfortable soon."

"Who are you?" It was Linda Barnes behind him. "Where are you taking us?"

The tall man seemed to consider her questions. He allowed a tolerant smile. "You may call me Angel," he said, using the Spanish pronunciation. "And as for where we are going, why not call it Paradise?"

111

The man who called himself Angel smiled and held something up in his hand. A watch, Deal saw. *His* watch. "I will keep this for you," he said to Deal. "It is a good one, I think," he added.

Deal stared back, saying nothing. It was a no-name watch his father had brought back from Switzerland twenty years ago. "Made right there in the Rolex factory," he'd told Deal. "Same damned Swiss dwarfs, they just don't put the three-thousand-dollar name on it." His old man, all right, blow twenty grand on a trip to Europe, another thirty in the Salzburg casino, but he knew a bargain when he saw one.

Angel didn't care about the monetary value of the watch, though. He didn't want Deal calculating time and distance, or trying to somehow clock the sun's movements, get some kind of fix on their location. Or maybe he just wanted to make a point.

"I can trust you, is that it?" Deal said.

Angel gave him a laugh. "Yes, my friend, that is one thing you can do."

Deal heard the sound of retching beside him and knew that Linda Sheldon had finally lost her fight with the nausea. Angel's gaze traveled to where she lay, watching with mild interest as her heaves continued. Maybe just checking to be sure she didn't choke to death, Deal thought.

The boat had dropped to near-idle speed now, and Deal felt something brush along the hull. There was a momentary whine from one of the engines as a correction was made, and they were gliding free again. Linda Sheldon's racking heaves had subsided, but her breathing sounded harsh and labored. The sweet-sour tang of vomit hung in the air.

Angel straightened, slipped Deal's watch into his pocket. "We are arrived," he said, with a glance at Linda. "You will be feeling better now."

He grasped the sides of the open hatch then, and pulled himself up with the grace of a gymnast, an instant's blur against the sky, bluer now with the onset of dusk, and then he was gone. Deal stared after him for a moment, catching sight of a sliver of moon, of a soaring shore bird. The stink of beached seaweed came to join the odors inside then, and he had a glimpse of an overhanging limb: a feathery Australian pine, he thought, the ubiquitous junk tree of the Florida Keys, of the Caribbean out-islands.

He turned back to Linda Barnes, who had twisted away from the pool of her own vomit and lay with her eyes closed, her face still pale. "You all right?" he asked.

She turned and opened her eyes. "I'm sorry I couldn't puke on him," she said. "The bastard. The polite sonofabitch."

"Don't waste your energy on him," Deal said. "He's not who we have to worry about."

She turned and stared in disbelief at Deal. "Is that right?" she said. "Then who *do* we have to worry about?" The engines died altogether, and there was a soft thud as the boat drifted into a set of pilings. Deal could hear orders being shouted in Spanish, the thump of lines being tossed, the creaking of wood as the boat was made fast.

"Us," Deal said. "We have to worry about us." She was still staring at him when the rear hatch doors flew open and four men in camouflage fatigues were there to take them out.

**Angel was not in sight** when Deal and Linda Sheldon were brought on deck, then prodded onto a spindly-looking dock where the Cigarette had been tied off. He glanced around at their surroundings, saw nothing remarkable. It could have been any of a hundred tiny islands he'd anchored off of in his life, and there were hundreds more just like it scattered about the Caribbean: on one side of the dock a ragged shoreline of mangroves that curved as far as he could see, a couple miles or more. On his left, a few feet of narrow beach littered with trash, sea scum, and ropes of seaweed deposited by the tides.

Further along, the land rose higher, a coral shelf that had once been sea bottom hove up into a mini-cliff that loomed half a dozen feet over the sheltered waters. The shelf was studded with the feathery Australian pines he'd glimpsed earlier, and he noted a low-lying house tucked amongst the trees. They'd entered the bay from that direction, he thought, which would have been the east.

The tall pines cut off any further view in that direction, and when he tried to turn to look directly behind him, he felt something strike him hard between the shoulder blades. "*¡Ándale!*" he heard as he staggered forward. Then, redundantly, "Let's go."

Another man caught him by the arm and a second came forward to point an automatic weapon in his face. Deal looked at the man with the weapon. Though they'd taken the ropes from their feet and throats, their hands were still bound behind their backs. He couldn't imagine that he presented a very threatening pose.

"They have seen American movies," a voice behind him said. Deal saw that Angel had joined their party. "A man who guards the President is to be greatly feared."

Deal glanced at Linda Sheldon, who had her mouth open in surprise. When she saw the expression on his face, she stopped whatever she was about to say.

"Tell them I'm not Arnold Schwarzenegger," Deal said.

Angel shrugged. "I think I will not tell them anything," he said. "I would prefer they worried too much instead of too little."

They walked in silence then, over the uneven planking of the dock and into the cool shade of the pines, where they assembled into single file, following a narrow path that rose up through the undergrowth. A series of sharp switchbacks that mounted the coral shelf, and then the path leveled out. Deal counted three men in front of him. He smelled cooking odors from somewhere, and realized that he'd had nothing to eat since morning. He felt the sting of something biting his neck. And then another. And another. The whining of the insects was burning at his ears and he willed his hands to stop jerking reflexively at the ropes that bound him.

"So tell me, Mr. Deal, if that is your true name," Angel said from somewhere behind him. "Are you of the Secret Service or are you with the CIA?"

Deal wanted to tell him to check his driver's license, then remembered what had happened to his wallet. He nearly laughed at the irony of it. He'd been carrying no ID except for the security badge pinned on him by Monroe Fielding. He'd blown away a couple of Angel's men, had been caught while shepherding the First Lady down a secret passage, away from the carnage. What good was it going to do to protest?

"I'm a building contractor," he said.

Angel laughed appreciatively. "And I," he said, "am a Negro aviator, is that not how your joke goes?"

Deal tried to turn his head, but he felt another tap between his shoulder blades. "Not my joke," he said.

"Well, Mr. Deal," Angel said. "The precise name of your agency is not a matter of great concern to me just now. We will have time to discuss the matter further."

Just wonderful, Deal thought. There were probably special interrogation techniques reserved for CIA types. Something else to look forward to.

"You want to tell us why you're doing this?" he asked.

Angel laughed shortly. "What does it matter?"

"If it doesn't matter, why not let us in on the plan?" Deal said.

"Enough talking," was Angel's reply, and when Deal tried to turn, a hand slammed roughly between his shoulders, jostling him forward.

They had finished climbing, it seemed. The undergrowth thinned and the path was taking them along an old quarry pit cut into the rock at what seemed to be the island's ridgeline. Vine runners and trash trees choked the abandoned site now, and a great pile of cut stones, some of them the size of small cars, had been left near the edge of the pit. The path veered around the jumble of stones, back into the underbrush, where the insects resumed their attack.

They hadn't gone far when Angel called ahead in rapid Spanish and one of the men who'd been leading the way stopped to swipe aside a thick spray of Brazilian holly that hung over the path, nearly obliterating it. The other two men made a turn into the passage and Deal felt another tap at the top of his spine.

The side path led a few feet through the thick holly and choker vines, then opened into a clearing where a raw cinderblock structure loomed. There was an angled corrugated tin roof rusted to a dull orange, littered with needles drifted down from the pines. The structure's unfinished windows were covered with concrete reinforcement mesh. There was an entrance with a steel door propped open by a bowed two-by-four, the wood gone gray in the pounding sun.

Deal felt hands fumbling at his back then, felt something cold at his wrists. He was vaguely aware of a sawing motion, then sensed his arms swinging free. But before he could bring his numbed hands up before him, he was being propelled roughly toward the building. He managed to keep his feet under him until his shins cracked against the elevated jamb. He felt a bolt of pain, then his legs were numb, and he was down and rolling on the raw concrete floor of the place. He came up in time to see Linda Sheldon tumble inside after him, throwing her hands out to break her fall. A second later, the heavy door had slammed shut and they were alone again.

Deal heard muttering in Spanish outside, then a laugh, followed by the sounds of men receding through the brush that they'd fought their way through. He sat up, rubbing the rope burns at his wrists, then the twin bruises on his shins.

Linda Sheldon was sitting Indian-style, inspecting the palms of her hands in the dim light. She glanced at Deal. "I'm having a hard time making out my lifeline," she said, rubbing her palms on the tails of her suitcoat. The coat was filthy now, but there was no mistaking the streaks of blood her palms left behind. "What's your prognosis, Mr. Deal?"

Deal tried to sound convincing. "Like I said, we'd already be dead if that's want they wanted."

She gave him a nod. "I keep telling myself that." She glanced around the single room, which was virtually bare. A listing stool, a scruffy mattress in one corner, a five-gallon plastic bucket in another. The label on the lidless bucket claimed there was drywall compound inside, but the odor that hung in the air told Deal otherwise. He could hear the angry buzz of flies all the way across the room.

"I liked the rooms at the Grand Bay better," she said wearily.

Deal gave her a bitter laugh. It was a grim inventory, all right. Bucket, mattress, stool, that was about it. A lightbulb dangled from the rafters, but something told him it had never cast its first glimmer. He saw a candle stub on the floor near the mattress, but he doubted there were any matches around. Someone had scrawled something in wavering Spanish along the back wall of the room, but Deal couldn't make it out at first.

"*Matanzas*," he read finally. He turned to Linda. "How's your Spanish?"

She shrugged. "I can usually get through ordering dinner," she said. "I don't remember that ever being on the menu."

He nodded.

She glanced at the message. "What do you suppose he used to write it?"

Deal shook his head. What were the possibilities? Blood? Excrement? A charcoal stick?

"I don't remember if I said thank you."

He turned back, considered her words a moment. "For this?"

"You know what I mean."

"I wish I'd have done better," he said.

"You did more than most people would have."

"We were lucky, that's all."

"It took more than luck for you to come after me." She stared at him earnestly.

Deal shook his head. The wife of the President, kidnapped, dumped in a cesspool, she wanted to explain how valiant he'd been. He wanted to call the reporter who'd dubbed her the "Barrenness," discuss a few things.

"There was a guy sitting in front of me, some cop from Queens, maybe. He stood up when the shooting started. He took a lot of fire, fell on top of me, or else I'd be dead, too, that's what I'm talking about."

"Still," she insisted. "You could have just stayed where you were." She gave Deal an odd look. She paused. "It looked like you knew what you were doing with that gun . . ." She trailed off again, left the question hanging.

"I'm a building contractor," he said evenly. "I have a friend who was a cop. He took me to a firing range once."

"You're John Deal," she nodded. "That's just fine with me."

He managed a nod of his own. Given the circumstances, given the possibilities for company, he supposed he'd come out all right. It could have been Nancy Reagan, after all.

Linda Sheldon's gaze had turned inward. "I wonder what happened to Leslie," she said. She glanced up at Deal. "My assistant," she explained. "And Monroe . . . "

Deal had forgotten all about Monroe Fielding. The man would have been front and center when the shooting started, but Deal hadn't seen what happened. He shook his head and she looked away.

After a moment she turned back to him.

"Assume these people, whoever's behind all this, they want to make some kind of deal. Release all the political prisoners in turn for us, or whatever it is. How long before it would happen?"

Deal shrugged, forcing away memories of various hostage crises. "Who knows? They probably have to wait until they're sure we're tucked away. Maybe somebody's e-mailing the White House even now."

She shook her head. "Poor Frank," she said.

"Poor Frank?"

She gave him a look. "That's right. How is your wife going to feel when she hears? And Frank's going to have to deal with this in public. He has to be the President, too."

Deal nodded, trying to comprehend it. He also tried to imagine what would happen when Janice got the news, *if* she were to get it. There was no certainty the world was going to learn he was part of the proceedings, after all. Maybe the only reason he was still alive had to do with Angel's misapprehension that he was part of the President's security force. Maybe that's what wearing the suit had gotten him. Their captors had brought him along as a potential source of information to these terrorists, or an added bargaining chip. And if the truth were established unequivocally, there'd be no further need to keep a building contractor on the roster, would there? He'd seem pretty small potatoes compared to the President's wife.

He took a breath, glancing about their surroundings. "Well, I wouldn't worry too much about your husband," he said. "Like I told you earlier, it's *us* we have to focus on. Maybe there are people on their way after us right now. Maybe these assholes already have their deal cut. Maybe they'll get cold feet and let us go."

She stared at him. "Wouldn't it be nice to think so," she said. She sighed and stood, somewhat unsteadily.

She glanced down at him. "Anyway, I don't think we're going to get rescued soon enough."

"Soon enough?" he shook his head.

Her hands were behind her, working at the clasp of her skirt. She nodded over her shoulder, toward the corner where the bucket sat, though her eyes stayed fixed on his. "I could wait a couple more minutes . . . *maybe*," she said, "but it's just going to come to the same damned thing now, isn't it?"

Deal understood finally, and he felt his face coloring. "I'm sorry," he said, struggling to his feet.

He made his way to one of the windows, waved away a wasp that hovered by the rusted mesh. Outside was a tangle of undergrowth that seemed alive with the hum of insects. "I wish there was something I could do," he said over his shoulder.

"There is," she was saying. "You can get us out of this somehow."

Something in her tone suggested she might be kidding, but on the other hand, he couldn't bring himself to look.

**20**

"Can someone have beeped me?" Salazar's voice drifted over the secure line as clearly as if he were phoning from a nearby office.

He gripped the phone tightly, fighting his anger. The voice was purposely light, that of a salesman responding to an everyday summons. And Salazar had used his accent to shade "beep" slightly, had turned it more toward "bip." Ricky Ricardo blithely checking in from the road.

"Humor is not called for," he responded, fighting to keep his voice even. There was a pause. Wasted moments, he thought. Even on such a line as this, encoded in, decoded out, jumping channels by the millisecond, there was always that element of risk. "What in God's name has possessed you?"

"Calm yourself." Salazar's voice over the ether once again, somewhat more soothing this time. "All our samples are secure."

He paused when the words registered. He willed away his urge to shout. "We were very clear on what was to happen," he said. "We had an *agreement!*" He fought to keep his voice under control.

"We *have* a common interest, my friend. I did what was necessary to secure that interest," Salazar said.

He paused, fighting light-headedness. "A *disturbance*, that's what we agreed upon. Not a massacre. And as for the rest of it . . ." He broke off, unable to bring himself to utter the words. Unthinkable. Inconceivable. And worst of all, himself an accomplice.

"Why have you done this? Who's paying you? Who's put you up to it?"

Only silence on Salazar's end.

"Do you want more money, is that it?"

"More is always better, my friend."

Madness, he thought. Utter madness in that voice. And yet *he* had opened the way for Salazar, had he not, held out his hand, pulled them both through the door of no return? He felt giddy for a moment, a tingling spreading through his body, a writhing current of madness inside him, a serpent all his own.

"How much is it? Tell me what to do."

"We will let the world steep in these juices for a while," Salazar said, "and when it is time, I will let you know. All may be made whole again."

"I don't see how that would be possible," he said, weary beyond belief.

"*I* have the means," Salazar said, his voice dripping with disdain. "Meanwhile, there is nothing for you to do, nothing that can be done . . . "

"I could take steps," he protested. "I have certain information . . . "

"Yes?" Salazar said. "And you would want your information known? I doubt that very much, my friend. Now go about your business, leave me to mine." And then the line was dead.

It was nearly dark, and Deal was at the window, dolefully inspecting the heavy mesh and the thick staples that held it fast against the wooden frame. If he'd had a hammer and chisel, he was thinking, or a pry bar, or even a nice long screwdriver, any of the everyday tools of his trade, he could have had them out of this excuse for a prison in minutes. As it was, he might as well be inspecting a row of titanium bars.

And even if he could get them out, what next? Where was there to run, after all? The island they were on seemed little more than a glorified sand bar, one of hundreds of such flyspecks in this shallow sea.

He turned from the window, stared at Linda, who was slumped on the wobbling footstool, her head down, her gaze turned inward. Deal fought the urge to jump in, start a stream of chatter going.

He heard footsteps then, someone pushing through the screen of brush outside. Keys rattled, a bolt was thrown, and then the door opened. Two men with automatic weapons stood at the ready, peering warily inside, as if they expected a full-scale assault from their prisoners.

"Wrong movie," Deal called.

One of the men gave him a dark look, then turned and used the barrel of his weapon to gesture at someone out of sight. Another dark-haired man in camouflage fatigues came forward and placed a plastic pail down in the doorway, then quickly withdrew. Deal noticed that he'd been unarmed.

The door slammed again, and the bolting and locking sounds repeated themselves.

Linda glanced up at him, uncertain.

Deal walked to the pail, glanced inside. At first he couldn't believe what he was looking at. He picked up the pail, moved to one of the windows where the light was better.

"What?" she said, standing unsteadily. "What is it?"

He reached into the pail, turned, held out one of the packages toward her. "Big Macs," he said.

She stared at him. "Come on."

"Feels like a gut bomb to me," he said, handing it over. "Go on, have a look."

She finally took the thing, peeled the paper away gingerly, peeked inside. "It *is* a Big Mac." She raised the sandwich, lifted the bun, sniffed, then tested it with her tongue.

121

Deal shook his head. He tried to imagine where the sandwiches had come from. "Excuse me, miss, but could you put a rush on that order, we're fleeing the United States with the First Lady . . . "

Deal unpeeled the sandwich that was left in his hand. Sure enough.

"Are you going to eat it?"

He glanced at her. "Why not?"

"They could have put something in it."

He took another look at the sandwich. "Right. Two all-beef patties, special sauce . . . "

"Funny," she said. "They really could have done something."

"For what purpose?"

"I don't know," she said. She sat down, still holding the sandwich. "I don't know anything about any of this." She glanced up at him. "Why the hell *is* this happening?"

Deal shook his head. "You're in a better position to know than I am."

"What do you mean?"

"Your husband takes a big interest in Latin American affairs, maybe he's got something cooking, ticked the wrong person off."

She shook her head. "Frank's not a meddler. Just the opposite." She tossed her hair. "He wants developments in other countries to take their natural paths. He came to Florida to tell Jorge Vas as much."

Deal shrugged. "Maybe meeting with Vas torqued the other side."

She sighed. "But what would that have to do with it? What could anyone hope to gain?"

Deal shook his head. "I'm not sure." He glanced at their surroundings. "And as our friend Angel says, I'm not real sure it matters a lot right now."

"If we knew what they wanted, we might be able to reason with them, strike some kind of bargain . . ." She trailed off.

"Maybe," Deal said, "but Angel seems to have us right where he wants us at the moment. I'm not sure he's interested in negotiating much of anything."

"Then what are we supposed to *do*?" she asked, the exasperation clear in her voice.

He took a deep breath. "I don't know . . . get out of here somehow. Find a boat, a place to hide, throw them off somehow."

She glanced at the window where he'd been standing. "Can you? Get us out of here, I mean."

He shrugged. "I don't know."

She stared back at him. "That wasn't the answer I was hoping for."

He nodded. "I could use a presidential aide or two right now. That would make things a lot easier."

"Touché," she said. She sat back, her shoulders slumping.

"You hungry?"

She glanced up at him.

"If I was hungry, I'd eat that sandwich," he said. "I don't expect there's a whole lot more where that came from."

She stared at him for a moment, considering things. Finally she held up the sandwich. "My husband actually likes these, did you know that?"

"I think I read it somewhere," he said.

She shook her head, took a bite, chewed. "Cold," she nodded, swallowing.

He nodded, bit into his burger. It was cold, but he didn't care. How long had it been since he'd eaten?

"Did they bring anything to drink?"

He glanced back in the pail, shook his head. He looked again, saw something at the bottom, reached in to pull out a matchbox. He glanced at the candle stub, shook the matchbox. Maybe two or three matches inside.

There was a pounding at the window behind him then, and they both started.

"Look," she said, pointing over his shoulder.

Deal turned to see a hand at the mesh, dangling a plastic water bottle. He had almost reached the window when the bottle dropped. He managed to catch it, then uncapped the water, brought it to his nose. He turned to Linda and shrugged.

"What's the worst that could happen," she said.

"Nothing like a little dysentery to liven up life in a prison cell," he said. He took a first, tentative sip, then a bigger swig. He handed the bottle over to her.

"It's wet," she said when she'd finished drinking.

They finished the sandwiches then, Deal leaning against the rough concrete wall, she sitting on the stool, her legs splayed out before her. Another context, he'd say they were pretty good legs, though now he simply registered that they'd picked up plenty of scrapes and bruises. There was a particularly vivid scratch that ran up the inside of her thigh, disappeared under the hem of her skirt. She glanced up, noticed him looking.

"Isn't this something," she said. She drew her knees up finally, wadded her sandwich wrapper, tossed it into a corner.

She turned back, gave him a quizzical look. "I keep telling myself it's impossible, it's just a bad dream." She sighed, propped her chin on her hands. "But then I look and you're still there."

It brought a laugh from him. He wadded his wrapper, tossed it toward the latrine bucket. She glanced at it, then back at him.

"You have to use that?" She glanced away. "Don't worry, I had brothers."

"Not yet, thanks."

She shrugged, then seemed to think of something and turned back to him.

"I'd almost forgotten why you were a part of that ceremony. All those refugees from Cuba you saved. What's your position on the issue, Mr. Deal?"

"That it was a goddamn shame they were out there to begin with," he said, staring out the window.

"Granted," she said. "But what's going to stop it from happening again and again?"

He turned back to her. "Nothing," he said.

"That's pretty cynical."

"Why should they stop coming? Most of the people down here don't live a lot better than this." He waved his arm about their cell. "Some bastard tells you he'll take you to El Dorado for a couple hundred dollars, why not give it a shot?"

She nodded, glum.

"So what's your husband's notion?" he said.

"He feels bad about the people, just like you do. He's got a whole staff working on it."

"That should take care of the problem."

She glanced up. "Spare me, okay?"

"Sure," he said. "I'm sorry. It's just the mood I'm in."

She turned away. They were quiet for a while, Deal listening to the whine of insects, waiting for some idea to strike him. After a bit, she turned back to him.

"In the mood for a story?" she asked.

He glanced at where his watch had been. "As long as you make you quick," he said.

"I went to Europe once, a trip my folks gave me for college graduation. It was a bus tour, a whole bunch of spoiled rich girls, mostly, everybody surly because canned Coke hadn't made it to Italy yet, and neither had ice, as far as we could tell." She paused. "We were somewhere between Florence and Venice when one of the girls started complaining she couldn't wait 'til the next stop, so the escort talked to the driver and finally we pulled over at some Italian gas station out there in the middle of nowhere, some ratty kind of a place, you know?"

Deal nodded. He'd never been to Italy, but he'd been to those gas stations. Ask his old man to pull over in the middle of a road trip, it was sure to be the scrungiest place in sight. His old man's way of revenge, Deal thought.

"Anyway, the escort points the way to the john and a few of us decide we may as well go since we're stopped. So we go trooping into this room and look around and we're sure we're in the wrong place." She gestured as if this were the very room. "I mean, there's nothing but four walls in there. No stalls, no commodes, no sinks or mirrors, no nothing. We were about to walk out when I noticed."

"Noticed what?" Deal asked.

She paused. "You're a good audience."

"I'm not going anywhere, if that's what you mean."

"I just mean you're attentive. I gave you that little pause," she said, "you knew you were supposed to ask." She shook her head. "Not everybody's so obliging," she added.

"People aren't obliging to the First Lady?"

She gave him a look. "Sure, some people are. All the suck-ups, as Frank calls them."

"Sounds a little jaded," Deal said.

She glanced up at him, shrugged. "It happens, once you get in. You work against it, but still . . . "

"I expect," Deal said after a moment. They were just rattling on, trying to fill the void, but he felt a little disoriented. They'd been held only a few hours, he already sensed a strange lassitude building. He glanced at her, trying to will himself toward action, even though he didn't know what could be done.

"You haven't finished your story," he said finally.

She seemed to have been drifting too. "Right," she said. "I *was* telling a story, wasn't I?"

He nodded, and her eyes turned inward. "The gas station from hell," she said. "Why am I telling you this, anyway?"

"There's usually a reason," Deal said.

She blinked, wiped her lips with the back of her hand, swiped it against the back of her skirt. "Italy," she said, after a moment. She glanced at him again, as if to show him she really could hold the thread of a thought.

"So we were ready to walk out and then I looked down and noticed something on the floor. There were these footprints carved into the cement, one for your left foot, one for your right, and just behind them this hole in the floor."

She looked up to make sure he understood. "I wish you could have seen the expressions on those girls' faces when they figured it out."

Deal was thinking about something else, the tenor of the whole story she'd been telling. "Those girls?" he said after a minute. "Sounds like you weren't really with them."

"I was and I wasn't," she said. "My folks owned a clothing store there in Columbia. They made a little money, but I grew up watching bratty kids come in and buy the same skirt in all five colors."

He nodded.

"Anyway," she said, indicating the room about them, "I really liked seeing those girls made so uncomfortable, that's what I thought then, and I never forgot it. It made me feel so superior. "

"It was probably good for them," he said. "I wouldn't feel guilty."

"I've actually been feeling sorry for them. Something like this happens, you remember so many petty things you've done," she said.

He nodded, glancing at their makeshift latrine. It was nearly dark outside now, and the insects and tree frogs had set up a deafening chorus.

"Well, go when you have to," she said, glancing away. "Maybe that was the point. We're not in a position to stand on ceremony."

She stood up then and walked to the opposite window, clutched her hands at the mesh as she stared out. Something in her pose seemed so forlorn, Deal thought. They could keep this up for a few days, sure, so long as the Big Macs lasted and their witticisms came steadily to their lips. But just how long could they bear up? How long would they have to bear up? Better not to think those thoughts, he reminded himself. Better not to think that way at all.

"Not what we expected, was it," he said.

She turned, her wistful smile back again. "Not what we expected at all."

## "Oh God, oh God . . . "

Deal woke to the panicked sound of her voice. Still dazed and groggy, he pushed himself off the rancid-smelling mattress, trying to orient himself in the darkness. He could sense her moving somewhere close by, could hear slapping sounds, tiny gasps.

"Linda?"

"They're all over me," she moaned. "Don't you feel them?"

Deal groped in the darkness for their candle stub, finally found it, still warm to his touch. He couldn't have been asleep for more than half an hour. In his pocket he found the matchbox, hurriedly fumbled out their second match. He struck it, got the candle going, held it up to see her slapping wildly at her arms.

"What is it?"

"Bugs," she said, staring wildly at him. She glanced down at the mattress as if she had finally understood what had taken place. She stood up quickly, began slapping at her legs. "Dammit! Goddammit!" Tears glistened in her eyes now. "Bedbugs! Goddamned bedbugs. What else? What else is going to happen?"

Deal put the candle down, stood to calm her. He caught her wrist, pulled her to his side. "They don't stay on you," he said. "They just bite where you're lying on them."

She glanced angrily at him. "How do you know?" she said. "There could be anything in this mattress. Some awful insect we don't even know about . . . "

She broke off then, as if she were suddenly aware of how she sounded. She closed her eyes, took a deep breath. "No bugs," she repeated. "There are no bugs on me."

"That's right," Deal said.

It took a moment while her breathing gradually calmed. Finally she opened her eyes and looked at him mournfully. "So where?" she said. "Where am I going to sleep?"

Deal glanced around the room, which danced with eerie shadows now. He was still trying to come up with a suggestion when they heard the sounds of footsteps approaching once again.

There were muffled voices outside, what sounded like cursing, and then fumbling with the keys and door bolt. When the door opened this time, the men were not so cautious as before. One man stood boldly in the doorway, his weapon in one hand, a flashlight in the other. Two others stood nearby, peering over their partner's shoulder. One had his weapon slung over his shoulder and seemed nervous, shifting his glance from inside the shed to the brush behind him. The first man had fixed the flashlight beam steadily upon Linda Sheldon. He seemed to lose his balance momentarily, and the beam shifted focus as he reached out to catch the doorjamb.

"They're drunk," Deal said quietly to Linda.

"Dear God," she said. Her voice equally subdued.

The first man mumbled something in Spanish to his companions, handed off his weapon. He stepped up onto the concrete floor of the shed and stood wavering for a moment, his shadow sliding about the wall behind him.

"I don't think this is good . . ." she began, her voice fearful.

"*Silencio*," the man blurted. He glanced at Deal, then turned and motioned one of the others inside.

The second man seemed unsure of all this, Deal thought, but he had his automatic rifle at the ready. As the first man moved on inside the room, the gunman stepped between Deal and Linda, the muzzle of the weapon now level with Deal's chest.

"Linda . . ." Deal began.

"Don't worry," she said, trying to keep her voice steady. "If this worm so much as touches me, I'm going to puke in his face."

"*Silencio*," the first man said, and strode forward, sending a backhand across her cheek. She cried out as the blow sent her reeling backward, her heels catching the edge of the mattress. She went down hard, her legs flashing in the beam of the first man's flashlight. The man tossed his flashlight onto the bed and moved toward her, fumbling at his belt, guttural noises sounding in his throat.

Deal lunged forward instinctively, but the gunman swung the butt of his weapon toward his jaw. Deal tried to duck, felt a bright jolt of pain, saw the room turn sideways as he went down. He was trying to right himself when he saw a boot—enormous boot, he found himself thinking—growing bigger with every millisecond until it passed somewhere beneath his shoulder and he felt pain drive deep into his chest, his breath flying away with the force of the blow. He was on his back, his side, then his stomach . . . Finally he managed to lift his chin, found himself a foot away from the mattress where the first man had wedged himself between Linda Sheldon's flailing legs.

He heard screams as the man fell upon her, then she was silent as a meaty palm clamped down over her lips. He saw her fist banging on the man's broad back and Deal lunged forward, caught the man's flapping shirttail and fell backward, pulling for all he was worth.

He heard the man's grunt of surprise, felt his weight shift, and then they were both tumbling together over the rough surface of the floor. Deal felt a blow between his shoulder blades, another in his ribs. The second man up there, trying to drive him off his partner. At least he wouldn't shoot, he thought. Or would he?

Deal twisted away from the blows, rolling the first man atop him, and heard a groan and a sudden outrush of air from the man's lungs. The bastard had taken one of the kicks, Deal thought with satisfaction. But hardly had he thought it than there was a stunning blow at his temple and he felt his fingers, his hands, his arms going numb.

He slumped back to the floor, saw vaguely that the first man was astride him now, his face twisted into a grimace of fury. The man drew back a fist, drove it down, past Deal's useless arms, past the edge of his blurry vision.

He managed to turn his head aside so that the blow glanced away, but still he felt his lips flatten, the warm bath of his blood in his mouth. He heard Linda Sheldon cry out again, caught a glimpse as she came clawing at the man atop him, saw a hand lash out, heard her groan as she went down.

The man turned his attention back to Deal, brought his hands into a knot, raised them high, as if he held some imaginary axe. The man brought his hands down in a pile-driving motion against Deal's chest and he felt pain compounded upon pain. He saw the fury on the man's face as he raised his hands again and knew that the man intended to beat him to death.

He saw the man raise his hands even higher above his head, saw his face redden with fury and effort, saw his eyes widen with anticipation . . .

. . . and suddenly everything changed. What had been a face transformed itself into a froth of tissue simultaneous with an explosion that rocked the tiny room. The man went over sideways, what was left of his face bouncing wetly off the unfinished concrete.

Deal turned aside, looked up blearily at a tall man—*Angel?*— who towered over him, a smoking pistol in his hand. *And I am next*, Deal found himself thinking. But Angel turned from Deal and said something to the man who'd been holding the gun and extended his hand, and the second man held out his weapon uncertainly.

Angel took the weapon, nodding as if to say that all was well. There was another explosion then, and a burst of flame that seemed to leap straight from Angel's hand. The man who'd given over his weapon threw his hands to his chest and fell backward. He struck the wall and slid slowly down into a sitting position, an amazed expression frozen on his sightless face. Angel watched him for a moment, then holstered his pistol.

Deal felt something hard against his chin, realized it was the tip of Angel's boot. A flashlight beam struck him in the face, and he blinked and tried to raise his hand to block the light.

"*Bueno,*" he heard Angel say softly. The boot moved away from his chin and Deal's head settled back against the concrete.

The flashlight beam slid over the filthy mattress to where Linda was pulling herself up. She got unsteadily to her feet, pulling her rumpled skirt over her legs. Her blouse was torn at the collar and there was an angry welt on her cheek. She started to say something to Angel, but nothing seemed to come. Then she shifted her gaze to Deal and started toward him.

"You bastards," she muttered as she knelt over Deal. "Filthy bastards."

"This is nothing I would permit," Angel said. He waved his flashlight at the man who still sat slumped against the wall. A dark streak marked his path down the rough surface to where he rested.

She glared up at him. "You think that matters?" She turned back to Deal, lifted his head into her hands.

Deal felt a tingling in his fingertips, felt his arms dangling like heavy lumber at his shoulders. As if he'd slept in all the wrong positions at once, he thought. He swallowed, tasted blood, tried to force his tongue to work.

"You shouldn't have tried to stop him," Linda Sheldon said, staring mournfully at him. "I could have lived through it."

"Mr. Deal is a soldier." Angel's words drifted down from up above. Deal thought he heard a note of approval there. The coach who watches the player limp back into the huddle, the boxer stagger out sideways to answer the bell.

"He needs help," Linda insisted.

Other men were in the room now. One pair lifted the man who'd held the gun from his rest against the wall, someone else was dragging the man without a face out of the range of Deal's vision.

Angel let the flashlight roam over Deal's face. Even the touch of the light felt painful, Deal thought. With a steadfast effort, he found he could turn his eyes from the searing beam.

"No," Angel said, "I think he does not. He is a soldier," he repeated. "If soldiers live, they live with pain."

Coach Angel, Deal thought, his mind beginning to fog over. Put a little heat on those fractures, those bullet wounds, run it out.

"You're insane," Linda Sheldon was crying. "*This* is insane. What do you want?" Linda Sheldon was shouting now, but the words seemed to come to Deal as from a great distance.

"What do you want from us?" Her voice again, echoing down a long dark tunnel.

"From you?" he thought he heard Angel say. Deal thought he heard the man laugh. "I want nothing from you."

*Nothing?* Deal thought, his head swimming. *All of this for nothing?*

"You are my little proofs of chaos," Angel was saying. "And that is all you are."

Deal thought that he had only blinked his eyes then, but when he opened them again, Angel was gone, and the door was closed and locked, and sometime after that, the rain began.

**22**

"And what makes you so sure this Deal person is with the First Lady?" The man Driscoll had been brought to see regarded him with the bored indifference an emergency room nurse might give anyone still able to stand. Utter self-certainty, Driscoll thought. Not a good quality for a cop, but then maybe being a Fed had something to do with it.

Driscoll stopped himself from offering his characteristic shrug. "You and I can agree he was up there on the presentation stand, right?"

The man nodded, glanced at his watch. They were in an airless room in the Federal Justice Building, where the local command center had been established. Only ten-thirty and the guy looked like he was in a hurry for lunch.

"And he's not among the fatalities, he's not in any of the hospitals . . . "

"These emergency rooms have been pretty busy," the Fed offered. "Maybe he's unconscious, somebody took him in as a John Doe."

Driscoll shook his head. "There were a few of those, homeless types who hung around Victory Plaza, I'd guess. But none of them were Deal. I saw 'em all." Driscoll added the last in response to the guy's how-can-you-be-sure look.

He'd been in nearly a dozen hospitals over the last fourteen hours, seen more dead and dying than he'd ever expected to look at the rest of his life. The gunshot victims were one thing—he'd seen plenty of that before. But the victims of the as-yet-unidentified gas were something else again. Many of them comatose, many on respirators, most of them with skin lesions, as if they'd been dunked in boiling water. Whatever the stuff had been, it worked like a combination of mustard gas and nerve gas: if it didn't put you out, it made you look so ghastly you wish you had been, that was Driscoll's take on it. Something sure to spread panic on the battlefield. And in downtown Miami, he thought.

At Gables General, he'd caught a glimpse of a bundle of bandages that had once been Gina Lozano, the stylish Channel 7 reporter who'd been on the scene when the gas was released. One of the nurses had confided in him that only the machines were still keeping her going. Aurelio Pincay was outside the building doing a blustery standup when Driscoll left . . .

"Your friend will turn up," the Fed in the airless room was saying. "He could be out there somewhere, walking around in a daze. We've seen that kind of trauma before."

"And he could be up at the North Pole tuning Santa's sleigh bells," Driscoll said. "Reason I came in here, I think there's a good chance he's been taken along for the ride."

The Fed leaned back in the office chair he'd likely appropriated from some hapless staffer, tented his fingers at his chin. "Let's say you're right, Mr. . . . " He broke off to consult the business card on his blotter. ". . . Mr. Driscoll. Say whoever is responsible for this did kidnap your friend as well. What I'm not clear on is what you'd like us to do about it."

Driscoll stared at the man in disbelief. Before he could say anything, the man had rocked forward in his chair, was jutting his chin defiantly at Driscoll. "The President's wife has disappeared. We assume she was kidnapped by the same people responsible for everything else that's taken place over the last twenty-four hours in this hellhole you call a city, but we're not even sure of that, since nobody's bothered to deliver any kind of ransom note. Nobody claiming responsibility, no scuttlebutt on the international terrorist hot line that anything was in the works. Meantime, there's threescore people dead, a quarter of them federal agents, and a like number headed for the same destination. We have every available resource assigned to the matter of finding the First Lady, Mr. Driscoll. If your friend is with her, then you can be sure we'll bring him back as well. But in the meantime, there are more than a few matters that need attending to." The guy pushed himself up from his desk, letting Driscoll know the interview was over.

Driscoll didn't budge. "Seems to me," he said, "that in a situation like this—never mind that John Deal is a human being whose life is every bit as worthy as the First Lady's—I'd want to know anything and everything about what I might be looking at, who I might be looking for, under what circumstances I might find them when and if I did."

The man closed his eyes momentarily. "I gather you were a cop," he said finally.

Driscoll nodded, thinking he heard a bit of emphasis on the *were*.

"That's the only reason you're in here to begin with," the guy added. "Somebody talked to somebody and now I'm talking to you, and everything I've said is in strictest confidence, I might add."

Driscoll nodded again. There was nothing the guy had said so far that couldn't be inferred from what was on television. He was trying to keep himself calm, trying to remind himself that assault on a federal law enforcement officer was a serious matter.

"Well, rest assured that what you've told me will be passed along. The information will be evaluated, and if it's determined that we need to speak with you further, then someone will get in touch."

Driscoll threw up his hands then and stood. No use continuing with this guy. After all, Driscoll had delivered the same speech himself, hundreds of times. People come in wanting to help on a case they've read about, or demanding action on it, or wanting to confess to doing the crime, you make a quick assessment. Time demands it. And ninety-nine percent of the time, you're right, you've saved your energies for more likely leads. It was just that he hated feeling like part of the one percent who had something important to be considered.

"Here's my card," the agent said. "Something turns up, feel free to call."

Driscoll glanced at it. "Harvey Clyde," it read. No agency, no address. Telephone number written out in blue pen below his name.

Driscoll nodded. "Sure," he said. "Deal turns up, I'll give you a buzz."

If Clyde heard any of the irony in Driscoll's voice, he chose not to acknowledge it. "Thanks for coming in," he said, and extended his hand. "You might want to file a missing persons report on your friend," he added.

Driscoll forced himself to smile. He made a gun of his fist, closed the hammer that was his thumb, then turned and walked out.

He used the stairs going down, wanting to work off some of the heat he felt still burning at his neck, telling himself he could have managed the same three flights going up, he was going to have to do something about the old waistline somehow, was about to step out into the busy lobby when he felt the beeper began to rumble at his belt. He checked the readout, found an unfamiliar number. He'd left his own with several nurses over the course of the night—maybe someone *had* found Deal, after all. Irrational as it was, he found his heart rate accelerating as he moved toward the bank of pay phones just outside the stairwell.

"Doctor *who*?" Driscoll called into the phone. He held a finger to his ear to block out the clamor in the lobby. His heart was pounding now, and he felt his throat go dry. He didn't remember speaking to any doctors the previous night, but that didn't mean anything. Doctors liked to be the ones making the important calls, didn't they?

"Jameroski," the voice on the other end repeated. "Leo Jameroski."

Driscoll tried to remember. "Yeah, you're over at Cedars, right? I talk to you last night?" Driscoll shifted the phone to his other ear, glanced over his shoulder as a squad of plainclothes types jostled their way out of an elevator, began striding for the door. All of them in suits, good haircuts. Places they'd gone to college, Driscoll thought, he could buy a car for what they'd spent on a semester's tuition, and yet none of them looked like the kind of guy he'd go to in a pinch.

There was a pause. "We talk some long time ago," Jameroski said. "You help me out about some things."

Jameroski. The name had finally registered with Driscoll. Doc Hammer. Junkie Doctor. Doctor Pump 'Em Up, get your steroids while they're hot. He'd drawn a five and dime in a scandal that involved several ex-Dolphin football players at least fifteen years back, had lost his license in the bargain. Driscoll had investigated the case, found the good doctor a somewhat addled type who'd been manipulated by his partners. Driscoll had helped the doctor bargain a reduced sentence in return for his testimony regarding his co-conspirators. The last time Driscoll had seen Jameroski, he discovered the man had somehow managed to get a pharmacist's license and was running a pharmacy out on the beach. That was Doc Hammer for you, cut out the middleman, go straight to the source.

"You remember," Jameroski was saying. "I help you get those pushers couple years ago."

"Right," Driscoll said. Jameroski had, in truth, called to tip him about some kids selling stolen Dilaudid out of a van up and down the beach. "As I recall, you were trying to get rid of your competition."

"Nah, nah," Jameroski protested. "Were selling to kids, those punks. I *never* do something like that."

Driscoll's pulse, meantime, had dampened considerably. Whatever it was, the call couldn't be about Deal. No self-respecting hospital would allow Hammer within rifle shot, not even as a patient.

"So what can I do for you, Doc? I'm a little busy here."

"I think's important," Jameroski said.

"So tell me," Driscoll said, his voice weary. He watched the quartet of trimmed and suited Feds push through the doors and hustle down the steps of the building where a dark sedan was parked. They moved like movie cameras might be trained on them, he thought.

"The phone," Jameroski said, a note of protest in his voice.

"What about the phone?" Driscoll said.

"I tell you, 's important."

Driscoll sighed. He knew Jameroski didn't want to talk about this "important" matter on the phone, but he wasn't in the mood for a drive to the beach. Besides, what could it be? The doc wanting to rat out somebody he was writing downer scrip for? "You know I'm not with the department any longer?"

"Sure I know," the doc said, sounding offended.

Not bad, Driscoll thought. It wasn't every seventy-year-old junkie he knew who was capable of taking offense.

"I'm pretty busy here," he said. In fact, he'd been wondering just what his next move was. Take out an ad in the paper, solicit leads? Consult a medium? He knew he should do what Harvey Clyde said, just go home, or go see what he could do for the Zaragosa brothers and their charcoaled charcoal hut, but it just wasn't in him to walk away. He'd rather spin his wheels than give up.

"This kid I work on," Jameroski persisted. "Was talking in his sleep, you know?"

"Uh-huh," Driscoll said. The momentary rush was gone altogether now, had left him feeling even lower than when he'd walked out of Harvey Clyde's office. Or was it Clyde Harvey? Probably a bogus name, the phone number probably hooked up to a machine that invited callers to take a howling leap at the moon.

Driscoll realized that Jameroski had been rattling on while his thoughts wandered. "Hold on a second, Doc," he said. "You were *operating* on this guy?"

"I didn't say that." Jameroski's voice had turned guarded.

Of course the doc didn't want to incriminate himself, Driscoll thought, but he'd been busy trying to recombine everything he'd just heard. "Yeah, well forget about why, Doc. What were you saying about *police* uniforms?" Jameroski began to go through it all again, but he didn't get far before Driscoll cut him off. "You're absolutely right, Doc. You bet. You did the right thing. Right. That's right. I'll be there in fifteen minutes. Exactly. Don't let him out of that room, no matter what."

**23**

"Assuming that air traffic is too obvious, too easily controlled, and ground transportation is too risky and too limited given the local topography, probability suggests we're looking at a waterborne escape from the area," the general in charge of the briefing was saying. *Waterborne*, Chappelear thought. Odd choice of words, but then that was the military for you. Turn the kidnapping of the First Lady into a science project.

The general punched a button on his remote and another vast black-and-white satellite image filled the screen before them. They were using one of the hotel's conference rooms, and the size of the image only made the quarters seem more cramped and airless to Chappelear, who was accustomed to the spacious briefing rooms in the White House. The President had been adamant, however. No time would be wasted shifting the base of operations back to Washington. It was the electronic age, after all. Information was infinitely portable, infinitely malleable. It was people who were difficult to move.

"What this gives us is a composite of the boat traffic from twelve hundred hours all the way into the evening," the general was saying as the image came into focus. The satellite map seemed an impenetrable maze of white threads overlaid on a dark background that must have been the sea. "You can see what we're up against," the general said.

"We can factor out for size," he said, punching another button. The maze transformed, leaving what must have been a hundred or so lines that crisscrossed wildly in all directions. "That's your commercial traffic, for instance. Cruise liners, freighters, fishermen of size, easy enough to trace using the port records, but unlikely targets, most of them."

He clicked another button. "Here's the real problem," he continued. The maze re-formed itself, became a spaghetti-like tangle again, nearly as dense as it had seemed in its first incarnation. "Pleasure boats. Day fishermen. Anything bigger than a wave runner."

He turned to face the assembled group: the President, Lawrence Chappelear, John Groshner, representatives of the FBI, the Secret Service, the CIA, assorted aides. No one from the agencies seemed expectant. This was old news, grim news, a courtesy briefing primarily for the benefit of the President: we're out there doing our best, Chief.

"It's not just the volume of traffic," the general continued.

He pushed another button and the view pulled back, leaped alive with color. The sea was suddenly blue, the boat trails a more vividly defined white. The southern edge of the green-shaded peninsula of Florida curved into focus, along with a few nearby dots of land that were the Biminis. Cuba—the entity that Chappelear could blame for all this—lurked there to the south, but most of its mass was shrouded by a dense gray cloud cover that arched on northward into the Bahamas, obscuring most of those tiny islands from view. The great majority of the boat trails disappeared into the thick cloud mass as well.

"The storm system's not only played havoc with surveillance," the general said, maneuvering an electronic pointer over the cloud mass, "but we'd pay hell getting any kind of craft down there right now, even if we had a destination in mind."

He clicked something else on his device and the cloud mass transformed itself into a mad whorl of color: bands of green twisting at its outer edges, shading to yellow further in, bursts of angry red glinting at the edges of the imagery. "We've got a hurricane headed this way," he said, sliding his pointer southeastward, toward the outcroppings of red. "Category One as she stands, but the tracking center in Coral Gables is predicting it'll strengthen steadily through the night."

"Good God," the President murmured. "What else can happen?"

"The storm could turn north," the general said, "miss most of the islands altogether. It's a little too early to tell."

"So we're sitting on our hands, waiting?" the President asked.

"Well, sir, I wouldn't say that," the general replied. He pushed a button, and the image onscreen dissolved. He motioned to one of the aides and the overhead lights came back on. "We've mobilized SEAL units, special land response units, we've been screening the commercial traffic, as I said. We've got Coast Guard units in the Biminis where the weather's still holding. We've had voice contact with most of the marinas where fuel might have been dispensed, we've got agents checking every marina on the mainland, from the Palm Beaches all the way to Key West . . . "

"And we have nothing to show for it?"

"Some things," the general said. He gestured at the aide again and the lights went down. He pressed another button and a new image grew on the screen, this an actual photograph, an aerial shot of a small scrub-covered island, the Miami skyline in the distance. He clicked his controller again and the image tightened in on a lagoon sheltered by the island. Something seemed to hover there just beneath the surface of the water.

"We've discovered a cabin cruiser scuttled in shallow water off Soldier

Key, just a few miles off the coastline," the general said. He paused. "It's being raised as we speak."

"Did we send divers down?" Chappelear asked.

The general heard something in his voice, glanced nervously at the President. "We had a quick look," he said. "There was no one in the cabin, nothing else readily apparent, but once we get it up and can get our technicians to work, we'll see if there's any evidence to suggest it was used by the terrorists."

"What about the local authorities?" Groshner asked, glancing around the room. "I don't see any representatives here."

"Local law enforcement is mobilized to the maximum," the general said. "They have primary responsibility for airport and marina surveillance, checkpoint control, ancillary services."

"I don't care about the groundskeeping," Groshner said. "Have they come up with anything we can *use*?"

The general turned to one of the agency types at his side. "Mr. Clyde is the Special Agent in Charge. He can tell us about these matters."

Harvey Clyde stood ponderously, adjusting his suitcoat on his broad shoulders. "We're still in the process of evaluating Metro-Dade and City of Miami data," he said, casting a nervous glance at the President. "As well as the smaller agencies, of course. We're taking a look at a break-in at a police supply house a couple of nights ago, which we suspect was the source of the uniforms used by the terrorists."

"Any suspects in that robbery?" the general asked.

Harvey shook his head. "There's a break-in about every thirty seconds in this part of the world. They don't take them too seriously. By the time anyone realized the significance of this incident, the scene had already been contaminated, the owners boarded up and back in business the next day." He shrugged, glanced again at the President as if to see if he'd seemed too cavalier.

"We're also looking into a car bombing in south Dade County, checking residues against materials lifted from the plane that was blown up at the airport . . ." He trailed off for a moment. "There was a subject transported to one of the public hospitals who may have been involved in the car bombing, that's what the locals tell us, anyway, but he was never ID'd." Clyde threw up his hands. "He seems to have disappeared. We've got a team working that matter, but again, we're talking pretty cold leads at this stage of the game." His expression left no doubt as to his opinion of the local authorities.

"Thank you, Mr. Clyde," the general said. He glanced around the table as if hoping to see an eager face, someone with good news to share, but the others stared up or down or off into the distance, anywhere but at him. The general might have been about to utter some hapless statement when something finally happened to galvanize everyone's attention.

"I've heard enough," the President said, rising from his chair. He turned to Chappelear. "Next time you bring me down here, make sure it's for a reason, Larry."

He strode out of the room then, flanked by a pair of Secret Service men, leaving all eyes on Chappelear, except for the general, who knew enough to avert his eyes. John Groshner's gaze seemed particularly penetrating. "Well," Chappelear snapped finally, "you heard the President. Do something. Do any goddamned thing."

"Bomb that hurricane off the map?" Groshner asked mildly.

Chappelear stared at him for a moment. He felt the eyes of the others upon them, not much different from the promise of a schoolyard scrap, really, everyone gathered around, waiting for the fists to fly. "If that's what it takes," he said to Groshner, his voice cool.

He stood then, surveyed the others arrayed about the conference table. "There's a trail out there somewhere," he said. "And by God, we need to find it. Is that understood?"

Grudging nods around. "Dismissed, then," Chappelear added.

The general looked up at him. "Sir?"

"If you've got a moment?"

"Absolutely," the general said. He left aside his paper shuffling, let his briefcase fall shut.

"You're the one who wrote the report bemoaning our diminished defensive posture on the Caribbean, aren't you?"

The general colored. "Well, sir, I know we've had our differences . . . "

"Never mind that," Chappelear said with a wave of his hand. "You're a man of conviction. That's what matters at a time like this. We need men we can count on. *I* need someone I can trust." Chappelear stared at him evenly.

"I'll do everything I can, sir." The general straightened, clasping his hands behind his back.

"Good," Chappelear said. "I'd like a rundown on just what gear we've got at the ready down this way."

The general nodded. "We've got everything, sir. Now we do, that is. Anything and everything. Men and material all in place. You want a missile up Castro's behind, just give me the okay and stand back."

"That's fine," Chappelear said. He liked a man who was eager to please. "Have a seat. I want you to tell me everything about it."

"Watch your car for a dollar, man."

Driscoll was locking the Ford when the voice came over his shoulder. He turned, found a guy materialized right there in the street, about six feet, weighed maybe a hundred pounds. The street had been deserted when Driscoll had pulled into the space, a rare non-metered spot sheltered by some overhanging banyans a block or so off Washington Avenue where Doc Hammer kept his so-called pharmacy.

Where had the guy come from? Driscoll wondered. Manhole? Up from one of the storm drains? He had another look at the guy's clothing: blue T-shirt that had once had a pocket, pair of shorts looked like they'd been peeled off a truck lane on I-95, rubber flip-flops that reminded him uncomfortably of his own favorites, 99-cent bargain bin, K-Mart of your choice. He was thirty-five, maybe, looked about fifty.

"Why would I need someone to watch my car?" Driscoll asked.

The guy stared back at him, blinking, eyes that might have been blue once, now the color of nothing. Zero. Zip. Zotz.

"'Cause I need a drink, man," the guy said.

Driscoll sighed. There was something to be said for honesty.

"Say I don't give you the dollar," Driscoll asked.

The guy stared off, thinking about it. Perfect blue sky, perfect summer day. Looked like he was staring straight up into the sun, Driscoll thought. No wonder his eyes were bleached out.

The guy turned back to him. "I dunno," he said. "Take a whiz in your gas tank?" He stared at Driscoll like he was wondering if that was the right answer.

"What you been drinking, I'd probably get better mileage," Driscoll said.

He dug into his pocket, found his money clip, examined the notes folded there. Two twenties, two tens, two fives. He glanced up, noticed the guy was looking, too.

"Bummer," the guy said.

"Yeah," Driscoll said. He could stiff the guy, and probably nothing would happen to his car. Or maybe there was some change in his other pocket. He had important business—where did it say he owed this loser anything?

He stared off into the sky, same place the guy had been looking, couldn't find his answer. He peeled off a five, handed it over.

"I could do your windshield," the guy said. He held up a wad of his T-shirt, made a wiping motion.

"Next time," Driscoll said. He gave the guy a wave, already on his way toward Jameroski's. "Just keep an eye out for the bad guys."

"You bet," the guy called after him.

Driscoll didn't bother to look back. He knew there'd be no one there.

A **"CLOSED" sign** hung behind the steel-grated glass of Jameroski's pharmacy. There'd been a Rexall decal stuck on there once, but big chunks of it had disappeared, probably gnawed off by one of the doc's customers looking for a new high, Driscoll thought. Driscoll checked his watch. Closed at 11:30 A.M. on a Thursday. Sure.

He pounded the door frame with his fist and after a minute the doc showed up—snowy-haired, skinny Doc Hammer in a baggy pharmacist's coat that had probably been white several years ago, all hunched over and squinting out at him over his granny glasses and his big broken-veined nose like some character out of Dickens. Jameroski had to throw at least three locks, jerk his five-foot-plus self mightily against the door to get it open.

"Goot, goot," Jameroski was saying as Driscoll walked inside, out of the warming sun and into a netherworld of shadows and mildewy smells that took him back about forty years in the space of a footstep. What was the essence of it, anyway? Driscoll wondered. Faintly medicinal, but certainly not sterile. Like maybe somebody'd swabbed the wooden floorboards with Mentholatum, then started over again with shoe polish. Musty paper and baby powder and cistern water in there, too.

He blinked, his eyes adjusting to the light. The shelves were dusty and half empty and a big faded box of surgical cotton lay open on its side, spilling white stuffing like a tiny pillow someone had shot. There was a dangling fluorescent fixture with two of its three bulbs gone and the other one sputtering blue. A wooden ceiling fan just behind it turning so slowly you could see the flies sitting motionless on the blades. There had to be a ceiling up there someplace, but it might have been cathedral height for all Driscoll could tell.

A wire paperback rack with three books total, their yellow pages fanned and dinged. *The Stranger. Hoyle's Rules of Games.* Something called *Street Eight*, with palm trees and a gun and a babe on the cover. There was a wooden counter, an old-fashioned brass cash register the size of a baby carriage, a display card full of Sen-Sen packets propped beside it. On the wall there, a line of sample trusses that looked like they'd been nailed up by old man Rexall himself.

Driscoll stood as if paralyzed, barely able to shake his head. It was the kind of place, you plugged in a modern appliance, the walls would explode. He wanted to sink down in the dusty wheelchair at the end of the counter, suddenly, and weep for all the days past, for all the days of our lives.

He wanted to be a kid again, come into the place to spend a dime for a Nehi soda, shoplift whatever was handy. He wanted Deal to be waiting outside on his bike, they'd peel off somewhere, smoke cigarettes, argue arcane rules of card games, look at the pictures in their stolen copy of *Dude*, *Nugget*, or *Gent*, jack off in their socks. He wanted that life back, the life he couldn't put a name to, the life that had damn well been right here once but was now out there in space somewhere, every last image expanding, whistling off in the void at the speed of light, on and on and on, never mind poor Vernon Driscoll, never mind all the terrible bends in the road.

He turned to Jameroski, who'd had to lean into the door to get it closed again, was snapping all his locks shut. "I bet you got a dial on your phone, Doc."

"Sure I got a dial," he said, offended. "What do you think? You want to use the phone already?"

Driscoll shook his head. "How about *Look* magazine? You carry that?"

"No magazines." Jameroski shook his head. "No good. All the kids steal them."

Driscoll nodded. Why *couldn't* he dial back the clock? he was thinking. Notch it a couple days in reverse, anyway. None of what had happened would have happened. Bring Deal over to see this place. Buy out Jameroski, send him to the Keys with a U-Haul full of drugs, open up this place as a museum-*cum*-clinic, good for what ails modern you. He'd been to Ponce de Leon's supposed Fountain of Youth in St. Augustine, paid five bucks for a bottle of the very water, he and Marie had chugged it, still couldn't get their sex life started.

But this place . . . half an hour inside, you could forget time had ever progressed past Ike. Mom would be cooking in the kitchen, Dad knocking down a big-time two-seventy-five an hour at the plant, the vacuum cleaner'd suck up all the bad shit in life.

Sure. He sighed again, put his arm out, hung it over Jameroski's frail shoulders.

"Okay, Doc. So tell me, where's this jerkwad hiding?"

"*Isn't* hiding," Jameroski said.

"No?" Driscoll said. Anything was possible, Jameroski could have dreamed the whole thing up. "Then why'd I come all the way over here?"

"*I* hide *him*," Jameroski said, making the distinction clear.

"Whatever," Driscoll said wearily. He was feeling the onset of a headache now. All this time travel back and forth.

"I *show* you," Jameroski said. And off he went.

"This was taken from the body of one of ours," Agent Knowles said, leaning to place the wallet on the desk of the Special Agent in Charge.

Harvey Clyde, the SAC, stared down at it. A workingman's wallet, it appeared. Dark stains marred the leather surface. There was a dimple on one side of the wallet, a tattered eruption on the other, where the bullet had exited.

"This the shot that took our man out?" Harvey Clyde asked, fingering the ragged edges.

"I don't think so," Knowles said. He consulted a slip of paper in his hand. "Agent Gerald Casenovich. With the Service less than a year. He took fourteen rounds, including that one. The wallet was found in the front pocket of his pants."

Harvey Clyde nodded. Fourteen rounds. He tried to imagine it. If there had been pain, it would have ended quickly. Please, God, let it have ended quickly.

"And we've found no trace of this John Deal?"

"None, sir."

"What's the story on . . ." Harvey Clyde broke off, consulted his own notes. ". . . on Vernon Driscoll?"

Knowles shrugged. "An ex–Metro Dade homicide detective. A friend of Deal's, apparently. Deal was/is a tenant in a duplex owned by Driscoll."

"Driscoll is convinced Deal was taken with the First Lady?"

"If that's what he told you."

Harvey Clyde took another look at the notes. "Do we find this plausible?"

Knowles shrugged, and Harvey Clyde nodded in agreement. Who knows? Who cares? John Deal was just a citizen. A hero, of course. Probably a great guy. But compared with the First Lady . . .

"But we've got someone watching Driscoll?"

Knowles nodded reluctantly.

"You figure he's some kind of nutcase?"

"I dunno." Knowles glanced away. "But we got a lot of people down here, most of them looking for something to do."

Harvey Clyde nodded. "This is one hell of a situation, isn't it, Knowles?"

"The worst, sir."

"We're all dressed up, there's nowhere to go."

"Something'll break," Knowles said. "They call in, we'll find them."

Harvey Clyde nodded and checked his watch. Despite Knowles's confident words, they both knew the statistics. Ninety percent of kidnappings still unresolved after forty-eight hours went unresolved forever. First Lady or John Doe. Statistics really didn't give a shit. If the people who took her didn't make contact, if they didn't want her to be found, well . . .

He glanced again at his watch. "Okay, Knowles. I'm late for a briefing at Command Central. I'll tell them about Driscoll, that ought to take up a good ten seconds."

Knowles nodded. "Watch yourself out on the streets. Drivers are crazy in this town."

"They're not the only ones, Knowles," Harvey Clyde told him. "They're not the only ones."

The rain had come in waves through the night and continued without letup into the day, torrents that turned the corrugated metal roof into a roaring drum at times, gentling off to a feathery whisper at others. Deal had come awake two or three times, gazed up groggily to find Linda Sheldon looking back at him in concern. This time—he sensed it was already afternoon—he'd found her asleep, still in a sitting position, her arms cradling his aching, cement-heavy head.

*The hero,* he thought. *Flat on his back, fresh out of bullets, fresh out of tricks.*

The rain was still pounding, coming down in sheets that sprayed through the open-mesh windows, forming rivulets and puddles on the concrete floor. He raised his head gingerly, felt something on his forehead, realized she'd torn a sleeve from her suit jacket, soaked it in water for a compress. He peeled the cloth away, lifted his hand gingerly to his face.

Hard to tell without a mirror, of course, but it felt like someone had inflated the side of his head with an air pump. He worked his tongue around inside his mouth, found a couple of teeth that wobbled, but everything seemed intact.

He held himself steady on one elbow for a few moments, letting the throbbing in his head settle, the memories of the night reclaim him. He glanced across the room to the wall where Angel had executed the man who'd held the gun. Blast mark where the bullet had struck the wall, broad dark streak down the uneven courses of block. All in all, Deal thought, things could have turned out worse.

He turned back to Linda, found her coming awake. She brought her hands to her eyes, rubbed. Finally she looked up at him, shook her head.

"Your head's lopsided," she said matter-of-factly.

"Thanks," he said. Smiling seemed out of the question.

"It's not too bad," she said. "It was worse last night, kind of horror show. Now you're almost back to human."

He nodded slowly. Very slowly. He felt his puffy cheek.

"How do you feel?" Linda Sheldon was asking him. There was concern in her voice once again, and she raised her hand gently to his cheek.

He pushed himself into a sitting position. "A lot better than the guy who hit me," he said.

She nodded, shook her head at the memory.

He picked up the soggy coat sleeve, dabbed at his swollen jaw. There was a throbbing ache in his jaw, and he felt a little light-headed but otherwise clear, as though he'd come through a fever. He got a knee underneath himself, stood and moved to the windward side of the room, raised his face to the cool spray of the rain sweeping through the mesh.

He felt something, looked down, realized the fly of his shredded trousers was gaping open. He started to zip himself reflexively, found the tab stuck in a gather of cloth. Something dawned on him then, and he glanced up at Linda.

"You had to go," she said. He stared at her, checked his zipper again.

He dislodged the cloth that had jammed the mechanism, zipped himself up, wiped the mist off his face. "I find myself speechless," he said after a moment. "But thanks."

"You can make a contribution to the campaign," she said. "If we get home," she added.

*When* we get home, Deal wanted to say, but false bravado had never been his strong suit. Instead he nodded.

"Just don't mention why you felt compelled," she said.

Deal could imagine the kind of saloon talk Driscoll could manufacture out of this one. *What does the First Lady say when she's been kidnapped? No big Deal.* Har-de-har-har.

It occurred to him that there was not much likelihood that Driscoll would ever have the chance to turn any of this into a joke. *But would that he gets the chance,* Deal thought, stepping out of the suddenly chill draft. *Would that he gets the chance.*

"... right here in Great Inagua, where the outlying storm bands are beginning to affect the local
weather ... "

There was a mackinaw-clad reporter on the screen of the tiny television
as Driscoll followed Jameroski into the storeroom. Raindrops spattered
the camera image and winds were whipping the background harbor
waters of some Caribbean port into a frothy mass. "SPECIAL WEATHER
ADVISORY . . . SPECIAL WEATHER ADVISORY . . ." went a banner scrolling
along the bottom of the screen.

Driscoll wasn't paying much attention to the television, though. His
eyes were on the guy tied to the cot.

"Is him," Jameroski said. "Ray Brisa."

The guy, who had his back and shoulder and a chunk of his face in bandages, looked up at Driscoll, then shifted to Jameroski. "You brought the
frigging cops?"

Driscoll gave him a mirthless laugh. "You wish I *was* the cops, dickhead. Just wait a little while. You're gonna be begging me to call one for
you."

"What's going on?" Brisa demanded of Jameroski. "Who is this guy?"

Driscoll settled down on his haunches beside the cot. He could smell
the tang of burn ointment, and also the sour hint of Brisa himself.
Driscoll wanted to think it was fear. "My name is Vernon Driscoll," he
said. "And you are going to tell me everything I want to know."

"Get fucked," Brisa said.

"No," Driscoll said. "You are the one that is fucked, my friend." He
turned to Jameroski. "Iddn't that right, doc?"

Jameroski nodded absently. His eyes were on the television. "You know
there maybe comes a hurricane," he was saying.

"A hurricane?" Driscoll said, glancing at the set.

There was a studio shot there now, a weatherman standing before a
satellite map of the Caribbean. The Florida peninsula seemed clear, but
the islands to the south and east were another story. There was a huge
mass of yellow- and green-pixeled clouds blanketing the farther reaches
of the Caribbean, doing a steady crawl northwestward. Behind that was a
tightly packed red-banded whorl with a black dot at its center. The weatherman was dancing in front of the map, pointing here and there with a
computer pen like an enthusiastic John Madden diagramming NFL plays.

"What else, huh?" Driscoll turned back to regard Brisa, who had his chin set toward the wall, staring off into some world where hurricanes were irrelevant, where punks got only respect and cops sucked wind the livelong day. "Ever read the Bible, Ray? Maybe we got us a Second Coming on the way. Maybe you're one of the weasels it talks about in there, gets puked up out of the bowels of the earth right before the scourge."

"Not my Bible, man," Brisa said, his eyes steady on the wall before him.

Driscoll nodded. "I didn't think so."

He glanced up at the television where John Groshner, ubiquitous special advisor to the President, had replaced the weatherman. Groshner, who bore an unfortunate resemblance in Driscoll's mind to Bob Haldeman, was at a podium somewhere, heading up what looked like a press conference, speaking earnestly into the camera. *Enough for the calamity to come*, Driscoll thought. *Back to the ones we already have.*

". . . a plea from the President to those responsible to come forward, for anyone who has information that might be helpful to come forward . . . "

Driscoll tuned out the pleas, which sounded pathetic, even desperate to him. He passed his hand over his face, trying to rub fresh feeling into the flesh there. Why couldn't he just sit back and let other people take care of things? Leave the Ray Brisas and the bomb makers and gas leakers and First Lady kidnappers to their work and just wait for the old screen to go dark? He supposed he could, if it hadn't been for Deal.

"Yo, Doc," Driscoll said to Jameroski, who seemed immersed in the weatherman's continuing dance. "Whyn't you tell Ray here why you called me up. I think he's having a hard time with the code of criminal conduct, trying to get it straight how a fellow offender like yourself might give him over."

Jameroski looked at Brisa like he was a worm crawling through snot. "The President," Jameroski said, shaking his head.

Brisa cut a surly glance at Jameroski, turned back to his wall.

"I can tell that explanation eludes you," Driscoll said. He poked one of his stubby fingers into Brisa's bandaged shoulder, and Brisa howled in pain.

"What the doc is getting at," Driscoll continued when Brisa's cries had died away, "he's different from guys like you and me in that he still has ideals, right, Doc?"

"This country." Jameroski nodded. "Goot country."

Driscoll poked Brisa once again, just to be sure he was paying attention, had to wait again before he could continue. "What we got here is a guy who grew up with Hitler. Ever hear of Hitler, Ray?"

Driscoll poked him again, so it was difficult to tell whether Brisa was nodding yes or just writhing around in agony. "So anyways, the doc may have made his own mistakes, but he realizes that back where he came from somebody would have turned him into a lampshade for a hell of a lot less."

Driscoll found a fresh spot, poked again. "Pity you didn't know the doc was a patriot, that's what I'm trying to tell you, Ray."

Driscoll picked up a bottle of Pine Sol out of a scrungy-looking bucket, held it up to the light. "This looks pretty well aged, Ray. I'll bet it feels pretty good on a burn, what do you think, Doc?" Driscoll uncapped the bottle, passed the pungent neck under Brisa's nose.

"Goot." Jameroski nodded.

"What the fuck you want from me?" Brisa screamed, tears leaking down his face now.

"You knocked over the Southern Police Supply couple of nights ago, right?" Driscoll said.

"Fuck you," Brisa said.

Driscoll tilted the bottle and let a stream of liquid splash on Brisa's shoulder. Brisa arched up as if electrified, setting his cot into a dance on the dingy tiled floor.

It took Brisa a minute to catch his breath. His shoulder was still twitching when he spoke. "I thought you weren't a cop." His voice was a breathless rasp.

"I'm not a cop," Driscoll said mildly.

"Then why are you trying to pin some number on me?"

Driscoll held the bottle close to Brisa's face, swished what was left of the Pine Sol around. "Ray, I don't give a flea's fart about you. I just want to know who you were working for."

"You gotta be crazy," Brisa said.

Driscoll capped the Pine Sol with his thumb, gave it a vigorous shake. He caught a corner of bandage on Brisa's shoulder, yanked it up, shot a fizz of cleaner underneath. Ray's howl was enough to set Driscoll's teeth on edge.

"Looks a little nasty under here, Doc," Driscoll said when the noise had dropped away to muffled groans. "Maybe you got something stronger, we can get it good and clean."

"Sure," Jameroski said. "Got plenty things."

"Okay," Brisa croaked, catching Jameroski going out the door. "For God's sake. It was Eddie Left."

"Eddie Izquierdo?" Driscoll said. Another noted sleazewad, best known for the string of escort services he ran. A former Miami mayor and a couple of his cronies had been run out of office for diverting several thousand dollars of campaign funds into Eddie's tony brothels. Eddie would do anything for a buck, but he was nobody who'd kidnap the President's wife.

"Eddie must've brokered the deal," Driscoll said. "Who'd you deliver the goods to?"

"I don't know, man."

Driscoll raised the Pine Sol into the line of Ray Brisa's vision.

"A bunch of Colombians, I think. Drug scammers."

"Bullshit," Driscoll said. "See if you got any carbolic acid, Doc."

Jameroski nodded, went on out the door. An eager exit, Driscoll thought.

"I don't *know* who they were, man. I'm telling you the truth. I'd tell you if I knew who they were. They killed two of my guys, they tried to kill me. Give me a frigging break."

"How about I break your neck, Ray, do the world a favor?"

Jameroski was back already, an uncapped pharmacist's jar of something purple in his hand. "Put this," Jameroski said eagerly.

Driscoll waved his hand to fan away the ghastly smell. "Christ, Doc. Put the top on that thing. I think Ray's told us as much as he knows. That right, Ray?"

"Go see Eddie," Brisa said. "Maybe he knows who they were." Some realization seemed to pass over Brisa's face. "Maybe Eddie knew they were going to waste me, the bastard."

"You got a mind like a steel trap," Driscoll said, clapping Ray Brisa on the back as he stood. He ignored the fresh groans of pain. "Shame to waste it on these criminal pursuits," he said.

He passed back through the time warp of Jameroski's pharmacy, thinking that he would go see Eddie Left, all right, and after Eddie the next scumbag and the next, keep on slogging no matter what, as long as there was a trail to follow, unless somebody got lucky and found a way to stop him.

"What I should do with him?"

Driscoll realized it was Jameroski on his heels, the bottle of ghastly purple stuff still in his hand, little junkie doctor cum pharmacist looking more like some poor man's wizard, ready to do his bidding. And it was a good question, he thought. He'd been so concerned with Eddie Left, he'd already dismissed Ray Brisa. But he might need Brisa, he thought. Like you need the aftermath of anything awful, just to prove that it had happened, if nothing else.

"You gotta open up now?" Driscoll asked.

"Open up?" Jameroski asked.

"The store, this place, as in 'open for business,'" Driscoll said, impatient.

Jameroski looked around as if he'd just noticed where they were standing. "Ach," he said, waving his hand in dismissal. "I have a customer now and then, most by appointment."

Driscoll nodded. Customers by appointment. There was a twist. "Well, maybe it wouldn't hurt to keep Mr. Brisa on ice for a while. Would that be something you'd mind doing?"

Jameroski gave a look in the direction of the storeroom. That expression, Driscoll was thinking. Anybody else might have called it revulsion, Driscoll saw a strange kind of glee.

"Sure," Jameroski said. "On ice as long as you want."

"Good," Driscoll said.

He had also remembered one other piece of business, one more sorry job he had to take care of before he tracked down the infamous Mr. Left. "Now, you mind if I borrow your phone?"

**"Vernon?** Is that you, Vernon?"

Driscoll standing at the counter of Jameroski's time-warp pharmacy, heavy ebony phone receiver from another era in hand, assuring her that it was indeed him, listening to the catch in her voice, listening as she tried to stop herself from sobbing. "Just hold on a second, will you?"

He heard the sound of Isabel's voice, of Janice saying something in an urgent tone, the sound of a door closing, then she was back.

"I wanted Isabel in the other room," she explained. He could hear the intake of her breath on the other end. "What's happened, Vernon? I've been calling the house, the police, the hospitals. No one will tell me anything . . . "

He nodded. He'd already heard that same panic-stricken litany when he pulled her message off his machine before coming to Jameroski's.

"Nobody knows anything, Janice," he cut in. "I'd have called you earlier, but I didn't know where to reach you. I've been out doing the same as you, just trying to get some answers."

"Was he there, Vernon? Is he . . . " She faltered then, her sobs breaking over the line. He was about to say something when she found her voice again. "Please, Vernon. Tell me the truth!"

"John's not on any casualty list. That's pretty certain. I been to all the hospitals, talked to some people . . . "

"Then where *is* he?" she cried.

"I don't know, Janice."

"I'm up here in Fantasyland," she continued, "trying to pretend to Isabel that everything is just fine while the whole world's turned upside down. Can you imagine what that is like?"

"I don't want to imagine," he said. "I wish to God I could do something, that's all." He heard more sobbing on the other end of the line. "You gotta think the best—. That's what I been."

"The best *what?*" she fairly shrieked. "Is he dead? Is my husband dead?"

"Janice, you have to calm down," he said. "He's not dead. At least that's what I think, what I hope, anyway."

"Vernon," she began, a steely edge in her voice suddenly, "speak to me in a direct fashion. Tell me what you're talking about. If you don't, so help me, I am going to come absolutely and totally apart."

He took a breath, glanced at Jameroski, who stood by the shuttered door of the shop, staring out onto the sunny Miami Beach brightness as if he'd turned to stone. "I think that maybe they took him, too," he said.

There was a long silence on the other end of the line. Thumps of someone pounding on a door. A distant child's voice. "Just a minute, sweetheart!" Janice's voice, muffled. Then clear, as she came back to him. "That's not possible."

He didn't say anything. It seemed a universal sentiment.

"Is it true, Vernon? Is this something you're making up for my benefit?"

"Janice," he said, "I'm looking into it. I hope I'm right . . . or maybe I don't," he broke off, furious at himself for not being more adept. "Look, I'm going to call you back the minute I find out the slightest thing, okay? Meantime, you gotta hang in, take care of Isabel."

He heard her blowing her nose, clearing her throat. "I understand, Vernon."

"I dunno," he said. "Maybe you ought to bring her on back to Miami, maybe Mrs. Suarez can help . . . "

"Then Isabel would have to know." Driscoll heard the alarm in her voice.

"Yeah, well . . . "

"If we stay up here, I can keep her occupied," Janice continued, her voice steadier. "I'll just take her to see Minnie and Mickey, you know? It's hard to believe, Vernon. I mean, Peter Jennings is on TV all day long, even the cartoon channels are having news breaks, but the Magic Kingdom's business as usual, Mickey and Minnie are still dancing, they'd be dancing if bombs were falling, for God's sake."

A little humor, Driscoll thought. A good sign. "You're probably right," he said. "Keep her occupied. Keep yourself occupied. I'm going to call the minute I know anything. Just pray I'm right."

Another pause. "Sure, Vernon, I think I can manage that," she said. "And thanks."

For what? he wondered. And then the connection broke.

It was the tree crashing onto the roof that got Deal's attention. He'd been inspecting the door hinges, thinking idly about *The Prisoner of Zenda*, where he thought he remembered that the guy had managed to tunnel out of a dungeon using a spoon, except it had taken him twenty or thirty years, or maybe it had been *The Count of Monte Cristo . . .*

Suddenly there'd been a sharp splintering sound from somewhere close by outside, and another, then a breathless *swoosh* of needles sweeping the rain-striped air, and the crash of metal when the branches slammed against the roof.

He'd turned in time to see the branches fly up in recoil, then settle back toward the ground, slinging a fresh shower of water through the open windows as they whipped about. There was a gaping hole now where two sheets of roofing had buckled, and the rain was already cascading through.

"What? What was that?" Linda came out of a doze, her face panicked. While Deal had canvassed the place, searching for nails, crevices, anything that might suggest the possibility of escape, she'd dragged the mattress into the driest corner, propped herself into a sitting position, and nodded off. Maybe she'd had a half hour of rest, he thought. It couldn't have been more.

"A tree," he said on his way to the window. He glanced out. "A big tree," he added.

He saw now that it was one of the Australian pines he'd noted as they'd arrived on the island, not really a pine at all, but some shallow-rooted weed of the tree family, which had been brought halfway around the world earlier in the century. About as steady as a fifty-foot man doing a handstand, they'd been the first trees to come down when Hurricane Andrew had swept into Miami. And then—as Deal stared out over the fallen tangle of branches, the shattered trunk, the great clod of root and earth that loomed up out of the storm like some shaggy creature thrust to life—it finally occurred to him what was really happening.

"We're in trouble," he said, as much to himself as to Linda.

She'd gotten to her feet, was on her way to the window. She laughed at what he said. At least it was a sound that resembled laughter.

"Because there's a hole in the roof?" she asked. She glanced dolefully at the water splattering onto the floor.

"The weather," Deal said. "We could be looking at a hurricane."

She stared at him, uncomprehending. "It seems like one to me."

He started to say something, then stopped himself. *She wasn't there, Deal. No one who wasn't there can understand.*

For a moment he wavered, fighting against the fear rising inside him. Just a patch of bad weather, he wanted to tell himself. Another tropical wave, characteristic of the season down here.

He might have been able to dismiss his troublesome thoughts, but he'd felt the same thing when Andrew had made its final approach toward Miami a few short years back, some subtle shift in his inner chemistry that told him that it was no false alarm: he'd had this same sick feeling in his gut—as if the bottom had fallen away, as if the all the cells were clamoring for something to hold on to. The utter certainty of his body that this time was no false alarm. Duck and cover, John Deal. Find someplace to hide.

He hoped he was wrong. But he hadn't been then. And if he were right again now . . .

"This is nothing," he said to Linda, waving his hand at the fallen tree. A branch just outside the window continued to whip strangely about, and he saw that a two-foot Cuban lizard had emerged from the tangle, probably wondering what had happened to its home. The bright green thing was dangling upside down, its claws clamped fast to the slender branch, its ponderous head swiveling about like some tiny dinosaur looking for someone to take out a grievance upon. They were surly creatures, and Deal had been bitten by them more than once, clearing rocks, felling trees. He decided not to point it out to Linda Sheldon. There were plenty of worse things to talk about.

"It starts this way and you think you're getting nailed," he found himself saying. "Then when the storm really hits, you can't believe how bad it is."

"If you're trying to cheer me up, it's not working," she said, staring at him uncertainly.

"I don't want to frighten you," he said. "I just want you to know."

She stared at him, the tough countenance she'd maintained so stolidly a little shaky, it seemed. "Know what?" she asked, her voice quiet.

Deal took a deep breath. He noticed that the lizard had disappeared. Maybe it was trying to dig a hole, he thought, pull the top in after itself.

"I don't think this island's very big. I doubt that where we're standing is twenty feet above sea level, if that."

"So?"

Again he hesitated. *Keep your mouth shut, Deal.*

"I have to tell you these things," he said. "If it is a hurricane, I want you to know what we might be in for."

Her eyes widened slightly, but she was nodding assent.

"It's not so much the wind," he said, glancing about them at the walls of the makeshift prison. The concrete block had been laid haphazardly in places, but the seams were solidly mortared even if they wavered drunkenly along. A solid concrete cap beam had been poured atop the top course of block, and there were lengths of half-inch steel rebar jutting from the cap to hold the roof rafters down. "This place isn't very pretty, but I don't think it'll come down on us."

"I'm glad to hear it," she said, her eyes still fixed expectantly on him. "Are you going to tell me the bad news now?"

"It's the storm surge," he said.

"Storm surge?"

"The wind gets going hard enough out there over the water," he said, waving his arm, "it pushes a wall of water up in front of it, just piles it up, drives it forward."

"A tidal wave?"

"Something like that." He shrugged.

"As in how big?"

"I don't know," he said. "It depends on the wind speed, the size of the storm . . ." He broke off. "We had fifteen feet come ashore ahead of Hurricane Andrew, maybe more in some places . . . "

"Fifteen *feet*?"

He met her stare, nodded.

She glanced around. "How high up are we?"

He shrugged. "Six feet, maybe. Maybe eight, I'm really not sure. All of this is just speculation, you know."

She glanced out the window, then back at Deal. "We have to get out of here." Her voice had taken on an edge of panic.

It was what he'd warned himself against. *Way to go, Deal. Scare her good. Misery loves company, was that it?* "There really isn't any way to know if I'm right," he said.

She studied him for a moment. "How about Angel and his people? They must be concerned about this storm. They must have a radio . . . "

"Maybe," Deal said.

"So if there was a hurricane coming, they'd know, they'd have moved us."

Deal shrugged. "You'd like to think so. But maybe they've got bigger things on their minds. Or maybe there's no place else to go."

She stared at him. "You think that's possible? That they just wouldn't tell us?" She broke off, stared up at the rattling tin above their heads.

"Whatever's happening," he said, "it's too late to try and get off this island now. Not in the boat they used to bring us here. If we had an ocean liner, maybe we could put out to sea . . . "

"Stop it!" she cried.

He stared at her.

"I'm sorry," she said. "I'm scared, that's all. *You* scared me. I don't want you to joke. I want you to do something about . . ." She broke off, staring about them. ". . . about *all* of this," she finished.

"Yeah, me too," he said.

She glared at him in frustration. "I should have told Frank to forget it," she said. "I should have let him pass out his own damned medals. I should have been a selfish person just once in my life and done just exactly what I wanted to do, which was go down by the pool of that expensive hotel and park myself in a chaise longue and read a book and let myself be pampered just like all the rest of the people with any sense."

Deal nodded as she finished. "Right. It could have been Frank and me sitting right here hashing things out. Maybe we could have made some progress on the Cuban situation." He glanced around. "At least the bathroom situation wouldn't have been so awkward."

She had her mouth open to say something else, but that stopped her. She took a breath. "Okay, Mr. Deal. What do you propose?"

Deal gestured up at the gap in the corrugated roofing. "We could wait for the wind to blow that tin away," he said. "Or we might try giving it a hand."

She looked. "How would we get up there?"

He glanced at the wobbly stool in the corner, but knew it wasn't tall enough. A five-foot ladder, that's all he needed. And why not a cellular phone, too, since he was wishing?

"Come on," he said, kneeling down on his hands and knees. "I want you to stand on my shoulders." He glanced up at her.

"Come on," he repeated. He indicated the wall with a jerk of his head. "Steady yourself against the wall with your hands."

She gave him a doubtful look, then hiked her skirt up and stepped forward.

"Okay," he said as he felt her bring her feet together in the middle of his back. "Now lean forward."

"I'm trying!" He felt her feet stutter-stepping about, as if she were doing some kind of dance step up there. "This isn't going to work," she cried.

"Come on," he called back. "Lean into the wall, steady yourself with your hands."

After a moment he felt her weight settle, her movements even out.

"Okay," he said. "I'm going to stand up now. Keep yourself leaning into the wall, move your feet on top of my shoulders."

"I flunked gymnastics," she called to him. "I just want you to know that."

"Put it in your autobiography," he said. "Here goes."

He strained against her weight, got one foot beneath him, rose up as slowly as he could. "Let yourself slide," he called. "Come on."

He felt the resistance lessen then, got his other foot under them, rose into a crouch. "Can you touch the rafters yet?"

"You mean the wood things across the ceiling?"

"Right," he called. "The wood things."

"A couple more inches," she said. He felt her wavering on his shoulders and willed himself still. He could do this. He could turn himself to stone if that's what it took.

"Okay," he said. His face felt like it might blow out from the pressure. "When I straighten up, grab hold of the rafter that's closest to you."

"Got it," she called. He felt one foot dig into his shoulder, then straighten. "What now?"

He clasped a hand over each of her ankles then. He wanted to glance upward, guide her movements, but worried that the movement might dislodge her. "I'm going to back away from the wall," he said. "I want you to reach out for the next rafter with one hand. When you've got it, bring your other hand along, and let me know. We're going to walk ourselves over to where the hole is, just like that."

"I'll try," she said, her voice doubtful.

"You're going to do it," he said. "Just get yourself ready."

"Right," she corrected herself. "I *will* do it."

He felt her lurch then, heard the smack of her hand on wood. He staggered back, trying to keep himself centered beneath her.

"You okay?" he called, gasping for breath now.

"Got it," she answered.

He sidestepped more neatly this time, spread his legs for balance. He felt the spray of rain, caught sight of the gap in the roofing from the corner of his eye. "One more," he said. "You can do it."

"Go," she said. And he staggered under her once again, feeling his foot slip in the water that had puddled beneath the hole.

For a moment he thought they would both go down, but then his sole caught on a ridge in the poorly troweled concrete. *So there was something to be said for poor craftsmanship,* he thought, steadying himself. *What do you think about that, old man?*

"So what do I do now? It's hard to see up here. The rain's splashing in my face."

"Try pushing up on the panel that's already loose, see if it gives."

"It's hard," she said. Then she cried out.

"What happened?"

"I cut myself. This stuff's all rusty."

The water was cascading directly down upon him now, and he felt himself beginning to waver. He turned his head from the torrent as best he could and shouted. "Can you push harder? Go ahead, give it everything you've got."

His breath was coming in shorter gasps now, and his legs were going leaden. It was the beginning of the end, he knew. The last time he'd struggled this way had been twenty years and twenty pounds ago, he was on the football field, wearing full pads, and was at the peak of physical condition.

"What if they're out there?" she was calling.

"It doesn't matter," he cried. "Come on!"

"Here goes," she said.

He felt her feet dig into his shoulders, felt the tendons and muscles in his shoulders quiver as she strained upward. He heard her cry—whether from effort or pain he couldn't tell—then heard metal buckling.

"It's giving a little," she cried.

"Push, goddammit," he said. "Don't stop. Push."

He drew his legs together as close as he dared, stiffened his spine, threw his chin up so that the water poured fully into his face. He felt her cry out again, but the crashing water drowned it out and he wasn't sure what had happened until he heard the rending shriek of metal and felt the pressure on his shoulders lessen, and he knew then that they still had hope.

Driscoll piloted the Ford due west out Sunset Drive, his eyes wary on the line of thunderheads that blanketed the horizon, about to rush up to meet him, or so it seemed. It was angry weather, steel gray and blue and black, but it had nothing to do with whatever was brewing in the tropics, that much he knew. These storms were a clockwork phenomenon this time of year, fueled by a blistering sun that cooked the Everglades like a shallow pot all the hours of every morning, June through October, until these monster clouds were born and the sky seemed too swollen and bruised not to split.

Driscoll stopped at an intersection, watched a couple of long-haired kids push a battered VW bug through the intersection, hustling to make the light, one guy at the driver's door, one guy at the rear. A couple of surfboards were lashed to the top, and Driscoll wondered if maybe they were intending to push the thing all the way to the beach, which would be about twenty miles from where he sat. Two more people for whom the world continued to turn. *Good,* he thought. *Good for them.*

There was a backfire, and a plume of blue smoke out of the rear end of the VW, and the two kids were suddenly racing after the car, which was picking up speed, jouncing up over the curb, heading toward the crowded parking lot of a Publix supermarket on down 117th Avenue. Driscoll couldn't see anybody behind the wheel. It didn't surprise him that the car was now driving itself away. He'd read about it tomorrow, if the casualty count was high enough, that is.

He had the light now and pressed the accelerator down, getting a last glimpse of the two kids still chasing their car, which had careened off a coconut palm and was now heading toward a drive-in branch bank on the edge of the lot. Only in Miami, right?

He'd been listening to some guest of Ted Koppel's on *Nightline* last night, this "terrorism consultant" talking about the history of corruption in the Miami Police Department, the sorry, confused response by the city in the face of the triple disaster, making it sound as if it were the place itself who'd kidnapped the President's wife, as if the event could have taken place exactly nowhere else in the world. As if that weren't bad enough, the guy'd closed his stint by reminding Ted that wasn't everyone lucky, it could have just as easily been the President who'd been taken, and still no mention of anyone named John Deal.

Well, Driscoll thought, so much the better if such lamebrained thinking kept the Clydes and terrorism consultants of the world in Washington or Beirut or wherever they felt more comfortable. Let them lambast Miami, give the hundred-best-places-to-live-in awards to the Orlandos and the Duckburgs, let the walking oatmeal of the race go live in such places and leave Driscoll to his Doc Jameroskis and Ray Brisas and the guys off the street who'd take a dollar not to steal his hubcaps. What had happened was dreadful, but it had been born of the twisted impulses of human beings, not by geography, not by the design of some sentient landscape.

Speaking of landscapes, Driscoll realized that the one surrounding him at the moment had taken a marked change. Since he'd passed under the elevated bridge carrying the Florida Turnpike, the strip malls and condo developments had fallen away, replaced now by nurseries and day schools and sprawling estates surrounded by the kind of whitewashed rail fencing more typical of Kentucky than South Florida.

"Horse country" was what the locals called it, an oasis of grassy farms on the far western verge of buildable land where horses were kept and bred and presumably ridden, though the latter was an impulse Driscoll couldn't fathom. The day a horse would deliver a verbal promise to him not to try anything funny, that was the day he'd mount up. He'd had a couple of friends on the Mounted Patrol, the horses were always biting them and stepping on their toes and aiming kicks at their heads, and those animals were city employees, the next thing to commissioned officers, for Christ's sake. Imagine what civilian horses were capable of.

A couple of fat raindrops hit the windshield of the Ford as he swung off Sunset, traveling northward now along a narrow lane that ran between a palm grower's fields and a sod farm. The rain began to pick up then, and after a while the farms fell away and the sawgrass took over, a ten-foot wall of green rising up on either side of him. The grass, which seemed to need about a week and a half to take over any patch of untended land in this part of the county, was for Driscoll a reminder of the area's natural state of affairs.

Do your worst, it seemed to suggest, set off your explosions, spread your gases, litter the landscape with bodies, and when you tire of it all, in a few thousand years, the grass will come back, the roots will split the seams of the concrete, the heat and the moisture and the rot will do the necessary work, and all will be as it was before anybody got any big ideas.

The rain had become a blinding, roof-thrumming downpour, and Driscoll flipped his wipers onto high, slowing the Ford to a pace just above reverse. Hard enough under the best conditions to find the entrance to Eddie Izquierdo's compound, which is the way Eddie must have intended it, Driscoll thought. He gave a glance in his rearview mirror, just to be sure that no produce truck was about to flatten him from behind, then looked ahead in time to see it, a break in the sawgrass and Brazilian pepper that was what he was looking for.

He hit the brakes at the same time he twisted the wheel and the Ford took the turn more like a skidding luge than an automobile, bottoming out in a mammoth pothole that stretched the width of the driveway. The Ford coughed, then caught its rhythm again, the wheels chewing and sliding along the ruts. God help him if the vehicle bogged down, Driscoll thought. He might as well be in the middle of the Amazon jungle now.

He goosed the accelerator and the Ford lunged forward, spitting mud and rock fragments up into the wheel wells with a clatter. And God help him if anyone were on the way out of the compound, he thought as the Ford wallowed around a curve in the narrow road.

It wouldn't be Izquierdo, of course. He wouldn't be caught dead using this miserable excuse for a driveway. If Eddie had to go out, he'd use his helicopter, and pray that no ground-to-air missile encampment had been set up nearby by one of his competitors. Though Eddie didn't go out much these days. He'd finally achieved the dream, Driscoll thought. He'd made so much money, had come to exert so much influence in the Miami underworld, that he risked annihilation any moment of the day, so he'd become a virtual prisoner in his compound, had taken up more or less permanent residence in what had originally been an afterthought: a thoroughbred farm where Izquierdo could launder a significant portion of his ill-gotten gains as well as party down with some of his ladies and henchmen in relative privacy whenever the mood struck.

Abruptly, the muddy track turned solid beneath his wheels, and the wallowing Ford stopped its boatlike pitching. Getting close, Driscoll knew. The road was still a tunnel through the underbrush, but it was a brick-lined tunnel now, a couple hundred yards of roadway paved with what had once been the walls of some factory or school or apartment building in Chicago, knocked down, demortared, and shipped by the trainload to become the driveway of a rich South Florida pimp. About a hundred dollars a yard to lay this road to nowhere, Driscoll guessed. Too bad Deal hadn't gotten any of the work.

He pulled the Ford to a stop outside a set of iron gates that looked like they'd been stolen from some European baron's castle, and probably had been. Driscoll had passed through this portal once before, but it had been nighttime, and the gates had been swung open then, and there had been a squadron of thugs directing traffic to a party that Izquierdo had tossed back in the days when such a gathering was still possible. Just like the old days in one respect, however: Driscoll wasn't on any guest list of Eddie Izquierdo's.

The rain seemed to let up for a moment, and Driscoll rolled down the window of the Ford, reached out, mashed the button of the driver's-side intercom with his thumb. He waited, hit the button again, and finally a voice crackled out of the speaker.

"*Quién es?*"

"It's Vernon Driscoll," he said. "I need to talk to Eddie."

There was a pause, then a crackling of static and the voice was back. "*No esta*. Eddie gone. *Véte.* "

Driscoll sighed. The person doling out Spanglish on the other end probably knew as much English as he did, could use it better, too. He reached to push the button again. "Cut the shit," he said. "Tell Eddie I'm here to save his ass from Ray Brisa, see how that plays, all right?"

Another pause, a gust of wind and a splatting of water from the over-hanging branches onto the Ford, then finally a different voice on the line. "This Vernon?" Suspicion there, but not necessarily dislike. Driscoll had never hidden his disdain for the man, but he'd never had to nail him, either. Maybe that made him a friend, in Eddie Izquierdo's view.

"Eddie," Driscoll said affably. "Open the gates. "

"I'm pretty busy, man."

"Open the gates, Eddie, or I'm going to turn Ray Brisa loose on people that matter, you hear me?"

Another pause, then Izquierdo again, sounding resigned. "You by your-self?"

"No, I got Bobby Kennedy and Eliott Ness here with me. Now open the goddamned gates, Eddie."

Izquierdo didn't bother to answer, but Driscoll heard a squeal of metal from somewhere and saw the gates starting to glide backward. He rolled his window up and urged the Ford on down the lane.

"Good thing I got those intercoms rigged on a hard wire," Izquierdo was saying. *Izquierda* meant "left" in Spanish, something it had taken Driscoll a while to figure out, despite Eddie's nickname. When he had finally managed that feat, a few years back, it had doubled his vocabulary in the language. To *cerveza* had been added *izquierda*. So now he could go anywhere in the Spanish-speaking world, order a "left beer."

Izquierdo, who resembled a younger Charles Bronson except for the dense clusters of acne scars on his dark-skinned cheeks, was standing by the window of his den, turned to give Driscoll an annoyed glance. There'd been a couple of goons in the room when the doorman brought Driscoll in, but after they'd patted him down, Izquierdo had sent them away.

"You say things like you did over a cellular, you don't know where it ends up," Izquierdo continued.

"God hears everything," Driscoll said, unconcerned. He was leaning at the corner of a bar that had been done up to look like an English pub. There were a pair of spigots back there, big porcelain jobs, one for Bass Ale, another for Double Diamond. Driscoll wished it weren't raining outside. The weather was perfect for it, made him ache to go behind the bar, see what it would be like to draw himself one.

Izquierdo stared at him, finally shook his head. "You're one of a kind, Driscoll, you know that?"

"I'm glad to hear it, Eddie. I'd hate to think there were any more of me out there running around."

Izquierdo nodded, but Driscoll could tell he wasn't sure what to think. Eddie spoke English fairly well, but there was a certain parrotlike quality to him. All the words were there, but you weren't always sure if he caught all the nuances.

"You want something to drink?"

Driscoll had another look at the big ceramic taps. "No thanks, Eddie, I can't stay."

"Sorry to hear that," Izquierdo said. He turned his gaze back out the window. The house, a massive neo-Tudor—and God knows what drug-addled fantasy had inspired Eddie to pick Tudor—sat on a slight rise, a rare variation in what had once been undifferentiated shallow sea bottom. In South Florida terms, the three-foot hump passed for serious elevation. Several acres behind the house had been cleared for the stables, the exercise fields, a training ring. Portable bleachers were scattered about the grounds, and some accoutrements of a steeplechase course. Maybe Izquierdo had envisioned becoming part of the horsy set, Driscoll thought. A person gets rich enough, he might convince himself of anything.

Driscoll also wondered if Eddie, who looked like he was dressed for company, sleek gray silk suit, a dark shirt open at the neck, mightn't have meant it, that he really was sorry. Holed up all alone out here, hookers and horses and bodyguards for company, how long before that got old?

"So what's this crap about Ray Breezes?" Izquierdo said.

"Breezes," Driscoll said, thinking about what Eddie had just said. "That what Brisa means?"

Izquierdo turned to him. "You come all the way out here to work on your Spanish?"

Driscoll shook his head, distracted momentarily. *Beer, left, breeze.* How could you make a sentence of that? Maybe, if he spent a couple more years hanging around this crowd, he could become a Spanish conversationalist yet.

He came out of it, noticed that Izquierdo was swirling the glass of scotch in his hand hard enough to clatter his ice. Not quite 3:00 P.M., Driscoll thought. Maybe it was just boredom, but then again maybe he *had* touched a nerve.

"I ran into Ray earlier today," Driscoll said.

"Yeah?" Izquierdo said. "Where was that?"

"Forget it," Driscoll said. He walked over to the window, stood beside Izquierdo. It looked like maybe the rain was letting up. "He told me you set him up with some work."

"Is that right?" Izquierdo's expression didn't change, but there was something new in his voice, a tightness that suggested Ray Brisa's life expectancy had dropped a few notches down the criminal's actuarial scale.

"I thought maybe you could tell me who wanted all that stuff from Southern Police Supply, Eddie."

Izquierdo laughed. "I don't know what you're talking about. I haven't seen Ray Breezes in I don't know how long. The guy's a head case. Tell me I'm responsible for the things he dreams up."

Driscoll shrugged. The rain had picked up again, but he thought he saw a horse poke its head out over one of the stable doors. Maybe it wanted to see if the ark was on its way.

"You know I quit being a cop, don't you, Eddie?"

Izquierdo gave him a speculative look. "That's like saying Michael Jackson got married, he don't care about little boys anymore."

"This thing with the First Lady," Driscoll continued, "I think a friend of mine may have gotten tangled up in it. That's all I'm doing, Eddie. I'm trying to help my friend out of a jam."

"Yeah?" Izquierdo said. "So you think I know something? Forget it, Driscoll. This is some serious, bad-news, *terrorista* shit. Anybody who even thinks they talked to somebody who might have *heard* about this business is in deep *chingada*." He took a healthy slug of his drink. "I do whores and emergency lending," he said. "I don't get involved with politics."

"I hear you, Eddie," Driscoll said. "But I find myself standing here looking out at all that pretty green grass, I wonder what it's going to look like when the *federales* turn it into a landing strip, cuz that's exactly what's going to happen, my friend, the minute I get back to town and sic 'em on your ass."

Izquierdo gave him a look. "What if you was to maybe have a riding accident while you were out here visiting, Driscoll? Say you hit your head on a big limb, fell off out in the swamp someplace where nobody could ever find you?"

Driscoll stared back at him. "Horses don't turn me on, Eddie. Besides, it's not me who's important. It's Ray Brisa. He's scared shitless. He doesn't need me to tell him how to cut a deal with the Feds."

Izquierdo regarded him for a moment. Crunch time, Driscoll thought. Would Izquierdo make the natural assumption, no way an ex-cop would be stupid enough to walk into the lion's den, not without some kind of insurance backing him up?

Izquierdo sighed, and by the sound of it, Driscoll could guess that his bluff had carried.

Driscoll walked to the bar, flipped up a hinged section of burnished mahogany, stepped through to where the bottles were arranged on glass shelves. He found a bottle of Scotch with a label that looked like medieval monks had printed it by hand. He brought it down on the bar, then selected a pilsner glass from a glittering array on another shelf. He drew himself a Bass, skimmed the head with one of his fingers, topped it off. He tasted the beer, made a sound of approval from deep in his chest, then turned and saluted Izquierdo with what was left.

"Come on," he said to Izquierdo, wiping foam off his lip with the back of his hand. "I'll buy you a drink, you point me in the right direction, everybody stays healthy, everybody stays friends."

Izquierdo hesitated, but came toward the bar. He hiked himself up on a stool, slid his glass across to Driscoll. "You know what that stuff costs?" he said, nodding at the bottle.

Driscoll poured for him, sniffed the bottle before he corked it. He shrugged. "About what it costs for fifteen minutes with one of your girls."

Izquierdo ignored him. He took the bottle, turned it so the label was there for Driscoll to see. "It's a hundred years old. You can't even buy it down here, man. I got a guy in Connecticut ships it to me, three grand a case."

Driscoll nodded. "That's about what I spend on beer in a month."

Izquierdo nodded as if it were true, still inspecting the label on the bottle. After a moment he put the bottle down and turned to Driscoll with some interest. "What did you do to Ray, man? Make him say all this crap, I mean."

"I reminded him of his duty as a patriot," Driscoll said.

Izquierdo shook his head, still finding it hard to believe. He took a sip of his drink. "This ain't going to do you no good, you know?"

"Let me be the judge of that, Eddie."

Izquierdo sighed, put his drink down. "You know what? Let's forget this shit. Let me call a couple of girls over, you and me, we'll have some drinks, some dinner, we'll have a little party, man. Take a helicopter ride you want to. You ever fuck in a helicopter? Come on, man, what do you say?"

Driscoll put his glass down, started around the open end of the bar. "I'm out of here, Eddie. I gotta see some people down at the Federal Building."

"Okay," Izquierdo said, his voice taking on something of a whine. "I'm sorry I offended you."

"I'm tired of wasting time, Eddie." Driscoll hadn't broken stride.

"I thought it was about drugs, man," Izquierdo cried. "Colombians and drugs, you know how they are."

Driscoll paused. Izquierdo had turned on the barstool, palms turned up in a gesture of innocence. "Or maybe home invasions, you know, where they dress up like cops? I didn't know it was gonna be something like this."

Driscoll nodded. "So you're a patriot at heart, too."

"What are you talking about, man? I wouldn't mess with the President, blow up airplanes, put nerve gas on the streets, that's all. I'm happy right where I am."

"Just tits and ass and a hundred percent interest," Driscoll said. "What's not to like?"

"Fuck you."

"Never mind," Driscoll said. "Who was this Colombian you talked to?"

"Maybe he was Colombian, I'm not sure," Izquierdo said.

"You need to do a little better than that," Driscoll said.

Izquierdo glowered at him, but finally reached into his coat pocket, pulled out an address book, flipped through the pages. He found what he was looking for, glanced up at Driscoll. He rolled his eyes, tore a piece of paper off a pad, pulled out a pen, and scribbled something. He handed the paper to Driscoll, a sour expression on his face.

"Angel?" Driscoll said, examining the note. "This is the guy you dealt with."

"*Ahn-hel*," Izquierdo corrected him, nodding. "How long you lived here?"

"An-*hell*," Driscoll repeated. "Whatever." He folded the note. "It mean the same thing as it does in English?"

Izquierdo managed a laugh. He shook his head. "Not this guy," he said. "Not even a little bit."

Driscoll nodded, held the folded note up between his fingers. "Two-four-two, that's the area code for the whole Caribbean."

"I didn't need his address. It was all cash and carry, okay?"

"You want to stay friends, Eddie?"

Izquierdo gave him a pained look. "I think he was in Nassau. You got ways of finding that stuff out, man."

"I got lots of ways, Eddie. I find out you forgot to tell me something, I'm going to come at you from all of them."

Izquierdo nodded. "You see Ray, you tell him I say *hasta la vista.*"

"As in goodbye?"

"Like that," Izquierdo shrugged. "Also I'd watch my ass if I was you. "

"An-hell is no angel," Driscoll said. "I got it. I got it in English *and* Spanish."

Izquierdo shook his head. "Just keep my name out of it, man."

"Don't worry," Driscoll assured him. "I find this guy, that's one thing you don't have to worry about."

He tucked the note away, went out the door of the study. One of the goons was in a chair just outside the door while the other was down the hallway, engaged in a muttered conversation on a cellular phone. Something that had to do with girls and helicopters, Driscoll guessed.

Driscoll shouldered his way past the second goon, ignoring his growl of protest. *Brave words,* he was thinking, recalling his parting shot at Eddie Left. But one thing at a time. First he would need to find this Angel. After that, there'd be plenty of time for the worrying.

**He had stopped** at a pay phone in front of a Farm Store, a mini-mart with a Guernsey cow on its sign. "Cow store" was what Deal's little girl Isabel called the places. "Let's go to the cow store, Uncle Vernon. Can we? Can we?" Her voice rang clearly in his mind as he listened to Harvey Clyde's number ring and ring and the ache he felt transferred itself directly into frustration at Clyde. By the time the machine picked up, he was ready to break the connection.

A woman who sounded to be in her eighties told him in a recorded voice that Mr. Clyde was not in his office, that he could leave a message if he chose. "It's Driscoll," he told the machine after it beeped at him. "Maybe I found something of interest with that break-in at Southern Police Supply." He hesitated, checking his watch. Did Clyde keep regular business hours during a crisis? Was Driscoll supposed to go home and wait for a call? If Dedric Bailey and the entire Special Investigative Section was on traffic detail, where did that put Vernon Driscoll and his suspicions?

"I'll get back to you," he said to the machine, and hung up.

The thunderheads had dissipated now, but the light was nearly gone. Bugs were already swirling in the glow of the sign, and he reached to slap something stinging the back of his neck. Maybe he'd come down with malaria, Driscoll thought idly, wiping a smear of blood from his palm onto his trouser leg. He stood for a moment, staring up into the purpling sky, glanced once more at the phone, then made up his mind.

An ice cream bar and a quart of beer, he thought, glancing at the number Izquierdo had given him. And as soon as he finished dinner, he'd take step two.

**Osvaldo Regalado** lived on the ground floor of a mildew-encrusted apartment complex just off the Palmetto Expressway. It had been attractive once, Driscoll supposed. Now an expressway connector cut through what had been its parking lot, and the developer had had the adjoining green belt rezoned for storage and light industry. Unending roar of traffic on one side, the whine of a cabinet fabricator's plane on the other.

"It gets a little quieter on the third shift," Osvaldo told him. "The cabinet business is on the downswing."

Driscoll nodded. It was hard talking over the noise.

"You want a Yoo-Hoo?" Osvaldo had wheeled himself over to a tiny refrigerator that propped up one end of a makeshift door-desk jammed with computer equipment. He reached into the fridge, held up a yellow can of something.

Driscoll shook his head. "You think you can trace that number for me?" he called.

"You kidding? Ask me for something difficult, like dance the tango."

He gave Driscoll a goofy smile as he popped the top on his drink, then deftly turned his chair with one hand, scooting back toward his computer. The man had reclaimed his beefy torso, Driscoll noted, and had built up a pair of powerful arms, presumably with all the Nautilus gizmos crowding the other half of the living room.

Osvaldo was a computer hacker whom Driscoll had met during an extended period of bank-wire surveillance. They were about to go to trial with Osvaldo the star witness when somebody pushed him off a Metrorail platform into the path of a train. He'd survived but lost both legs, then his job with Southern Bell in an alcoholic aftermath. The bad guys, of course, had walked.

Driscoll, who'd felt a certain responsibility, had done what he could for the man. He'd stayed in touch, talked Osvaldo into a rehab clinic, had later sent him as much freelance programming work as the department could hand out. In turn, Osvaldo had evidenced no bitterness: he had always been willing to help Driscoll out whenever modern technology was required. "Any asshole I can help you get, that's one for me, too."

He arranged himself in front of a keyboard, wiped his thick glasses on his T-shirt, then took another look at the paper Driscoll had handed him. "I oughta get myself over to the islands," he said to Driscoll. "What's their take on crips, you suppose?" He glanced up, his smile intact.

Osvaldo's way of dealing with it, Driscoll supposed. The man had been dry for a couple of years now. Whatever worked.

"They like the ones with money," Driscoll said, handing him some bills.

"Everybody does," Osvaldo said. He began tapping his keys.

Deal staggered back, shielding his face from the spray of rain, saw that Linda was half in, half out of the fractured roof, her legs kicking wildly beneath her. The loose section of corrugated metal had ripped away with the gusts, leaving a gaping hole behind. The rain was driving into their cell in torrents now.

"I'm slipping," she cried, the words tearing off in the wind.

He glanced into the corner, ran for the battered stool. He rushed back, clambered onto the stool, then steadied himself against its rocking. The rain washed over him in sheets and the sky lit up in formless lightning, the same eerie greenish glow he hadn't seen since the onslaught of Hurricane Andrew. He reached up, caught her legs, steadied her.

"Pull yourself on up, turn around toward me," he called, his voice firm. "I'll steady you."

She gave a cry of anger, of frustration. He felt her legs stiffen beneath his touch, and for a moment he thought she might be about to kick him off the wobbling stool.

"This is *awful*," she cried.

*Yes,* he thought. *Beyond awful.* "Come on," he called. "One leg at a time . . ."

He urged her on, his hand levering one heel, knowing that she would only need to give the slightest nudge, he'd go flying himself . . .

"Catch hold, now . . . that's it! I'm going to let go . . ."

He boosted her other leg up, heard a muffled thump as she disappeared . . . and then he saw her other hand groping at the edge of the torn metal. She pulled herself around until her head appeared. She ducked through the gap, away from the force of the rain, and stared down at him, a sodden, angry latter-day Kilroy.

"Can you see anything? Anybody moving out there"

She glanced up, had to fling her hand before her face to shield it from the driving rain. "Are you crazy?" she called. Rain was pouring off her chin, and her blouse billowed up from her back like a wind sock.

"I'm coming up," he called. He was down off the stool, dragging it along the rough floor under the gaping hole to a point where the roof sloped a bit. Not much, but even a couple of inches might help. He checked the positioning of the stool, tried to get its legs arranged in a position approaching steadiness.

He backed off a few paces, then made as much of a run as he dared across the puddled floor. His jaw was throbbing again, his head seeming to swell with each beat of his heart. Maybe the effort would blow an artery, he thought, all the worrying, all this effort could end.

In the next instant, he was launching himself upward, one foot banging hard onto the top of the stool, jamming down, giving it all he had, his hands thrust up, fingers extended . . .

. . . there was a splintering sound and he felt the stool blow apart beneath him as he pushed off . . . *You won't have this to do again, son . . .*

. . . and then his hands caught ragged metal—both hands digging in, or wasn't it the other way around, the metal slicing into him? It didn't matter: he gripped furiously and pulled himself up against the pain.

The tendons in his arms were searing. He flung one elbow up over the edge, brought his head up after, felt his cheeks go rubbery with the force of the wind, felt the stinging tattoo of the rain against his face.

*Outside*, he told himself. *You're outside.* But his feet were windmilling beneath him, threatening to pull him back down again. He clawed about with his free hand, but the roof was slick with water, and there was nothing there, nothing to hold on to.

He sensed movement at his side and caught sight of Linda, dragging herself hand over hand along the gash in the roof until she was beside him at last. She reached out, snatched a wad of his shirt in one fist. She pulled for all she was worth, her face working with strain, but it was no good. He could feel himself beginning to slide backward, and he knew where that slide would end.

He turned, about to utter some last-minute encouragement to Linda Sheldon, some inanity out of the old movies—"You've got to go on without me, kid . . . "—found her struggling to untangle her blouse from something. She pulled herself free, and he saw the nail then, a sharp, headless spike left behind when the metal sheeting ripped away.

He thought about what he would have to do, but he didn't think long. She yelped in alarm as he flung his arm toward her, slammed his palm down. The she screamed in earnest when she saw what he had done.

"Linda," he called to her. The pain was electric, beyond anything he'd felt . . . but he wasn't falling.

"I'm going to need your help here." He fought to keep his eyes off the spike that protruded from the back of his hand. His breath was coming in gasps, and a wave of blackness threatened to claim him.

She turned to him, her face pale.

"I want you to grab hold of my arm . . ." He nodded his chin, scooted his free hand forward as far as he could. "With both hands," he added. His own throat was tightening; the waves that pulsed up his arm from his hand were pure agony.

Her eyes widened as if he were suggesting she throw herself off the building. "Your weight's going to anchor me," he said, trying to keep his voice even. "I want you to hold on to me and let yourself slide on down the roof."

She was still staring at him as if he'd lost his mind. "It's the only way," he said. Oddly, the pain was lessening, but he felt the darkness closing in again. Maybe it was shock, maybe he'd simply worn the synapses out.

Not much time left, any way he figured it.

He fixed his gaze on Linda Sheldon and said it simply, forcefully. "It's the only chance we have."

She gave him a look, then clutched his sleeve with one hand, dug her other into the fabric at his shoulder.

He felt his weight shift at once. *Physics, my boy, the simple laws of physics . . .* some unbidden voice doing a W. C. Fields impression to cheer him on. She was sliding slowly toward the lip of the roof now, working the wind, the wind working her—and somehow he had managed to heave his chest fully onto the outside surface.

There was a hesitation as his belt buckle hung up on the rusted metal beneath him, but he closed his eyes and wrenched his hand free of the spike he'd impaled himself on. Once more a bright sheet of pain flooded the darkness behind his eyes, but this time he could stand it, for they were sliding free.

She cried out, caught a handful of his hair as they picked up speed, and then they were over the side and through the air, crashing breathlessly, deep into the tangle of fallen limbs below.

They lay there motionless for a moment, Deal on his back, Linda Sheldon facedown atop him. After a few seconds, he felt her breathing start up against his chest and he realized he'd been holding his own breath as well. A branch was jabbing him painfully in the back, but when he tried to shift his weight, the tangle of limbs shuddered in response, threatening to send them tumbling again. He eased himself back against the limb and took that pain.

*Stay a moment, Deal.* No one was shooting, no alarms were ringing. He could still himself that long.

"Are you okay?" he asked. He didn't have to shout. They were sunk deep in the clutch of the feathery limbs, and though the force of the wind was enough to rock the tangle of fallen trees, they were shielded from the worst of the blast. *A cave,* he thought. *A blessed haven.*

She didn't lift her head from his chest. "I told you not to ask that question," she said.

He felt something warm trickling down his left arm. The pain was still there, searing his palm, but it was nothing to what he'd felt when he'd been holding all his weight against the spike. He turned his palm toward his face and tried gingerly flexing his fingers.

More pain, enough to send comets and pinwheels across his vision, enough to send his head back against the pillowing needles. But he forced himself to keep on until he knew each finger still worked. At least until tetanus or some other godawful tropical island rot-your-flesh-to-ribbons set in.

"You're bleeding pretty badly," Linda said. The limb they were tangled in gave a dip, then steadied.

He nodded. Nothing he hadn't already figured out. After a moment, he began to grope about the tangle with his good hand, caught hold of a solid branch, moved his fingers until he found an oozing fracture in the bark. He dug up a glob of the sap with his fingers, took a breath, then bought his hand up to jam the sticky stuff against the wound, just as another blast of thunder rattled the world about them.

The pain was searing, but he had braced himself for it this time. Before the pounding could subside, he'd taken another swipe of the oozing sap, clamped it to the back of his hand. He lay back then, holding his jury-rigged blood plugs tight, trying to breathe through his clenched teeth, willing himself to think of anything other than the liquid fire that ringed his brain.

He felt her hands at his shoulders, felt her draw herself tightly against him. "God, it must hurt . . ." she said.

He opened his eyes, about to muster some kind of an answer, when he saw her go rigid, her hand pointing over his shoulder.

There was a rustling of limbs, a snapping sound, a cry . . . and he turned in time to see a pair of boots and a blur of camouflage-clad leggings plunge past, a yard in front of his nose. The man who belonged to the boots and the pants stopped suddenly, giving another sharp cry as a shattered limb dug into his groin. And then he and Deal were staring face-to-face.

The man, still clutching an M-16 over his head, had been clambering over the debris looking for them, Deal realized. He registered it all in an instant: the rifle, the man, stunned expression still on his face, struggling to bring the weapon down into firing position. But the sling was hung up in a tangle of branches, and when the guy glanced up to see what was wrong, Deal got a foot planted in the crotch of a limb and lunged forward.

He hit the man in soft flesh beneath his chin, and a burst of fire flew high into the sky. Deal hit him again, felt something give under his fist, and this time the firing stopped. The guy was making gargling noises and dropped his weapon to claw at his throat. His eyes were still open, but he wasn't seeing any more.

Deal was reaching for the rifle, which still dangled from a pine limb, when he heard a shout, someone screaming in Spanish nearby, and an answering cry at his back.

"Deal." It was Linda, her hand pointing to show him. He glanced up to find a second man in camouflage fatigues clambering over the fallen limbs toward them. The second man spotted Deal at the same instant and swung his weapon into position, searching for a clear shot through the branches. He fired, but hurrying had sent his aim wide. Deal sensed the rush of slugs, a warm tickle through the pine needles at his cheek.

He lunged for the sling of the dangling M-16, then felt his feet sliding off the rain-slick limb he had been perched on. He went over sideways into the tangle, the rifle flying out of his grip.

The second man saw what had happened and ducked beneath an intervening bough, steadied himself, raised his weapon carefully. There'd be no mistake this time, Deal thought. He lay on his side, wriggling like some poor-sap insect caught in a giant web, while the guy sighted down on him.

A matter of seconds, and that was all the difference, wasn't it? Deal's entire life reduced to the span of a few heartbeats: he'd never been late for an appointment, could count the number of projects he'd completed behind schedule on one hand. He'd been the one to nudge Janice along all the years of their relationship, hustling her out the door toward parties and movies and concerts well ahead of time. He liked to show up at the grocery with his check already made out, only the amount left to fill in, thank you very much. He was never, ever late, except he was going to be a half-second off this time, and there'd be no need to write any note of apology, either.

He could see that man's trigger finger tensing, could see rainwater skirling off the tip of a dirt-ringed nail, rain glazing an intervening dangle of pine needles, rain silvering the blue-black metal of the barrel and the trigger guard, also had a fragment of some poem from freshman English, chickens and wheelbarrows and rainwater . . . so long, Deal, you always talked too much in class . . .

. . . and then there was a burst of gunfire at his shoulder, bark and wood fiber and pine needles exploding in a steaming froth before his eyes, and the man who would have killed him went over backwards, his weapon flung away.

Deal swung about, found Linda Sheldon lying across a thick branch of the fallen pine, the automatic weapon he'd been trying to reach clutched in her white-knuckled hands. She stared at him through the haze her firing had left, her eyes wild.

"You're all right?" she cried.

Deal glanced at the two dead men, then back at her. The wind seemed to pick up a notch, and the boughs of the fallen tree groaned in response.

"I'm all right," he said, and reached for her hand.

She lay down the weapon and wept.

**31**

"You telling me that *nobody's* flying to Nassau?"

"You're welcome to try elsewhere," the Bahamas-Air clerk said. She tilted her head, made a shrugging motion that made Driscoll think of his own. "Though I don't think 'tis going to happen." She was a black woman, with the accent of an islander. "It's the weather, you know?"

A group of people were seated in a waiting area nearby, most of them watching a blaring TV program where several analysts debated why no one had yet come forward to claim responsibility for the First Lady's disappearance.

Driscoll gestured past them toward a bank of windows that overlooked the runways outside. When he lifted his own arm, Ray Brisa's rose along with it. The clerk must have noticed the set of cuffs that linked the two of them together, but she didn't say anything.

"Look at it," he said. "It's clear as a bell out there." It was a lovely evening, the thunderheads long gone, the sky so pristine that a sliver of moon and a single star were already visible.

". . . may very well be that they've botched the job, that they've actually killed her," the voice of one of the television pundits drifted over. This from a young guy with a British accent, a vest under his coat, a bow tie. His tone of voice suggested it was an intellectual problem. Driscoll stared at the television for a moment.

He'd glanced at a paper on the way into the airport. Charles Hollingsworth, the President's opponent in the upcoming election, had called for an attack on Libya, on general principle alone. The senator seemed to think that America had gone soft, that some indiscriminate bullying was in order. The message was that the liberal President had brought this all upon himself. Pretty soon they'd have Charles Manson on, checking his opinion on the matter.

"Sure, it's calm out *there*," the Air Bahamas clerk was saying, her eyes already on the next person in line. "Down in the islands there's a storm coming."

"Listen," Driscoll said patiently. "If you had to get to Nassau, what would you do?"

She looked at him impassively. "Nothing," she said. "I'd stay right here."

". . . avoid jumping to any conclusions," another TV pundit was saying.

"We learned that lesson after the TWA disaster . . ." His counterpart, the guy in the vest, rolled his eyes, made a dismissive gesture. Tom Brokaw leaned in to separate the two. Driscoll was glad they hadn't invited him on the show.

"Come on, man," Brisa said, his expression—what you could make out for the bandages, that is—a pained one. "You heard what the lady said . . . "

"Shut up," Driscoll said.

He started to reach into his pocket, then stopped when he realized he was pulling Ray Brisa's hand along, too. He reached in his jacket with his other hand, found his "SONNY CROCKETT—CHIEF OF DETECTIVES" shield, flipped it open, let her take a look. The thing had been a joke, a going-away present from his peers on the squad, but they'd used an official-looking blank and Driscoll had found it handy more than once since his retirement.

"Where's your pilot's lounge?" he said, flipping the shield closed quickly, stowing it in his pocket.

"We can't give out such information," she protested.

"Do you know the penalties for obstructing an officer during the performance of his duties?" Driscoll said. "If you're not a citizen, we . . . "

"Hey . . ." Brisa began, but that was all that came out before Driscoll ground his heel down atop the little bastard's instep.

". . . the limitations of this country's power and the essential helplessness of the human condition," another TV voice was saying, the phrasing clear even over Brisa's groans. Driscoll glanced to see which set of teeth and hair had been so profound, but a Buick commercial had already begun to play. He thought of Janice Deal's comments then. The world gone to hell in a handcart, and the Buicks were still rolling off the line. Was that what it had come to, then? Even disaster was a media opportunity.

"What's the matter with him?" the clerk asked, bringing Driscoll back. She was staring at Brisa in concern.

Brisa was bent over the counter, still gasping. He probably would have been on the floor, rubbing his stomped foot, but Driscoll wasn't about to give him the slack. "He needs medical attention," Driscoll said brusquely.

"In the Bahamas?" she asked.

Driscoll leaned in toward her. "Point me in the right direction, now. Then you can go ahead and give all the rest of these people the bad news."

She hesitated, glanced at the surly, ever-growing line behind the restraining ropes, then gave in. She tore a slip of paper from a pad, jotted something down. "That's down C Concourse, now," she said. "But you won't get in without the proper clearance."

"Thanks for the tip," Driscoll said. He was already off, dragging the protesting Brisa after him.

**"You think** you can haul me anywhere you want?" Brisa was saying. They were standing against the wall of the broad concourse, opposite the entrance to the Air Bahamas pilots' lounge. "This is like kidnapping, man. You're not even a cop anymore."

Driscoll stared at him mildly. "Let's get something straight, you little prick," he said. "I got a use for you."

"Which is what?"

"You're my eyewitness, okay? You don't like it, you want me to take you downtown, hand you over to the Feds, you just say the word."

Brisa stared back, trying for a bad-ass look, but even he must have realized how pathetic he appeared. He turned away, working the foot Driscoll had stomped. "I'm hurting, man. This isn't, like, humane."

"Humane?" Driscoll repeated. "That's something that applies to humans, isn't it?"

"Fuck you," Brisa muttered, but it wasn't really an insult.

"I'm doing you a favor, Ray. Try to keep that in mind."

Brisa scoffed, but he didn't say anything more. After a moment, he turned back to Driscoll. "Why don't you go knock on the door?" he said. "You wait much longer, all the guys'll be gone, man."

Driscoll nodded. It was true that they'd already seen two pilots hustle out, wheeled suitcases in tow, heading back the way he and Brisa had come: one tall black man in his forties—uniform immaculate, shoes gleaming—who moved with the snap and precision of a military officer; then a younger Latino guy with his pilot's cap under his arm—he'd had an Errol Flynn look about him, a broad smile on his face, was jabbering into a portable phone as he walked.

"So what are we doing here, man? Couldn't we at least sit down somewhere?"

"That'd only happen if we went to Plan B," Driscoll said.

"Yeah?" Brisa said, cocking his good eye at him. "So what's Plan A?"

"For you to shut your face," Driscoll said. He nodded across the concourse, where the door to the pilots' lounge had opened once again. Driscoll lifted their common hand, used his thumb and forefinger to fire an imaginary round at the pilot who emerged.

This one was a short, overweight man in his fifties, his coat slung over his shoulder, part of his shirttail hanging out in back. The network of exploded veins on his broad face was vivid, even at their vantage point. "Now *there's* a fucking loser," Brisa said.

"Yeah," Driscoll said. He pushed himself off the wall, jerking Brisa along after him. "But he's *our* loser, Ray."

They were hurrying down the concourse then, Driscoll sidestepping a porter rolling an old woman in a wheelchair, hustling after the pilot, who was moving quickly toward the terminal, his bright nose cocked up as if he'd caught the scent of whiskey somewhere.

"Yo, Billy," Driscoll called.

The pilot turned, saw who it was. He groaned and closed his eyes as Driscoll approached. "Good to see you back at work, Billy."

The pilot cut a glance about them. "Keep your voice down, Driscoll. And stop calling me Billy."

Driscoll shrugged, took the coat off the pilot's shoulder, inspected the name tag clipped over the breast pocket, where a whitish stain and a cigarette burn formed an accidental kind of crest. Driscoll glanced up, clapped him on the shoulder.

"Captain Michael Cudahy, is it, then?" He gave the pilot a smile. "Well, Captain Cudahy, what do you say we go have us a little chat."

**The three of them** sat at a table in one of the brightly lit restaurants in the main terminal, Driscoll and Ray on one side, Cudahy on the other. Cudahy toyed with an unlit cigarette, scanning the room carefully as a waitress refilled their coffees. She glanced at the handcuffs, but the look on her face suggested she'd seen a hundred men chained together that week.

When the waitress left, Brisa turned to Driscoll. "You think I'm getting on a plane with this guy behind the wheel?"

"It's not a wheel," Cudahy said.

"I think you'll do whatever I say to do," Driscoll said.

"He doesn't even have a real *name*," Brisa said, his voice rising.

"Can you shut him up?" Cudahy said.

"Sure," Driscoll said. He put his free hand on Brisa's injured shoulder and squeezed. Brisa's face went pale. "Try to keep your voice down, Ray."

Driscoll turned back to Cudahy. "So you can appreciate my problem, right, Billy?"

"I appreciate all kinds of things," Cudahy said. "That don't mean I can help you."

Driscoll nodded. "How much weight you moving in from the islands these days, Billy?"

Cudahy stiffened. "All that's over with. A long time ago."

Driscoll shrugged. "I know that, Billy. Besides, I'm just a private citizen looking for a little help." He turned to Brisa. "I ever tell you about Captain Billy here? He was a star in his day. The man practically opened up the Colombian pipeline, him and a bunch of other airline employees."

"I got backed into that . . . "

"And that's how I got you off so easy," Driscoll said, turning aside to Brisa. "We used the captain's testimony to put some big fish away, Ray."

Cudahy leaned closer. "Nobody's going to rent us a plane to fly to Nassau with that weather coming in. Forget it."

"So we lie," Driscoll said.

"There's not an airport over there that'll let us land," Cudahy said.

"What are they going to do, shoot us down? They got a hurricane to worry about."

"Now there's another good reason to fly," Cudahy said.

"Billy," Driscoll said patiently, "I got great faith in you."

"My ass," Brisa said.

Driscoll nudged him in the ribs with his elbow. Brisa's breath left him in a gasp.

"I gotta get to Nassau, Billy."

Cudahy looked him over. "It's not like you to beg."

Driscoll tossed a wad of bills on the table. "I ain't begging, goddammit."

Cudahy gave him a pained look, dropping his napkin over the bills. He glanced around the room, then checked under the napkin, riffling the corner of the wad with his thumb. "You know what a plane rents for these days?" he asked.

Driscoll sighed. "They take credit cards, don't they?"

Cudahy met Driscoll's gaze, smiling for the first time. "You must really want to go to Nassau."

"I'm going to take that as a yes," Driscoll said. And then he was pulling Brisa to his feet.

**32**

Deal moved down the dimly traced path, fighting the wind, the lashing foliage, hoping he was headed toward the docks and the house he'd seen when they were brought to the island. Not only was his visibility limited by the storm and the failing light, but the very topography itself seemed changed, as if the wind were remolding landmarks before his eyes.

He lurched forward in a slow crabwalk, pulling himself along through the storm from tree limb to root to shrub. Slow going, but the only way to keep himself from being toppled by the force of the wind, and it had the added advantage of keeping him out of the path of flying debris. Most of their prison roof had already torn loose, the great corrugated sheets soaring away in the gusts like tissue—seventy-pound sheets of tissue, each with a razor's edge.

He pulled himself close to a sturdy pine, trying for a moment to shield his face from the full force of the wind. Limbs snapped, vague shapes flew past overhead, greenish lightning crackled everywhere, and the thunder was an unabated background roar.

He could have stayed huddled with Linda beneath the boughs of that great fallen tree, but they'd nearly died there once already. Maybe the two men they'd killed were the only ones who'd been out, of course. Maybe all the others were battened down inside that shoreside house, waiting for the storm to pass. But he knew only one way to find out.

He'd been trying to watch for more of Angel's men as he moved along, but he couldn't keep his head up for more than a few seconds at a time. The M-16 he'd taken from one of the dead guards was slung securely across his back, useless if he ran into anyone with a weapon at the ready, but he needed both his hands free to pull himself along. He would just have to hope that they wouldn't be moving about in such weather, or that if they were, they'd be moving just as blindly, just as hamstrung, as he was.

He wiped his sleeve across his face, but the movement only squeegeed more water into his eyes. Still, he could hear the pounding of surf up ahead, and knew he couldn't be far from the point where the path branched, one arm leading down to the docks, the other twisting along the waterfront toward the house. He was about to push himself on, toward a sodden clump of Brazilian pepper that thrashed Medusalike in the gusts, when he felt the hand on his shoulder.

He lurched away from the touch, already down on one knee and clutching for the rifle at his back, *No use, Deal, no use . . .* was swinging the rifle up to fire when he found himself staring at Linda Sheldon, her face frozen, her hands outstretched.

He dipped the barrel of the rifle, closed his eyes, let his breath out in a rush.

"Goddamnit, Linda," he shouted. "Goddamnit!"

A squall of rain swept over them and he found himself trembling, as angry at himself as at her.

She caught his soaking shirt to help him up, guided the two of them, stumbling, into the shelter of the big pine. "I'm sorry," she cried as they leaned there. "I couldn't stay. Staring at those men . . ." She broke off then, shuddering at the memory.

"It's all right," he said. "You scared me, that's all."

He grasped a knob on the trunk of the pine with his free hand, wrapped his other arm about her shoulders, held her until her tremors began to calm.

"We better get moving while we're still able," he told her finally.

She nodded, might even have said something in return, but he was already on the move. Half stumbling, half sliding through the mud, he made it to the screen of holly, caught hold of one of its lashing branches, then turned, waiting for her to join him. From there, the trail took a zigzagging plunge through thick undergrowth, carrying a deluge of rainwater downward.

He motioned for her to follow, then turned back, sitting himself down in the mud. He used his hands to shove himself off, and in moments he was sliding freely, skidding down the twists and turns of the rutted path as if it were some ride in a water theme park. A rock cracked his pelvis, his shoulder thudded off a jutting tree trunk, his injured hand raked over outcroppings of coral, but he was moving too quickly for any pain to register. Near the bottom of the slope, his heel dug into a crevasse hidden by the rushing water, and he went up and over, his arms outflung, leading the last several feet of his slide with his chin, face down in the muck.

He came groggily to his knees and turned as Linda came tumbling sideways toward him. He threw up his arms to catch her, then both of them were down and rolling again, until finally he felt his hips slam against something unyielding and they were stopped at last.

They lay there for a moment, breathless, and then Deal felt her stir atop him. He was about to struggle up himself when she flopped back down on him.

He was about to speak when she pointed at something. "They're right out there," she said.

She eased off his chest, and Deal rolled over onto his stomach. He raised his head carefully and peered through the undergrowth. They had come to rest on a narrow shelf that had kept them from tumbling all the way down to the shoreline. There were several larger pines clinging to the shelf, their big trunks breaking the force of the wind and affording them a view of below.

He could make out the spot where the trail emerged and split, one branch leading toward the pier where the Cigarette had docked, the other snaking along the battered shoreline to the house. Much of the narrow shingle of beach in between had already eaten away by the pounding surf.

Shutters blanked the windows of the house, which he saw now to be larger than what he'd remembered. It had been built partly into the hillside, partly raised on pilings that were sunk just above the waterline. It also had a nearly flat roof, its slight angle canting down toward the water, which helped it shed the wind. At the back of the structure a guard stood, his back pressed to the wooden siding, his shoulders hunched as if he were shielding himself from a blizzard. He was staring directly their way, but he was at least fifty feet away and the rain and the intervening brush hid them from sight.

The guard glanced off in the direction of the pier, and Deal followed his gaze. Wave after wave slammed into the pilings, sending surf and foam flying, some of the spray carrying as far as the shelf where they lay. Four more men in fatigues struggled about the pier, struggling to raise the Cigarette up on a set of davits that loomed against the dark sky like miniature white derricks. Raising a boat that size would be a tricky enough job under the calmest of circumstances, Deal thought. Now it seemed madness.

The tide had risen so high that the breakers were swamping the floorboards of the pier, and the men had tied themselves to pilings to keep from being swept away. They were working in pairs, at either end of the boat, using hand signals to communicate. The two at the prow of the boat had succeeded in bringing their end up, but the two working aft had not been as lucky. The rear of the boat dangled precariously, just above the reach of the waves, and there was much arm-waving going back and forth.

One of the men near the prow worked the forward davit controls, trying to hold that part of the boat steady, while the other struggled to secure a line that was fastened to a cleat on the Cigarette's foredeck. The rocking of the boat had him teetering precariously at the edge of the planks. His partner leaned out from the controls and tried to steady him without being flung off himself.

One of the men near the stern pummeled his partner and pointed out at the swaying, sagging boat. The second man shook his head. His partner hit him again and the second man threw up his hands in a gesture of defeat. He turned toward the boat, moved to the edge of the pier, balanced himself with a wild circling of his arms, and then jumped. Like being made to walk the plank, Deal thought as the man tumbled into the open cockpit of the lurching boat.

The man pulled himself up and began inching himself toward the stern, toward the place where the davit cables were attached, when the rear cable suddenly snapped, and the stern lunged toward the water, tossing him out of the cockpit into the water. The snapped cable lashed across the pier deck with something—a cleat, a fractured piece of pulley—tangled in its end.

The man who'd been directing from the pier never had time to move. The heavy metal whipped into him, snapping his chin over his shoulder. He flew off the pier like a broken doll. With all the weight of the boat on the forward davit, some gear, some set of bearings, gave way, and the spindle drum began to freewheel backwards. The heavy manual crank, a four-foot length of steel used to lever up lighter loads, broke loose from its catch and spun wildly, striking the man at the automated davit controls squarely between the shoulder blades. He went over as if he'd been slugged with a crowbar.

The fourth man, the one who'd been trying to loop the prow line around one of the pilings, hadn't seen anything. When the boat dropped, it left him trying to hold ten tons in his bare hands. The few feet of slack in the rope disappeared, jerking him off his feet and against the thick piling, his hand pinned hopelessly in the thick tangles of rope. His screams were loud enough to carry above the howling of the wind and the pounding of the surf.

"Dear God," Deal heard Linda gasp at his side.

The guard at the house had seen the catastrophe unfolding, and had dragged himself along the porch railing to hammer at the door of the place. How many inside there, Deal wondered? Would they all come streaming out? He glanced at the weapon slung across his back. Even if he could bring them down, would there be others nearby, lurking somewhere at their backs, ready to descend the instant they'd blown their cover?

He was still pondering when Linda clutched his arm. "What is *that*?" she cried above the thundering wind.

He swung his head about, following her gesture.

"Out there," she shouted again, raising her hand to seaward.

He blinked against the needlelike rain and strained to see in the ever-dimming light. The same roiling ocean, the same dark backdrop of sky, the flashes of blue-green lightning that fed the endless thunder.

Finally he saw it: a thin, continuous band of white, dividing the horizon where sea met sky. In the few seconds that he watched, the band seemed to widen, to grow a pale fraction and then another . . .

. . . and understanding came upon him. Let biblical scholars debate the parting of the seas as much as they wanted, what Deal was looking at explained it all.

"That's it," he said, trying to get his leaden feet beneath him, trying to scramble up. "Christ almighty, that's it!"

He reached down, caught her arm, pulled her up roughly. "Let's go," he said, glancing over his shoulder at the ever-widening, ever-advancing band of white. "Now!"

No men coming out of the house at the shoreline yet, but he couldn't have cared if they were pouring out by the hundreds. He wouldn't wait for them if he'd had a Gatling gun in place, or a howitzer, or a god-damned atomic bomb. He pushed Linda toward the muddy slope they'd tumbled down. Pushed her hard, and he didn't care about that, either.

"Up the hill, now!"

"What is it?" she cried, stumbling ahead of him now.

"The storm surge," he shouted as he ran after her. "That fucking wall of water I was talking about."

She glanced out to sea as she staggered upward, and in the moment she was turned, he saw the flash of recognition—the same look that must have flashed over all the weary folks who'd been fool enough to follow Moses to the shore of that damnable sea, the impossible become real.

Now Linda Sheldon, too, had seen. She began to clamber upward without his urging, yanking herself up the slope through the underbrush, oblivious to the vines, the thorns, the whipping limbs. He was right behind her, boosting her when he could, gasping with exertion already.

He wasn't sure how much time they had, but every step, every foot of elevation they gained gave them that much more of a chance. And hardly had he had that thought than she was going down, toppling sideways into a thick clump of brush. Rain splattered on his back like exploding gravel as he bent over her, wrestling her foot free from a tangled clutch of roots.

He slung one of her arms about his neck, clutched his other arm about her waist, and dragged her forward. They burst out of the underbrush then, and he realized that they'd crested the hill where they'd begun their mud slide just minutes before.

*Progress, progress*, he thought, but he sensed they hadn't climbed nearly high enough. He didn't know if there was enough climbing to be done on this entire miserable island to save them.

A new roaring had sprung up somewhere behind them, an ominous low grinding sound that rode some level below the wind and the thunder in pitch. A roar and a scourge to cleanse the earth, he thought. To wipe all troubles clean.

He forced himself onward, holding fast to Linda's hand, grasping the waistband of her skirt now to hold her up. *Step at a time, step at a time*, the voice inside him chanted as he ran, ignoring the burning in his lungs, the numbness in his legs. His strength would last only so long, but he told himself that every step might be the one that saved them.

The wind flung them from tree to tree and the stinging rain was also doing its part to shove them forward. He passed the tall pine where they'd rested earlier, might not have recognized it but for the knobby protrusion he'd used to hold himself against the wind. Most of the tree was down now, snapped at head height like a matchstick, its shattered trunk steaming in the last of the light, its branches splayed out in the underbrush.

Lightning, he thought. Another swipe they'd narrowly missed.

The grinding and the roaring at his back had grown, the ground shuddering, shifting beneath his feet like a funhouse floor. A strange luminosity washed their surroundings: some objects had been effaced in the gloom altogether; others, like the blasted stump, seemed to glow. As if even the light were being shoved forward, he thought, his mind growing bleary with exhaustion. The light also racing the wall of water at their backs, not wanting to be swallowed.

He veered onto the dark ribbon of path that would take them up the last rise toward the quarry. A dozen steps more and the wind belted them again, sent him sprawling, both of them sliding through the muck again.

He heard the roaring behind them, felt the threat of a new coolness approaching in the air, sensed the light going altogether, and he forced himself up and pulled her to him, and was running again.

He hit the first of the tumbled boulders squarely, without seeing it, but when they fell this time, he was ready before they stopped rolling. Everything nearly dark, the sound behind a frothing explosion of snapping timber and grinding rocks, a monster mouth gnashing at his heels.

He saw an impossible tendril of foam, fifty feet or more, soar through the dark sky at his shoulder, saw an entire uprooted tree sailing overhead, its tangled bare roots mirroring the wind-stripped branches on its opposite end. The thing flew just ahead of the skein of foam like a giant insect chased by a silvery tongue. He saw what might have been the roof of a house twirling through the sky beyond that—like Dorothy now, he thought—and was on his feet again, his arm under Linda as if he were lugging a sack of grain, up over another boulder, and then one more, until, finally, he saw two huge stones that loomed up before them like something out of Stonehenge, with a gap of darkness between.

He staggered forward, dropped Linda into the crevasse—no time to check just how deep, how rugged the fall, what were the choices anyway . . .

. . . and though he shouldn't have, though he told himself he wouldn't do it, he paused and turned and gave that last look backward, the one all the coaches tell you not to take, and now he knew why:

. . . *nothing there, nothing, the world gone, swallowed, nothing but a dark wall above him . . .*

. . . and then he was down, and spinning in the grip of the sea.

"I told you," Driscoll said to Brisa as the tiny plane took another sickening lurch, its engines groaning. "The man is a consummate professional."

Brisa tried another of his ugly looks, but he was too pale to pull it off. "I'll never forget this," he managed. "Long as I live, man."

"Jeez," Driscoll said to Brisa, glancing around the bouncing plane. "I guess that means I got about fifteen minutes to worry."

"Real funny," Brisa said.

"Uh-huh," Driscoll said. "You gotta puke, make sure you do it on your own side."

The plane rocked wildly in the unpredictable updrafts, but its engines whined steadily on. Driscoll peered out over Billy's shoulder, trying to see what he might be fixed upon, but the sky outside seemed only darkness. All Driscoll could see was the reflection on the inside of the windshield glass, the less-than-reassuring image of a squinting, florid-faced man in a disheveled pilot's shirt, an unlit cigarette dangling from the corner of his mouth.

Driscoll tried to check his watch, but it was hopeless in this light. He guessed they'd been aloft over an hour. They couldn't be too far from land, assuming Billy had maintained anything resembling a proper heading.

"How close, you figure?" Driscoll asked, raising his voice over the whine of the engines.

"I thought I saw our marker beacon a minute ago," Billy called from the pilot's seat.

"He thought?" Brisa cried.

"Quiet," Driscoll said. "Let him concentrate."

"I could use a drink," Billy said, still hunched over the wheel.

"Get us down," Driscoll said, "I'll buy you one."

"Man, oh, man," Brisa said. "This is not the way they talk at the airlines."

They were lost in a cloud suddenly, a cloud that exploded in greenish-white light and sent a dancing spark out the left wing of the plane. Brisa gave a moan that made his earlier whining sound brave.

"Just so you'll know, Billy," Driscoll called, "there's not enough left on my plastic to pay if this airplane crashes."

Billy's shoulders lurched as if he'd found the remark funny, but he kept his gaze ahead. "Don't sweat it," he said. "All those rental outfits carry insurance."

"Even if you lie on the flight plan?" Driscoll asked.

"They'll just say we got blown off course."

*Yeah,* Driscoll thought. The paperwork said they were going to Jacksonville, but once they'd cleared Miami airspace, Billy had swung them some ninety degrees, dead on toward Nassau. That'd be quite a stiff breeze. They'd spent the first half hour waiting for some query, some chase plane to appear, but so far their luck had held.

Another bombshell of light strobed through the passenger cabin, and Driscoll had a glimpse of Brisa gripping the arms of his seat like a man who'd caught sight of hell.

In the next instant, the plane tilted sideways, sliding sharply away to the right as if the sky had collapsed beneath them. Billy wrestled frantically with the stick and the engines screamed with the strain of the dive. Even Driscoll, who had glommed on tightly to the armrests of his seat, wondered if the lightning blast had disabled something, wondered if it were all coming to an end. Still, it would be better than dying in bed, he told himself. Better than sitting around with the other old farts in the home, waiting for your prostate to explode.

Some of the noise in his ears was coming from Ray Brisa's mouth, he realized, and another thing had occurred to him in the midst of the chaos: What if there were an afterlife, and what if the handcuffs didn't snap on impact? What if he had to go through eternity chained to the ghost of Ray Brisa?

"You gonna pull her up, Billy?" he shouted.

"Whatever you say, boss," Billy called back. Driscoll thought he saw a madman's grin reflected from the windshield glass.

Billy leaned back hard on the stick and, miraculously, the plane's nose picked up. Moments later, they were back in clear skies, leveling out, the whine of the engines dropping back what seemed about a hundred notches. A few miles ahead, Driscoll saw the lights of what looked like a hotel or condo tower rising up out of the darkness. A moment before, the view was of impending death. Now, by all appearances, they were homing in on a tropical resort.

"Sorry about the dive," Billy said, glancing quickly over his shoulder. "Had to get us out of that crap in a hurry."

"You're the pilot," Driscoll said, holding up his hand in surrender.

"That's not the hurricane, you know," Billy said. "Just garden-variety bad weather. The real storm's kicking north. You might get lucky. The worst stuff might miss Nassau altogether."

Driscoll nodded. "I won't feel too bad if that happens."

He glanced over to see what Brisa thought of the news, found him with his eyes closed, his head thrown back.

"We're dead now, right?" Brisa said.

"If we were, I'd kill myself," Driscoll said.

Brisa opened his eyes, gave him a look. "That makes no sense, man."

"I'll explain it to you sometime," Driscoll said.

"Just get me on the ground," Brisa said.

Driscoll glanced out the window. "Don't tempt me."

Driscoll was thinking again of the ignominy of going through eternity chained to this punk when he saw a brilliant flash of light spearing through the dark sky just ahead. Driscoll glanced anxiously at Billy, who seemed to have been expecting it.

"Roger that," Billy said, and leaned hard on the stick. The plane banked again, swooping low over the combing waves toward land. The flashing lights shot up from the ground once again. Someone down there with a hand held beacon of some kind, Driscoll realized, signaling Billy in.

The plane was dropping rapidly now, and a screen of feathery limbs rushed past, so close to the starboard wingtip that Driscoll had to fight the impulse to throw up his arm.

"Jesus," he said. "We that low?"

"What are you talking about?"

"Those trees we almost hit."

"What trees?" Billy glanced over his shoulder, then turned back quickly as a draft rocked the plane again.

"I'm not looking, man. I am not opening my eyes."

"Shut up," Driscoll said.

When the plane steadied, Driscoll saw what he supposed was the landing strip laid out in front of them, a dim set of multicolored Christmas lights laid out in vague parallel lines running off into the darkness.

"Number seventeen fairway," Billy said. He nodded at the skein of lights without turning. Driscoll thought that the ground seemed to be rushing up very quickly.

"You landed here before?"

"Sort of," Billy said.

"Sort of?" Driscoll thought he was beginning to sound like Ray Brisa, but he couldn't help himself.

"Before they turned the nines around," Billy said, shrugging, calling over the noise of the straining engines. "It used to be number eight. Long par five. A real tough mother, too. You want to stay out of the traps down the left side."

"You bet I do," Driscoll said, feeling a mounting pressure from his own bladder. Maybe he'd been a little tough on Brisa, after all.

"I landed on it before, I played on it, too, back in the old days. I reached the green in two one time," Billy was saying. "Driver and a three iron, stopped three feet from the cup." Billy shook his head, made what seemed a sudden adjustment to something on the control panel. The engines were making a sound Driscoll didn't remember hearing before.

"Missed the goddamned putt, though," Billy said. "That's the kind of luck I have."

"Should we be talking about golf?" Driscoll said, watching Billy's hands dance about the controls.

"Sorry," Billy called. "I get a little nervous, I tend to rattle on, that's all."

*Nervous?* Driscoll started to say something, gave it up. Billy was pointing out the windshield now. "They're running those landing lights off batteries," Billy said. "That's why they're so dim."

"I'd just as soon not think about it," Driscoll said. He saw the vague silhouettes of trees waving to the left and right. They were roaring down a chute of tall pines now. He wasn't a pilot, but even he knew there'd be no chance to pull up now.

"The ganja boys get pissed off at a pilot, think he's been running his own scam, they'll string those lights right up against the trees or up to the side of a cliff," Billy said. He shrugged, and Driscoll could see his smile in the reflection of the glass. "Upside of it is, you never even see it, you never know what hit you until it's all over."

Driscoll heard Brisa groan softly. He stared at Billy, his hands turned to steel on the armrests. "I like an optimist," he said. He had to swallow hard before he could get the words out. He could be home at the fourplex drinking beer, he thought. He could be flying helicopter circles with Eddie Izquierdo and the trapeze girls.

"Hang on now," Billy said. He flipped a switch and powerful landing beams shot out in front of the plane.

Driscoll caught his breath as the ground seemed to erupt just beneath them. The good news was that there was no cliff, no wall of trees rising just ahead: only a gently undulating ribbon of green fairway that rushed up to the wheels of the plane before he could think further about it. They skipped once, a light, foot-high hop, then were down for good, skidding a bit when the port wheels dug into a soggy section of grass.

"The members'll be pissed off about the tire tracks in the morning," Billy said. He was wrestling with the stick, pulling the plane into a steady taxi as the engines ground down to an almost-lull.

"I guess it won't be the first time," Driscoll said.

Billy laughed. "You guys gotta step smartly, once I make the loop down here by the green," he said. "It'll be what we call a quick turnaround."

Driscoll turned to Brisa. "You hear that?" Brisa gave a grudging nod.

"What about the guys who set up the landing?" Driscoll said to Billy. "They okay?"

"For what you're paying, you got nothing to worry about," he said.

Driscoll nodded, was about to turn away, when Billy took his arm. "Look, Driscoll, you're a pain in the ass, but you always did right by me. I hope you find out what happened to your friend. Whatever you need, these guys'll take care of you. Consider it a favor."

"I appreciate it, Billy."

"Captain Michael Cudahy, okay?"

Driscoll stared at him for a moment. "Captain Cudahy," he said, nodding. "Just make certain you get this plane back to Miami before my plastic melts, okay?"

Billy gave him something of a smile as he slowed the plane for its turn. Driscoll saw what must have been the seventeenth green out his window, caught a glimpse of a yawning sand trap, of a flagstick and a red pennant with a number stenciled, waving wildly in the prop wash . . . and then the plane was turned around, its nose pointed down the fairway in the direction they had come.

He leaned across Brisa, opened the door, jerked on the cuffs. "Where's the steps?" Brisa grumbled, coming slowly up from his seat.

"*Banzai,* asshole," Driscoll said, and took them flying out the open door.

They rolled over the soft grass together, the cuffs digging painfully into Driscoll's wrist as he dragged Ray Brisa after him. He pulled himself to his feet, forcing Brisa up as well. The plane was already well down the fairway, its engines whining, picking up steam. A few more moments and the landing lights had snapped off. The engines kicked into a snarl, and Driscoll saw the plane's dark silhouette rise up against the lightning-strobed sky. No rain, he thought, which seemed odd, given what they'd flown through. Despite Billy's reassurances, Driscoll suspected there'd be plenty of weather to come.

They stood quietly together until the sound of the engines had disappeared and there was only the rush of the wind through the tall, feathery pines, and the rumble of approaching thunder in the distance. Even Brisa seemed chastened by the silence, by the realization that they were on their own.

"You have any idea what you're doing?" Brisa said.

Driscoll sighed. "Stop trying to think, Ray. It doesn't suit you." The truth was, he wasn't sure if what he was doing was worth all the effort. But he didn't have many options, now, did he? If he thought this trip was a long shot, what were the chances of interesting any government agency in following up his tenuous skein of suspicions? *"Sure, Mr. Driscoll, we'll get right on that, just as soon as the First Lady checks in."*

His hacker friend Osvaldo had done as much as he could. Recordkeeping in the Caribbean nations was not as tidy as Driscoll might have hoped, but they'd finally discovered that the number was a Nassau listing, for an outfit called Tradewinds, Inc. There'd also been a street address, which meant nothing to Driscoll, of course. Then, a few keystrokes later, Osvaldo had tapped into Metro-Dade's database, had run Tradewinds through the department's crime files, but nothing had come up—no mention of the firm, no apparent connection with any of the sleazewads on file.

Driscoll got on the phone and convinced Dedric Bailey's assistant to call their Bahamian counterparts, but with similar results. No files on Tradewinds. It had been too late to try any business association offices, though Driscoll doubted that would have yielded anything, either. When he'd finally dialed the number of Tradewinds itself, there had been nothing but the odd and endless series of double rings.

Of course, Driscoll could have simply left Bailey's offices and gone home then, waited for a call from Harvey Clyde, or for a bright morning to start anew, but it just wasn't possible, simply wasn't in his makeup. Assume Driscoll were trapped in some collapsed building; would John Deal go home for a hearty meal and a good night's sleep before seeing what he might do?

A man who had used Ray Brisa to steal police uniforms had used a telephone here in the Bahamas to make his initial contact. Driscoll had exactly that one lead, and he intended to pursue it as far as he possibly could. If this pursuit finally led him nowhere, to the blank wall of a cliff, then he would accept that fact. But he would not rest until he had brought himself to that pass, he simply could not, and if it meant melting a couple of credit cards and taking a near-hurricane plane ride with an idiot hoodlum to get there, then so be it.

"You must be crazy, man," Brisa said as if he'd been reading Driscoll's thoughts.

"I am, Ray," Driscoll said. "Just keep it in mind, how crazy I am."

He reached into his pocket then, found the key for the cuffs. He twisted his arm up, trying to catch some light reflected from the dim runway lights, but finally had to do it all by touch. He slid the key into his cuff and twisted his hand free.

"What're you doing?" Brisa asked warily.

"I'm tired of smelling your breath," Driscoll said.

He worked his wrist for a moment, trying to get the feeling back, then snatched Brisa's free hand and snapped the cuff in place. He looked like some unlikely choirboy suddenly—or a sullen undertaker.

"Stick close now, Ray."

"You can't do shit like this," Brisa said, raising his clasped hands in protest.

"So file a complaint," Driscoll said. He grabbed Brisa's manacled hands and had turned in what he hoped was the direction of the hotel when he saw the dim lights bordering the landing strip blink out and, at the same time, heard the soft thudding of footsteps running across lush turf.

He sensed movement behind him, and spun about to find a massive silhouette blocking the sky, a few feet away. He tensed, his hand going automatically inside his coat.

"Mr. Driscoll." A deep voice issued from the darkness.

Brisa, who hadn't noticed the guy's approach, staggered backward, giving a yelp of fright.

"Who is that?" Driscoll said.

"No time for talking," the voice said. "You want to come with me, come quick."

Driscoll hesitated, then heard the sound of motors approaching in the distance. "That would be the policeman," the deep voice said. "Say come or go, right now."

Driscoll glanced again in the direction of the approaching motors, then regained his hold on Brisa. "Come on, dickhead," he said, and they began to chase the big man through the darkness.

**There were four** of them in the bed of the pickup: Driscoll and Brisa in the forecorners, two dark-skinned youths in the rear, all of them holding on desperately as the truck crashed and wallowed up the rough hillside terrain. Driscoll supposed they were following some sort of road that led up from the seaside golf links through the sandy pine barrens, but the clatter of gravel in the wheel wells and the ache of his tailbone as it slammed against the metal flooring suggested that it wasn't any paved thoroughfare.

Driscoll ducked as a limb whipped over the cab and downward, heard

Brisa curse as it slapped against him. "Come on, Driscoll, undo these cuffs," he whined.

"Dream on," Driscoll said. He clutched the top of the bed as the truck shot over a rise, leaving them as weightless as astronauts for a few moments. Brisa had his cuffed hands curled over the bed holding on for all he was worth, his chin clamped against the metal edge in desperation. When the truck slammed back down, Brisa took every bit of the force. His head snapped up off the edge of the truck bed as if he'd taken a Mike Tyson uppercut. He went over backward without a sound, sprawling unconscious over the coils of runway lights the two kids had loaded.

The two of them stared down at the handcuffed Brisa, then back at Driscoll, their expressions betraying nothing. "This is a guy who never listened to his mother," Driscoll said.

One of the kids glanced indifferently again at Brisa. The other lifted an eyebrow, then turned toward the forest. They were fourteen, Driscoll thought, fifteen at most, doing the grunt work right now, but give them a couple of years, they'd be doing things that were beyond Ray Brisa's imagination. Driscoll had run enough of the island brothers through the Miami justice system to know.

The pickup broke through another screen of pines, careening out of the forest onto a crumbling asphalt road in an impressive power slide. The big guy behind the wheel—Gavin, he'd finally said—hit the accelerator in earnest then, and Driscoll felt his head lean toward his shoetops as whatever was under the battered hood caught hold. By the time he straightened up, the slipstream around the side of the cab was enough to whip his breath away. The two kids at the tailgate had bent their heads forward against the windblast, as if in prayer.

It wasn't long before he saw one streetlamp whip past in their wake, then another and another, and soon ramshackle houses were looming up, more and more of them crowding together and pitching their tottering porches forward toward the street. Saw through his tearing eyes a scrawny yellow dog trotting indifferently away, as if unaware of their passage, a white-haired man in a scoop-necked T-shirt leaning against a lamppost, solemnly watching them fly by, old guy, dog, and houses dwindling rapidly into nothing as they whisked away from that settlement and down a long tunnel of overhanging trees.

Scenes from an old Robert Mitchum film he'd caught on cable flashed past in Driscoll's mind, Kentucky moonshiner Mitchum outrunning the feds down Thunder Road. Judging by the way he handled the deceivingly superpowered pickup, Gavin had probably seen the same movie.

Downhill now, slowing, and the streetlights snapping past overhead again. He blinked as they rolled onto an urban boulevard, a palm-lined, gently curving street that carved its way through a different world. He saw a clutch of exclusive shops set back from the street in a discreetly lit pedestrian mall, and a few yards further on, the grandly landscaped entrance to something called Atlantis, taxis full of white folks piling in, racing to beat the arrival of the storm. He caught a glimpse of the gleaming hotel towers he'd seen earlier from the air, and then they were up and over the steep hump of a bridge spanning a narrow river or canal and back down again, slowing to a stop at a tollgate.

Driscoll heard some quick back-and-forth between Gavin and the man in the booth, but they had lapsed into a singsong dialect that might as well have been Portuguese. He propped his leg atop Ray Brisa's still-inert form, trying to hide the handcuffs, but he needn't have. The guard didn't look in the bed as they slid by. Driscoll noticed that one of the heavy truck batteries that had been stowed in the back had tumbled against Ray's head, and he moved to shove it aside. Brisa stirred, and Driscoll gave him a pinch on the cheek that was enough to get his eyelids fluttering open, kept after it until Brisa had blinked awake and scrunched himself back into a sitting position in the truck.

They drove on uneventfully for a bit, down a street that was a slightly more dilapidated version of U.S. 441, the alley of ticky-tack that stitched South Florida from Miami all the way to West Palm Beach: a rundown gas station here, a grungy market there, sagging cars from other eras piled along the streets and jamming every possible space in the lots of blank-eyed businesses, a few pedestrians moving in their flapping clothes like shades haunting the litter of hell . . . the landscape was a testament to the failure of free enterprise, Driscoll thought. If Karl Marx saw it, he'd pop triumphant from his grave. The two kids in the back still had their heads bent on their knees. Maybe they were asleep, maybe the vision was too much, even for them.

A few minutes later the truck pulled off the main drag and eased to a stop in a residential area. It was several steps up from the rawboned settlement they'd passed through, but no place you'd be thrilled to call home. Rows of room-sized, paint-peeling houses, a wan streetlight every block or so, the sweet-sour tang of raw sewage in the air, a dog barking incessantly in the distance. There was a rotting sofa on the sidewalk before the cottage where they'd stopped, its cushions vomiting yellow foam stuffing everywhere.

"Looks like my neighborhood," Brisa said.

Driscoll gave him a look. "Cockroaches have a neighborhood?"

"Fuck you, man. What'd I ever do to you?"

"Guys like you piss me off, Ray. Just looking at you sets my teeth on edge."

Brisa shook his head. "These people you're looking for tried to kill my ass, too. You ever think about that?"

Driscoll stared at him, nodded finally. "Sure I thought about it, Ray. The good news is, you're my finger man. The bad news is, you're still alive."

Brisa turned away. "I'm just saying I wouldn't mind a shot at the ass-holes myself. I never even got paid."

"I'll keep that in mind, Ray. I find the right assholes, I'll toss you in a room with them, see who walks out."

The passenger door of the truck opened then and a wiry guy who'd been riding shotgun with Gavin got out. The guy had his head shaved, wore a waffle-weave, collarless polo shirt that clung to a chiseled physique. He gave Driscoll the same affectless stare the two kids in the back had. "Gavin say, where you want to go?"

Driscoll reached into his coat, saw the guy's eyes careful on his every move. He drew out a slip of paper, handed it to the guy, who glanced at the address, then back at Driscoll, suspicion in his eyes. The little guy walked around the hood of the truck, handed the slip through the window to Gavin.

Driscoll heard mumbled conversation, then the little guy was back, smacking the two kids on the shoulders, motioning them out of the truck. The two jumped down from the truck without question and vanished into the darkness. The wiry guy fixed Driscoll with a glare. "Gavin say okay." He shook his head, then went back to the cab and got in.

Driscoll wondered where he'd asked to be taken. "We can get a cab," he called, whacking the glass in the back of the cab for attention. But neither of the men up there turned to look at him, and his offer was lost in the squealing of the pickup's tires as it tore away from the curb.

**A light rain** had begun to fall as they left the shabby residential area and passed through another genteel shopping district, this one exuding a certain colonial flavor that contrasted with the flash of the first tourist enclave they'd passed through. This one reminded Driscoll of a section of Charleston Jean Ann had been fond of. She'd leave him cooling his heels on the sidewalk while she popped in and out of a similarly quaint series of jewelers, boutiques, and notions purveyors, seldom purchasing any of the overpriced merchandise but loving the process of inspection, a pleasure that had always eluded Driscoll.

He broke off his reverie as the truck made a quick turn, and they left the shuttered enclave of shops behind. They were climbing a gentle hill now, Brisa seemingly fully conscious but off in his own world, his manacled hands clasped about his knees, his surly gaze focused somewhere between his shoetops and the clutter on the truck bed between them. They had entered a far different sort of neighborhood than he'd seen so far, Driscoll saw. The deserted streets were actually cobbled here, and had become twisting tunnels draped by dense-leaved limbs of banyan and ficus, high whitewashed walls rising up on either side.

He caught sight of a consulate's plaque mounted on one wall, some Latin American country whose name he didn't catch, the brass face dimly illuminated and glistening with the soft rain. The next compound bore a discreet barrister's shingle, while a gate in the wall opposite gave him a glimpse of a neatly tended courtyard and what resembled a French country home: mansard roof, massive toothing stones and cornices, an elegant brass lamp burning in a bow window downstairs.

The truck had scarcely passed the gate when he heard the engine die. He felt a soft bump as they drifted to a curb. Driscoll glanced through the rear window into the cab, but he couldn't see much. An overhanging limb dripped moisture down his neck, and the truck's engine ticked against the silence. After a moment, one of the truck doors opened and Gavin stepped down.

"Here it is," he said to Driscoll.

Driscoll heard the other door open, sensed the wiry guy at his back. He stood, clutched at the curved roof of the truck's cab for support, kicked the kinks out of his legs. Getting a little old for these shenanigans, he thought. Couple more years, he wouldn't be able to get out of an easy chair.

He clambered down from the bed to stand beside Gavin, glanced about their surroundings. It looked like a neighborhood where people might actually live, but there were no sounds to suggest it. "This the high-rent district, is it?"

His eyes had adjusted to the darkness enough to see Gavin's big shoulders rise in a shrug. "Use to be," Gavin said. "Most people don't like the old houses anymore. They like to build a new place out on the island where we was, you know. Most of these come to be offices now, and like that."

Driscoll nodded. "Which one's Tradewinds?"

"What we just pass," Gavin said, pointing at the place Driscoll had taken for a country home.

"You sure?" he said.

Gavin stared at him, but didn't reply. The wiry guy had come to join them. Driscoll heard Brisa sigh, mutter a curse, rearrange himself in the bed of the truck.

The wiry guy reached into the truck, found something, handed it to Gavin. A flashlight, Driscoll realized as a beam of light shot from Gavin's hand to illuminate another of the tasteful brass plaques set into the brick-work on the opposite wall. Driscoll's eyesight wasn't what it had been, but he could make out the two-inch letters well enough.

There was a bell button set below the plaque. "Well, thanks for the ride," he said. If nobody answered the bell, he thought, he could cuff Brisa to the gate, find a way inside, have a look around.

"You got somebody to see in there?" Gavin said.

Driscoll turned back. The big guy seemed in no hurry to leave. He gave him his shrug. "It's possible."

"Looks like everybody gone home to me," Gavin offered. "Maybe you ought to find a place to stay, come back here tomorrow."

"I'm in a little bit of a hurry," Driscoll said.

Gavin nodded. "That's what I thought." He turned, nodded at the wiry guy. "Go on ahead, Tilton."

Driscoll stared as the wiry guy scurried across the narrow street and disappeared through a screen of shrubbery that masked the wall of the Tradewinds headquarters up the hill a few yards. He heard rustling sounds and ducked down as a shower of droplets fell from the limbs overhead.

Moments later there was a soft metallic thunk and Driscoll turned to find a pedestrian gate swinging out from the wall of the Tradewinds compound. Tilton stood just inside the gate, waiting.

"Okay," Gavin said, ushering him toward the opened gate.

"You don't have to do this, you know," Driscoll said.

"Captain Billy said take care of you," Gavin said. "A man don't know his way around down here, he can use some help."

Driscoll thought about it for a moment. "Just a second," he said. He leaned into the bed of the truck, caught hold of Brisa's manacled hands, found his key. He unsnapped one of the cuffs and Brisa started up, grumbling, but Driscoll jerked him toward the back of the truck bed and snapped the cuff shut around the heavy safety chain that dangled at the tailgate.

"Hey," Brisa protested. "Let me loose."

Driscoll hesitated. "You saying I can trust you not to run away?"

"I told you, man. I'm on your side."

Driscoll thought, but he didn't think long. "No can do," he said. When Brisa hesitated, Driscoll reached over the tailgate and clipped him behind his knees. Brisa went down with a groan.

"Man having his troubles," Gavin said as they moved off toward the gate.

"His troubles are only beginning," Driscoll said.

Gavin made a chuffing sound that might have been a chuckle. The three of them moved quickly through the gate, then walked quietly toward the house along the graveled driveway, Tilton leading the way. They were out from under the canopy of trees now, and the rain seemed to have picked up, hissing at the thick carpet of grass.

When they had drawn even with the window where the lamp was burning, Tilton eased across the driveway and pulled himself up by the sill. He stared inside briefly, then dropped down and came back to join them, shaking his head.

Driscoll moved on toward the broad terraced entryway, wondering if he was doing the right thing after all, then just as quickly dismissed those doubts. At least he'd fallen into the right hands, it seemed.

He moved quietly up the smooth stone steps and over the threshold. "I need to go inside," he said when the two had joined him on the terrace. He gestured at the doorway. "I need to find out what kind of place this is, what kind of business they do, and who's involved. It might take me a little while . . . "

"Only midnight," Gavin said mildly. "We got plenty of time. And Tilton get you in, no problem."

"I appreciate it," Driscoll said, "but you don't have to . . . "

"Say, chief." Tilton's voice came to them then, not much above a whisper, but carrying a note of concern that brought both their heads around.

"See here," Tilton said. His hand pushed lightly at the door, which swung inward at his touch.

"Not locked?" Gavin said. His tone suggested it wasn't a charming local characteristic.

He motioned Tilton inside with a nod, then started after him, holding Driscoll back with his trailing hand.

"Sorry, pardner," Driscoll said. He put his hand on Gavin's wrist and they stared at each other for a moment. Finally, Gavin allowed a doubtful lift of his brows and dropped his hand.

Driscoll came in quickly on Gavin's heels, noting the smell right away. Something of it was the slightly musty, damp-wood odor that all old houses seemed to have. Anytime he visited a place that provided the least whiff of it, Driscoll found his mind filled with images of himself as a child, puttering about his grandparents' sprawling Victorian home in Ocala. Though the absurdity of such a Northern-style structure being imported to Florida had not struck him until adulthood, he'd loved it as a child: wooden staircases, fore and aft; dumbwaiters and laundry chutes connecting its three floors; window glass that bubbled and wavered in spots, warping the normal Ocala outdoors into a landscape of magic and mystery . . . probably another clue to how he'd gone wrong, Driscoll thought, watching Gavin move carefully down the hall away from him.

No sign of Tilton, and even though he heard what sounded like the creak of a stair tread somewhere above, the staircase itself was empty. Driscoll turned toward the front of the house where he'd seen the light burning, easing his way along. He knew that the oak floorboards, the plaster walls, and the age of the place were primarily to account for the smell, but there was something else there, some tang of machine oil, maybe whatever it was they used to wax all the wood, he thought: not only was the floor gleaming in the soft reflection of the light from the parlor up ahead, but so was the dark molded paneling that lined the hallway.

He reached the parlor door, which leaned a few inches ajar, leaking the lamplight that guided him. He waited for a moment, listening, but there was no sound, and besides, Tilton had already looked inside this room from outside, hadn't he?

Driscoll nudged at the door with his hand, but nothing happened. Something seemed to catch at the bottom. A doorstop, he wondered? Or a bunched rug? He pushed harder, felt the door give a little. Something heavy sliding across the polished floorboards inside there.

He shoved again and nearly fell as the door gave way, sending him into the room in a drunken stumble. It might have been some granny's parlor once, he thought as he blinked, adjusting to the glare. But now it had been converted into a waiting room of sorts: a couple of leather easy chairs flanked the table that held the lamp he'd seen from outside; there was a leather sofa hunched against one wall, a coffee table littered with magazines. There was an area rug on the burnished floor all right, a tightly knotted Persian rug in a dark pattern, the real thing, or so it seemed to his eye.

But the rug wasn't what had been jamming the door, Driscoll noted. It was the guy lying behind it, facedown at the edge of a vast, muddy stain that had been smeared up considerably when he'd pushed the guy through it. Now he realized what he'd been smelling. If this *was* a waiting room, then this man was going to be waiting a long, long time. He glanced about the otherwise empty room, then circled the mess on the floor to get a look at the guy's face.

A mistake, he thought, turning away from the mass of splintered bone and tissue where the bullet, or bullets, must have exited. He guessed that the guy had been Latino, but he couldn't be certain even of that much. He was bending down, about to search the body for identification, when he heard hurried footsteps coming down the corridor.

Gavin came through the door, glanced at the body, took in Driscoll's hand that hovered inside his coat. "Tilton's upstairs," he said simply. He turned, and Driscoll presumed he was supposed to follow.

The big man was already halfway up the stairs by the time Driscoll made it to the hallway, and had disappeared altogether by the time Driscoll hit the first landing. At the top of the staircase he paused, looking right and left, seeing nothing but darkness.

"Here," Gavin's voice came, a harsh whisper from the darkness straight ahead.

Driscoll realized there was a room opening directly across the hallway from him, could make out Gavin's vague bulk in the doorway. He stepped forward and felt Gavin's big hand on his arm. There was another rank odor in this room, a hint of what he'd noticed downstairs, but this time it was overshadowed. Kerosene, he thought. Or lamp oil, like the scented stuff Deal sometimes used in his outdoor tiki torches.

"Show him," he heard Gavin say.

A vague nimbus of light sprang up, and Driscoll realized that Tilton had snapped on his flashlight, keeping one hand cupped over the lens. It wasn't much light, but it was enough. More than enough.

Tilton stood a few feet away from them on the other side of a broad and gleaming cherrywood desk. Driscoll had a glimpse of a credenza, its files tossed wildly, a tumbled computer monitor with its screen shattered, its processor smashed by what might have been hammer blows.

There was also someone else behind the desk, a guy flopped in a high-backed swivel chair, this one frozen too in the eternal waiting position. He was an Anglo, a fair-haired guy with what you might mistake for a dark mole in the middle of his forehead, another such dot high on his cheek. Two neat little dots, Driscoll thought, glad that he didn't have to look at what was on the wall behind the guy.

"See here," Tilton said. He grabbed the dead guy's hair and pulled his head forward, toward the light. The guy's jaw gaped open and what Driscoll saw inside his mouth made his stomach heave.

"They took his teeth," Gavin said. "Tore his teeth out, man. And look at his hands."

Driscoll didn't especially want to look at the guy's hands, but he turned back anyway. Tilton had let the guy's head fall back, now stood holding one of the corpse's palms to the light. Five fingers, all right, but each one ending in a bloody stump. The palm had had most of its flesh hacked away; something waved from the thumb pad like a white worm.

"Both hands like that," Gavin said. "Man still warm."

Driscoll had turned away, swallowing against the gorge that threatened at his gut. Too old, he thought. Getting too old. He nodded finally, turned back to the two of them. Tilton, thankfully, had left the corpse's side, was walking around the desk toward them.

"Some voodoo shit, maybe," Tilton said.

"You think?" Gavin said.

Driscoll was shaking his head, trying to make sense of it. "No prints, no dental ID," he said, as much to himself as to them. "Maybe the guy downstairs wasn't in the bank."

"What you say?" Gavin cocked his head at Driscoll.

"The data bank," Driscoll said, still trying to get past the ghastly images, get his mind fixed on the matter at hand.

"Whoever this guy was, somebody didn't want him identified. Maybe the guy downstairs was just a nobody." He glanced up at Gavin. "Or maybe there wasn't time to finish the job," he continued.

He registered the stink of the lamp oil again. "Maybe whoever did this got scared off. In fact, maybe *we* . . . "

He might have continued, but he'd heard the creak of a stair tread again, the same sound he'd heard when he entered the place. He broke off and turned to the doorway of the room, sliding his hand inside his coat for his pistol. He saw Gavin moving toward the doorway as well, and turned back to Tilton.

"The light," he whispered.

"Yo," said Tilton, realizing, and he might have snapped it off if he'd been just a little quicker.

There was no sound to speak of, but Driscoll saw the muzzle flashes, saw Tilton fly forward, gasping as if a battering ram had cracked against his spine. The flashlight flew out of his hand, spinning a crazed zigzag about the room before it crashed to the floor and blinked out.

Driscoll was going down as well, rolling to his left by choice, still trying to get his hand on the .357. He saw another pair of muzzle flashes, heard a groan behind him, then a heavy thud: Gavin, he thought. Gavin hitting the wall and sliding down with a sigh.

Driscoll finally felt the cool grip of his weapon and came up on his knees, squeezing off two rounds of his own in the direction of the muzzle flashes. The explosions were deafening in the airless room. Driscoll went down again as he fired, rolling back the way he had come.

He thought he had the desk between himself and their assailant now, thought that even if his shots hadn't hit home, they might be on somewhat equal terms. He tried to quash his harsh breathing, tried to will away the slamming pulse in his ears. Give him anything to lock onto, he thought. A stumble, the slightest scuff of leather on wood.

He heard a wet, rattling sigh behind him. Tilton, his wounds sucking air, sucking hard. He heard another groan from further away, where Gavin had gone down. And then he heard a door slam on the opposite side of the room, heard a strange soft popping noise, and next, the sound of footsteps rapidly descending stairs.

It couldn't be, he thought, his mind rebelling for a moment. The stairs were at his back. The gunman would have had to run right over him to make it out the door and down those stairs . . .

But in the next instant he understood: there was a service stairwell on the other side of the room, just like the one in his grandmother's house.

He was on his feet and out the door, bounding down the front staircase three steps at a time, one hand steadying himself on the banister, something else he'd done at his grandmother's house nearly forty years ago, except this time the silver pistol raised in his other hand fired real bullets, and the bad guy who'd taken the back stairway in an attempt to escape was no figment of a childhood imagination.

He hit the landing with one foot and launched himself all the way to the bottom with his next step. He bounced off the opposite wall, steadied himself, then turned and ran toward the back of the house at full tilt, hitting what he hoped was the same swinging door of his youth with his leading shoulder.

As it turned out, it wasn't a swinging door, but other things were different as well. He probably had put on a good two hundred pounds—maybe two and a quarter—since the time he'd done this as a child, enough weight, at least, to splinter the frame and send the door rocketing back on its hinges.

He went on into the kitchen sliding on one knee, the .357 braced in both hands. There was light from a distant streetlamp, light enough for

Driscoll to see the door from the service stairwell shuddering on its own hinges, enough to see the shape of a tall man at the back door of the house turned and firing his way.

He saw the silent muzzle flashes and knew it was good that he saw those brilliant flowers, that he had registered them without pain, or even worse, an icy numbness. He was still sliding across that highly polished floor as he fired in return, was still moving as he emptied his weapon and the tall man who'd tried to kill him flew out the doorway, shattering its glass panes as he went.

Driscoll rose unsteadily, moving toward the open doorway, cursing himself for not holding at least one round back. He hesitated with his back to the jamb for as long as he could stand it, hearing nothing but the hiss of the rain, then finally spun out onto the landing holding an empty gun in his hand as if it might accomplish something, as if he really were ten again, he thought.

But it wasn't an imaginary man who came forward to meet him. He saw the underhand pass coming toward him, the glint of steel in the light of a distant streetlamp. He staggered back, watching the blade slice an arc an inch in front of his gut. The force of the thrust pulled the tall man slightly off balance and Driscoll cuffed him with an awkward left, sending him into the side of the house.

The guy bounced hard, but kept his grip on the knife. He came off the wall with a loopy grin on his face, might have missed the first time, but was eager to try again. Driscoll steadied himself with one hand on the doorjamb, considering his options: stand there, take it in the gut, try to run, take it in the back.

The guy made a feint, hesitated when Driscoll pulled his hand from the doorframe. A momentary standoff, Driscoll thought, this guy too good to be making some foolish pass. He'd wait until he had things just the way he wanted them, then make his move. Driscoll's eyes had adjusted to the dim light by now. He could see the guy's face, some of it, at least. Half a grin in shadow, half illuminated in the reflected light.

"I know you," Driscoll said, the words coming unbidden.

"Do you?" the man said.

Driscoll nodded slowly, his eyes never leaving the face. Never mind watching the blade. When the guy was ready, he'd see it coming in his face.

And he did know the guy, he was certain of it. The cop's curse never to forget a scumbag's face. Though he couldn't place this particular face right now, and there was some odd psychic static surrounding the memory that wasn't quite right.

Another feint, another countermove by Driscoll. No way he could get out of it whole. Best case, he could give up a little, hope to take something on an arm, a shoulder, he could get in close, a chance for one straight shot. If he could hit the guy, he could put him down, that much he was certain of. The guy was tall, but slender. Driscoll outweighed him by fifty pounds at least. And Driscoll had a punch. Only trouble was, he didn't want to trade a right cross for major surgery.

"I am sorry, my friend. Sorry our acquaintanceship must end."

The voice, Driscoll thought. Something about that voice. But never mind all that. It was coming now, he had seen the slightest tremor in the man's cheek, the pulsing of a vein in his temple.

He sensed movement in the dim background. There was a strange whistling sound as something rushed through the air nearby, and a metallic flash in front of Driscoll's eyes. He lurched backward, tumbling through the door of the house. He heard a crack, and the tall man cried out in pain.

Driscoll was on his back, still confused as to why the tall man wasn't through the door after him, couple of nifty swipes of the blade, this would all be over . . . and then he saw why it wasn't happening that way.

It was Ray Brisa there, moving in on the man who'd been about to gut him. The tall guy had his knife hand clutched in his left, knife long gone it seemed, and was still groaning in pain as Ray Brisa came at him, readying himself for another awkward backhand with what looked like a length of chain clutched in his manacled hands.

"Come on, dickwad," Brisa called, and sent the chain in a another whistling arc.

The tall guy ducked and came in on Brisa, took him in the solar plexus with an elbow. Brisa's breath left him in a gasp. The chain flew from his hands, went chewing and chattering through a hedge. Brisa was backpedaling, trying to keep his balance, when the tall man hit him in the face with his good hand.

Brisa went over just as Driscoll was shoving himself off the floor of the porch. They both went down in a tangle.

By the time Driscoll rolled out from under Brisa and got to his feet, the backyard was empty. He heard scuffling feet receding down the alleyway that bordered the back of the house, then a car engine, tires squealing away in the night.

He cursed, brushing gritty dirt from his palms onto his trousers. He coughed and felt a pain in his side where some part of Ray Brisa had crunched into him when they went down. Brisa was on his hands and knees, trying to push himself to his feet, a clumsy move with his hands still shackled.

He glanced up, noticed Driscoll staring at him. "Don't help me, asshole," Brisa said.

Driscoll reached down, pulled Brisa to his feet. Brisa worked his shoulders, glanced in the direction the tall guy had taken. "You want to take these cuffs off now?" he said, turning back to Driscoll.

Driscoll regarded him for a moment. "That was the tailgate chain you used, huh?"

Brisa shrugged. "Piece of shit truck, man. I could've brought the bumper over here, hit him with that."

Driscoll nodded. "I wish you would have. You got a little excited with that chain. You could have put him to bed, now look what happened."

Brisa stared at him. "Look what happened? I saved your fat ass is what happened."

"Guy got away, though."

"I can't believe it."

Driscoll shrugged. "How come you didn't take off once you got loose?"

Brisa looked around. "I'm in fucking Nassau, man. I never even been on an airplane before. I got no passport, no money, nothing. I figure you got an obligation to get me back home."

"An obligation," Driscoll repeated.

Brisa shrugged. Not like his own shrug, Driscoll thought. Brisa's move was abrupt, combative, really.

"I told you, I wouldn't mind a crack at those assholes myself," Brisa said. He glanced off in the direction of their departed assailant. "I got him, too, didn't I. He hadn't ducked, he'd be talking to the angels right now . . ." Brisa broke off, listened to sirens in the distance.

Driscoll heard the sirens, too, but he'd been taken somewhere else suddenly, a dozen years or so, a farm in the Virginia countryside, rolling hills, horses, and vague flashes of the face of the tall man in there, too, like snippets from a crazy dream. Angel, Driscoll found himself thinking. But not like that, not like the mythical creatures with bright blonde hair and fluttery wings. He'd mispronounced the name even then. *Ahn-hell*, was how it was said. Sure. Ahn-hell Salazar. *Dear God*, he thought, fighting what had flashed through his mind.

Angel Salazar, who had been his teacher, no less. Driscoll packed off from Miami to rural Virginia a dozen years ago on a government-sponsored training mission, Reagan-inspired aid to local law enforcement.

Salazar, not really an agency man, but a mercenary they'd trained, a creep brought in fresh from Salvador, the ghoulish half of a team-taught seminar on interrogation techniques, and all his classroom references to what was justifiable in service of the forces of freedom had been the mildest part of the course.

A few of the assembled cops had expressed some minor disagreement about the measures Salazar suggested as being within the limits of the law, or at least undetectable, but most lapped up Salazar's act like week-end athletes who'd suddenly found themselves in the company of Ray Nitschke during a male bonding retreat: "Why don't you tell us again how you chewed off that guy's finger in the pile-up, Ray."

Last night of the stay, Driscoll had wandered back to the dorm late, found a group gathered around a TV in the rec room, a grainy video running, the color so bad it could have been black and white. Some guys in fatigues were hanging around a scummy-looking room with a battered table and two weary-looking guys with the high cheekbones of the Indios slumped and tied in wooden chairs. Driscoll poked his head in just as a guy tall enough to have been Salazar made his appearance in the video, though it was hard to tell, being that he was wearing a ski mask on his head.

The guy in the ski mask stepped up to the table, grabbed one of the subjects by his hair, shouted something in Spanish that came out like underwater gargling talk on the lousy tape. It didn't matter what he'd said, though, Driscoll knew that much already.

It looked like the guy who'd had his hair snatched had spit at the one in the ski mask. And that didn't matter, either. All this had been preordained, probably several million years ago when Angel's ancestors had slithered out into the light.

Angel, if that's who the guy in the ski mask was, reached into a back pocket and came up with a plastic bag that he jammed down over the poor bastard's head. Somebody else in the interrogation room was ready with a roll of tape.

The guy in the ski mask was clearly practiced. He had everything wrapped tight in seconds. The guy in the chair was thrashing about, even managed to get the chair kicked over backward, get himself down on the floor where even though his hands were still bound behind him he could beat his head against the cement.

It wasn't really clear whether the guy managed to knock himself senseless before the end, but Driscoll suspected he hadn't. He didn't know what happened to the other guy at the interrogation table, either, because he'd stepped on into the rec room and kicked the TV's power plug out of the wall before the tape could get to that point.

There had been a chorus of complaint, somebody up to bang on the set before the group saw Driscoll coming after Salazar and it dawned on everyone what had happened. Just as well they had caught him before he'd reached Salazar, Driscoll thought. Somebody might have died. It might even have been him.

"You takin' a nap or something?" It was Brisa's voice, cutting into the memory that had flashed before him.

He looked at Brisa then, still trying to piece it together, what it meant to find Salazar involved in this, then noticed how bright it seemed to be for this time of night, how odd flashes of light danced over Brisa's face. Driscoll glanced upward and remembered the smell of kerosene inside the room where he'd found the dead men and the soft popping sound he'd heard during the gun battle. And then he saw the reflection of flames in the second-story windows.

He was running again, Ray Brisa on his heels. Inside, running as fast as his weary legs would carry him. Through the kitchen, down the hall, once more up those stairs, struggling upward, Brisa following after him, until they were finally blocked by the wall of flames.

No chance of going further, no hope for anyone caught in that cauldron, he thought. Angel's murderous grin danced before his eyes, and sirens wailed in his ears. He turned to urge Ray Brisa away, then saw movement from above and a form falling through the flames and suddenly there was Gavin, sleeves ablaze, smoke rising from his hair, hurtling down upon them like a smoldering angel.

"Get me gone," he called as he tumbled to the landing below. "Get me from those sirens."

And they did.

# Part 4:
# Homestretch

"I want to talk to Dedric Bailey. Right, *Chief* Bailey, for Christ's sake." Driscoll was trying to keep his voice down, but he didn't know why he bothered. The vast lobby of the hotel where he and Brisa had been directed by Gavin was deserted at this hour. No bellmen, no one behind the endless stretch of check-in counter. Even the all-night casino, which sat on the opposite side of the cavernous lobby, was nearly deserted.

"Somebody went to get him, just hold tight," the voice on the other end of the line said. There seemed to be an inordinate amount of static, even more than there had been when he'd spoken to Bailey earlier, from the hospital.

"Tell me who I'm talking to," Driscoll said. He'd replayed the memories of Salazar over and over during the long cab ride to the hotel, getting his paranoia into primo shape.

"Is this Driscoll?" came the response.

"Who is *this?*" Driscoll demanded, glancing nervously about the lobby. A wave of static filled the line, leaving Driscoll to fume. He needed Bailey. His old pal Bailey who'd agreed to run the checks on Salazar, find out who the bastard was plugged into. Bailey he could trust. That much he was certain of.

"This is Ellenberg," the voice on the other end came finally. Another wave of static. A distant alarm bell ringing, some diehard hitting a jackpot on one of the hotel casino slots.

"Why don't you tell me where you are," the voice said. "We'll have Bailey get right back."

More alarms ringing in Driscoll's head now, but not from any slot machine. Salazar and his connections. Bailey's stories about the Feds, how easily they steamrolled local law enforcement.

"Give me somebody I know," he said. "Rogier. Or Pete Rodriguez."

"There's nobody else right now."

"Who went to get Bailey?"

A pause. "Holden."

"I don't know any Holden, either," Driscoll said.

"Just hold on, I think Bailey's coming," the voice said. A new urgency there. The alarms a corresponding blare in Driscoll's head. How many times had he strung a caller along, waiting for a phone trace to complete?

"Forget it," he blurted. "Tell Bailey I'll call back."

"Just one more sec . . . "

Driscoll slammed down the phone.

215

"You consider Vernon Driscoll a reliable individual, do you?"

Dedric Bailey stared back at Harvey Clyde across the briefing table, reminding himself to keep his composure. He was a cop, Bailey counseled himself, chief of the City of Miami Special Investigative Section.

However, over the past few hours he had begun to understand what it was like to be on the other end of a process he had conducted a few thousand times in his career. "Of course I do. We've been over it again and again."

Clyde shrugged. He was the third man who'd been in to interview him through the night. Same routine, same questions. Wear your subject down, wait for the inconsistencies to crop up. Bailey understood the drill. But he was here trying to help, not hide anything.

Bailey stole a glance at his watch, noted it was almost six. No windows in the room, an anonymous cubbyhole in the basement of the Justice Building the Feds had turned into their command center. He assumed it'd be growing light outside.

If he hadn't answered the phone last night, he'd be pulling on his sneakers right now, readying himself for his morning run. With Robert away at college, he and Dorothy had sold the house, moved into a condo that was part of a sprawl around a series of dredged-out lakes on the west end of the county. It was pretty white bread out there, but Dorothy felt safe, and he'd come to enjoy his new jogging route, along a series of asphalt paths that bordered the lakes. Mist rising up off the water some mornings, the occasional heron wading the shallows for breakfast, a fellow jogger now and then to nod a welcome . . . quite a contrast to the tightly packed neighborhood they'd left behind, a place where he'd see someone else running, he'd have to assume they were leaving the scene of a crime. He felt a little guilty about leaving sometimes, but not too guilty. He'd worked hard, he'd earned a little peace and quiet.

"We keeping you from something?" Clyde asked, noting Bailey's glance at his watch.

Bailet couldn't help himself. "The Montel Williams show," he said. "I'm supposed to be on right now, explaining why you guys couldn't find your ass with both hands."

Clyde gave him a look, then turned back to the pad in front of him.

Though Clyde had not identified himself, Bailey suspected he was with the Bureau. Too many of them shared that wrapped-way-tight, holier-than-thou affect; no good cop/bad cop orchestration for these characters. They were bad actors all the way. It could be the stress everyone was under, he supposed, but something told him the guys he'd had across the table were happy to be jerks in any weather.

"You took the call at 1:00 A.M.?"

"Around then," Bailey said. "I was still in the office, the call was logged in. You could go check the records if it's important to you."

"I appreciate your patience," Clyde said. "We're just trying to establish a few things."

Clyde went back to studying his notes, like maybe he wasn't quite sure what this was all about. Bailey took a deep breath, let it out in a sigh. When he did this to a suspect, the purpose was to exasperate, to agitate, have the subject blurt out something unintended, something incriminating. Problem was, he was no suspect and there was nothing to blurt.

"The caller identified himself as Vernon Driscoll. You have any reason to doubt that's who it was?"

"The man has a characteristic way of speaking," Bailey said. "Listen to him for twenty years, you wouldn't forget."

Clyde nodded. "And he informed you he was in the Bahamas."

"It came up during the conversation."

"And that he had illegally entered that country in an aircraft obtained under fraudulent pretenses?"

"I don't recall Vernon using any of those kind of adjectives. He's not an adjective kind of guy."

Clyde flipped a page in his pad. "Let's get back to this business of Angel Salazar."

"Whoever he is," Bailey said.

"Vernon Driscoll told you that he'd encountered a man whom he identified as Angel Salazar at a crime scene in Nassau?"

"He did." Bailey was feeling groggy. He wondered how many times he was going to have to answer these questions. He was ready to leave now, was going to leave.

"And Driscoll asked you to run Salazar's name through the system, correct?"

"As I must have said about a hundred and fifty times."

"I'm going to assume that's a *yes*," the interrogator said.

Bailey nodded. "Are we finished?"

Clyde seemed not to hear him. He stared at Bailey, waiting for more.

"And I ran the name," Bailey continued wearily, "which returned a couple of petty criminals, neither of whom seemed to be the guy Vernon was interested in."

"Did you speak with Vernon Driscoll again?"

"No," Bailey said. "Driscoll said he'd call me back."

"Then why did you make the assumption that you hadn't found the person he was looking for?"

"Because he indicated we were looking at something different here, some kind of a major player. And . . . "—he nodded across the table— ". . . because it wasn't an hour after I got into the computer that your guys showed up in my office."

"So you haven't spoken to Vernon Driscoll since that phone call about one last night?"

"Maybe you should check your notes," Bailey said. "I could have sworn I just told you that."

"Are you trying to be evasive with me?"

Bailey felt the muscles in his jaw tightening again. He willed himself to relax, clasped his hands on the table before him. "I have not spoken to Vernon Driscoll since we hung up on that call I told you about."

Clyde nodded, but there was no indication on his face that he necessarily believed what Bailey had said. There was a tap on the door to the room then, and Clyde rose to open it.

Bailey got a glimpse of a military uniform before Clyde stepped out into the hall, closing the door behind him. Bailey heard muffled conversation, a couple of rising inflections there, and then Clyde was back through the door. He picked up his notepad, flipped it shut. He gave Bailey a disinterested look. "We want to thank you for your cooperation, Chief Bailey. We know it's been a hardship, but you'll appreciate what we're up against." He made a gesture with his pad. "You're free to go."

Bailey rose, fighting indignation. *Free to go?* "So what happened? You guys find Vernon Driscoll? The First Lady phone home?"

"Nothing's happened, Mr. Bailey. But you'll let us know if you hear from Vernon Driscoll again."

"Sure," Bailey said. "The very minute."

"Then that's all," Clyde said, and motioned him out the door.

Billy had been fighting a bothersome stutter in the starboard engine of the Cessna for most of the last leg home. If he'd known it was coming, he could have made the adjustments while he was laid over at the untended airstrip in Bimini, waiting for a break in the weather and the onset of dawn, when his return to the mainland was less likely to draw attention. But he hadn't known, of course, and even though he should have gone over the plane while he was on the ground, instead he'd taken the opportunity for a tiny sip or two from his pocket flask and a few hours of sleep, upright in his seat.

The stutter was nothing of major concern, a chronic problem that he'd experienced before with that particular engine. But it, along with dodging the patchy weather, had kept him busy, constantly adjusting the fuel mixture, lean to rich and back again, trying to find a setting that would keep the beast happy, let him settle back into Billy-pilot mode, the state where he simply existed as a part of the machinery, a nudge of the stick here, a glance at the dials there, but essentially just another cog in an interlocking set of gears.

It hadn't been until the last fifteen minutes that he'd managed to achieve that near-satorial state. He'd broken into the clear just east of the Gulf Stream, and the engine had evened out about the same time. He'd finally gotten the opportunity to zone out the way he liked: wrap himself up inside the drone of the engines, stare out mindlessly at the view while he glided home.

He still loved to fly after all these years, all these bends in the road. Ferrying passengers, running dope, smuggling Vernon Driscoll into the Bahamas, it didn't really matter. He wouldn't have chosen to make this evening's run, perhaps, but now that it was almost over, he didn't begrudge it, either. He smiled, thinking of the look on Driscoll's face when he'd dropped them down through the chute toward the golf course landing. "What trees?" he'd said to Driscoll. He'd been down that tunnel of trees fifty times, at least. The perfect setup. A perfect moment.

He was still chuckling about it, so lost in his reverie that he very nearly missed the fighter's approach. Not that he'd have had much chance to react anyway. He was flying low and slow, doing his best to stay off the radar screens—maybe a hundred and fifty feet up, about the same in airspeed—and the jet had to be coming at him at four-fifty or five. He had a moment's glimpse of the jet's underbelly as it screamed overhead, the sound rattling him in his seat.

Billy pulled back hard on the stick, lifting the Cessna's nose against the sudden cyclone that wanted to send them hurtling down to that black water. The plane rocked crazily in the downdraft, its balky engine coughing in protest, but in the next instant they were through it, and steadying once again.

Billy glanced over his shoulder in the direction the fighter had taken, hoping it had been chance, a near-miss, two disparate ships passing by accident in the starry night. Maybe the pilot was one of the rocket jockeys from the Naval Air Station in Key West out there practicing his fuck-you-Fidel moves, hadn't even noticed him.

But then he saw the glow of the jet's afterburners soaring up in a graceful loop behind him, and he knew it wasn't going to go down that way. He sighed and goosed up the volume on his radio, and heard just what he'd heard the last time he'd taken a big fall:

". . . request you identify yourself, repeat, identify yourself at once."

Billy shook his head sorrowfully, picked up the microphone, keyed in. "Captain Michael Cudahy here," he said. "Bound for Tamiami Field from Key West." Maybe they'd let him pass, Billy thought. Fly on, Captain Billy. But given recent events, that was likely a forlorn hope. They'd check Key West, the inconsistency would be noted, he'd find himself flying on in with an escort, probably find a few hundred security types waiting to talk to him at Tamiami. His philosophy on the beauties of flight took a sudden downturn. Goddamn Vernon Driscoll anyway.

"You are in breach of United States airspace," the pilot's voice came. "You have ignored repeated warnings. Repeat. You have ignored our warnings. You must turn back at once."

Billy stared at the radio. "What the hell are you talking about," he shouted into the microphone. "This is Billy . . ." He broke off, cursing himself. "This is Captain Michael Cudahy. Repeat, Michael Cudahy. Cessna aircraft, tail number Beta Charley Alpha seven niner six. Do you read me?"

". . . a breach of United States airspace and refusal to acknowledge repeated warnings," the pilot's voice droned.

"Wake up, you asshole," Billy shouted, keying and unkeying his mike. "This is Michael Cudahy . . ."

He broke off, staring in astonishment as the fighter reached its apogee and began a dive toward him. He saw a spark of light beneath one wing of the fighter, then a matching spark from beneath the other.

PRESIDENTIAL DEAL

Missiles? The asshole was firing fucking missiles at him? Impossible. A dream. A bad, bad dream.

He sent the Cessna into a dive toward the black water, pulled into a roll just above the wave tops, dropped back on his speed, tried frantically to kick the pilot's door open. He glanced up as the fighter screamed past, its wingtips glinting silver as it peeled off toward the moon.

"You sonofabitch," Billy screamed. He would have screamed something more, would have squeezed off rounds with a sidearm if he'd had one, would have chunked a few rocks as well, but he did none of those things.

For the Cessna had ceased to exist. It transformed first into a brilliant blossom of fire, and then a hail of molten fragments that disappeared hissing into the dark water, and finally it was only a plume of dark smoke that rose lazily into the purpling sky until even that was gone.

"I can confirm that incident, sir," the general said. His posture was erect, frozen, his gaze evasive, darting everywhere in the room but at his audience.

"You can relax, general," Chappelear told him. "This area's been swept by the best we have. This is just you and me here."

The general didn't seem reassured. "We can confirm the crash of a civilian aircraft over the Florida Straits at approximately oh-six-hundred hours," he said, his eyes fixed on a spot high on the wall while he recited.

"Warning shots fired. Subject aircraft lost due to mechanical failure while fleeing lawful interdiction. Debris recovered suggests subject aircraft payload consisted of baled cannabis in an amount exceeding recommended payload for the craft and which in all likelihood contributed to the crash. No survivors, no bodies recovered. Aircraft registered to Pan-Aeronautica of Bogata, leased by Vernon Driscoll, a private investigator and former Metro-Dade homicide detective, and piloted by one Michael Cudahy, also known as William 'Captain Billy' Nolan. Nolan a known drug trafficker who avoided sentencing via plea bargain in the Colombian Airlift sting in 1989, and now a contract pilot for BahamasAir."

"Very good," Chappelear said. "Of course, we're going to sit on this report for the time being, General."

"Yes, sir," the general said.

"One more drug runner gone south, that's all it is. But any incident in this arena could become a distraction. We don't need anything like that, do we?"

"Absolutely not, sir."

"So we understand one another, do we?"

"We do, sir."

He turned, just to be sure there wasn't anything of riveting interest that had appeared high on the wall behind his desk. "And what has become of this Vernon Driscoll?"

"We're not certain, sir."

"We were following him at one point, but lost track of him when he left the airport?"

The general cleared his throat. "He was under surveillance by another agency, sir. The plane filed a flight plan for Jacksonville, as I understand it. Driscoll was a low-priority target. Jacksonville was alerted. But there seemed no reason to continue surveillance to the destination."

Chappelear nodded. "We can't confirm he was on board the aircraft when it went down?"

"We cannot."

"And the third man involved?"

The General shrugged. "A petty criminal named Ray Brisa. Driscoll had him manacled. We don't know why. Driscoll was in contact with some individuals prior to his departure from MIA. We have our own people looking into those contacts as we speak."

Chappelear tented his fingers, thought for a moment. "We've alerted our people in Nassau, have we?"

The general nodded. "There's been no commercial air traffic outbound from any port in the Bahamas since late yesterday afternoon. But the storm's turned northward and that's about to change."

"Very good, General," Chappelear said. "You'll keep me informed."

"Yes, sir," the general said. "And one more thing, sir. Who *is* Angel Salazar?"

"A product of someone's imagination," Chappelear told the general. "Angel Salazar has been dead for fifteen years."

The general nodded. " I see," he said. But the look on his face suggested he actually saw nothing at all.

"You are hurt," the mate said, watching Angel step stiffly from the crumbling concrete dock onto the rail of the boat.

The mate hurried to extend a hand, but Angel lowered himself onto the deck without assistance, dropping the bowline as he came. He steadied himself at the rail, waiting for the streaming constellations above to steady themselves.

They were tied off at an abandoned ferry stop just off the cut between old town and the island where the new tourist hotels had been built. A mile or two behind him, the privileged and beautiful were gathered. Music. Torchlights. Food. Flowers. Ease.

Here was darkness. Above him, pilings and battered oil drums lined the docks, their shadows looming like abandoned spirits waiting to be beckoned aboard.

"Is it done?" the mate asked him.

Angel turned from the dock, from the still-throbbing stars, to regard the man. Over the man's shoulder, across the broad cut, glittered the lights of old town. Roberto this mate's name. One he had brought with him from Salvador many years before.

"There is no one left here," Angel said evenly. "And nothing left to find."

Roberto nodded. After a moment, he turned to the controls of the boat, and the engines thundered to life. He ran to the stern and cast off the last line that held them, then returned to the wheel.

Angel raised a hand to the wetness beneath his shoulder. Too much blood, he thought. Blood everywhere.

He had recognized the man who'd shot him. From where, it was impossible to know just now. Only a scrap of memory, and that the most essential: an airless room, and others there, and Angel's eyes locked with that man's in the elemental bond of hatred. A moment impossible to forget. Timeless. And time come around again, he thought.

"We will go south now," Roberto said, turning as they approached the mouth of the channel and the broad cut opened out before them.

Angel shook his head. "Not south," he said. "Not yet."

Roberto hesitated, turned to him. "Then where?"

"Something yet to do," he said, pointing in the direction that had brought them here.

Roberto shrugged and turned the wheel, urging them on toward the open channel. The engine coughed, and the mate worked the throttles. Another cough and a lurching beneath their feet as the swells from the open water caught the boat and threw them.

The mate glanced at Angel, then throttled back. The engines held there, and the mate left them nosed at near idle against the swells, and went to check the engine compartment. He raised the hatch, ducked his head inside the compartment, waved his light about, then came up again, motioning Angel forward.

"Have a look," he said to Angel.

Angel came toward him, uncertain. Roberto gestured toward the open compartment, guided the torch beam downward. Angel was about to lean inside himself when he saw the glint of steel at his side and lurched away.

The blade in Roberto's hand dug into the underside of the engine hatch and snapped in half. Roberto glanced at the ruined blade and cursed.

Only a moment's distraction, but enough. Another person might have scurried backward, fighting for distance, but Angel knew that such instincts would have doomed him.

He stepped forward instead, shot his elbow out, felt the crack as it struck Roberto's cheekbone. Roberto staggered backward, his head twisted aside with the force of the blow. Angel hit him again, this time with the heel of his hand.

The blow caught Roberto at the hinge of his jaw, lifted him off balance, up against the transom, and over. He teetered for a moment, his hands clawing as if at invisible ropes. Then he toppled backward, into the dark water that boiled with the action of the props.

There was a sharp cry, cut off as Roberto was jerked under. Another lurch of the engines, a shudder as the props struck, then struck again. Angel steadied himself at the rail, saw something pale shoot to the surface, float away in the wake of the boat: Roberto's hand, floating free, palm up—a grotesque flower thrown up from the depths.

Angel turned away from the sight, picked up the tumbled flashlight, bent into the compartment to find the fuel valve Roberto had tightened nearly to full stop. He opened the valve and the roar of the engines grew steady.

He raised his hand absently to the wound beneath his shoulder, felt the wetness and the fiery pain. Perhaps he'd made it worse when he'd struck Roberto, he thought. But no matter.

Nor did he feel any real sense of betrayal as he stared out over the now-blank waters behind the boat. He might have expected it of his employers. No loose threads, no unfinished business, was that not the law in affairs such as this? He who tidies up, survives. He who does not, dies.

Angel nodded and went to the wheel of the boat. He pushed the pain from his mind. He gripped the twin throttles tightly. He aimed himself where fate decreed. He drove.

**39**

She awoke, unable to catch her breath, her hands clawing the air as if she were trying to pull herself up through dark water. It took her a moment to shed herself of the dream . . . though she would never leave it behind, she thought.

She sagged against the rough-hewn wall of rock at her back, felt the drip of water cool against her skin. She was slick with sweat, the air still and stifling. And a quiet so total that her ears rang.

She swallowed and felt a soreness in her throat and heard tiny popping sounds in her ears. She blinked and realized that the darkness had taken on a different character . . . as if light might be drifting down from somewhere, but nothing definite, only the vaguest hint of other-than-darkness.

She remembered running from the storm, remembered tumbling down the crevasse to land somewhere deep in the jumble of rock with her head below her feet. She had still been trying to right herself when the water cascaded down and covered her. The buoyancy of the water had allowed her to right herself, but then, when she'd clawed her way up toward the surface, there'd been no surface to find.

Her head had cracked painfully against a ceiling of rock, and her hands had thrashed in a panic, finding nothing but rock and more water. She'd been certain that she would die in that liquid darkness.

And then, just as she felt her lungs about to explode, her face burst up into a pocket of damp, salty air and she could breathe again.

She'd clutched herself against the rough wall in a panic, waiting for the next wave, the next surge of water that would swallow her, but even though the wind outside continued its roaring and rain sluiced down through the rocks in torrents, the next wave of seawater never came. After what seemed like hours, she'd relaxed enough to sink down against the rocks again, where she lay and listened to the howling of the storm and tried not to wonder what had happened to John Deal, nor what she would do if she lived through this night, nor how she would stay sane if she were in fact alone.

She'd found herself dozing off in fits and starts after that. Not really sleeping. More like periods of blackout that she'd willed upon herself. Something to do with exhaustion, surely, but just as much a way of refusing to consider what might lie ahead.

She wiped at her sweaty face then, and reached out, searching for a handhold to pull herself into an upright position, felt her fingers brush against something wet and warm and yielding. She sensed movement, something alive there, something looming up in front of her face. She jerked her hand back, her throat locked. In the next instant she was screaming, the sound redoubling inside the tiny chamber.

There was an answering roar that had her screaming even louder, trying to escape the hands that clutched her shoulders, shaking her, and that other voice roaring in her ears . . .

. . . until finally she heard her name, "Linda . . . Linda . . . "

John Deal, she realized, crammed into that tiny, stifling space with her . . .

. . . she felt relief flooding over her, warmth that touched her to the core . . . she let herself go into his arms . . . could find comfort there at last.

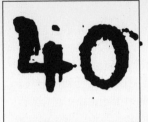

"I say we just go to the airport, take our chances."

"Go right ahead," Driscoll said. "There's a bunch of taxis right out front be glad to deliver you there."

Brisa stared back across the table at him uncertainly. They were sitting outside on one of the terraced decks of the Neptune, the same sprawling seaside resort they'd viewed from the air during their approach to the island the night before.

Driscoll understood something of Brisa's urgency. The storm had swerved north and east of the island, sparing them the worst of its effects. Air traffic had resumed, and they'd already seen a couple of passenger jets lift off from the nearby airfield. Driscoll felt a powerful temptation to climb aboard one of the great birds, settle back with a Bloody Mary, grab a few winks, find himself in Miami inside of an hour.

"So what's your problem? You like hanging out like this, pretending you're a tourist?"

Driscoll glanced down at the outfit he was wearing: matching tropical print shirt and boxer-style swim trunks, okay on a skinny guy, maybe, but in his size made him look like a jungle's worth of migrating parrots. Brisa was wearing a turtleneck that hid most of his burns and a pair of warmup pants, a pair of knockoff Fila wraparounds perched on his nose. Anybody glancing down from his hotel room at the two of them would probably think, *There's some fat-boy tourist getting himself all pimped up.*

And that'd be just fine, Driscoll thought, given they had no choice but to wait, despite what he'd heard on the phone earlier. After that, it had struck him that his stained and scorched sportcoat might just make him easy to spot. Nor did battered Ray Brisa present the image of the typical tourist.

He'd bought the clothes in the hotel's gift shop, the place being open around the clock, ready to serve any customer lucky enough to win at the never-sleeping slots and gaming tables. He might have gone for something a little more stylish, but in the end they'd made their choices from the sale rack: using plastic seemed out of the question, and he needed to keep hold of what cash he had left—there was no telling what obstacles lay ahead of them.

He'd already dropped a couple of hundred at the hospital where they'd taken Gavin, enough to turn the emergency room personnel around, get them convinced they could take a look at the man's charred backside after all. Another deuce for Gavin's cousin Cork, whom Gavin, even in his pain-addled state, had insisted they go see.

Cork, it had turned out, ran the beachfront concessions along the stretch by the Neptune. And through Cork, he'd divested himself of another four bills for the guys who were going to help them out of their present predicament, that being how to get out of Dodge. Four bills was a bargain, Driscoll thought, but Cork would only take what he called "necessary expenses," given that Driscoll had saved Gavin's life. Saved it, assuming Gavin could survive treatment at that shitheel hospital, Driscoll thought. He broke off his thoughts, rousing himself to answer Brisa's question at last.

"I'm going to like it a lot better if that bar ever opens," Driscoll said, pointing at a nearby tiki hut perched in the dunes above the beach. A bartender in a shirt even more ridiculous than Driscoll's poked about, opening and closing cooler doors, rearranging liquor bottles on shelves. "Then I'm going to have a big-ass drink and one for you, too."

Brisa looked away, out over the water that had begun to shade from slate toward blue as the sun climbed above the towers behind them. "I just think you're paranoid, man. Like maybe you watched too many spy movies or something. We could take ourselves out to the airport, give them somebody else's name, man. "

"You may be right, Ray. I'd let you go find out, but if I'm the one who is, then there wouldn't be any second chance. The guys I'm talking about get their hands on a guy, they got a way of making him share his deepest feelings."

"I just don't get it. So what, this Bailey guy don't answer his phone. Maybe he's asleep, like some normal person. Give him another shot, he ought to be up by now."

"I already left enough in the system," Driscoll said. "We'll talk to Dedric when we get home."

Brisa turned away then, clearly out of patience. He was a savvy enough kid, Driscoll thought, and whatever else he thought of Brisa, he owed him one for last night. But no matter how street smart he was, the kid couldn't be expected to appreciate the dark suspicions in Driscoll's mind.

And maybe Brisa was right, maybe it was all paranoia to think Angel Salazar was still connected the way Driscoll thought. Maybe all that weirdness on the phone meant nothing. Maybe it was the kind of thinking that was fueled by cynicism, by thirty years of viewing the inhumanity of the species at too close a range, but as Driscoll had already pointed out, there wouldn't be any second chances if his suspicions were true.

He heard powerboats in the distance then, and glanced up to see a pair of sleek racing-style boats clipping the waves a hundred yards or so offshore. The boats came abreast of the Neptune's beach, then began angling toward shore.

"Look alive," Driscoll said, nudging Brisa.

"What are you talking about?" Brisa said.

"These got to be our guys," Driscoll said. He was already pushing himself up from the table.

"Those are toy boats, man," Brisa said.

"Sometimes your bigger ships have these tender boats," Driscoll said. "Little ones take you out beyond the reef, you get on your cruiser, go where you have to go."

Brisa glanced up at him over the rim of his phony Filas, hardly convinced. Driscoll shrugged and moved off toward the wooden staircase that zigzagged down through the dunes toward the water.

By the time they hit the beach, the two powerboats had anchored just beyond the breakers. There were pilots at the wheel of each boat, while a third guy had jumped out to wade through the mild surf to shore. The guy was unfurling a banner between a wooden platform with a ramp that led down toward the water and a pole jammed into the sand several feet away when Driscoll approached.

"You want to take a ride, mahn," the guy said. It didn't sound like a question.

"Cork says we should," Driscoll responded.

The guy nodded without looking at him. "We can do that," he said. He finished tying off the banner, finally turned around. He pointed at Brisa, who stood a few feet away, studying the wording of the banner.

"How about your friend? He want a ride too?"

"Cork says we both ought to try it," Driscoll said.

"Then tell him come on," the guy said, motioning toward the anchored boats.

"You have to understand that the sanctity of the individual life is a fairly recent historical development. The concept didn't gain much force until the Renaissance," the man in the tweed coat was saying. He wore reading glasses, a closely trimmed gray beard, and sported a good haircut. He'd been identified at the outset of this *Good Morning America* segment as a professor of humanistic studies at the New School of Social Research.

Lawrence Chappelear, who sat with the President in the living area of his suite, watching the program, thought the man probably rated his own life fairly far along up the scale.

"It's something that certain cultures, our own included, value much more highly than others. To give you an idea of how these notions evolve culturally, just watch some of our own films made in the forties, when the concepts of valor and duty held so much more weight. Then try to imagine selling the American public of today on the wisdom of dying for one's country. You'd never get such a film made. We've become so much more self-oriented. Heroes perform only out of self-interest nowadays," the professor said. "Or because they're paid to."

The hosts of the program nodded as the television camera panned their faces. Charlie Gibson looked like he might be willing to take the professor on faith, but his female cohort seemed disturbed. "How much of this thinking is male-oriented?" she asked. "For instance, I can't imagine any mother anywhere, in any time, who wouldn't do anything to save the life of her child."

The professor paused. "Well," he said, "that's a good question. I doubt very much that it's women who are responsible for these atrocities."

He gave her a sympathetic look. "Do understand, the very point of terrorism is to undermine a culture's belief system, to cast doubt, to cause uncertainty."

"But for what reason?" she persisted.

The professor raised his hands. "Sometimes for no other reason than that itself," he said. "I call it the Iago Syndrome."

Charlie Gibson seemed to sense trouble. "You've been involved with the assessment of a number of hostage situations," he cut in. "What does it suggest to you that there's been no ransom, no demands, no communication of any kind since the disappearance of the First Lady?"

Chappelear stole a glance at the President, who was slumped in the side chair of the desk he'd been using, staring impassively at the monitor. He was wearing yesterday's suit, a shirt without a tie, still hadn't shaven. The look of a man coming off a weeklong bender, Chappelear thought, though he knew the man hadn't had a drink in his presence, at least.

The professor stared into the camera before he answered. His voice softened, as if he knew who was watching. "We're into our third day now. Studies tell us the prognosis becomes less optimistic the longer the passage of time," he said. "This is a rather special case, however. I'd hesitate before making any assumptions."

The President held up a remote unit, clicked *Good Morning America* into oblivion, then turned to Chappelear. "How about you, Larry? You made any assumptions yet?"

Chappelear drew himself up, a wad of the most recent reports in his hand. Much sound and fury in all these printed words, he thought. All of it come to nothing so far.

"She's still with us, sir," he said finally. "Everything I know tells me that."

The President stared back at him. "That's good, Larry," he said. He flipped the remote unit over his shoulder. It hit the corner of the desk and split open, sending its batteries flying to the floor. "You keep me away from the television now, you hear?"

Chappelear nodded. He thought he'd felt something give inside himself as well.

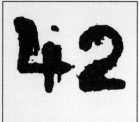

"What's left out there?"

"It's okay," Deal called down to her. "Come on, take my hand."

Her hand emerged from the darkness then, groping about, the skin pale and shriveled from the damp, her nails ragged and ringed with dirt. He fought off a wave of sadness at that sight and took her hand and pulled, bringing her blind and blinking into the light. He steadied her with his hands at her shoulders, waiting for her eyes to adjust.

"Dear God," she said at last, her voice barely above a whisper.

"You want to sit down a minute?"

She shook her head groggily, shading her eyes. The sky was still overcast, but compared with the darkness they'd been in, it seemed ablaze out here. "Where are we?" Her voice was dazed.

"The same place we were last night," he said. He sensed something of what she had to be feeling.

She turned completely around. A slow circle. He'd done the same thing himself.

"But there's nothing," she said. "Everything's gone. Everything." He heard the protest in her voice.

He nodded. She was right. It couldn't be. But it was.

Twelve hours before, they'd run for their lives up a forested trail. Now they stared down a slope that had been blasted clean, defoliated as if by a bomb blast. Here and there a shattered stump rose up a few feet into the steamy air and huge clumps of brush and uprooted trees were strewn about, but not a single tree had been left standing. The view down to the waterline was unobstructed now, but it was difficult to believe they were looking at the same place where they'd spied on men trying to save themselves and their boat the night before.

The short pier where the boat had been tied off had vanished. To the east, where there had been a house, there was nothing. When he looked closer, he could make out the vague outline of concrete footings, saw perhaps a length of white PVC piping jutting into the air, but it was a little too far away to be sure.

Behind them, where there had been the hollow of a deep vine-choked quarry site, there was now a lake, maybe two hundred feet across, filled to the brim with seawater left behind by the big wave. Where their makeshift prison had stood, there was a tumble of block and the spar of a shattered timber poking from the rubble.

The air, which was improbably calm, was sodden with humidity and sea smells. He noticed a fish on the rocky ground at his feet, a sizable grunt already bloating up in the heat. He saw another and another, and realized that the ground was littered with them, smaller fish for the most part: grunt, mullet, snapper, among those he recognized.

Here and there something larger. A silvery barracuda lay a few feet from the lake, easily four feet from tip to tail. Another couple of flops, he thought, it might have made its way to that new inland sea where it could have survived, for a little while at least.

He sensed her staggering at his side and reached out to steady her again. "I think I will sit down," she said.

He helped her to a seat on one of the boulders that had not been displaced, then sat down next to her. "There's so much sky all of a sudden," she said, glancing up.

"That's what we all said after the hurricane went through Miami," he said.

"Really?" she said. Her voice was hollow. Doing her best, he thought. Fighting that despair that threatened to explode at any second. He knew the feeling.

"You don't realize until all those trees are gone." He sat quietly, thinking how he'd felt when he'd come out of his home after Andrew, found his lifelong landscape suddenly transformed.

They sat quietly for a moment before she turned to him again. "You think we're the only ones left?" she said, glancing up at him, finally.

He gave her a look, swept his arm about. They were perched on the highest part of the island, hardly a hilltop, but enough to give them a view of what they'd inherited: a chunk of coral that jutted up out of the water, maybe a mile from east to west, half that in width. Men could hide in the tangles of trees and brush that had been left behind, he supposed, but what would they be hiding from?

"What are we going to do, John?"

He laughed mirthlessly. "I've been waiting for you to ask that question," he said.

"Then you should have some snappy answer ready for me," she said.

He nodded. "What I've been trying to do is tell myself how lucky we are. That we lived through it."

She glanced around them. "The old half-full, half-empty thing, right?"

"Something like that."

"Okay," she said. "After that, then."

"It's rule number one," he said. "You have to start off telling yourself what's positive. Otherwise . . . " He trailed off.

"If you try to tell me about all the fish we've got to eat, I'm going to scream," she said.

He nodded, tried to give her a smile.

"The weather's clearing," he said. "There ought to be search planes out soon enough."

She nodded. "I'm thirsty," she said after a moment.

"So am I," he said.

"I wish I'd thought of it last night, all that rain . . ." She broke off, staring down into the crevasse. "Maybe there's a pool down there."

He shook his head. "I thought of that earlier," he said. "It's all broken rock where we were, the water just percolated on through."

She nodded, licked her lips. "It's worse now that I mentioned it."

"I'd try to think of something else," he said.

"So tell me about these search planes," she said.

"Lots of them," he said. "Guy from the cavalry in every one."

"Uh-huh. You're thinking about something else, aren't you?" she said.

He gave what he hoped was a blank look.

"Something worse than the water," she said.

He studied her for a moment. "My wife used to do that," he said.

"Read your mind?"

He nodded. "She said I should never play poker."

"She was right," Linda told him. "You going to tell me now?"

He shrugged. "There's not much we can do about it . . . "

She thought for a moment, then recognition came over her features. "You think there are more of them somewhere, don't you?"

He shrugged again.

"You think there are people somewhere who know where we were taken, that they'll show up wanting to see what's happened."

"It's possible."

She glanced about the barren skies nervously.

"Nobody's shown up yet," he said. "Maybe that's a good sign, or maybe there's heavy weather between us and them." He shrugged. "Like I said, though, there's not too much we can do about it."

"So I should try to think about something else, is that it?"

He stood up, took a deep breath. "I was thinking maybe we could poke around a little bit." He indicated the crevasse. "All that rainwater has to go someplace," he said. "Maybe there's some kind of a spring that pops up closer to the shoreline."

"A spring?" she said doubtfully.

"Come on," he said, reaching for her hand. "It's a long shot, but that's rule number two when you've just been hammered."

"What is?" she said.

"Get off your ass and move," he said. Then started down the path.

"John Groshner must be out of his mind," the President said. He stared at Chappelear in disbelief.

Chappelear glanced down at his shoe tops. "I know how you feel, sir, but he feels it's essential. Senator Hollingsworth will be featured on every network news program this evening. Groshner got a look at some of the tape. He manages to come off as sympathetic to your personal plight, but he comes down hard on the administration in general."

Chappelear threw up his hands helplessly. "He doesn't implicate you personally, of course. But he talks about a climate of ineffectuality . . ."

"Bullshit!"

". . . the old soft-on-communism line . . ."

"This is incredible."

"He wants to be the President, sir."

"You think the American people are going to listen to such bullshit at a time like this?"

Chappelear swallowed. "They're shell-shocked, sir. Malcolm Jesse's got some figures, a small sample really, but . . ."

"But what?"

"The nation's distraught. They'll listen to anyone who can promise them nothing like this will ever happen again."

They stared silently at each other then. After a moment, the President looked away. "What in the hell would you have me do?"

Chappelear drew a breath before he spoke. "Groshner's certain he can get full network coverage. Schedule a national heart-to-heart. Present the image of a man determined . . ."

"Turn all this to my political advantage, is that what you mean?"

Chappelear ran his fingers through his hair. "The sharks are out there, Frank. Groshner's a shark. He knows how they operate."

The President closed his eyes, snorted. "Unbelievable," he said. After a moment he opened his eyes again, sighing. "But the thought of turning this government over to a man like Hollingsworth . . ." He broke off, shaking his head.

Chappelear nodded. "You want me to tell Groshner to go ahead, then?"

The President had his gaze out the window at the overcast sky, but his chin made a nearly imperceptible nod.

"I'll do it. I'll stay on top of it, sir."

Another, almost invisible acknowledgment.

Chappelear turned to leave, but hesitated, feeling the need to inject something positive into the moment. "The weather's clearing in the Caribbean, sir. We'll be able to expand our search down there today."

The President nodded again. "Let's find her, Larry," he said. He kept his eyes on the water. "Just let's, please God, find her."

"I think you need a new travel agent," Ray Brisa said, bracing himself against the boat's wild pitching. They had moved out of the shallow seas surrounding the islands, were well into what was called the Tongue of the Ocean by now.

"Next trip, I promise," Driscoll said. He checked his watch, noted that they'd been out just over an hour. According to the guy behind the wheel, who had turned out to be Cork himself, the trip would take about six hours altogether, if the weather didn't get any worse, that is.

He'd started to feel a little green himself. There were a couple small portholes in the boat's tiny cuddy cabin, but trying to see anything that way was like staring into a front-loading washer gone spastic. He was doing better keeping focused on the square of sky he could see out the hatch behind him. Not much there—the sky had gone gray again, the bland view interrupted now and then by a flash of Cork's red windbreaker fluttering back from where he stood at the wheel—but the pitch and yaw of the craft seemed lessened somewhat that way.

He found himself trying to recalibrate the odds, factor in the weather. Maybe it would knock down some of the surveillance craft, lessen the chances of a routine stop. On the other hand, wouldn't it make them that much more obvious? What kind of diehards would be out on a pleasure cruise in crud like this? Of course, the weather might clear the closer they got to the Keys . . .

. . . and on and on. He knew he was just spinning his wheels, trying to distract himself from the frustration he felt, nothing he could do until he was back on land and meantime just another sack of potatoes in the hold of a groaning boat.

"Why can't we stay on top?" Brisa asked. "We see anybody coming, we can just duck inside."

"Time we saw anybody coming, it'd be way too late, Ray," Driscoll told him. They had gone belowdecks to don the rumpled sweat clothing that Cork's mate had provided, but Driscoll thought it best that they stay out of sight now that they were approaching more isolated waters.

He'd had a look at some of the imaging technology during his last visit to Washington, cameras up in space that could just about read your watch while you walked down the street on a moonless night, and that had been a dozen years or more. Who knew what they were capable of now. Maybe x-ray vision, they could be peering down through the top deck of the boat, watching Ray Brisa hustling his balls at this very moment.

"We get back, you seen the last of me," Brisa said, noticing his gaze.

"Soon as we finish up, Ray."

"No way," Brisa said. "I did my part. You are looking at a ghost. Ray Brisa is gone from this world. I am somebody else already."

Driscoll nodded. "I thought you wanted a shot at the guys who tried to kill you."

"I took my shot," Ray said. "If they're as bad as you say, I don't need to be messing in that business."

"Too late, Ray. You already messed."

Brisa gave him his uncertain look, the one that was supposed to be a sneer. "No too late about it."

"You think they don't know who you are? You think they won't find you?"

"I'm out of town, man. I already forgot my own name. I done that before."

"You could get yourself an operation, start dancing in a titty bar, Ray. These people will find you."

The boat clipped a wavetop, landed hard in a trough. Driscoll felt the wallop from his tailbone to his neck.

"You're just guessing about all of it. So this Angel guy was a CIA spook once. Maybe he retired."

"Sure, just like if he was mobbed up, Ray. Wiseguy turns in his resignation, he gets a pension, nice little place in the country, raises flowers and volunteers for the Community Chest. You know how that goes."

Brisa sat up as straight as he could on the narrow seat that doubled as a bunk, worked his head around like a fighter. "Even if you were right, what good would it do going against guys like that? How do you expect to win?"

Driscoll nodded. He noted that the sky was darker all of a sudden. Maybe a squall to ride through. Maybe a typhoon, or was that something that only happened in another part of the world?

"I don't know, Ray," he said finally. "But it's like what happens when you find a bad dog snapping at your butt. Don't matter how fast you run, the dog's gonna get his. Only chance you got is to turn around, make your stand."

Brisa stared at him, thinking about it. The boat had evened out, Driscoll noted. He prayed it might last.

Finally Brisa nodded. "I had a buddy was taking down a fancy-ass joint over on Star Island, that very thing took place."

"Is that so."

"Yeah. Big dog came after him when he was almost at the gate, and my friend with all this loot in his arms, you know, when he hears all this slob-bering dog noise behind him."

"So what'd he do?" Driscoll asked. Outside, the rain had started, dark sheets that looked like smoke plumes peeling away in their wake.

"Like you said," Brisa told him. "Guy turned around, stared right in the bastard's eyes. Big dog, too, they were almost nose to nose."

"Then your pal backed right out the gate with his loot, huh?" Driscoll felt the boat launch itself off the top of a wave, felt like they were heading out into space.

"No," Brisa said, the engines whining, churning nothing but air beneath them now. "Dog ate his fucking face off."

"That's it for me," she said, collapsing in the sand Indian-style. Her skirt had hiked far up her legs, but she seemed not to notice.

Deal noticed, but it was only an intellectual point. She was an attractive woman, all right, but ... so much for all those stranded-on-a-deserted-island jokes. He'd trade a conga line of Penthouse pets for a jug of water right now.

She pointed out over the water to where what *looked* like a section of roof poked up from the shallows. She stared up at him, wiped sweat and grime from her face with an even grimier, more sodden sleeve. "This is where we started." She sagged back on her elbows. "Now I'm really thirsty."

Deal nodded, trying not to think about his own cottony tongue. They had been all the way around the island, found nothing but fish and more fish.

He stared out over the water at the improbable sight jutting up from the now-gentled waves: the roof he'd seen flying off Oz-like the evening before, a sizable chunk of it, at least.

"Looks like a house that went down at sea," she said.

"I wish it *was* the whole house," he told her. "Those guys had to have something inside to drink."

"A house blows away, wouldn't you think there'd be something left behind?" she asked, closing her eyes wearily. "A refrigerator, a cooler with a can of Coke, a canteen, *some*thing."

Deal wanted to remind her how cleanly the house on the windward side of the island had been lifted away. He wanted to tell her other stories, dip into his endless stock of hurricane lore. Like how he'd gone with a friend to check out what had happened to the home in far south Dade the friend had fled as Andrew had approached.

Country Walk, the name of the development. A series of wood-frame houses built by people with the instincts of the first two Little Pigs. He and the friend had had to park a mile from the development's entrance, in the middle of a six-lane boulevard blocked by deadfall, clamber over and around endless massive piles of debris, had struggled all the way past the friend's home site until they'd realized they'd reached the end of his block and had to double back. Easy enough to become disoriented, after all: not a house left standing on that street, not a wall, not a tree.

They found his friend's house by dragging away fallen limbs and studying the numbers that had been painted on the curb. And then, still disbelieving that they were on the right street, they'd walked up the sidewalk to a bare concrete pad where once a house had stood, a couple of tendrils of electrical conduit waving in the air, not a scrap of anything else left to see. Deal had had to hold the man tight to keep him from falling over—his whole world had been jerked out from under him, after all.

Not so different from what had happened here, except that he'd had the luxury of returning to civilization with his friend, stopping for an icy beer along the way. He swallowed again, turned back to Linda.

"Maybe there is something," he said, gesturing up the slope behind them. "Under a pile of bush somewhere, something behind a rock. We have to keep looking, that's all."

"Go right ahead," she said, her eyes still closed.

He stared at her for a moment, debating. Give her a pep talk, never give up, never give an inch . . . ? He shook his head finally, then turned and started up the rocky slope.

"John?"

He stopped, glanced over his shoulder. She'd pushed herself up on one hand, was staring after him, her face drawn.

"I'm just tired," she said.

"It's okay," he said. "Rest awhile."

She gave him a grateful look. "For a minute," she said.

He nodded, was about to turn away, when something caught his eye, a little blip farther out on that leeward horizon, a tiny irregularity. He shaded his eyes, squinted hard. Something there, he thought, but he wasn't quite sure.

"Linda," he called.

Whatever she heard in his voice brought her up quickly. "What?" she called, scrambling up from the sand. She hurried up the slope toward him, brushing grit away from her skirt.

"What is it?" Her voice was breathless with anticipation.

"Something in the water," he said, pointing. "I can't make it out."

She turned, scanned the horizon in the direction he indicated. "I don't see anything," she said.

He leaned over her shoulder, nudged her chin into line with his forearm. "Right out there, over the peak of the roof jutting up from the water."

"I see it," she said, her voice thick with excitement. "Something's out there."

She turned to him briefly, her face shining. "A boat," she said. "I think it's a boat."

"Maybe," he said. He turned his ear in the direction of the object, tried to catch the sound of motors.

"We have to signal them somehow." She glanced about them. "If we only had matches . . ."

"Shhh . . ." He motioned her quiet, and a stricken look came over her features.

"Oh God. You think it's *them* . . ." She'd been unbuttoning her blouse, ready to use it as some kind of flag, he supposed, but now her hands were frozen at her breast.

He shook his head. "I'm just trying to hear." He turned back toward the distant object, cupped his ear, then shifted about, tried the other. Still no sound above the gentle wash of the surf.

He glanced at whatever it was again, squinting until his eyes burned. Again he caught it, the dot swelling, becoming an oblong shape momentarily, then subsiding once more. Whatever it was, it didn't appear to be moving closer.

"I don't know," he said, as much to himself as to her. "It could be a boat, maybe someone circling around out there, but I don't hear any motors."

"Maybe the wind's blowing the sound the other way," she said.

He gave her a look. "Do you feel any wind?"

She gave him a look, then turned back to scan the horizon. "Well, maybe there's wind out there."

Deal started to respond, thought better of it.

"Maybe it's another piece of the house," she said.

He nodded. He supposed it could be more wreckage carried out by the winds. Or perhaps it was a shallow reef that barely jutted from the tide, its mass alternately rising and sinking with the waves. That would account for the swelling and shrinking, all right. But the timing seemed off for that explanation to hold.

He dropped his hands then, and started back down the slope toward the narrow stretch of beach. He had his shoes and socks off by the time he hit the sand, paused there to step out of his ruined slacks.

"What are you doing?" It was Linda at his side, her voice tight with concern.

"I'm going to swim out aways," he said, struggling out of his shirt.

"Swim?" Her voice had risen another notch. "That thing—whatever it is—is miles away."

He glanced out over the water. Nothing visible at all from this angle. "I doubt it," he said. "It's hard to judge distance over water. No points of reference."

Her expression was wild by now. "You're just going to jump in the water, leave me here? What if there are sharks, what if you drown . . . "

He tossed his shirt down atop his slacks, took her by the arms. "I'm a good swimmer," he told her. "I'm just going out far enough to get a better look."

"I'll go with you," she said.

"Linda," he said patiently, "I won't go out of your sight, I promise."

She stared at him, still uncertain.

What he saw in her eyes kindled something inside himself. He paused, drew a breath, raised his hands to her shoulders. "I won't leave you," he said, his voice softer now. "Not after all this."

She opened her mouth to say something, but the words seemed to catch somewhere inside. They stared at each other silently for a moment, and then he felt her moving toward him, felt himself lean toward her. His arms encircled her, he felt her hands on his back. They held each other without words, a spontaneous gesture that seemed to hold a long time.

Finally she stepped back, managing something of a smile. "You're really a good swimmer?"

"Fishlike," he said.

"Fishlike," she repeated. "Well, go on, fish," she said, putting a hand on his shoulder.

"I'll be back here before you know it," he said.

And then he was in the water.

**The first hundred yards** were easy, the second more like work, the third hundred downright tough. He eased off on his stroke, rolled onto his back, gave a few easy angel sweeps with his arms, raised his head up to look back toward shore.

He was well past the spot where the roof jutted up from the water now. Linda had climbed the slope to stand where he'd spotted the thing, and was waving. He lifted a hand to return the gesture, holding it until she'd seen him.

He lay on his back a moment more, waiting for his breathing to even out, waiting for the dull ache to subside in his shoulders, then flipped over finally and once again launched into his crawl, trying to notch it down just a bit, trying to settle in for the long haul.

He broke off his crawl for a moment, glancing over his shoulder to see that he'd more than doubled his distance from the shore since his last break. That was good, he thought, turning his mind from the ache in his shoulders. Put the mind on mental overdrive, let it drift to something else, let those muscles do the work. Forget the pain.

The jutting peak of the sunken roof had become a vague hump, and Linda's form had become indistinguishable. He turned back to seaward, shifting into a breaststroke that lifted his head up far enough to see over the wavetops.

He saw nothing at first, and wondered if Linda had somehow been right. Was whatever they'd seen miles away, in fact? Or had it truly been a shallow reef, one that the tide had already risen up to cover? Or maybe it had been a mirage altogether, some sign of hope born of their very desperation. His shoulders were aching now, and his breath was coming in gasps and pants. He caught a little seawater from an unexpected wave and found himself gagging suddenly, salt water and bile burning his throat and nose.

*Calm down,* he told himself. *Go on your back. A little rest. You can float all the way in if you have to.* And then he was rising up on the crest of another wave, twisted about by a swirl of current . . .

. . . and he saw it there, riding the waves out ahead, now swinging toward him with the tide, now swinging away . . .

. . . and he understood, as his aches and pains vanished in an instant and the bile that had burned his throat whisked away: He had lied to Linda Sheldon. He would not be coming right back to her. Not for a little while longer, at least. Not until he had reached what he saw lolling in the waves a hundred yards or so up ahead.

**Deal had seen** his share of displaced marine craft following Hurricane Andrew's sweep through Miami. In the backyard of one Gables by the Sea job he'd been called to, he'd found a twenty-eight-foot catamaran lifted from its nearby moorings, bobbing serenely in the homeowner's thirty-foot pool. Driving down Bayshore Drive toward Coconut Grove, he'd had to detour onto the grassy median to get around a huge shrimp boat, perfectly intact and lodged upright between a tumbled eighteen-wheeler and an uprooted banyan, all of it blocking the southbound lanes several hundred yards inland from the marina. At a home in Saga Bay, he'd given an estimate for the reconstruction of a storm-devastated house, then had gone outside with the owner to marvel at the sizable cabin cruiser lodged high in the branches of a backyard oak, a mile or more from the nearest body of water.

So what he saw now was not really beyond his ken at all: the Cigarette lay there, bow-heavy in the shallows of an outlying reef, somehow snagged and swinging to and fro with the swirling motion of the currents. He treaded water for a minute or so, waiting to catch his breath, still a few yards shoreward of the craft.

He glanced backward toward the island where he'd left Linda, but could see nothing from this vantage point. A bit too soon to get too excited, wasn't it?

He kicked himself forward, approaching the boat cautiously, even though it seemed crazy to be concerned. Still, something about the boat had spooked him. The odd way it sat in the water, perhaps, a boat on the way to full fathom five, unaccountably interrupted in its descent.

The craft swung slowly toward him, and he found himself close enough to touch the portside hull now. Deal saw the line that was holding the boat, pulled taut by the current, disappearing into the water a few feet from where he floated. He made his way around the prow, caught the line in one hand, then took a breath. He upended himself and dove down, using the rope as a guide.

The water was murky, but by the time he'd pulled himself a dozen feet under, he felt his hand strike something hard and bulky. He steadied himself, running his hands over the object, felt shards of wood, then a huge chunk of concrete. The line was tangled fast to a piece of one of the pilings, he realized as he released himself and churned back toward the surface. That was what had finally stopped her. Otherwise the boat would probably be in Key West by now.

He came up, caught another breath, then dove directly under the boat this time, using his hands to probe the hull for damage. He moved backward along the shadowy hull, from bow to stern, then forward and back again, finding a scrape here, a gouge there, but nothing that indicated serious damage, on that half of the boat at least.

He came up for air, went back under to find the twin props and their outdrives still seemingly intact, then worked his way forward, checking the port side of the hull this time. He made a couple more passes before he was satisfied that all was intact below the waterline, then swam back to the stern and levered himself up over the broad transom.

He rolled on his side, then flopped over into the cockpit and landed in a crouch, his hands splayed on the roughened surface. He found himself breathing heavily as he stared about the empty space, his back jammed against the motor compartment as if he were still awaiting an all-out assault . . . the cabin door bursting open, a hoard of assassins piling onto the tiny deck space.

But no one came, of course. He stared at the motionless cabin door, the wheel that yawed with a ghostly motion of its own as the currents worked the outdrives. Not even the sounds of water sloshing on the deck, for this was one of those self-bailing cockpits, with ports that allowed for the runoff, and, with luck, a tight seal that would keep serious water from belowdecks.

He pulled himself up by the wheel, found that he could make out the island once again. He massaged his aching shoulders, checked the angle of the sun, guessed he still had a few hours of light. He wished desperately that there was a way to signal Linda.

Maybe there was a flare pistol down below, he thought. He moved quickly to the cabin door, found the heavy, nickel-plated hasp and sprung it, then pulled the door open. He started down the steps quickly, but stopped when he felt his foot plunge into water.

Watertight deck or not, the cabin below had been swamped. Either there was a breech in the hull that he'd missed in his cursory examination, or the deck seals had proven less than hurricane-proof. He paused, twisted around in the narrow passage to glance toward the aft engine compartments. Another sealed setup, but if the bilge area had been swamped as well, he could forget all his hopes.

Deal sent a silent prayer skyward, then moved toward the engine compartments. He undid the hasps, folded back the starboard engine cover, glanced down into darkness. He fought the urge to simply thrust his hand down there, see what he might find, instead turned and threw back the opposite cover. A shimmering oily mirror that threw a dim shadow up from the bilge—his own silhouette reflected in water down there, he realized.

He bent over, shielding his eyes against the glare from the sky, and peered into the recesses of the compartment. Not as bad as he'd thought at first, though. He could see the engines—twin 454s, probably, most of their bulk jutting up above the water that had leaked into the compartment: From this angle he could see that it was no more than a foot, maybe not that much. Had those cylinders gotten submerged, he'd be out of luck.

All that water in the forward compartment had been a blessing after all, he thought. The weight of it had levered the stern higher, reversed the normal slant of the craft, helped keep the engines out of the water.

Most important, though, would be the batteries. He lowered his shoulders all the way into the engine well, twisted his head.

There, in the forward part of the compartment, he found them. Four big marine batteries, two for each engine. The forward member of each pair was half-submerged and a third looked to have had one of its terminal cables ripped free. But the fourth battery was wedged atop its twin, well out of the water, its cables intact.

Deal pulled his head up, reeling from the pressure of his inverted position. He waited for his dizziness to pass, then went to the control panel and undid the catch. He raised the cover, found the ignition key still in its protected niche. Most boaters would have done the same, especially if they were tied up on a private dock where a bunch of guys with Uzis were keeping an eye on things. He glanced up to check the angle of the sun, thought once again of Linda Sheldon, then bent to study the controls.

He checked and double-checked, making sure that nothing was switched on but the engine compartment bilge pump—he couldn't take the chance of wasting one speck of power, after all. He closed his eyes again, and turned the master key. When he heard the whine of the pump from behind him, he felt his breath go out in a rush. First problem taken care of . . . if the battery held out, that is.

He listened to the steady whine of the pump for a few moments, then turned back to the cabin hatchway. Back down the narrow passageway: feet, legs, groin, one quick gasp of air and then under the tepid water. He groped about, found a door on his right, realized it led to the tiny head.

He pulled himself up for another breath, then went under again, this time finding another doorway. He yanked it open, felt objects float out about him like some colony of strange sea creatures. Something descended softly onto the top of his head, sending its long tendrils over his face, and he clawed at it, his heart racing again, until he realized it was only a mop. He shrugged the thing away, dug his hands inside the closet, felt the lip of a plastic bucket, jerked it past the frame, and surfaced with it.

He rested until his breathing had evened out, then pulled himself up into the cockpit, bringing his precious bucket along with him. He stood, listened to make sure the bilge pump was still going. Then he glanced about until he'd found the hump of the island again.

Nothing to do but go to work. He emptied the bucket overboard, then leaned down the stairwell, dipped it full again. Water seemed to ooze from everywhere, a new bucketful for every one he dumped, and for a while he wondered if there weren't some hole up on deck that was sending what he bailed right back down again. But finally he was sloshing about the cabin in ankle-deep water.

He tossed another bucket of water up out of the cabin and lay his head against one of the steps in exhaustion. When he felt that he could move again, he tossed his plastic bucket aside and moved toward the tiny refrigerator he'd had his eye on. He pulled open the door, which did not quite clear the water, sending a small wave up his shins.

No light popped on, of course, but a rancid smell lifted toward him and he caught sight of something—a chunk of fish or a days-old sandwich, wadded at the back of an otherwise empty shelf. He was about to slam the door shut in disgust when he heard a tinkling sound and glanced at the door rack, which hung partly submerged in the water. Something tumbled over there, two somethings, he realized. His hand was trembling when he thrust it into the murky water.

He came up with a small bottle of juice on his first pass, found a similar container with the second. *JUGO DE PAPAYA,* the gelatinous label read. He lay one of the bottles carefully in the now-dry sink above the refrigerator, took the other and wedged the cap against the counter. He hit the top so hard it sheared a chunk of wood and formica off the counter's edge, but the cap popped off as well.

He forced himself to wait a moment, then raised the bottle to his lips. One swallow, two, three . . . he willed himself to stop, lower the bottle while the warm, sticky juice went down his throat. Right now, *jugo de papaya* tasted just wonderful. He raised the bottle, finished the rest. He thought about drinking the second, but he forced the impulse away. Even if the boat didn't start, even if all he brought back to Linda Sheldon from this expedition was one bottle of papaya juice, she would have that much, at least.

He wiped the back of his hand against his lips, then willed himself up out of the compartment and across the cockpit to check the progress of the bilge pump.

He moved across the tiny deck space in a crabwalk that was the result of his endless bailing crouch, ducked his head inside to find that the engine compartment was dry now, or virtually so. He stood, then moved stiffly to switch off the pump. With the cabin and bilge bailed out, the bow of the boat had risen considerably. The stern had swung around to the south, and the Cigarette had its prow raised toward the distant island like some water hound eager for the word to go.

He glanced back at the engine compartment and hesitated. "What the hell," he said, and turned to throw the starter switch. The first engine coughed, then caught hold. When he tried the switch for the second, there was a weak grinding sound, a second echo, then nothing.

He released the switch, hanging his head with frustration, with exhaustion. Only the battery that had powered the bilge pump was providing any current in this circuit, he suspected, and in its worn-down state, there simply wasn't enough juice left to kick the motor over. With only one engine, they'd have to move at near-idle speed. And if they encountered any heavy weather, well . . .

He sighed, went back to the engine compartment, eased himself down, groped about until he found the ripped cable, used it to pull himself toward the disabled battery again. He got his hand around the battery casing, managed to tilt the heavy thing until he could jam the two broken ends together. He pushed and twisted, doing his best to tangle the wires into some kind of bond, but it was hopeless. The minute he released his grip on the battery casing, the whole thing fell back into its place again, breaking the tenuous connection.

He hung upside down like some distraught circus performer for a moment, his hands dangling free, the blood thundering in his temples. Finally he swung himself up again, made his way dizzily to the control panel. Again, he twisted the starter switch. Again the weak, reluctant grinding. He released the spring-loaded starter, stood thinking for a moment.

He shook his head as if to negate the thought that had occurred to him, but it was really more a gesture of resignation. Get down to the short strokes in such a situation, there wasn't really such a notion as choice. You'd have to try anything.

He climbed back down into the soggy cabin, kicked about the murky water until his toes cracked against the handle of the mop that had fallen on him earlier. He pulled the thing up, wrung some of the filthy water out of its head, pulled himself back on deck.

Back at the panel now. Pulling out gelatinous mop strings until he found one that wouldn't part. Tying that string around the starter switch. He twisted the starter until it engaged, then eased the mop head out of his hands.

The idea was to let the weight of the sodden mop hold the spring-loaded starter in the engaged position. And it seemed to work just fine.

He waited for a few extra seconds, listening to the groaning starter, then hurried back to the engine compartment. He would have liked a pair of linesman's pliers, or a rubber glove, or anything dry. But that was a laugh, wasn't it? He hesitated, then peeled out of his soggy briefs, wadded them in his hand.

He ducked carefully into the engine compartment, peered about until he caught sight of the parted cable. He reached out, cupped the battery, pulled it hard toward him. He gritted his teeth, arranged the briefs one last time, then reached out for the waving cable and jammed it against the matching end that sent its little copper tentacles out from the terminal.

The jolt flung his head back as if he were the heavy bag and some fighter had planted the last, best shot of a hateful workout squarely on his forehead. Before he'd even had time to register the pain, the recoil sent him forward, bouncing his face off a housing flange.

But it didn't matter that his head was icy with pain or that he was spitting blood between his broken lips, because he'd held his grip until the arcing current had melted the copper strands, fusing the cable together— and the roaring that had sprung up in his ears was coming from the second of those mighty engines only inches from his nose.

He pulled himself out of the engine compartment, gasping, fell back against the wheel housing, feeling the numbness gradually leaving his hands, feeling the irregular beat of the engines shuddering through the hull. Finally, something going his way, he thought as he managed to pull his grimy briefs back on. Just maybe there was a way out yet.

Hardly had he thought this than there came a loud bang, followed by a series of farting sounds. He froze, listening.

One of the engines clearing moisture grudgingly, the pistons cranky, but, thank God, continuing to fire. Blue smoke puffed up from the waterline at the transom, and he glanced toward the island-smudge on the horizon, wondering if it were something that Linda might possibly see.

He hurried back to the control panel, worked the mop head off the starter switch. He worked the throttles delicately, fighting the urge to call out to the engines, beg them to behave.

There was another bout of coughing and farting, then he was able to work the pair into a rough but steady idle. "That's it, boys," he found himself murmuring. "Good work. Just hold tight now."

He glanced nervously at the engine compartment, then hoisted himself up on the foredeck of the boat and made a quick crabwalk out to the prow cleat where the line still held them tied.

He pulled against the line to create some slack, then slung it free with the quick motions of his wrist that he had learned as a child. His old man would have been pleased, he thought. Lots of good boat work, Johnny boy. Maybe he was watching right now, sipping from a bourbon and branch and nodding approval.

Deal found himself glancing skyward as he made his way quickly back toward the cockpit. They were drifting free now, but that meant new danger, didn't it? Shallow reefs here, after all. That was what had hung the boat up in the first place.

If he ran aground, all the effort would be for nothing. He cast a nervous glance out over the water, which was beginning to lose its differentiating hues as the sky darkened, then jumped down into the cockpit and took the wheel. He gave the engines some throttle, holding his breath against another failure, then steadied the nose of the boat toward that distant hump on the horizon.

"Stay the course," he called into the wind that was gathering against his face now, edging the throttle more. *No new disasters now, Johnny Deal.* "Just stay the course."

"This look like someplace you know?" It was Cork, helping Driscoll out of the cramped cuddy cabin where he'd spent the past five hours with Brisa. The latter had gone blissfully off to sleep the moment he'd finished with his story of the flesh-eating Doberman, leaving Driscoll to a contemplation of his dour thoughts, a stomach that seemed constantly on the verge of emptying itself, and Brisa's racheting snores, which carried clearly even above the roar of the engines.

Driscoll got his stiff legs under him, turned to glance ahead at the huge mass of land that rose above the western horizon like some unlikely volcano. With its bulk silhouetted by the setting sun, it seemed as if it could be a volcano, but in fact it was nothing of the sort. "Mount Trashmore," Driscoll muttered, and Cork nodded. It was an enormous aboveground dump that had been given its name by local residents amused by the status of the pile as by far the highest landmass south of Orlando. Though he couldn't see them at this distance, it was a place well favored by enormous flocks of gulls and the eternally circling buzzards who'd turned up in Florida from all corners of the country to find the graveyard of their dreams.

"We'll go in here, then?" Cork said.

"That'd be best," Driscoll said. He could see the first of the channel markers a few hundred yards ahead. A mile or so from land, he thought. One hundred and seventy-nine down, one to go. So why was he so worried?

"We could go on up to Matheson," Cork said. "Or Coconut Grove. The River if you want."

The Miami River, Cork meant. Not really a river at all, but a deadwater estuary that bisected the central city. Driscoll glanced at Cork, admiring his balls, if not his good sense. "Too many of the wrong kind of people around those places, Cork. This'll do just fine."

Cork nodded. "Okay, then."

They'd come across the Straits of Florida on what Cork called the Gulf Stream Freeway, the most heavily traveled pleasure craft lane in the Caribbean. It was a straight heading from Chub Cay, where they'd broken out of the weather, to the mainland, and it had taken them a little over four hours in the twenty-eight-foot craft. He might have saved them another thirty minutes or so, Cork had explained, but running the twin

350s at maximum would have halved the engine life. The things had been bored and tuned, capable of exceeding sixty knots in an emergency, but they'd lucked out and Cork needed to get back home without stopping to rebuild his engines. You had to save top end for outrunning the visible law.

That was fine, Driscoll had assured him. What was a half hour, more or less.

They were well into the channel now, the engines cut way back, a couple of open fishermen passing them on the way out for some evening angling, or maybe just a run to see the skyline or southward to Alabama Jack's for a beer and burger dinner at bayside. Sure, Driscoll thought, he could remember the part of life where you simply did things for pleasure. He'd done it himself, though it seemed about a hundred years ago now.

The other boaters had passed them with bland glances or the typical boater-to-boater wave, the water being the last place in South Florida where such folksiness still prevailed. No shots across their bow, no helicopters swooping down. So far so good, but still he would have to be careful.

The channel had narrowed considerably by now, swinging northward to parallel a long scrub-covered jetty that ran for a mile or more into where the sprawling Black Point Marina lay. It was a county-owned park with a huge dry storage facility, public docks, restaurant and concessions plunked down in a mangrove and pine wilderness shadowed by the hulking landfill a mile or so further inward. Driscoll knew the area well, for it was an area greatly favored by miscreants coming ashore. Too much wild country for law enforcement to cover, even if you'd been tipped that there was a load of dope or rafters or weapons landing there.

Driscoll checked the channel up ahead, saw nothing coming their way. There was a big right turn up there a few hundred yards, the part of the channel where they'd have to swing northward, idle the last quarter-mile to the docks. He put his hand on Cork's shoulder, gestured at the jetty boulders a few feet on their right.

"Any way you can put off here?"

Cork gave him a look. "Don't have to worry about me, man. I'll take you on in."

"I'm not worried about you," Driscoll said. There was a pause and Cork nodded, his eyes dead ahead now. "But if you could get us ashore here without messing up your boat . . ."

Cork looked at him again. "No problem," he said. "Go get your man."

Driscoll, who was about to duck down into the tight cuddy cabin, found

Ray Brisa crouching at the entrance. "End of the line?" Brisa said, looking up at him.

"That wouldn't be my choice of words," Driscoll said. "But this is where we get off."

Brisa nodded, came stiffly up on deck. Cork had cut the engines back to idle, now was throttling one into reverse, swinging them expertly toward a spot where the jumble of coral slabs dumped as a breakwater had formed a kind of shelf. Cork's man was at the prow of the boat, gaff in hand.

The man thrust the gaff forward then, hooking the corner of one of the boulders. Cork turned to Driscoll. "There you go," he said simply.

Driscoll nudged Brisa toward the rail of the boat. Brisa put one foot up, glanced back at Driscoll. "How deep's this water here?"

"Jump before I push you," Driscoll said. Brisa gave him a last glance, then raised his other foot and jumped. He hit the rugged breakwater on all fours, was clambering up toward the screen of mangroves as Driscoll turned to Cork. "I owe you one, pal," he said.

"Don't owe me nothing," Cork said, his face expressionless.

Driscoll handed him a card. "I hope Gavin's okay," he said. "You let me know if there's anything I can do."

Cork nodded. "Boat coming," he said, nodding toward the bend in the channel.

Driscoll glanced ahead, saw the prow of a cabin cruiser nosing its way into the channel. He gave Cork a wave, then hoisted himself onto the rail and followed Brisa's lunge onto solid ground.

Deal could see her from a quarter-mile or more away: the tiny figure waving his shirt for a beacon, her shape growing more and more distinct until finally he could make out her anxious features. She stood on the slope beside one of the deadfalls, her hands clasped now, intent on his approach. He passed the prow of the sunken roof, cut the engines back to idle, swung the boat into a steady broadside perhaps thirty feet out from where the waves lapped placidly against the reef-protected shore.

He ducked inside the cabin for the prized bottle of *jugo de papaya*, came back up to find her still watching from her place on the rocky slope. He held up the bottle with a grin, then vaulted over the side, landing chin-deep in the silty water.

He slogged as fast as he could manage through the shallows, holding the bottle toward her like a trophy, giddy with exhaustion, with his success. When he stumbled onto the shore, he found her still on the slope above, staring down at him with a wary expression.

"You believe it?" he called, sweeping his arm toward the Cigarette. "We're out of here, dammit . . ."

He came up the rocky slope toward her, thrusting the bottle toward her like some knight errant home from the quest. "Their boat," he said, unable to wipe his grin away. "It was their fucking boat, hung up on the reef out there. The one those guys were trying to tie off . . ."

"John," she said, shaking her head, her face a ruin.

He couldn't fathom her reaction. He'd come back with sweet nectar to drink, a mechanical steed to carry them home, its engines rumbling anxiously over his shoulder. What on earth could be wrong?

He stopped, glanced down at himself, at his filthy briefs, gave her a look that was meant to pass for a loopy apology. "Hey," he said. "I'm sorry I'm not dressed . . ."

She was still shaking her head when he heard the voice behind him, felt the press of steel at the base of his neck. The juice slipped from his hands and shattered on the coral at his feet. Sticky nectar slithered down his calves.

"Very, very carefully, Mr. Deal," the familiar voice intoned. "Step forward, now."

Deal did as he was ordered, his eyes still on Linda's distraught face.

"I'm sorry, John," she said, her voice strained. "He came ashore on the other side while I was watching for you. I didn't hear him until . . ."

Deal started to turn, felt something clip him above the ear. He staggered forward, went down on his hands and knees against the rock. He steadied himself on all fours for a moment, waiting for the static filling his head to clear. He felt Linda kneeling at his side, felt her hands at his sides. He could still hear the idling engines of the Cigarette, but they seemed to come from miles away.

"Are you all right?" she asked.

Deal managed a nod, looked past his shoulder at the blurry shadow standing there. The shape swelled into utter fuzziness, then congealed into the form of a man. A very tall man with handsome features. He seemed to be leaning on something—a stick, a makeshift crutch—and there was also a pistol in his hand.

"He can stand if I tell him to stand," Angel said mildly. He waved the pistol in their direction.

"Stand," he said after a moment.

Deal turned away from Angel. Linda lay her cheek against his back, her arms tight about him. A gunshot sounded and hot shards of rock blew against his ribs. Linda flinched, but her grasp grew tighter.

"I gave you permission to *stand*," Angel repeated.

"I'm so sorry, John," she whispered.

"It's not your fault," he said, struggling to his feet.

He stood, helped her up, turned to face Angel. The man had been hurt, Deal realized. Blood soaked a circle beneath his shoulder, and he leaned heavily against the branch he'd fashioned into a cane. But his other hand held the pistol steadily upon them.

"I'm glad you came in, my friend," Angel said. He was trying to maintain his smile, but it seemed difficult.

Deal stared at him. "You thought I wouldn't?"

Angel coughed and winced, giving a little sideways step. When Deal leaned forward, Angel lifted the pistol on a line with his chin. "The woman tried to convince me you had abandoned her, that you had gone for help," he said. His smile grew again, though there seemed a shadow behind his eyes.

"Noble of her, wouldn't you say? I reminded her that we both knew better. You are a hero, after all." He tried a bitter laugh, but the sound dissolved into a gargling, wracking cough.

Deal wanted to go for him, but the pistol stayed level at his chin.

"You need a doctor," Deal said.

Angel nodded. "I have been told that before," he said, his smile flickering back.

"You should put the gun down."

Angel nodded, looking at Linda now. "Spoken like a champion, no? Too bad we have no medals here. You could drape him with his proper laurels before he dies."

"Stop it," she cried. "No one has to die "

Angel fired again, and Deal felt scalding splinters of rock on his bare legs. *A hero,* he thought bitterly. *Sure. A hero with his pants down . . .*

Then it registered.

"How'd you find out?" Deal asked.

"Find out?" Angel said, wiping at his chin. His eyes seemed glassy for a moment, but regained focus quickly.

"You thought I was Secret Service, some kind of government security," Deal said. "That's why you took me along in the first place."

Angel paused for a moment. Thinking, perhaps, or waiting for a wave of pain to subside. Then, the tolerant shake of the head, that all-knowing smile.

He held up his hand, displaying the watch he'd taken from Deal days earlier. "I told Chappelear about you. The idiot informed me as to who you really were." He shrugged. "I thought about killing you then, but there was no urgency, was there?"

Deal heard Linda gasp. "Chappelear?" she repeated. "Larry Chappelear? You've spoken with him?"

Angel glanced at her. "For a number of years now."

Deal felt her hands tightly on his arm, but he kept his eyes on Angel. One moment, one slip, that's all he prayed for.

"What do you mean . . . ?" Linda was saying, her voice faltering. "Who are you? Who are the people you work for?"

"He works for us," Deal said, breaking in. "Isn't that right, Angel?"

Angel glanced back at Deal, something like amusement on his face. "Good with his hands, a good mind as well," Angel said. He turned back to Linda.

"Lawrence Chappelear and I have done business for years. As Mr. Deal suggests, one might even say that I work for your husband."

"My husband would never . . ." she said, starting toward him. Angel raised the pistol menacingly, and Deal pulled her back.

"Your husband is a politician," Angel said. "He needed the support of Jorge Vas, and Angel Salazar provided a way to get it."

"Angel Salazar? That's you?" Deal repeated.

Salazar shrugged, wincing, then continued. "I am a practical man. I approached Chappelear and explained how an incident could be staged that would bring these votes . . . "

"An *incident*?" Linda cried. "You call that massacre an *incident*?"

"Not what your Chappelear had in mind, I will grant you. But by then there were other considerations,"

"What are you talking about?" Linda seemed dazed by it all.

Salazar kept his gaze on Linda. "Your husband's true plans were discovered, I'm afraid."

"What plans?"

"Frank Sheldon is a mediocre politician, I will grant you. But he knew that opening relations with Cuba would give him a place in the history books."

"You're insane," she said. "Frank's been interested in normalizing relations, but . . . "

"No need to dissemble, Mrs. Sheldon. The issue, shall we say, is a dead one."

"But . . . "

"You found yourself another player," Deal cut in. "Is that what happened?"

Salazar simply smiled.

"Someone who wanted to short-circuit this business of normalizing relations with Cuba once and for all," Deal said, glancing at Linda.

"And who would that be?" Salazar asked, his grin teasing.

"Any number of people, Jorge Vas included," Deal said. "But I can't imagine anyone who'd authorize the things that you did."

Salazar shrugged. "The task was mine to accomplish. I did what was required to accomplish it."

"Work both sides of the street, screw them both," Deal said.

"I know what is necessary . . . "

"You're insane," Linda cried.

"I am *efficient*," Salazar snapped back. "The world has become inured to *incidents*. It gobbles them up with its corn flakes each morning. What I have accomplished will stand for years."

"Keep all the bad blood flowing," Deal nodded. "That ought to be good for the mercenary business."

Salazar nodded. "And you will help me, Mr. Deal."

"Not a chance," Deal said.

Salazar waved his weapon dismissively. "That the First Lady die was always a foregone conclusion," Deal heard Linda's intake of breath, but Salazar went on unconcerned. "That her work seem the work of leftists was another." He paused. "But imagine, what if she were to be slain by one of the so-called heroes she had come to honor? What if it should be discovered that this ultimate honorable man should have conspired in such perfidy?"

"You're not human," Linda said, her voice calm, her jaw thrust, her eyes fierce.

Salazar kept his eyes on Deal. "Chaos is the norm, Mr. Deal. It is my purpose to remind those who pretend otherwise." He glanced momentarily at the sky, then gestured with his pistol. "Now, stand a bit closer together, if you don't mind," he said. "We are beginning to lose our light."

True, Deal thought. The light *was* nearly gone, the sky shading from gunmetal to charcoal, the slight breeze cooling ever so slightly. The time of day he normally cherished most, when the light softened and all things slid toward the flip side of being . . .

. . . when you'd like to take a drink in hand and stroll about the grounds, any grounds, and dream that there is an order that prevails, that all things are forgiven and that tomorrow will be the golden day. Now a lunatic had appeared to wipe such thoughts away. Maybe it was a suitable enough time to die, he thought. At least as good as any.

And then the explosion came. Just another bubble of water vapor in the Cigarette's fuel line, really. But enough to send one of the finely tuned engines into a startling backfire that rang across the water like a gunshot. Enough to send Angel's head swiveling about in alarm.

Deal leaped forward, bringing his fist around hard, but trying to keep control. Aim was what was important, after all.

He knew he'd been putting on weight, up until the last few days, at least. Even with what he might have lost in dehydration, he figured he had to be carrying around 210, 215. Add that to the force of coming downhill, the frustration, the hatred, the desperation that was behind the punch, it would have had its effect on anyone, anyplace it struck.

But Deal had his sights on the stain spreading down Angel's chest: gunshot wound, stab site, whatever. His fist splatted into the center of that sticky circle, and Angel screamed and flew backward off the shelf where he'd been standing. He was airborne for most of the distance, but struck the rocky ground before he tumbled into the water, losing his grip on the pistol.

Deal was over the rocks and on him before he could come up from the shallows. He drove another uppercut to Salazar's injured shoulder, and the man went back into the water with a groan.

Deal fell upon him, his arm locked about Salazar's neck, forcing his head under, grinding his face into the sand. Salazar thrashed violently, managed one gasp of air, but Deal fell back upon him, digging his heels to lever them toward deeper water. Salazar flung himself about frenziedly now, but his movements were panicked, lacking any focus. Deal sucked a breath of air and pulled them both to the bottom, his arm locked about Salazar in desperation. *Whatever it takes*, he thought. *Whoever comes up . . .*

Finally he felt an explosion of bubbles at his side, a last spasm, and then all was quiet. He rose to the surface, pulled Salazar's inert form up by the hair.

"Sonofabitch!"

It was Linda Sheldon, her face wild, struggling through the shallows toward them. She had the pistol clutched in her hands, was sobbing now.

"Bastard," she cried, steadying the pistol, bringing it an inch from Salazar's face. "Bastard," she repeated. Her sobs shook her body now.

Deal pushed the pistol aside, let Salazar drop into the shallows, put his arm about her heaving shoulders. "We've got a better use for him," he said.

She glanced up at Deal, uncertain. He took the pistol from her hands, pulled Salazar up by his hair once more, and moved them on toward shore.

"You want to try and step a little more lively there, Ray?"

Driscoll stood with his hands on his hips, watching Brisa struggling down the path toward him. He felt something sting the back of his neck, swatted at it reflexively. He inspected his palm, found a dark speck that had been a mosquito, a smear of red beside it the size of a quarter. If he'd waited any longer to nail the thing, he might have fainted from loss of blood.

They had bypassed the marina complex, keeping to the heavily wooded canal bank opposite the buildings. There was an old utility road there, nearly overgrown now, but still used as a hiking trail, primarily by non-boat-owning fishermen willing to walk the two or three miles out the levee for some form of access to deeper channels. Driscoll had been on the road a couple of times before, but he hadn't been after fish. Not the marine variety, anyway.

He'd had to shoot a man in these woods once, a guy who'd promised to come out of his boat with his hands up, and had done so . . . though there was a pistol held in one of them as well. Not a memory Driscoll treasured. He'd had no choice, and yet he had been holding the man when he died.

Brisa, in the meantime, had caught up, stood panting beside him, his hands braced on his knees. Driscoll pushed his memories away, stared at his unlikely companion. "You must be about thirty years younger than me, Ray. You're starting to make me feel in shape."

Brisa glanced up at him. "I got a serious injury here. You ever stop to think about that?"

Driscoll shrugged. "How is it a burn on your ass affects your ability to walk?"

"Forget it," Brisa said. "I don't like talking to you."

"I really can't blame you," Driscoll nodded. "Come on, we got to get out of here before it gets dark. The bugs'll carry us off."

Brisa fell wearily into step behind him. "I saw a restaurant the other side of the canal back there. There's gotta be a phone. Why don't we just go call ourselves a cab?"

"Because I came too far already to chance getting picked up now," Driscoll said.

"You're paranoid, I'm telling you. Nobody gives a shit about you and me."

"Uh-huh," Driscoll said, bending to avoid a gnarly pine limb that drooped across the path. He judged there to be another mile or so through the brush. Then a series of housing developments, maybe another mile or so out to Old Cutler Road. They'd find a strip mall, he'd feel safe enough using a phone out there. He was about to turn and tell Brisa something of the sort when he sensed movement in the dim shadows ahead. Something in his cop's radar told him what was coming even before he heard the voice.

"You two hold it, right where you are." It was a deep voice, authoritative, calm. Not a trigger-happy voice, Driscoll thought.

"Aw, man," Brisa groaned, bumping into Driscoll's backside.

Driscoll lifted his hands slowly, spoke without turning. "Just do what you're told," he said.

Two uniformed cops were coming out of the underbrush toward them now, one on either side of the trail. "Keep those hands high," the cop who'd spoken first was saying. He had his service revolver drawn, but held it casually at his side. His partner, younger, advanced in some kind of step he must have seen on a television cop show, his pistol braced in both hands. Driscoll heard a helicopter rattling somewhere not far away.

"Tell that kid to ease off," Driscoll said.

"Oh yeah?" the older cop said warily. "And why should I?"

"Because it's *me*," Driscoll said.

The older cop stopped, found a flashlight, snapped it on. He waved it over Driscoll's face quickly, then snapped the beam off.

"Hell if it isn't you," the cop said.

"What's going on?" the younger cop said. He'd stopped a dozen feet away from Driscoll and Brisa, still had his pistol braced.

"It's Vernon Driscoll," the older cop said. If it meant anything to the younger cop, he didn't show it. The older cop holstered his sidearm. "Who's your friend, Vernon?"

"You mind if I put my hands down, Emmeling?"

The older cop looked surprised. "Oh," he said, smiling. "Sure, go ahead, long as he keeps his up." He pointed at Brisa, who scowled in return.

Vernon worked his shoulders for a moment. "This is Ray Brisa," he told Emmeling. Driscoll paused, glanced at Brisa. "Just somebody lending me a hand on a piece of business."

Brisa might have relaxed a bit at that, but he still seemed ready to go off any second. Maybe the young cop had good instincts, Driscoll thought.

Emmeling, meantime, was nodding affably, as if they were two old pals who had just bumped into one another at the supermarket. "I heard you went into the rent-a-cop business," he said.

Driscoll noticed that the younger cop had taken a step back, still had his pistol trained upon them. Emmeling glanced over, shrugged. "Kid's wrapped a little tight," he said. "So what are you doing down here, running through the woods?"

Driscoll hesitated. He'd known Bert Emmeling for more than twenty years. Emmeling wasn't the brightest, most ambitious cop, but he was honest and dependable. "I just got off a boat," he said, nodding behind them. "I wasn't sure who might be hanging around the marina, so we put in up the breakwater a bit."

Emmeling shook his head, turned to his partner. "That something?" he said. The younger cop's expression didn't suggest whether he thought it was something or not.

"What are you doing down here yourself, Bert?"

Emmeling turned back to Driscoll. "Surveillance," he said. "The feds had a tip a couple of guys might be coming in." He gestured upward where another helicopter was racing overhead, a search beacon spearing down through the gloom from its belly. "They never gave us any names, though." Emmeling peered at him through the gathering darkness. "Are *you* our guy, Vernon?"

Driscoll thought there was honest curiosity in Emmeling's voice.

"You want me to call in?" the younger cop said.

"Listen, Bert," Driscoll said. "Before you do anything, I want you to call Dedric Bailey, tell him . . ."

"Dedric Bailey?" Emmeling cut in, his voice rising. "You haven't heard?"

Driscoll felt his knees give ever so slightly. He glanced at Brisa, then back at Emmeling. "Heard what?"

"He got killed this morning."

"Killed?" Driscoll felt his heart beginning to race.

"Car wreck. Poor bastard been up all night, was on his way home, drove right into a canal out that way, is how I got it." Emmeling glanced through the screen of trees at the waterway beside them, shaking his head. "Must've fallen asleep," he said.

Driscoll felt himself sag, felt his breath leave him in a sigh. The prospect of explaining to Emmeling what was racing through his mind was impossible.

"Anyways," Emmeling said, "you can just come along with us now.

We'll take you out to the command post they got set up, you can get you a ride to wherever you're going." He turned toward the young cop, had to duck away from the still-upraised pistol. "What the hell are you doing, son? Put that gun down."

The young cop faltered, lowered the pistol. He was looking at Emmeling, about to say something, when Driscoll gave Brisa a nod. "Get that gun now," he said as Brisa moved past him in a blur.

Driscoll swung about, burying his elbow in Emmeling's solar plexus. The big cop's breath exploded from him in a *whoosh*. He went down, doubled over, his hands clutching his gut. Driscoll had Emmeling's sidearm out of its still-unfastened holster before the man could respond.

He heard a thudding sound behind him, turned to see Brisa standing over the young cop, the cop's pistol in Brisa's upraised hand. The cop was rolling about on the ground, groaning, his hands holding his head. "That's enough, Ray," Driscoll said.

Brisa glanced back, uncertain. "Get his cuffs for me," Driscoll ordered. He bent down beside the still-gasping Emmeling then. He got Emmeling's cuffs off his belt, snapped one around the cop's meaty wrist, then pulled his arm around a nearby tree trunk. When Emmeling pulled feebly back, Driscoll jammed the barrel of the service revolver against Emmeling's cheek.

"It's nothing personal, Bert," Driscoll said, snapping the other cuff, "but I can't go with you right now."

Emmeling was half sitting, half leaning, his arms thrown around the tree as if he'd fallen in love with it. He was trying to say something, but he still hadn't caught his breath and only strangled gasps came out. His eyes were another story, however. Pure hatred there.

"I'm sorry I can't explain it to you," Driscoll said. "I'm gonna look you up after this over, give you a free shot, any way you want to take it. You'll know why I did it, okay?"

Emmeling turned, as if Driscoll's words were too insulting to bear. And Driscoll could understand. He'd never laid hands on a fellow officer, and even though he was off the force for years now, what he'd just done shamed him. He'd known crooked cops himself. He knew what was going through Emmeling's mind right now. He shook his head, reached into his pocket, found his handkerchief, which he used to gag his old pal, the cop.

He pushed himself to his feet, glanced at where Brisa was working with the other one. The young cop's cap had fallen away and a dark trail of blood ran out of his hair and down the side of his cheek. His eyes were rolling around, and he was still groaning softly as Brisa finished cuffing him around a tree of his own.

"How hard did you hit him?" Driscoll asked.

Brisa glanced up. "He's not hurt."

"Yeah?" Driscoll said, moving toward him. "How about I try it on your thick skull? Just break out laughing when you've had enough."

"Fuck you," Brisa said, standing to thrust his jaw at Driscoll. "You said take his gun, I took his gun. What you want me to do, ask him for it?"

Driscoll closed his eyes for a moment. Once upon a time, in another dimension, another state of being, he had allied himself with cops, had dedicated himself to the apprehension—in fact, the annihilation—of such as Raymond Brisa. In that world had lived a man named Dedric Bailey. Another named John Deal. Things in that jolly place had gone more or less by design.

Now he found himself at the center of chaos. In fact, he had begun to wonder if he had not become its perpetrator. After all, here at his side was Brisa. There at his feet were Emmeling and another young policeman whom Driscoll and his new partner had assaulted and chained to trees with their own handcuffs. Overhead, helicopters churned the skies and strobed the land below, looking for him, for him and Ray Brisa. *How it turns,* he thought. *How the poor world turns.*

He turned from the sight of the battered cops then, and put his hand on Ray Brisa's good shoulder and patted.

"Okay, Ray," he said then. "You're right. I'm wrong."

He held up a ring of keys he'd taken from Emmeling's belt along with the handcuffs. "Furthermore, I have this feeling there's a patrol car not far from here. What do you say we find it."

Brisa stared at him for a moment. He glanced off into the near-darkness as if he had other options to consider. "I always wanted to drive a cop car," Brisa said finally. And then they went to find it.

"He's got to have something to drink on that boat," Linda Sheldon was saying.

"And dry gasoline," Deal said, swallowing thickly. "And a radio or a cell phone . . ."

"Maybe some clean clothes, something to eat . . . "

Deal nodded, feeling vaguely like a man who'd topped a dune in the desert to find a glistening oasis in his path. He'd donned his shirt and tattered slacks, stepped into his still-soggy shoes. They were standing on shore on the opposite side of the island where once a dock had been, staring out through the gloom. A second Cigarette, a near duplicate of the craft Deal had salvaged from the reef, bobbed serenely at anchor, perhaps two dozen yards away.

Linda glanced at Salazar's inert form, his hands bound with his bloody shirt. He'd started to come to as they dragged him across the island, but Deal had taken care of that. "I can't believe it. Larry Chappelear . . ." She broke off, shaking her head.

"We'll find out the truth. That much I promise you."

She stared back, long enough for that contract to be sealed. Then, abruptly, she was moving away from him, picking her way down the rock toward the waterline. Deal's gaze moved on out over the water toward the boat Angel had brought, still trying to put his finger on something that was bothering him. Then he glanced back at her, realized what she had in mind.

"Wait," he called.

She didn't seem to hear. She was at the water now, had tossed one of her shoes off, stood balancing herself as she tugged at the second.

"Linda . . . "

He hurried down the slope, caught her just as she was about to jump.

She came around at him swinging. "What are you doing?" she cried. "Let go of me." The heel of her hand banged off his chest. "Let go!"

"Linda," he cried, ducking another swipe of her hand. He caught her other arm, forced her away from the water. "Just wait a minute, all right?"

"I don't want to wait a minute," she cried. She was out of control now. "I'm thirsty. I'm starving. I want to get out of this place before more of them come. I want you to let go of me . . . "

"Just wait," he shouted, shaking her roughly.

The gesture seemed to stun her momentarily. He let go of her shoulders, turned, spotted a sizable chunk of coral rock lying just out of the water. He bent and hefted it, his eyes meeting hers briefly. Then he turned and heaved it at the boat. The rock struck the side of the hull and fell into the water with a splash.

"What are you doing?"

He held up a finger to silence her. He found a shard of timber half in, half out of the water, snatched it up by one end. He hefted it, decided it would be a better test.

"Get back a ways. Up behind that pile of brush," he said, pointing at a twisted clump piled not far from where they'd hidden earlier.

She stared at him in amazement.

"Go on," he commanded. She gave him one last glance, then moved reluctantly up the slope toward the pile.

When he was satisfied she'd gone far enough, Deal turned, gauged the distance again. Then he spun around like a hammer thrower, hurling the water-soaked timber out over the water. The chunk of wood soared across the intervening space, disappeared over the boat's gunwale, landed with a thud.

Deal didn't see it happen, though. He'd been running the instant the timber left his hand. He reached the pile of brush, dove, tackled Linda, drove her to the rocky ground beneath him.

They both heard it, the dull thud of the timber striking home. A strange crackling sound right after.

"What . . . ?" was all Linda had time to say.

She was fighting, trying to twist out of his grasp. Then came the thundering explosion. Where the boat had been was now a bright, angry flower, and for a moment the dark sky turned to day.

**"You want me** to ride out *there*?" Linda Sheldon said, pointing out the long prow of the boat, the Cigarette he'd nursed back to life. No radio on this boat, no cell phone, no case of Red Stripe. But there'd been no bomb aboard, either. Salazar prepared for every contingency, you had to give him that.

"Just for a little while, until we get past the reefs," he told her.

She glanced at the sky. "It's practically dark."

"You'll still be able to tell," he said. "You see something coming up like a bright shadow under the water, you just yell."

She nodded uncertainly. "What if I fall off?"

He appeared to ponder it. "Then I'll come back and get you."

She thought a moment, her expression softening. "That's right," she said. "You do come back, don't you?"

He stared at her: her face bruised and scraped, her hair a tangle. There was a sticky-looking smear on her cheek where she'd wiped her mouth from the one swallow of *jugo de papaya* he'd found for her.

He was reminded of something from that former life, the one when he'd been John Deal, building contractor, the guy who'd come home from work and prop his feet up on the coffee table and watch the nightly news. Most times it was the Prez who was on, of course. But sometimes it had been her. Tough lady, he'd always thought. And that had always appealed to him. But he'd always thought her a bit too patrician-looking for his taste. He made a soft sound that was almost like a laugh. The notion struck him as ludicrous now.

"What?" she said.

He stared at her. "Like the man said, we're going to lose our light soon," he said quietly.

She stared back. He thought he saw her waver. He thought she was leaning toward him, if ever so slightly. Her tongue ran over her dry lips.

"Maybe there's something to drink down below," he said. "Something I missed."

Her gaze had not left his face. "I'm not going inside there," she said.

He glanced down through the hatchway, caught a glimpse of Salazar's form where it lay inside the gloomy cabin, and nodded. "Sorry to put you to work," he said, waving vaguely at the sky. "But I've got to have help."

She closed her eyes briefly, put her hand on his. Then she turned, and was scrambling out the long prow of the boat.

**"What are those lights?"** Linda had to shout over the roar of the Cigarette's engines. She pointed out over the prow of the boat toward a vague glow on the northern horizon. Aside from the distant lights of a freighter they'd spotted as they came upon the shipping lanes, it was the first sign of life they'd seen in hours.

"Let's hope it isn't Havana," he called back to her. No radio, no range finder, no depth finder. He had only the vaguest idea of where they'd begun this voyage, and, other than that, a go-fast boat and a compass, and his rusty memory of navigation by the stars. Take us west, Captain Deal, wasn't that the American way?

Steady as she goes. If they didn't pile into something else first, they'd eventually find Florida. Now, judging by the lights ahead, it seemed they had.

He held their course steady until the glow brightened, gradually filling the horizon with a corona stamped on the night sky like a ghost's thumbprint. A few minutes later, and the first beacon came into view: Fowey Light, unless he were mistaken, the northernmost of a series of lights that marked the shelf of the continent itself.

From where they were, it was a minuscule blip on the distant horizon. In reality, the lights sat atop huge towers of fifty feet or more, anchored where the depth of the waters had shifted from six hundred feet to half a dozen in the space of a few hundred yards.

He checked his compass reading again, then swung the boat abruptly southward, away from the lights of the city.

"What are you doing?" she called.

"That's Miami all right," he told her, keeping his eyes straight ahead, watching carefully for Fowey Light to reappear. "But that's not where we want to go ashore."

"Why not?" Her grip on his arm tightened. "Let's get to the first place we can."

He caught sight of the light, checked the compass, adjusted course once again. At last he turned to her.

"If what Salazar said is true, if this thing really had Lawrence Chappelear's blessing from the beginning, then we don't know what might be waiting for us."

She stared at him in astonishment. "You can't be serious."

"Think about it," he said. "If you were in Chappelear's place, what would you do: go in, tell the President you made a little mistake, things just got out of hand?"

She shook her head slowly. "I've known Larry Chappelear since I was in college . . . He would never . . . "

"I don't want to be paranoid," Deal said, "but there's a way to find out the truth. If I'm wrong, then we won't have lost anything."

She opened her mouth to say something, then closed it again. She turned her face back into the wind, one hand gripping the side rail, another braced on the panel before them.

"What did you have in mind?" she asked.

"We'll put in someplace safe," he said. "I'll make a couple of phone calls. Then we'll see."

He could imagine what was going through her mind. A hell of a note, all right. So near to salvation and yet so far. He glanced at the distant shadows on the horizon, the first of the shallow islands that still lay between them and where they needed to go. He throttled back and called out to her.

"I'm going to need your help again," he said.

She turned to him, and he pointed over the prow of the boat.

"Some shallows up ahead," he told her. "It won't take long."

"I can't believe it," she said. But she was up and climbing again.

**"You sure** you folks don't want to come inside?" the waitress asked. "These bugs are pretty bad out here tonight."

Deal glanced at her, shook his head. He and Linda were seated at one of the plastic tables set far out on the sagging docks at Alabama Jack's, not far from the piling where they'd tied off the Cigarette. "We're fine," he assured the woman, who was waving her order pad at the cloud of mosquitoes circling her head.

"Kendall sprayed earlier," the woman said. "But sometimes I think they just get high off the stuff."

"I'll have another iced tea," Linda said, setting her glass down on the table between them. She'd ducked into the ladies' room the moment they'd docked, gulped tepid water straight from the tap, she'd told him. She'd done what she could with her face, tied her hair back in a knot.

Deal too had washed up, slicked his hair back, but there'd been nothing he could do about his clothes. His once-white shirt was gray and torn. The knees were out of his filthy pants, which he had tried to keep hidden under the table. Still, the waitress seemed not to notice. She'd probably seen far worse come drifting up at this dockside.

Jack's was the workingman's gateway to the Keys, dropped down on Card Sound Road, an out-of-the-way route not much used by tourists. The roadhouse sat just short of the graceful bridge that connected the mainland to sparsely populated north Key Largo, cheek by jowl with a raffish houseboat colony. The last time Deal had been in the place was on a Sunday afternoon a couple years back when a throng of day sailors, laborers, and bikers had jammed the place, no special celebration, just marking the winding down of another weekend in paradise. But that was back when there were such things as carefree moments in his life. Now, late on a sultry mosquito-laden night, aside from a few stolid drinkers hunched over the indoor bar, he and Linda constituted the sole clientele, and fun seemed in short supply.

He noted that the waitress, also serving as the barmaid at this hour, had been studying Linda carefully. "You sure look familiar," the waitress said. "You live over in Florida City?"

Linda managed a smile. "Just passing through," she said.

"Yo, Iris," a man at the bar called through the screening that separated outside from in. "I'm dry!"

The waitress glanced away for a moment, turned back to give the two of them a nod. "Your sandwiches'll be right out," she said. "I'll get you a refill on the tea."

"I just need a little phone change," Deal said, holding up a bill as she started away.

The waitress reached for it, then stopped. "This is Bahamas money," she said.

Deal nodded. "A five," he said. "Worth the same as ours. I'll trade you for a couple of quarters."

The waitress peered at him suspiciously. "How about this dinner you ordered? You planning to pay for that in Bahamian, too?"

Deal glanced at Linda, then back at the waitress. "It's all we've got," he said, wondering how she'd feel if he explained whose wallet he'd taken the money from. "Say I give you twenty to one. How's that for an exchange rate?"

"I ain't some bank, mister," the waitress said as she scooped up the menus from the plastic table. "The ice tea's on me," she said over her shoulder, "but maybe you and your wife ought to take it somewheres else."

"He's not my husband," Linda said abruptly. Something in her tone caused the waitress to turn. "The truth is," Linda continued, "I had a little trouble over in the islands. This man's been good enough to try and get me home."

The waitress had turned all the way around, was facing them once again now.

"Hey, Iris," the man at the bar bellowed.

Iris turned fiercely on him. "Shut your yap, Bean." She turned back to the table, drew a deep breath. She was a solidly built woman with hair that might have been red once, but had faded with years of sun and hard living. She stared steadily at Deal, who did his best to look honorable. After a moment, she let her breath out in a small explosion, reached one of her fists inside her apron, banged a mound of change down on the table in front of Deal.

"There's for the phone," she said, jerking her thumb over her shoulder. Deal followed her gesture toward a pay phone attached to a stanchion at the edge of the nearby parking lot. "As far as the sandwiches, they're already working anyhow."

"I appreciate it," Deal said.

The woman nodded wearily, as if she'd spent a lifetime listening to hard-luck stories and still hadn't found one she could resist.

"We're very grateful," Linda added as the woman left.

They watched her stride through a door in the screening, duck under the bar, go to snatch up the glass of the man she'd called Bean. She said something to him, pointing their way, and Bean peered quizzically out at them as Iris bent to pour him another drink.

"You think she recognized me?" Linda asked.

Deal looked her over. "A couple of days, it'll all come to her." There was a brief silence interrupted by the sound of a pickup speeding down the highway past the restaurant. After a bit, they heard heavy truck tires singing on the bridge approach, and finally there was silence once again.

"I hope you know what you're doing," she said finally. "I hope this is going to work."

He stared back at her. "I'm doing the only thing I can think of," he said, and stood to go for the phone.

**Driscoll had been** half asleep when the ringing began again. He came out of his daze with his heart pounding, his hand going automatically for the holster beneath his shoulder.

He blinked in the dim light, peering across the room at his friend Osvaldo, who had not only taken them in but had also overseen the rerouting of Driscoll's phone lines to his own condo. Osvaldo sat in a swivel chair, surrounded by banks of computer equipment stacked on old doors supported by plastic milk cases bearing the logo of the Publix supermarket chain. In another office chair beside him sat Ray Brisa, who watched Osvaldo's movements with fascination.

"That's Driscoll's phone," Brisa said, with some excitement.

"You're catching on," Osvaldo said.

"The feds again?" Driscoll called from his place on the couch.

Osvaldo shook his head, his hands flying over the keyboard. "They'll be listening in, though." he said. He sounded as enthused as Ray Brisa, but it was hard to tell for sure because his eyes were hidden behind the reflection of the monitors on his glasses. "Let's give them the sales pitch for the nursing homes, what do you say?"

"Works for me," Driscoll said, struggling to his feet. Osvaldo had helped him leave a series of untraceable messages for some of his old contacts within the department, but so far none had been returned. He was beginning to doubt they ever would, was beginning to feel very much alone.

Osvaldo punched a series of commands on a keyboard while Driscoll approached. "Who is it?" he said to Osvaldo. If he could get to Bailey's assistant Martinez, or Pete Rogier . . .

"One more ring," Osvaldo said, holding up a finger. "We've got the number now . . ."

He broke off, tapping more keys.

"A pay phone . . ." Osvaldo said as the next ring came.

"You believe this shit?" Ray Brisa asked, peering over Osvaldo's shoulder. Osvaldo was hammering a mouse button with the heel of his hand.

". . . on Card Sound Road," Osvaldo said, his eyes still on the monitor.

"Give me the phone," Driscoll said.

"Let the machine do it," Osvaldo said. "You don't know who it is."

"Fucking unbelievable," Brisa was saying. "The cops think they're listening, this guy's tracing the real call. He can do anything."

"Of course he can," Driscoll said. "Now shut up."

"What's with the volume here?" Osvaldo said, fiddling with a switch.

Suddenly the room was alive with static, the sound of a plaintive voice: "Don't tell me it's a machine, Vernon. Don't tell me . . ."

John Deal's voice. Driscoll stared about as if the sounds were coming from within the room itself. "Give me the phone, Osvaldo."

"It could be a setup," Osvaldo said.

"Right fucking now!" Driscoll said, extending his meaty palm. And the connection was made.

**When he got back** from the pay phone, the waitress was standing with Linda at the pilings where the Cigarette was tied off, a grease-spotted paper bag under her arm, her head bent in earnest conversation with Linda. Maybe she'd reconsidered her generous impulses, Deal thought.

She turned at his approach, gave him an appraising glance, shoved the bag toward him. "Keep your Bahamas money," she said. "Next time you're over this way, you can settle your tab in American."

Deal nodded, put the wad he'd withdrawn back into his pocket. "I can't tell you how much how much we appreciate this," he began.

"Oh, fuck off," Iris said mildly. "When it comes right down to it, you're just another man, okay?"

Deal stared at her. Linda smiled and put her hand on Iris's brawny arm. "Thanks, Iris," she said simply.

"You take care now," Iris said.

"We will," Linda said. She gave Deal a look.

"We need to hurry along." He nodded toward the boat. "Uncle Vernon's going to meet us."

Linda gave Iris a quick hug, then turned to follow Deal over the gunwale.

"Say, what's all that noise?" Iris said as Deal busied himself at the console.

A series of muffled thumps seemed to issue from somewhere in the hold of the Cigarette. Deal glanced up at her. "Fuel pump," he called, watching as Linda made her way into the boat. "It's been giving us some trouble."

The thumps seemed louder now, seemed to vibrate the deck beneath his feet. He flipped on the power, turned the ignition over while Linda struggled with the lines and Iris watched uncertainly.

"Thanks again, now," he called to Iris over the growl of the wakening engines. Moments later, they were gone.

"I'm getting a tremendous amount of pressure from the media, Mr. President," John Groshner was saying.

The President nodded distractedly. He turned from Groshner, looked vacantly at Chappelear, who'd been sitting silently at his side, the three of them the only ones in the parlor of the hotel suite where they were awaiting the start of the news conference to be televised from one of the ballrooms downstairs. "How's my tie, Larry?" he said.

It was an old joke between them. Frank Sheldon, then a candidate for governor, had gone on live television for his first-ever political debate with the knot of his tie fallen loose. It had dangled a good inch below his collar button for his entire presentation while Chappelear had danced about behind the cameras, making frantic gestures for his boss to straighten himself, until the producers had finally had him removed. Sheldon, the people's candidate, won the debate overwhelmingly, the election in a landslide.

"Your tie's fine, sir." Chappelear said glumly. "*You* look terrible." All his color gone, his eyes empty, his movements listless. A hollow man, Chappelear thought. A shadow wearing a thousand-dollar suit, a tie as perfectly knotted as a noose.

"Thanks, Larry," the President said, reaching to pat Chappelear softly on the knee. Something like a smile crossed his gaunt features. Chappelear wasn't sure when he'd last seen the man eat. Or sleep. He'd been awake for every meaningless update, taking calls from his counterparts on the other side of the globe around the clock.

"They're going crazy, sir," Groshner insisted. "Everyone's assuming you're going to announce some major development. Half of them are betting on the announcement of a suspect. The others are suggesting . . ." he broke off, threw his hands up. "Well, the worst."

The President glanced up at him. "Then nothing much has changed, has it, John?"

Groshner stared at him helplessly. "If you could just give me some cue, sir. You brought me on to manage a campaign. I'd like to think that my input could be valuable in an instance where . . ."

"There isn't going to be any more campaign," the President said, his voice firm, if uninflected.

"Excuse me, sir," Groshner said.

Chappelear leaned forward. "Frank . . . ?"

The President turned from the empty maw of the fireplace. A huge fireplace, Chappelear thought. Absurd for a hotel room in the tropics. But it was hewn from rugged coral rock and gave a kind of cavelike appearance just now. Maybe it seemed like the entrance to a lair where one might crawl to hide, lick the wounds, wait for another season, another life in which to emerge.

"That's what I'm going to tell the country, gentlemen." His eyes had taken on that vacant, faraway cast once again. "I'm sorry," he added, though he didn't seem to be directing his words to Groshner and Chappelear any longer. "But there just isn't anything else to give."

Chappelear glanced up at Groshner, who was staring open-mouthed at the President.

Sheldon had been holding his hands on the arms of his chair in stiff, Lincoln-chiseled-in-his-monument style. Now he folded them together in his lap. "I'd prefer to make this announcement myself, John," he said. He glanced at his watch. "Besides, there's not that much longer to wait."

He pushed himself stiffly up from the chair and Groshner took a backward step, his face a mask of confusion. "I'm not sure you're in the proper frame of mind, Mr. President. I understand the impact of these events . . . "

"I don't think you understand diddly, John," the President broke in. He put a hand on Groshner's shoulder. "But don't worry, there'll be another campaign to manage one of these days. I wouldn't be surprised if Senator Hollingsworth himself couldn't make a place for you."

"But, Mr. President," Groshner protested.

"That's enough," the President said, silencing Groshner with a wave. He turned to Chappelear then.

"I'll let you do the intro, Larry. Whatever you want to say is fine, just make it short and sweet."

He was striding toward the door, and in his movements, Chappelear had a glimpse of the old Frank Sheldon, the man who, once he'd made his mind up, would let nothing stand in his way. Almost enough to make him call the President back, beg him to reconsider, explain why things would not have to work out this way . . .

He dismissed those thoughts and stood to follow the President. He was nearly out of the room when an aide caught his arm. The young man held a cell phone toward him.

"General Williams calling from the command center, sir."

Chappelear shook his head. "It'll have to wait," he told the aide.

The aide held Chappelear's arm. "He says it's important, sir."

Chappelear sighed and took the phone. "This isn't the time . . ." he began, then stopped as the general's words sunk in.

"The first reports came in through customs, sir," the general was saying as he guided Chappelear through the crowded command center. The place was jammed with busy technicians and monitoring consoles, most of them displaying images of the ballroom and the empty podium where Chappelear should have been, where the President was about to make his speech.

Several others held stationary angles of the crowded public rooms of the hotel. A few, receiving imagery from tiny cameras clipped to the lapels of agents, reflected the urgency of cinema verité, the pictures waving and bobbing wildly as the agents moved about.

"Then we got confirmation from the DEA. The Bureau has a boat out there, too." He gave Chappelear a hapless glance, steering him into a glass-enclosed area with its own monitoring console. "I've ordered one of our cutters out and informed the agencies that we're in control, but I'm not sure I can order them from the scene."

"This is your bailiwick, General," Chappelear said. "I don't see why I . . ."

"Have a look," the general said, directing Chappelear to the monitor, where a technician sat. The technician had one hand clamped over his earpiece, shielding it from the hubbub in the outer room.

The monitor displayed a wavering exterior shot, from a plane or a helicopter swooping over the dark waters of Biscayne Bay. The helicopter swung about as Chappelear stared, its powerful searchlight focusing on something down below.

The image sharpened, and Chappelear saw a Cigarette cleaving the bay waters steadily, its nose pointed toward the glittering Miami skyline in the distance. In the vague nimbus cast by the beam, he saw other craft paralleling the Cigarette, presumably those of the agencies the general had mentioned. Between this convoy and the skyline, he could make out the search beams of the cutter, its lights sweeping over the dark waters as it approached.

"What the hell is this?" Chappelear said to the general. "I'm about to introduce the President on national television . . ."

The general held up a hand to stop him. He turned to the technician. "The chopper pilot's on the line?" The technician nodded and handed over his headset. The general made a motion and the technician stood, snatching up another headset for Chappelear.

". . . repeat, to the unidentified Cigarette, you are to cut your engines now," Chappelear heard as he clamped the set to his ear. "You are approaching restricted waters. Repeat . . . "

Chappelear impatiently checked the readout on the large digital clock hanging on a distant wall. Fifteen minutes to airtime, allow a few minutes for the President to get to the point. Inside half an hour, his life would be transformed.

"This is Williams," the general barked into the headset. "I have Lawrence Chappelear with me. Give us the rundown."

"Say again?" It was the pilot's voice, nearly obliterated by the roar of the helicopter's engines.

"This is Lawrence Chappelear," he blurted in exasperation. "What the hell's going on out there?"

The technician tapped Chappelear on the shoulder, directing his attention to a second monitor. The visage of the chopper pilot swam into view, bloating in fish-eye distortion as he leaned toward the lens.

"Sorry, sir, it's difficult to hear . . . "

"Goddammit, soldier . . . "

"This bogey down below," the pilot said. "We've got a man on board, identifies himself as . . ." There was a wave of static then, and Chappelear found his gaze drawn to the first monitor, where the image had tightened down on the open cockpit of the Cigarette. There was a tall sandy-haired man in tattered clothes at the controls of the boat, and a young Hispanic-looking man behind him, holding a pair of large plastic bags aloft in the search beams.

". . . apparently he called the DEA, Customs, the Bureau, told them he was bringing a boatload of drugs into the Port . . . "

"You think I should be concerned about some drug runner at a time like this?" Chappelear cried.

"It's not that, sir," the pilot insisted. "This man Deal got back on line, claiming to have information concerning the disappearance of the First Lady."

Chappelear paused. "You said this man's name is *Deal*?"

"John Deal, that's how he's identified himself, sir."

Chappelear stared at the general, who nodded glumly. Yes, that was peacetime for you, his expression read. Lull you, dull your senses, the moment things seem under control, chaos rears its head. Not like good old predictable war at all.

Chappelear stared at him meaningfully, then leaned to whisper something in his ear.

The general stood back. "You're certain."

"It is imperative."

The general turned to the technician, pointed at the monitor. "Whose cutter is that working the intercept?"

"Lieutenant Anderson, sir."

The general nodded. "Put me through to Anderson," he said to the startled technician, his voice the apotheosis of calm. "We have a national emergency on our hands."

**Deal banged** on the unresponsive cell phone, tossed it onto the Cigarette's console. No one was talking to him now. The boats that had initially zoomed out to intercept them had pulled back now, giving them a wide berth as they drew closer to the main channel leading to the port.

"Check out *that* big mother," Brisa said, pointing into the distance. He'd tossed aside their phonied-up "contraband" and was staring at the cutter steaming out the channel toward them.

Deal shook his head. What would they send out next, a destroyer? Any one of the boats that were escorting them had sufficient personnel to subdue a couple of drug-runners. He glanced at his watch. Driscoll and Osvaldo had had more than the allotted hour to get their part rolling. Plenty of time, Osvaldo had assured him as he and Driscoll took charge of their precious cargo, loading that bundle into the back of the equipment-laden van.

There was a Southern Bell relay station not far from the tiny Gables marina where they'd made the switch. "Nobody there at this time of night," Osvaldo assured them. "I got cameras, everything I need with me. Once I'm inside, if I can't get it done in an hour, then it ain't gonna work at all."

Osvaldo had said it cheerily, but by all appearances, he had not gotten it done, Deal thought. Time to pull his trump card. He was about to call down the hatchway when he saw the first muzzle flash from the big guns on the cutter.

"Whoa . . ." Brisa cried.

The shot was high and well forward of them, but the explosion was thunderous, sending a geyser of water high into the air off to port. He jerked the wheel hard right just as a second flash lit up the bow of the cutter.

This shot was lower, but trailed them by fifty feet. The shell tore through the hull of a Bayliner carrying a half-dozen Customs agents and exploded, erasing that craft and its passengers in a flash that sent fragments raining down on the deck of the Cigarette.

The force of the blast sent Deal to his knees, but he was up again, steadying himself against the wild rocking of the boat. He was back at the hatchway of the Cigarette, staring down at the frightened face of Linda Sheldon, then ahead at the cutter, now a hundred yards away, now seventy-five. All their efforts, all their desperate planning, he thought.

"Time to try plan B," Deal cried out, urging her up the steps.

"Whatever that might be," she called back, grasping his hand tightly.

"Good God," someone breathed as the image on the monitor wavered, then came back into focus.

The helicopter had swooped upward as the firing commenced, and the view was from a greater distance now. The Cigarette had clearly changed its course, was arrowing itself straight at the cutter.

"What's he doing?" someone else cried.

"He's a madman," the general said quietly, watching the drama unfold. "A terrorist."

The image soared away then as the chopper fought for altitude and all the close detail was gone.

The Cigarette might have been a toy boat now, closing in on a somewhat larger toy boat, all this laid out against dark waters with a horizon that might have been fairy-tale lights behind.

The command center had gone quiet. All of the monitors reflected the pair of distant boats, the Cigarette bearing down on the cutter, the cutter trying, at the last moment, to turn away . . .

. . . but the Cigarette launched itself off a swell like a missile: It hit the cutter squarely amidships and exploded. Then came the second blast, which sent a fireball high into the air, and wiped the dark seas clean.

Lawrence Chappelear stood in steely composure at the podium, waiting for the interminable sound and video checks to be completed by the bevy of technicians swarming about with their cables and cameras. He glanced around the crowded room, ignoring the shouted questions from the media personnel, all of whom were being kept at bay by a phalanx of Secret Service men. If they only knew what he had just witnessed, he thought, then just as quickly forced the thoughts away. One crisis at a time, he told himself.

Somewhere down one of the hallways behind him was Frank Sheldon, about to step before these baying hounds, lay himself open before all this attendant apparatus like a Japanese warlord disemboweling himself in shame. No grief so deep that it could be hidden from the public need to know, Chappelear reminded himself. No refuge. No place to hide.

And soon, no need to hide. No matter how monumental the tragedy, how awful its aftermath, all of it would pass, the events, the people become history, and, ultimately, footnotes to history, lost in all the outrage and tragedy to come.

All this would pass, and he along with it. Best now to begin the process of acceptance, to allow himself to be swept up as well, one more bit of flotsam carried along toward darkness and forgetting, and everything he'd done along with it.

*Go out with grace,* he told himself. He'd find some sinecure, some university post, some lobbyist's niche, nothing he hadn't anticipated, and though the need to come to terms with this future had presented itself sooner by some four years or so than he might have wished and despite everything he'd done to protect his own position, and, finally, Frank Sheldon's too, look what it had resulted in.

He should console himself with the fact that the damage had been contained to the extent that it had. He'd made a mistake, a miscalculation, but with Salazar gone, that unfortunate business out on the Bay behind him, no one would be the wiser. The general knew nothing of Chappelear's original involvement with Salazar; Williams was simply carrying out battlefield orders in an arena where covert operations were the norm, and he would have his battlefield promotion as a result.

Yes, Chappelear thought, he'd lost the battle, but he would survive. They would all survive. *"Being not the ones dead . . ."* he thought. Yes. Alive was always better.

Ignore the vast abyss that loomed just the other side of his scrambling thoughts. Don't look down, for there was madness beckoning with an enormous finger.

He blinked, and found himself staring dumbly at a microphone, one of what seemed a hundred affixed to a podium that seemed too frail to support their bulk. He reached up in reflex and tapped at the mike, tapped again, heard no sound disrupt the clamor in the airless room. Nothing but static from the sound booth lead clipped to his ear, and probably no one listening even if he were to shout into the invisible mike at his lapel.

He tapped again and bent to the microphone and spoke some mindless words, some ladies and gentlemen homily of testing, two, three, four, and still nothing. Endless waiting, up there in plain view as technology's stepchild, the President back there waiting, wanting to end his own agony too, and all these jackals eager for the flesh.

*Stop it, Larry,* he thought. *Get this over with one step at a time. Maybe a possibility for a life even yet.*

He had opened his mouth again, ready to demand that the technicians get their act together, flip their switches, open their gates, when he heard a murmur from the crowd, something new there. Shouts then. Arms raised, and pointing toward the giant monitors set up to flank the stage.

He turned toward them and felt his mouth open in surprise at the image that filled the screens. He heard a voice from the lead at his ear: "What the hell is that? Where's it coming from?"

"We don't know." He heard a technician's voice in his ear. "It's a pirate feed, someone's overridden the outgoing line . . ." Then silence, nothing more from control central.

Zigzags of distortion scrolled down the big monitor screens and there was a momentary blackout, but then, like something from his worst dreams, the image was back, and he felt the yawning blackness opening up beneath his feet.

The image onscreen now was that of Angel Salazar, swollen and battered, but Salazar nonetheless, his mouth opening and closing, mouthing soundless words as a burly man in a badly chosen sportcoat held him by the hair and directed Salazar's bleary gaze toward the camera's eye.

There was a sudden blast of noise then, and Chappelear felt himself clapping his hands to his ears along with the others in the room, but then the noise modulated just as quickly and he realized that what he was hearing were undeniably the words of Angel Salazar. What Lawrence Chappelear heard was the explanation of their plan, ". . . the First Lady a so much simpler target, our intention all along," and the proclamation of their doom.

A greater clamor arose then, and the doors to the room had flown open, a crowd of agents were flooding in, reporters stumbling in the wake of this tide, all of it lit in the glow of camera lights and flashes. Shouts and cries of amazement, for there, at the center of the throng of security men, *she* was:

The First Lady, Linda Barnes Sheldon, still soaking from the waters of the bay, her expression haggard, one hand thrown up against the glare of the lights, the other tight at the arm of a man just as soaked and even more battered-looking. In their wake, a weasel of a man with dripping bandages obscuring his face.

The words of Angel Salazar blared over it all: confession, explanation, and, where Lawrence Chappelear was concerned, annihilation.

Babel. Absolute chaos. Cameramen jockeyed for position. Reporters screamed questions, shouted into cellular phones. One or two might have been taking notes.

Hard to believe that anyone had his or her eyes on the podium on the stage where Lawrence Chappelear was standing, along with one amazed security officer. Though in the days to come, nearly everyone present would swear they saw it happen:

As the furor on the other side of the hall builds, this grim-faced man, who has spent an adult lifetime as advisor to his president, spins toward the distracted officer, snatches the man's weapon from his grasp.

Speculation still rages as to what target Chappelear might have had in mind. Was it John Deal? The First Lady? Or, as most argue, did he intend to turn the weapon upon himself?

All that will ever be known for certain is what happens next:

Chappelear pulls the weapon toward him; the astonished guard pulls back at last; there is a single shot expended . . . and Lawrence Chapplear falls in a spray of blood and bone at the podium, sending chaos into overdrive.

## Miami Beach: One Month Later

"Could've been me up there in Washington, you know that, don't you?" This from Ray Brisa, who's just opened a fresh beer from the ancient Coca-Cola cooler near the entrance to Doc Jameroski's emporium, is waving it at the tiny television set on the wooden counter.

"My aching ass," Driscoll says, readjusting himself in one of the webbed lawn chairs the doc has pulled down from a dusty shelf, some extra seating for their little gathering.

"Careful with such language," the doc says with a stern look at Driscoll. The doc points at Isabel Deal, age seven, who sits on a stool where once upon a time there was a soda fountain, with levered spouts that actually worked. She is bent intently over a coloring book, its pages yellowed with age: a moose, a flying squirrel in an aviator's skullcap, a little man with a raincoat and a pencil mustache saying something to a tall, dark companion named Natasha. Brown for the moose, gray for the squirrel, black for the evildoers, all of the work held neatly, perhaps even obsessively, within the lines.

Driscoll nods at the doc, contrite. He knows that it is true, that Isabel misses nothing. Intent as she may be upon her work, she glances up each time the CNN announcer mentions the ceremonies, which are to be carried by the network live and in their entirety this afternoon from the White House. And happy as he is to have Isabel here, something in Driscoll aches for her. He wants to push himself up from the flimsy chair that threatens to explode at any moment with his weight, lumber over to the counter and fold her up in his arms, squeeze her and assure her that her father loves her, that more than anything, he would love to have her with him on this day . . .

. . . but then the door behind the counter that leads to the storeroom opens, and Janice comes out from a trip to the rest room back there and gives him her rueful smile, and Driscoll simply nods and smiles a kind of a smile in return and bends for another beer of his own. He guesses he can't blame Janice for refusing to let Isabel attend, given all that's happened, the entire country still in fearful aftershock, but still it seems a shame.

The door to Jameroski's is shuttered and locked, the oblong of the CLOSED sign a mute silhouette behind the old-fashioned shade, and the junkies and the winos seem to know enough to stay their normal knob-rattling and foyer mutterings for this day. There, beer and several kinds of soft drinks are lined up vertically in the old-fashioned cooler, and Jameroski has rigged the mechanism so you can just open the rubber-gasketed door, reach in, choose one of the cylinders, and yank on the chilly neck of whatever you want and—forget the quarter—out it comes, with a clank and a thunk that sends another bottle down to replace whatever was there.

Something nice about that, Driscoll thinks. A suggestion of bounty, of a world that every so often gives, just for the hell of it.

The doc has ordered in food as well, great mounds of it, rich deli salads and carvings that reek of garlic and spice and threaten to send his cholesterol count soaring just from the smell alone. A celebration, Driscoll thinks, and shakes his head when he thinks about it. Amazing that he is here to celebrate, that any of them are.

And there will be no mention of Raymond Brisa this afternoon, and none of Vernon Driscoll, who turned a few of Salazar's interrogation techniques upon their inventor in that little phone company building where their impromptu studio had been set up. No mention of Osvaldo Regalado, whose considerable communications skills sent Salazar's confession beaming out into the world, if only a few minutes later than they'd intended.

No mention of Dedric Bailey, whose death remains attributed to accident, nor of Captain Billy—Captain Michael Cudahy, that is, shot down by the defenders of his country as a result of "tragic error." Of Tilton, or Gavin, or his cousin Cork. Of those nameless Bahamian kids who helped to hustle him and Ray Brisa off in the night, risking themselves for people they didn't know, for reasons no one could begin to explain.

There will be no mention of Angel Salazar, who sits now in the bowels of a facility unknown and unannounced, delivered from the hold of the boat Deal brought back into something like justice.

Nor will there be mention of Lawrence Chappelear. The story of his demise, of his ill-fated deal with Angel Salazar, has been aired in every imaginable form, in every media outlet the world over. One man who sought power, another who disdained it absolutely. Joined in unthinkable acts. Incomprehensible treachery. The legacy of antiquated cold war attitudes toward Latin America, et cetera, ad infinitum. Though the rumors of Jorge Vas's involvement never figured in the media circus, however. Salazar may have told them much, but he'd stayed mum on Vas.

Another escape for the seemingly invulnerable Jorge Vas, Driscoll thinks, another considerable irony. Though none of this confounds him. He finds no irony too great, no actions unthinkable, no betrayal beyond the bounds of comprehension. It is his strength and his curse. "The way my mind works," he mumbles.

"What did you say?" asks Ray Brisa.

Driscoll blinks, looks up into Brisa's disbelieving stare. "I don't know what I said." And it is true. He may as well have been dreaming.

"Funny," Brisa says, shaking his still-bandaged head. "I could have sworn you said it."

"Quiet!" Doc Jameroski commands them.

Isabel is sitting straight up on her stool now, her crayon work forgotten. "Daddy," she cries, clapping her hands. Janice stands behind her, her hands on Isabel's shoulders.

"Daddy!" Isabel repeats, pointing at the television screen, where a camera pans over a procession that steps lively from a door in the White House itself. Janice is nodding. There may be tears on her cheeks, but Driscoll can't be sure. He is thinking about what's unfolding on the screen before him, and all of a sudden, he's not seeing so clearly himself.

**". . . this highest** of awards, for heroism beyond reward, and beyond measure," the President concludes. "Though evil may persist, this greater spirit will prevail."

He moves to drape the medal about Deal's neck. There is an explosion of applause from those gathered in the Rose Garden, and, right on cue, the thunder of three Air Force fighters streaking in formation overhead. The President, all thought of his doomed campaign set aside for this day, embraces Deal, and despite his misgivings, Deal feels himself leaning to return the gesture.

Next it is the First Lady who steps forward to embrace him. Though he has spent a good part of the day anticipating this moment, Deal feels her in his arms for only the briefest instant. Memories crowd in upon him, so many that his head feels ready to burst.

"Not what the bad guys had in mind," he manages.

She steps back. "They didn't count on you," she tells him. And then she is gone, back to her place at her husband's side, and the band strikes up its stirring song.

Someone comes up to lead the President away. The President turns to Linda Barnes Sheldon, who is about to take her husband's hand. She glances back at Deal—one instant, but that's all there needs to be.

Deal watches her go, washed in the glare of photographers' lights and the wave of sound from the military band, and he wonders at the emotions that swell within him. *So many,* he thinks. *So much to contend with all at once.*

There is one thing above all, of course, one thing he no longer can escape. Pride, Deal thinks. Nothing he's asked for, nothing he'd ever flaunt. But pride, just the same.

He thinks of his daughter, hoping dearly that she has watched all this. Thinks of his estranged wife, Janice, and all her pain and fear. Thinks of the twisted course of politics, of all those women and children in the water who had given over their lives just for the chance to live in freedom. Thinks of the twists and turns his life has taken to bring him exactly to this place . . .

. . . and despite his knowledge that politics will grind on, and whatever the President's name, the boats and the rafters will keep coming, and the Chappelears and the Salazars as well . . . despite all this, he feels such gratitude to be here. He straightens. Today he'll be a hero. He bears himself away.

*Peabody Public Library*
*Columbia City, IN*

Peabody Public Library
Columbia City, IN